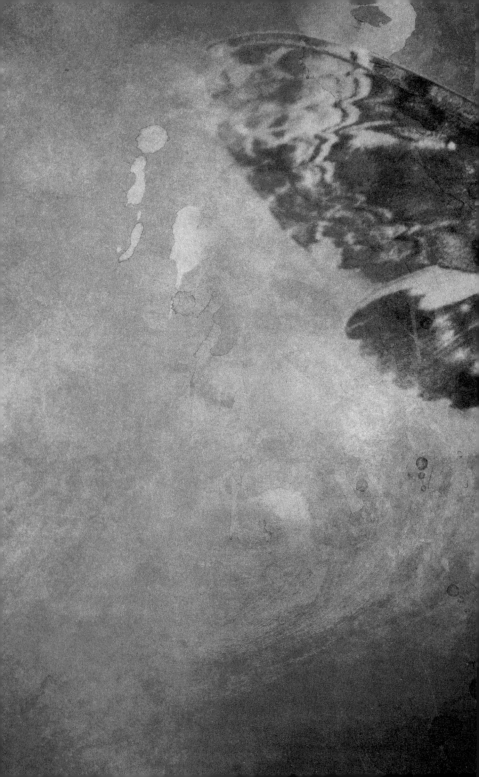

PINTIP
DUNN

SEIZE TODAY

Entangled Publishing, LLC
2614 South Timberline Road
Suite 109
Fort Collins, CO 80525

Entangled Teen is an imprint of Entangled Publishing, LLC.

Visit our website at www.entangledpublishing.com.

Edited by Liz Pelletier
Cover design by Mayhem Cover Creations
Interior design by Toni Kerr

HC ISBN: 978-1-63375-818-6
Ebook ISBN: 978-1-63375-819-3

Manufactured in the United States of America

First Edition October 2017

10 9 8 7 6 5 4 3 2 1

an imprint of Entangled Publishing LLC

For Aksara, my favorite girl.

1

Eleven years earlier…

I pull the lever of the cage, switching the tunnel onto a different track, trying to confuse the mice.

I know exactly how the future will play out, of course. I know which mice will fall down the trap and which ones will smack into the see-through glass wall. I know which mice will get hopelessly lost. I even know which ones will run the maze correctly on the very first try.

I like watching them anyway. They wriggle over one another like worms, and their whiskers twitch when they're at a corner between two paths. But what I like most is how they come to me when I call.

Picking up a mouse, I run my fingers over its soft fur and warm body. It looks at me with unblinking pink eyes, and I think it could be my friend.

Of course, I can see which mice will come, so I know which ones to call. Rodents are predictable like that. Humans, not so much. They have too many wants, too many feelings. I don't see any *one* future for people. Rather, I see them all—every single pathway their futures might take, flickering before my eyes.

So I have to guess which of my human classmates will want to play with me. Most of the time, I guess wrong.

"Are you bothering my mice again?" a little boy's voice says. "Fates, Livvy. How many times do I have to tell you? Leave them alone!"

Startled, I let go of the mouse and look up at Tanner Callahan, the other six-year-old who hangs around the scientists' labs. I'm here because my mom's the head of the Future Memory Agency, or FuMA, and he's here...I guess 'cause he has nowhere else to be.

He's got black hair that pokes up in the back, and his skin sticks too closely to his bones. I thought this meant he wasn't eating enough, but MK, our child-minder, said that grief over his parents' deaths had burrowed holes through his resources.

This makes me think of the mice digging through the straw, and my chest aches. I flash forward to his futures. He still has hundreds of branches remaining, but in most of them, one thing is the same: he will be sad and lonely until he kisses our classmate Jessa ten years in the future.

I don't know why kissing should change anything. But I do know how it feels to be lonely and sad.

We don't have to be like this. I could be his friend. I just have to figure out the right thing to say.

"Jessa and I are going to rule the world one day." It can't hurt to bring up the girl he smushes lips with. Maybe if he thinks she and I are friends, he'll like me, too. "You know Jessa, right? The girl with the teardrop eyes? She's my best friend." Not true. I think Jessa only talks to me because she's nice. But he doesn't have to know that.

"Oh yeah? Well someday, I'm going to be the inventor

of future memory," he shoots back. "And then we'll see who's more important."

I bite my lip. That wasn't what I meant. I wasn't trying to brag or compare or compete. The futures containing our friendship begin to fall away, one by one. I guessed wrong once again.

My thoughts whirl as I search for something else to say, but then I hear a pair of heels clicking against the tile outside the lab. My stomach drops. The door swishes open, and there stands my mother, Chairwoman Dresden herself.

Her hands go to her hips. Her short hair looks like icicles; her eyes are lumps of hail. "Tanner, what are you doing here? Get back to work before another one of my self-driving pods malfunctions."

Tanner suddenly looks like the tuft of hair on his head—all quivering and out-of-place. His parents died in a freak pod accident. That's probably what's gotten him so upset. "Th-this is where I work, Ch-chairwoman—"

She swishes her fingers through the air. "Does it look like I care? Be gone!"

Without another word, Tanner tucks his head down and scampers out of the room.

The door seals shut, and her shoulders droop. "I've had a rough day," she moans, covering her eyes. "I think we've found our key to future memory, but she won't cooperate. She won't send a simple memory to her sister. They say I'm so cruel. They think I'm a monster who tortures children. But what else am I supposed to do? How else can I make her comply?"

The words ring through the room and fall to the carpet. She's not expecting an answer, and I don't dare offer one.

She peeks at me through her fingers. "Come give Mommy a kiss, Olivia. You love me, don't you? You don't think I'm a bad person, do you?"

Obediently, I cross the floor and press my mouth against her cheek. A bit of powder comes off on my lips. It tastes bitter. I hold my face tight, but the grimace sneaks out anyway.

She goes perfectly still. "Did you make a face after kissing me?"

My blood runs cold. Colder than my feet when they stick out under the covers. Colder than the breath that puffs out in the winter air. All her futures flip through my mind, and over ninety percent of them end in the exact same way.

Still, I try.

"No, ma'am," I say haltingly. "I didn't mean to make a face. Your powder came off on my lips, and it tasted bad. Stale and bitter, like poison."

"I taste like poison?"

I wince. Clearly I'm not any better at guessing when it comes to my mother.

"No, ma'am. Not you. The powder—"

"Why must you look at me with those solemn eyes, Olivia? Children are supposed to be carefree and innocent. They're supposed to love you unconditionally. Just once, I'd like to come home from a hard day at work and take comfort in my flesh and blood. Instead, I'm greeted, night after night, by a daughter who stares at me like she sees every single one of my sins."

I *do* see all her future sins. And all her potential goodness, too. Which path she takes is up to her.

But if I say that, she'll just get mad at me for being precocious.

"I don't mean to look at you." Maybe she'll calm down if I change the subject to something more childlike. If I act more like the daughter she wants. "I had one of those visions again. You know, the ones you call nightmares? It was awful. People were dying. Everywhere I looked, people were confused and disappearing and dying."

A sharp glint leaps into her eyes. "Did you tell anybody? Did you tell Tanner?"

I shake my head. "Not yet. But maybe I should. Maybe, if he knows that I've seen horrible things, too, he'll want to be my friend—"

Her hand slashes across the air and lands squarely against my cheek.

Ow. The futures blow up, and stars blink in front of my eyes. I stumble, trying to find my feet.

"How can I get through to you? How do I make you understand? Nobody can know about your nightmares. You have no idea what will happen if the wrong person hears." She slaps me again. More explosions. More stars.

I cry out, even though I know it will only make her madder. The blows rain down on me. I scream, kicking out my legs, punching forward with my arms. Not because I'm trying to fight her. Not because I'll ever win. But because. It. Hurts. So. Much.

And then, all of a sudden, the walloping stops. Her heels *click-click-click* out of the room, and the door swishes shut. I collapse to the floor. My body aches in places I didn't know could ache. The skin between my toes. The muscles behind my knees.

My heart.

My mind, however, is not still. It races ahead, sifting, sifting, sifting through my futures until I find the one I want. The only one that will make this pain go away.

Closing my eyes, I live that vision as though it were real.

...

The door opens. My mother pads back into the room, but she is barefoot this time. She places her hands under my arms, lifting me to my feet. "Come on, Livvy," she says nicely, so nicely. Her voice is as light as a breeze blowing against my skin. As soft as a moth landing on my shoulder. "Let's get you on the couch."

"Can't move," I mumble against the tile. I taste dirt and chemicals and linoleum. "Don't think I can ever move again."

"It'll hurt for only a few moments," my mother says. "And then you'll be much more comfortable. I promise."

Because she is gentle, because she is kind, because all I've ever wanted is for her to love me, I try.

I stand and wince. Every movement shoots pain to my jaw and my legs, my stomach and my teeth.

My mom wraps an arm around me, and together we hobble to the couch. The fabric is coarse, but I melt into it as if it is the softest, most luxurious material in this time.

She rubs a salve into my face, kneading my aches with her fingers. From the past, I know that the salve is practically magic, and that tomorrow, I'll feel infinitely better. "I'm so sorry, Livvy," she says, tears strangling her words. "Can you ever forgive me?"

"Why should I?" Anger curls in my stomach. "You hurt me."

Her throat ripples. "I can't explain it to you. But believe me, it hurts me more than it hurts you. Every strike I lay on your body I feel in my heart tenfold. One day, you'll know the truth. One day, you'll understand why I have to be so hard."

"Tell me now," I beg. "You said yourself, I'm the most precocious little girl you've ever met. If you tell me, I'll understand."

"No." Her voice thickens, even as her hand moves lovingly down my arms. "You already have enough of a burden on your too-thin shoulders. If you learn the truth now, it will scar your soul forever. Just know this. Everything I do is because I love you."

"Do you mean it, Mommy?" I am sobbing now, although I don't know why. I bury my face in her lap, wetting her skirt with my tears. "Do you really love me?"

"With all my heart. With all my soul."

She continues to apply salve to my skin. I close my eyes. The fabric of the sofa scrapes against my arms, and the synthetic fiber of her skirt feels like sandpaper against my cheek.

But you couldn't move me if the world were coming to an end.

• • •

I open my eyes. Slowly, the real world comes back into focus. The cages full of mice, the cold linoleum floor, the bright white light shining above me. My pain.

My mother didn't actually apply salve to my aches. She didn't actually cuddle me in her lap and tell me she loved me. That was just one version of the future, a path that she could've picked—but didn't.

It doesn't matter. I wrap the vision up and hold it tightly against my heart. This is the way it's always been. All my life, it's like I'm being raised by two moms. The person Marigold Dresden actually is.

And the woman she could be.

2

Present day...

Across the control room, technicians stand at their com terminals, their hands moving busily over keyballs as they monitor the memories being transmitted from the future, right at this very moment. Right in this very building.

It's like we've gone backward in time, to the way our lives used to be eleven years ago. Once again, every seventeen-year-old in North Amerie is ushered into a government building on his or her birthday. Once again, the teens are instructed to open their minds in order to receive a memory from their future selves. Once again, these visions serve as an all-knowing guide for the recipients— and as a guarantee for everyone else: employers, loan officers, even prospective spouses.

It's as though Callie Stone never stabbed a syringe into her chest, as though the invention of future memory was never threatened. As though I didn't go into isolation for the last decade.

Nothing's really changed...except for one thing. Jessa

and I are now part of the system.

I look across the room at Jessa Stone—Callie's sister and, more importantly, my ally. She wears the same crisp navy uniform as me, but hers has three golden bars across her shoulders to indicate that she's the personal assistant to my mother, Chairwoman Dresden.

It's been six months since Jessa betrayed her family in order to gain my mother's trust. Six months since my mother asked me to come out of my cabin in the woods, where I had sequestered myself for ten years, so that I could follow Jessa around and determine her loyalty.

I didn't want to. Isolation is safe. Isolation doesn't bombard you with a million people's futures, with tragedies that you're helpless to change. But I set Jessa on this path. I convinced her that she would be the one to stop my mother's future plans of genocide. Of course, Jessa believes that the chairwoman is the ultimate bad guy, that she's nothing but pure evil. I don't agree. I *know* my mother. I've lived a thousand of her alternative visions, and I'm absolutely convinced she's got her reasons for making such bad decisions. They may not be *good* reasons—they may not justify or excuse anything—but in her mind, she's doing what's right.

I don't tell Jessa any of this. I doubt it would go over very well. But after dragging her into this situation, the least I can do is be her shadow.

That's what the FuMA employees call me when they think I'm not listening—Shadow. It makes sense, I suppose. I'm the strange girl who spent ten years by herself in the woods. I'm the meek employee who trails after Jessa from room to room, never acting and barely speaking. It's what I do best, what I've always done best: observe.

It's just too bad that I finally have a nickname from

someone other than Tanner, and it turns out to be "Shadow."

Jessa wanders over to me. "Want to take a break?" Her tone is so warm that I can almost convince myself that she likes my company. That we're not simply forced to work together. That she's actually my...friend.

I peek at grown-up Tanner, the third FuMA official in the room and the only other person who knows our true mission. "In fifteen seconds, Tanner will be joining..."

...*us*, I finish in my head. Ugh. Again? Six months ago, right when I rejoined society, I picked up this terrible tic of dropping the ends of my sentences. Not on purpose. My therapist at the Technology Research Agency, the one my mother forces me to see, thinks it's because I secretly think that my words are unimportant, that no one could possibly be interested in what I have to say. I don't know if she's right, but it's a habit I've been trying to break, without much success.

It's only because these are the first words I've spoken today, I reassure myself. *I'll be better once I get a little warmed up.*

"You think?" she murmurs, eyes brightening. "He's in the middle of a session. He can't just drop everything."

Five seconds...four...three...

Sure enough, Tanner glances up from his terminal and then swaggers toward us. Instead of a navy suit, he wears a white lab coat over his black thermal shirt and cargo pants—his unofficial scientist's uniform. Reaching us, he kisses Jessa on the cheek.

Almost without realizing it, I curl my shoulders forward and I back up one step, two steps, three steps, until I'm standing behind an empty com terminal.

"You're so predictable," Jessa says to Tanner.

"Well, of course I'm predictable." The black hair flops

over his forehead. "You're standing with the only true precognitive of our time." He flicks a glance at me—or at least, what he can see of me, since I'm mostly hidden by the metal structure. "She can see my future!"

"Correction," Jessa says mildly. "She can see the many different paths your future could take. She has no more knowledge than anyone else which path you'll actually choose." Her lips curve. "But it's nice to have proof that you can't resist me."

"*You* can't resist *me*." He grabs her waist, tickling her, and she shrieks with laughter.

I drop my eyes to the floor and try to make my body even smaller. Not because I want Tanner for myself—Fates, no. I've known him since before he knew how to make his hair lie flat. But because when I look at them, my chest aches.

This is what I want. What I've always wanted. Someone to love, and someone who loves me.

But for some of us, love exists in only a few measly twigs in the branches and branches of our possible destinies. I'm not like Jessa. I don't know how to open my heart to someone. Maybe I don't even have a heart. The only affection I've ever known is from a phantom mother who doesn't exist in this timeline. And my father? I don't know if I ever had one. Even as a child, I heard the snickers and gossip that the chairwoman's baby was externally incubated. Who would blame the world for finding me unlovable?

Not me. Not in a single one of my futures.

"So, what's your excuse for interrupting your work?" Jessa asks.

Tanner sobers. "I actually have one this time." He untangles himself from her but keeps a hand on her hip. "We've had another case. The third one this week. Like the others, the girl's fine when she's receiving her future memory. But afterward, she's confused. Mumbling to herself, walking into walls. Talking to people who aren't there." He moves his shoulders. "I don't know how to explain it."

I frown. Tanner Callahan, boy genius and the freaking inventor of future memory, admitting that he doesn't know something? Must be serious.

"Let's go talk to her," Jessa says. "Is she still in the recovery area?"

He nods, and the three of us troop down the hall. Well, to be more accurate, the two of them troop, and I drift behind, not wanting to intrude. Jessa looks over her shoulder, gesturing for me to join them. I flush and quicken my steps but continue to trail behind them.

We enter the recovery area. The patient is in the third partitioned section, staring blankly at the walls. She wears her black hair in two braids, and her left hand lays palm up on the table, a freshly inked hourglass tattoo gleaming on her wrist. Presumably, underneath the tattoo, a black chip containing her future memory has just been implanted.

A hologram floating in front of the partition displays her name. Danni Lee.

Jessa crouches down and takes her free hand. "Hi, Danni. My name is Jessa Stone, the chairwoman's assistant. Can you tell me what day it is?"

Danni's eyes focus not on Jessa but on a spot over her shoulder. "They say I live my life like a moth to a flame— attracted by bright lights and exciting moments," she says dreamily. "They say this will be the death of me, since the life of a moth who flies too close to the fire will soon be extinguished."

"O-kay." Jessa glances at Tanner. He shrugs, as if this was exactly what he expected, and sinks down next to her.

"Are these bruises from today?" He examines the marks

on Danni's shins. "How did you get these?"

"But I ask you: is this bad?" Danni continues. "Would you rather live a long, uneventful life, or seize the moment and leave this world in flames?"

My stomach feels like these very same moths are flitting around inside. Danni's not registering a word we're saying.

Jessa stands and gestures for Tanner and me to follow her out of the room. Danni continues to mumble about moths, and a nurse enters and injects her with an amber-colored syringe.

I don't want to leave her like this. I don't. But reaching into her future tells me that she'll soon recover from her symptoms and return to her regular routine.

"The bruises are from walking into a chair today," Tanner says, reading the hologram file floating in the air. "If her symptoms are like the others, she'll go back to normal after a few hours."

We step back into the hallway. "But where did her symptoms come from?" Jessa asks. "They didn't have these problems ten years ago, when future memories were processed as a matter of course. Is something different about the way memories are being received today?'"

"That might not be true," Tanner says, his steps slow, his words slower. "They might've had this problem ten years ago."

"What do you mean?" she asks.

"The amber-colored syringe that the nurse was injecting into Danni's arm. Look familiar?"

She gasps. "Oh dear Fate. You're right."

We continue walking, both of them lost in their thoughts. I have no idea what they're talking about. I should probably just ask, but my jaws seem to be fused shut, once again. No doubt they've forgotten I'm here.

As I try to work up my courage, Tanner turns to me

without prompting. "You know Jessa and I time-traveled to the past, right?" He rubs the skin between his ring and middle finger. "Well, we saw your mom. Even back then, ten years ago, she was medicating herself. She had a standing order for a formula, seven doses every week." He pauses. "It was amber, just like Danni's."

I frown, but I don't say anything.

He shrugs, as though he's read my mind. "It could be some kind of painkiller. Or maybe she and Danni are being treated for the same disease."

"There's more." Jessa's voice is gentle—too gentle. "I saw your mom walk into a door last night."

My mouth finally opens. "And I stubbed my toe on a…"

…*cleaning bot*. Fike. Not only did I drop the last part of my sentence, but the words I did say came out too fast, too loud. For years, I talked only to myself and the chipmunks, so I have little practice with voice modulation. I swallow hard, order myself not to break off mid-sentence, and try again. "Being clumsy's not a crime." Great. Now my words are so soft I doubt either of them heard me. At least I completed the sentence.

"That wasn't the first time I've seen her be clumsy," Jessa continues, unfazed. "When she came by my cottage, to show me the vision that I would be her assistant in the future, she almost crashed into a transport tube."

I lift my eyebrows, since nonverbal movements are an easier form of communication. Jessa's "evidence" doesn't prove anything other than that my mother might need new retinal implants. And yet, cement fills my veins.

I had no idea about the syringes. Not the first clue that my mother has a condition that reaches back ten years. For a moment, the old nightmares come back to me, the ones depicting a time that's dreary, desolate, *desperate*. People fading away. Our world stitched together by a single thread that's unraveling, unraveling, unraveling...

No! I slam shut the door to that vision and reinforce it with a fortress wall, brick by brick. No. I refuse to grant entry to those images. I refuse to let them rise to the level of conscious thought.

Ten years ago, I was teetering on the edge of madness, caused by seeing too much and too far into our possible futures. My mom whisked me to a cabin in the woods so that I could work on building the mental walls that would protect me.

She must've done something to herself, too, because shortly before my isolation, I stopped being able to reach into her future.

Gone was the phantom woman who loved me. Gone were the different versions of Marigold Dresden who rocked me and held me tight. Gone were the alternate realities I used to comfort myself. Maybe it was silly to mourn the loss of a woman who didn't exist, but I did.

And I never forgot her.

"Olivia, are you okay?" Jessa asks, concern etched in her lovely teardrop eyes.

I take a shaky breath. Nausea roils through my stomach, and a thousand knives jab into my brain. But I erected my mental walls just in time. I'm safe, for the moment.

"I'm fine," I mouth. My words don't rise to the level of audible hearing, but Jessa's been around me enough that she should understand what I'm saying.

Before she can respond, the head technician, Bao, flies out of the control room. "Miss Stone, I don't want to interrupt," he bursts out. "But we've got a late arrival who's just about to receive his future memory. And I think it's one you'll want to see."

3

We follow Bao back into the control room, where a knot of people is crowded around a single com terminal.

I frown. What in time? Aside from the technicians not working, there's a vibe in the air, a kind of gossip-fueled excitement that means people are gleeful and downright... celebratory?

"What's going on?" Jessa asks.

"It's one of the fugitives," a woman with freckles across her nose says. "The ones the chairwoman's been obsessed with tracking down. He's been caught at the perimeter of Eden City."

Another employee with burnished skin and a circuit board tattoo punches the air. "He walked right up to a pharmacy bot and tried to dispense some medication. Guess he didn't know about the bio-mapping we just installed."

"He's hot, too," a young female technician whispers to her friend. "If all the other fugitives looked like *that*, I wouldn't mind getting lost in the woods."

Sweat pops up on Jessa's forehead. "Exactly who are we talking about?"

"Take a look for yourself." Bao runs his hands over the keyball, and a holographic image of a boy leaps into the air.

He's tall. That's the first thing I notice. He must be six-two or six-three, although it's hard to tell because he's strapped to a chair, straining against the chains that cross over his biceps and thighs. Oval sensors, with wires emanating from them, are placed all over his head, and he's not wearing a shirt. Dark brown skin covers muscled arms and a chest that's ripped and corded. He could be a model for a gold-star boxing champion if it weren't for the angry slashes decorating his forearms and pecs. Either he's been resisting the guards—or those are just the injuries you get from living in the wilderness.

I swallow hard. I've been in isolation most of my life. For all I know, this is what teen boys look like. But somehow, I doubt it. He has such a...presence that I feel like I should avert my gaze. And yet, even though I've spent the last six months training my eyes to the floor, I can't look away.

"No," Jessa moans. Her knees buckle, and the only reason she remains standing is because Tanner wraps an arm around her waist. I glance quickly at the others, but the crowd's buzzing so excitedly they don't notice her reaction.

My mind whirls. A fugitive...his smooth brown skin... Jessa's despair...

Oh holy Fates. The boy in the hologram must be none other than Ryder Russell, Jessa's best friend...before she betrayed him. Before she pushed the red security button, alerting the Public Safety Agency to traitors in their midst. Before she forced him and the rest of her family to leave civilization and go on the run.

Sure, she gave them the supplies they needed in order to survive in the wilderness. She believed that betraying her family was her only way to infiltrate the system and stop the chairwoman.

And yet, the guilt of the last six months radiates deep in her eyes. She clenches her jaw, keeping her expression rigidly neutral. If I wasn't looking straight at her, I wouldn't see her pain. But I'm looking. I see.

The air in my chest burns. Fates, I didn't know. I didn't realize the betrayal affected her this strongly. Every day for the last six months, Jessa's been by my side. She's gone through the motions. She's more than convinced the chairwoman of her loyalty. And just now, I'm beginning to understand her calm, cool facade is only a mask.

"He's okay, Jessa," Tanner murmurs. Instead of drifting back, this time, I've moved forward. Away from the crowd, closer to Jessa and Tanner. "He's not hurt," my old playmate continues. "He's alive."

"He's in chains," she says softly, so that only we can hear. "Like an animal. What about the others?" Her breath comes out jerky, like she could use a paper bag. "What about Callie and my mom? Logan, Mikey, Angela. And oh Fates, baby Remi. Were they captured, too?"

He shakes his head because he doesn't know. And Fates help me, I don't know, either. For all my reputed powers, the only thing I could tell her is that in approximately two-thirds of the possible paths, Ryder's been captured alone. A lot of good that statistic does any of us.

"Okay, everyone," Bao announces. "We're going to retrieve the memory from the boy's head. If you want to experience it, put on your headsets."

All around us, people eagerly slip on their gear. One of the technicians hands me a metal contraption that looks like the inner skeleton of a hoverboard helmet.

I put on the headset. What did Bao mean, retrieve the memory? That's not the usual language. Ryder's supposed to open his mind, and then the vision's supposed to come to him.

Before I can figure it out, I am jerked into a different body and a different time.

I am in a narrow corridor. Deep underground, if the lack of natural light is any indication. The cool air chills my arms and blows against the nape of my neck.

Which means my hair is short. I look down at my forearms. I have thick, ropy muscles. The body of a boxer.

I walk a few steps. My hover shoes squish against the concrete floor. A dank smell fills my nose, and then I come upon an ornate doorway...

• • •

Without warning, I'm pulled out of the vision.

I blink, and the control room with its whirring com terminals comes back into focus.

"What in Fates was that?" Tanner asks, rubbing his head.

Bao's hands are a blur on the keyball. "The subject is resisting the memory."

"Why would he resist?" Jessa asks. "He's the one opening his mind to it."

A muscle ticks at the corner of Bao's mouth. "The subject's not cooperating. We're using the fumes to pry the memory from his mind."

My spine goes perfectly rigid. So Bao didn't misspeak. He's employing the same fumes that were used on Jessa's sister, Callie. The same fumes that were used on Jessa herself when the scientists kidnapped her as a child.

"Oh look, the memory's back!" the guy with the circuit

board tattoos shouts.

I've just put the headset back on when Ryder wrenches out of the vision again.

"We've got a strong one." Bao taps his fingers on his chin. "They aren't usually able to resist again so soon."

"How do you know?" I burst out, forgetting that I'm the Shadow. Forgetting that I'm not supposed to talk. "Has this happened…"

…*before?*

Bao chews on the inside of his cheek. "From time to time.'"

"How often?" Tanner presses.

"About once a week," he admits. "These days, not everyone wants their glimpse of tomorrow, you know. After what happened to Callie Stone, some of them feel like they're better off not knowing. But FuMA needs everyone to receive their memories—and follow through. So if they don't show on their seventeenth birthdays, we round them up. And force the memories out of them."

I want to throw up. This is terrible. They can't *do* that. They can't make people live memories they don't want.

But they can. And they are. This is precisely why we have to stop my mother, so we can end these practices— and worse. Much worse.

All of a sudden, the vision roars back, and because the helmet is still on my head, I'm thrown back into the corridor.

•••

Intricate designs are carved in the frame of the door, so detailed and precise that I assume the material is made of wood. But the doorway is not wood but metal—

•••

We are yanked out of the vision again. And then two more times after that. Each time shows us a little more of the door, builds a little more of the fear and anticipation at the back of my throat.

"He's getting weaker," Bao says into his wrist com after the third time we're pulled out. Who is he talking to? Is it—?

"Just stay the course, Chairwoman," the head technician continues. "He won't be able to fight much longer."

Of course. My mother. Since it concerns one of the fugitives, she's in the room with Ryder, administering the receipt of this memory herself.

A low moan escapes from Jessa's throat, and I bite my lip so hard I taste blood. Before I can swallow it, the memory's back.

•••

A beeping emanates from the other side of the door. I scan my biometrics, and the metal slides open. The smell hits me first—lemony air freshener mixed with leftover blood. I step into an arena.

A handful of people stand in the stadium seats. In the middle of the floor, a girl is chained to a throne-like chair, one made with cold silver metal and hollow glass legs. Clumps of hair fall across her face. Her clothes are tattered— but not because they're old. The rips look intentional and violent, and red scratches gleam through the gaping holes of the material.

My pulse races. My head pounds. It's all I can do to stand with my spine perfectly rigid, my hands clasped behind my back, as I've been instructed.

The perfect soldier. Or assassin.

A woman with brown hair and golden highlights steps around me and approaches the chained girl. After a few moments, the woman moves away again.

"On this fourth day of May, do you have any final words?" a voice intones from the stadium seats.

The girl straightens her shoulders and begins to speak. My ears start humming, a low, insistent buzzing that fills the entire capacity of my mind.

A few minutes later, she finishes. I step forward, catching a few glimpses of her face through her hair. A curve of her cheek. The corner of her lips.

As I pass, the brown-haired woman hands me a clear rectangular case, holding a single syringe. I remove the needle and hold it to the light. A clear liquid flows inside.

"Forgive me," I whisper. And then I inject the syringe right into the middle of the girl's chest.

Her limbs begin to convulse, her arms, her legs, her knees, her elbows—all with a life of their own.

The next few seconds pass in a blur. Sweat breaks out all over my body, the thoughts ricocheting inside my mind like ignited fireworks. Someone talks, but I can't process the words. I respond, but I don't know what I say.

When the girl collapses to her knees, I move forward to break her fall.

Her body goes limp, as though all her muscles have turned to liquid. I lay her on the ground.

I move the girl's hair, and finally, finally her features come into view. Her lips are relaxed, and her eyes are closed.

Olivia Dresden. The chairwoman's daughter. Dead. Just as the entire arena hoped.

4

The arena fades. The feel of the girl's hair—my hair—disappears, replaced by the sharp bite of my nails digging into my palm. My lungs contract, as though they're learning how to breathe again, and my heart's trying its best to break the gold-star record for sprinting. *I'm still here,* it seems to shout. *Still working, still beating.*

Still alive.

I open my eyes, clawing at the contraption on my head. It falls to the floor with a *clank*, but nobody flinches, nobody blinks. They're all too busy staring at me.

Instinctively, I back away. The crowd parts for me, and I duck behind a bot-charging station, because I have to get away from their looks. I have to get away from their eyes.

"That boy's going to kill you," the guy closest to me chokes out.

Maybe. Maybe not. The syringe had clear liquid in the barrel, just like Callie's. The future Ryder stabs it into my heart, just like one version of Callie did to Jessa.

But Jessa's not dead. She's standing across the room from me.

"Hot or not, I wouldn't want him in my life," the young female technician mutters.

"Is it...true?" Tanner asks. "Do you see that in your future?"

I rub my temples, struggling to clear the fog. Do I? I sift through my futures—and yes, there it is. Now that I've seen the future memory, all the other pathways fall away, so that there is one dominant branch left: the one where Ryder Russell injects the syringe into my body, and I collapse. But it is not the only branch remaining. Which means, like Callie's future memory, it doesn't necessarily have to come true.

In fact, the pathways where my future intersects with Ryder Russell are so varied that I don't know what to think. In my possible futures, he is everything from my enemy to my lover—a scenario that makes the heat flame up my cheeks. But the fact is, I have no way to guess how this boy will impact my life, if at all.

Except for one thing. A fact I've never revealed to anyone. Exactly twenty days from today, on May Fourth, my visions stop. Doesn't matter whose future it is: mine, Bao's, the Meal Assembler technician's. All my life, I've never been able to see a single future past this date. Instead, my vision smacks into a terrifyingly blank wall every single time.

There's only one explanation, really, and Ryder's future memory just confirmed it. May Fourth will be the day that I die. Mostly likely at his hand. That's why my precognition stops.

Which means I have only twenty days left to live.

All of a sudden, I'm shivering, goose bumps popping up along my arms. A delayed reaction to the vision? I guess. It's not every day I receive confirmation that I'm going to die. My body has no idea how to respond.

I look at Tanner, and the answer must be reflected in my eyes, because he takes a few steps back. I say it anyway. "Yes. Ryder Russell will kill me in the future." This time, the words aren't too loud or too soft. I don't drop the end of my sentence. I say it just right, because I'm saying it as much to myself as I am to the rest of the room.

"He would never do that," Jessa bursts out. "I know him, just like I know my sister. Callie would never kill me, no matter what the future told her, and Ryder wouldn't, either. This memory doesn't mean anything." Her voice pitches weirdly, bordering on hysterical. She knows, as well as I do, that the two situations are not remotely the same.

She is Callie's adored younger sister. And I am the unlovable daughter of Ryder's biggest enemy.

Jessa shoves a stray hair behind her ear. "Where is he?" she demands of Bao.

The technician swipes his hands along the keyball. "Sector Z-8. Room 628."

Without another word, Jessa spins on her heel and tears out of the room. Tanner takes off after her, and a moment later, I follow. I'd rather be running after Jessa than trapped in a room with all those stares in any pathway of my future.

We catch up with her at the elevator lobby. She bends over, putting her hands on her legs and breathing funny.

"I'm sorry, Livvy," she says, her head down. "I can't imagine how you must feel, seeing that. But there's got to be a mistake. Ryder wouldn't hurt a mouse. For Fate's sake, he used to put acorns in the squirrels' coffins so that they'd have something to eat in the afterlife. He'd never kill you. Never."

I don't respond. I can't. Because I feel the truth of this particular future in my bones. Because the more people who watch a memory, the more Fixed it becomes. That's why my mother ordered that future memories be implanted in a black chip inside every wrist. That's why she encourages prospective employees, loan deputies, and application officials to use these memories as a guarantee. That may even be a contributing factor as to why Callie was successful in changing her future—when so many others are not. Callie's future memory was seen by only two people, her and the administrating officer. It never had the chance to become Fixed.

And I'm very, very afraid—with a room full of people watching—that it's too late to derail my and Ryder's futures from this course.

The elevator capsules arrive, and we take them to Sector Z. As Jessa leads us to the right location, her steps speed up, while mine slow down. I'm not looking forward to coming face-to-face with my future murderer, but it's more than that. My mother is in that room. She's made it her life's mission to make sure every future memory comes true, in order to eliminate the "ripples" that might mess up our world.

Now that she's seen Ryder's vision, what will she do? Will she kill me in order to preserve her precious fabric of time? This wouldn't be the only branch where she sacrifices me for her policies. I should know. Those visions were the nightmares that had me screaming in my youth.

But no matter how slowly I walk, we eventually reach Room 628.

The room has the stark white walls and shiny tiles of every office in the FuMA building. Three reclining chairs with spherical cushions are lined up across the floor, and in the corner, there's a doughnut-shaped com terminal that will translate a vision across five senses.

Two of the chairs are empty. In the third, Ryder is strapped in place, with sensors on his closely shaven head. Instead of struggling against the chains, as we saw in the monitors, he sits calmly, his dark skin gleaming under the bright lights.

My mother poses next to the com terminal, one hand on her hip. With the other hand, she strokes a familiar metal case. A box that houses FuMA's instruments of torture. A case that contains black chips loaded with memories of all the phobias ever known to man.

5

The air feels heavy, wet. Saturated with sweat or tears—or some other moisture I don't want to know about. The smell assaults me, sharp and metallic, sterile and at the same time, disturbingly human.

At our entrance, Ryder emits a low, guttural noise. He attacks the chains, his biceps bulging, his chest flexing. So much force rolls off him I expect the bindings to snap.

They don't.

He sets his jaw and tries again, letting loose a snarl so desperate that it burrows inside me, digging its claws into my stomach. A sheen of moisture slicks over his skin, four parts sweat and one part blood. If my nerves weren't vibrating before, they are now.

My mother laughs in his face. "I see we have an audience," she purrs in the voice she reserves for the public, the one that layers a veneer of silk over thorns. "So much the better. More people to help me figure out which memory will make you scream the loudest."

Ryder bares his teeth at her. "I'm not afraid of you."

"You should be." She snatches one of the black chips

and holds it up to the light. "What should we try first, hmm? You falling headfirst into a pit of snakes? Or cockroaches crawling all over your skin?"

Jessa wraps her hand around my forearm, her fingers as cold as my core. Both she and Tanner have experienced this method of torture firsthand. For different reasons, when they were children, they were forced to live other people's memories, other people's nightmares, over and over again, in an effort to make them comply.

"You dare to execute the chairwoman's daughter," my mother storms. "You will be punished."

She shoves away the case of black chips, and I dart a panicked look at Jessa. Maybe he'll kill me in the future. That doesn't mean he deserves to be tortured.

Do something! I plead with her silently.

Jessa nods, takes a shaky breath, and releases my arm.

"Chairwoman, a word?" she says, her tone even and measured. You'd never guess she was the same girl who moaned inside the control room, the one who trembled like a kite outside the elevator capsules. "The prisoner hasn't technically done anything. The vision hasn't happened. As my sister showed us, it might never happen."

My mother's face contorts. "Callie's one of very few people who has ever changed her future."

"With all due respect, Chairwoman, you haven't given other people a chance," Jessa says. "Don't you remember? You've forced every other would-be criminal to fulfill their visions in order to contain the ripples."

My mother tilts her head, considering her assistant. Over the last six months, Jessa has slowly worked her way into my mother's confidence. She's impressed the chairwoman with her efficiency, demonstrated her loyalty a thousand different ways. If anyone can talk my mother out of this, it's Jessa. If anyone can save Ryder from this torture—

"You may be right, Jessa," the chairwoman says. "And if that were the entire reason for this punishment, I might desist. But there's more you don't understand. Ryder has information I need."

"I'll never give it to you," he spits out. "You can torture me as much as you want. I will never betray my family." He shifts his glare to Jessa. "Unlike some people."

She steps forward. "Ryder…"

"Don't talk to me, traitor," he growls. "I'd rather live a hundred nightmares than take any help from you."

Jessa's mask slips, and she shudders.

"Do you have any idea what you've done to our families?" His eyes are two black coals, burning into our skin, searing into our hearts. "While you've been sleeping in a cozy bed, eating your fill from the Meal Assemblers, we're barely surviving. Angela's so stressed that her body stopped producing milk. Remi doesn't like solid foods, so we go to sleep every night listening to her cries of hunger."

"But I packed formula," Jessa whispers, her lips so white I think she might faint. "There should've been enough to last six months."

"Fell into the river our first day on the run," he says. "And that's not all. Callie's pregnant. As joyous as that is for her and Logan, she's been as sick as our pre-Boom ancestors, and she's not receiving the proper nutrition. Mikey, Logan, and I have been giving her the best of our rations, to give this baby a fighting shot. But that doesn't even take into account her latest injury."

Jessa inches backward until her shoulders hit the wall. Even then, her feet continue to move, her heels rising and falling, as if the action can get her away from Ryder's words.

From Ryder's truth. "What happened?"

His jaw twitches, and I can tell he no longer gets any pleasure from sharing this news. "She cut her palm with a hunting knife. It's gotten infected, and we've run out of meds. That's why I came back to civilization, to get her antibiotics." He lifts his head and looks straight at his former best friend. "If she doesn't get proper treatment for the infection—both she and the baby will die."

A strangled noise works its way from Jessa's throat. Right in front of our eyes, her facade crumbles. Guilt leaches the color from her face, and even the navy blue uniform can't hide who she is: a girl who loves her family— and has lost them all.

"Just tell me where they're hiding," the chairwoman interjects smoothly. "That's all I need to know. You could save Callie's life—and yourself a world of pain."

Ryder sets his jaw. "Never. She made me promise before I left. She'd rather die than go back into your custody."

"How about just your father, then? And Jessa's father, too. Mikey and Preston, two of my very best scientists before they betrayed me. They're the ones I really need." My mother's eyes flash. "Turn over those two, and I'll let the rest of you die in the wilderness in peace. I'll even give you a pharmaceutical pack to take back with you."

He laughs, short and loud and harsh. "That's what you'll never understand, Chairwoman. We're a family. That means we stick together."

"Suit yourself." She shrugs, as if she didn't want him to cave so easily anyway. She fastens her eyes on her personal assistant. "I thought you'd cut emotional ties with your family, Jessa. That they were all but dead to you. At least, that's what you told me. Remind me again whose side you're on?"

Jessa blinks rapidly, as if she's being roused from a dream. "I'm on your side, Chairwoman. You know that."

"Prove it." My mother picks up the case of black chips and holds it out to her.

Jessa looks from Ryder to the chairwoman and then back again. "What...what do you mean?"

"Prove you're still loyal to me." The chairwoman's mouth twists, and it chills me to the bone. "Prove you won't let old relationships interfere with your duties. Prove you're the assistant I thought you were these last six months."

The breath whooshes out of my body, as the implications of my mother's words hit me in the stomach.

"How am I going to do that?" Jessa asks faintly, as though she knows exactly what the chairwoman is saying but is still hoping she's wrong.

"Easy. I'm not going to torture your friend by making him live other people's nightmares," my mother says. "You are."

Jessa slumps forward, and her shirt lifts, revealing the handprint birthmark at her waist and the curve of her spine.

I flash forward to her futures. This is an impossible situation for Jessa. Impossible. She can't jeopardize the trust she's built over the last six months. She's sacrificed so much to get this position, and now, she's poised to stop the chairwoman from committing genocide. And yet, she can't torture her best friend, either. She may have betrayed her family, but this would cross a line she won't be able to uncross.

This moment, this decision, will break something inside her. No matter what she chooses, she will hate herself for the rest of her life. I see the hollow shell she becomes. The shadow of the strong and selfless girl she used to be.

She'll turn into...me. A girl living on the edge of life.

Only observing but never acting. Helpless to bring about the change she so desperately wants. Reliant on other people to do what she thinks is right.

And it makes me want to weep.

I may never have loved anyone as much as Jessa loves Ryder. But I've seen a nearly infinite number of futures, and I know what love is. And, as I stand here beside Jessa, something happens to me. Her heart reaches inside my heart and squeezes, squeezes, squeezes. Until my entire chest is one big ache. Until my pathways shrink down to a narrow and precise tunnel.

Until I know that there's only one decision I can possibly make.

"I'll do it," I say, stepping forward. "I'll torture our captive."

6

They gape at me—my mother, Tanner, Jessa. Even Ryder. I don't know if it's because I spoke without being addressed. Or maybe because I volunteered to do something, anything. Most likely, it's because this is the first definitive action I've taken since I asked Jessa to fight with me—or more accurately, *for* me. But they all stare as though I'm a shadow that's suddenly turned solid.

And maybe I am.

I take the case and hug it close to my chest. The image of Jessa's spine drifts through my mind. So curved, so fragile. As though it might snap at any moment.

"It is my right to torture this boy." My voice is stronger and clearer than it's been in months, maybe even years. It has just the right amount of force, and I don't drop a single syllable. "I was in his vision. He stuck a syringe into my chest. I watched my body go limp, like it. I saw myself die."

Something bubbles in my stomach. It takes me a moment to realize that it's anger. Wow. I haven't felt like this in ages. Sad, yes. Horrified, lonely, even determined. But not angry. Because this emotion presupposes that you are entitled to something. That you've been wronged.

I may be used to taking what Fate's given me, but sometime in the future, some version of this boy will kill me. And I'm not okay with that.

"This is my right." I let my emotion leak into my voice. "If I have to wait for him to commit the crime, it will be too late. I'll already be dead."

My mother opens her mouth—and then closes it. Her eyes flash, a light so brilliant it is almost painful to see. She shifts, and all of a sudden, it is as though we are the only two people in the room.

Scenes of our past confrontations flow through my mind. In all of them, she stands before me, her glittery eyes testing me, daring me. Determining if I'm strong enough, smart enough, *good* enough to be her daughter. With all my foresight, I still don't know exactly what she wants from me.

"Fine," she says. "The job is yours. But be thorough. I want him to live every nightmare in that case, you got it?"

"I can't watch this," Jessa says miserably.

"Then you should leave," my mother snaps. "There're a million things you could be doing for me. Go make yourself useful."

Jessa sets her jaw. I can see her gathering her strength the way a tornado picks up the wind.

"Leave!" the chairwoman thunders. "And take your boyfriend with you."

"Go ahead," I murmur to Jessa. "Don't worry. I'll handle…"

…*it*.

She pulls me close to her. "You have to save him," she says directly in my ear. "You have to save Callie."

I nod, but inside, I'm trembling, trembling, trembling.

Isn't it enough that I've offered to torture her best friend so she won't have to? What else does she expect from me?

Suddenly, I want to take it all back. *I'm the Shadow!* I want to shout. *The Shadow. I don't know how to do this. I don't know how to do any of this.*

But she doesn't give me the chance. With one last glance at Ryder, she takes Tanner's hand, and they walk out of the room.

And then, it is just us. Me, my mother…and Ryder.

"You're making me proud, Olivia." The chairwoman rubs her hands together. "So proud."

Ryder lifts his chin. "That's right, Olivia," he says mockingly. "Make your mother proud. Make the long history of the human race proud. Show all those little girls and boys the kind of person they should aspire to be."

I adjust my sweaty grip on the case as the room spins lazily around me. "You will kill…"

…*me.*

"Not yet," he responds, his voice low and urgent, as though he doesn't notice that I've dropped a word. "If my will and my strength have anything to do with it, not ever."

Sweat gathers on my upper lip. My heart drills a hole in my chest. Never once in my life have I ever deliberately hurt—much less tortured—anyone. I don't know how it will change me. I don't know what it will destroy inside me.

But this isn't about me. I'm doing this for Jessa. For the countless boys and girls who will be wiped out if my mother's plans of genocide come to fruition. I'd never willingly torture someone. But for Jessa, I can. For Jessa, I will.

For Jessa. For Jessa. For Jessa.

Before I can change my mind, I move to the com terminal and insert one of the black chips into the slot. Immediately, Ryder's body arcs in the chair, and his arms and legs thrash violently.

"Which memory is it?" my mother asks, her tone not quite gleeful but close. Uncomfortably close.

I read the label through the slot. "Drowning," I say shakily.

Ryder's eyes bulge. His chest heaves, straining against the chains, but his lips are sealed tight. I want, with everything in my being, to look away. But I don't. If he has to live through this torture, then the least I can do is watch it.

Sixty long, eternal seconds later, the memory is finally over. Ryder collapses against his seat, the breath coming out of him in pants.

"Have you had enough?" my mother asks. "Go on. Tell us where they're hiding. We'll bring them in, save Callie's life. You have my word we'll treat them well."

He lifts his head, even though the action obviously pains him. "I can do this all day."

"And so we will." She turns to me. "Go ahead, Olivia. This time, find a memory that's not underwater. I want to hear him scream."

She smiles, small and tight and mean. Why is she smiling?

As Ryder glares at me, his eyes dark pools of rage, the answer dawns on me. I know what she's wanted all these years. I now understand that sharp look in her eyes, the one that slices up my insides. She thinks she's won. She believes I am no longer a shadow.

Instead, I'm turning out to be just like her.

No! The knowledge strikes me like a sledgehammer. We're not the same. She wants to destroy the world. I want to save it. But does it matter, if we use the same means to reach our goals?

I tremble so violently that my knees knock together. All these years, I've been hanging onto an idealistic image of the chairwoman. I've been fiercely loyal to the woman my mother could be. But that woman has yet to appear in my timeline. What if she never does? What if my mother's plans of genocide are not the misguided by-product of a person who means well—but the evil brainchild of a true monster? What then?

"That's right. Do exactly as your mother says," Ryder growls. "That's the only thing you're good for, isn't it? To be her little bot." His voice is ragged, raw. A few decibels above a whisper. And yet, the words pierce through my gut like a tranquilizer. "If I die today, then at least I'll know I was protecting my family. What will you die for?"

"Shut your mouth!" The chairwoman stalks toward him so that she's standing next to the empty recliner. "Do not speak to my daughter that way. She's worth a hundred of you. A thousand."

Why, I didn't know you cared, I think weakly. But it doesn't matter. I have to remember why I'm doing this. So that I can save the people of North Amerie from genocide.

Correction: so that *Jessa* can save the people from genocide.

In the majority of our futures, it's Jessa being close to the chairwoman that's important. Not me. It's Jessa who saves the world—not me. I'm simply an ally for Jessa. I'm the one who got her onto this course, but she doesn't need me anymore. This mission doesn't need me.

But maybe, just maybe, other people do.

Jessa's words drift through my mind again. *You have to save him,* she said. *You have to save Callie.*

All of a sudden, a single pathway lights up for me. It is only one branch in my thousands of possible futures, so remote that I didn't notice it before. But I see it now.

And I know what I have to do.

Without warning, I charge forward, striking my mother in the chest. She gasps and falls over, landing in the empty chair next to Ryder. Quickly, I move to the com terminal and push a button. Chains slither over her shoulders and thighs, holding her in place.

The chairwoman is now my captive.

7

"What the Limbo, Olivia?" my mother roars. "Let me out of here!"

I float somewhere outside my body. I must be, because that's not me confirming there are no security cameras, since the chairwoman likes to torture her victims in privacy. That's not me placing oval sensors all over my mother's head. That's not me crossing to the com terminal and setting up twenty black chips—and twenty memories—to play one after the other. That's not me watching my mother buck against the chains, letting loose an unending scream.

One of those weird pathways must be flitting through my mind—the ones that are so utterly remote that I usually filter them out as noise.

Vaguely, I note that my heart is battering against my ribs, that sweat is stinging my eyes. The me outside my body hears the sound of Ryder's ragged breathing, registers a bite on my tongue and the taste of blood.

My blood. But not nearly the only blood that's been shed in this room.

That's all it takes to make me return to my body.

I press the button that releases the chains that strap down Ryder. As soon as he slides off the chair, however, his knees buckle, and he barely manages to lurch to a wall. Fike. I guess the drowning messed with his body more than just mentally.

"What in Fates are you doing?" he manages to gasp.

"Rescuing you," I say.

My mother's writhing has made the shirt ride up on her waist. I stare. There, all over her stomach, are needle marks, along with bruises on top of bruises on top of bruises. Some look new; others look weeks—maybe even months—old. It's like my mother's been injecting herself on a daily basis in a place where nobody else will see.

Are Tanner and Jessa right? Has she been medicating herself for the last ten years? Why? To treat those strange symptoms Danni has?

Ryder shoves off the wall, pulling my attention back to him. I move forward, and he holds up a hand, warding me off. "I don't need your help—"

"Oh stop. You can hate me all you want, but I'm getting you out of here, aren't I? So let's go save Callie's life." The words spill out of me, smooth and uninterrupted.

He nods reluctantly, as if he has no choice but to accept my logic, and glances at my mother, who is nearly hyperventilating on the chair. "And the chairwoman?"

"She'll be fine." Guilt snakes into my veins. She…doesn't look good. But this is no worse than what she did to Tanner and Jessa when they were six years old. She'll recover.

Oh Fates, now I really sound like her. Before I can despair, however, the next black chip slides into place on the com terminal, which means my mother's beginning a new memory. A new nightmare scenario, a new set of moans and whimpers.

I grit my teeth. I cannot—I will not—melt into a pile of self-recriminations. We simply don't have time.

"I've set up approximately twenty minutes of memories." There. Another sentence without any dropped words. If rebelling against my mother is the reason, maybe I should've done it a long time ago. "We need to be out of here before the black chips stop playing. Can you walk?"

He gives me a withering look. "Of course I can walk."

Two steps later, he's sucking in air and grimacing. Aw, Limbo.

"Here, lean on me." I wrap his arm around my shoulder and tuck my own arm tightly around his waist. I'm about half his size, and it feels like most of me is pressed against him...and his bare skin. He smells, inexplicably, of evergreens.

I shiver—but only because the warmth and hardness of his body are so unfamiliar. I've never been this close to a boy, ever. My reaction means nothing. Doesn't mean I feel anything other than anger and pity toward him.

"I don't want your help," he says, even as he leans into me heavily. We walk forward, and he sucks in another breath.

"You already said that," I retort. "And I already said we're not going to discuss it."

"At least your skin is soft," he says under his breath.

I halt, glaring up at him. "What?"

"Never mind," he mumbles. "Clearly I'm still caught up in the nightmare you put me through."

I resolutely ignore him, and we shuffle out of the room and down the hall, still plastered together.

My mind whirls. Even if we find an exit without anyone seeing us, how will I get him out without setting off any alarms? FuMA's doubled up on security over the last few months, and no one gets in or out of the building without an identity scan.

I reach into his future, sifting through the possibilities for a way out of here. Limbo, Limbo, Limbo. In every pathway where I try to sneak him through a door, we're caught.

I flip faster and faster through the other branches, staying high-level and zooming in closer when a pathway shows promise.

And then, I see it. The slender branch that might actually get us out of here.

"We need to stop by the dispensary," I blurt out. I can't let him know—yet—what I'm planning. "There's one in this sector that should be unstaffed right now. We'll grab the antibiotics for Callie."

He narrows his eyes. "You think I'm just going to lead you straight to Callie and the others? No way. Torturing your mother doesn't prove anything. This could all be a big ploy to get me to reveal their location."

Seriously? My brows shoot up my forehead. So he doesn't trust me? Good. I don't trust him, either. We're talking about the boy who's going to kill me in twenty days, for Fate's sake.

"Fine," I say. "Don't show me where they are. I'll get you the antibiotics and then drop-kick you out the door. Better?"

His lips twitch. "Much."'

At that moment, a FuMA guard rounds the corner. He does a double take upon seeing a shirtless guy draped over my shoulders.

Ryder stiffens, and he scans the corridor wildly, looking for an escape route. I pinch the skin at his waist, hoping he'll let me take the lead.

"Shadow," the guard blurts out. "Ehrm, I mean, Miss Dresden. What are you doing?"

I draw myself to my full height, which is difficult while I'm supporting Ryder, and fix the guard with my best imitation of my mother's scowl. "What does it look like I'm doing? I called for transport half an hour…"

…*ago*.

Fike. The last thing I need is for this pesky habit to resurface now. I take a deep breath and center my thoughts. "No one came. So don't just stand there! Quick! Get me a gliding chair so I don't have to keep holding him."

The guard's jaw drops, probably because he's heard that the Shadow doesn't speak, much less give orders. "Is he a detainee? He doesn't have on electro-cuffs—"

"You dare to question me?" My tone climbs into the arctic range, as I repeat the words I've heard my mother say dozens of times. "I am the chairwoman's daughter, and I gave you a direct order. Now, before I report you."

He snaps to attention at the reminder of who I am. Of what my authority is, even if I've never used it. "Yes, ma'am! I think there's a gliding chair in the next corridor. Be right back, ma'am!"

He scurries off, and Ryder turns to me, blinking. "Wow. That was…impressive."

I flush. That's the first time anyone's ever followed my lead—but he doesn't have to know that. "Still think you can get out of here without me?"

"Oh, I could do it. Don't ever underestimate my will to survive."

We stare at each other, his eyes deep, dark, challenging. I shiver again—but before I can figure out why, the guard's back, nudging along a gliding chair.

"Here you go, ma'am!" he says. "Will you need anything

else? Happy to escort you wherever you need to go. Ma'am."

"No, thank you," I say, my tone softening. "And no need to call me ma'am."

He backs away, saluting me until he's out of sight. I maneuver Ryder into the gliding chair and then guide him down the hallway. "We have to hurry. The more people who see us, the more dangerous it'll be."

I look down warily. Ryder's sitting perfectly erect, a fierce glower on his face. Even in a chair, he's intimidating as Limbo.

"Play dead," I demand.

"What?" He twists, his shoulders brushing against my knuckles.

Sparks shoot through my skin, but I pretend not to notice. "You just lived through the memory of a drowning. It's feasible that you would pass out from the panic."

"Um, I don't think so," he says haughtily. "I never pass out. And I've experienced much more panic than that."

I roll my eyes. "I'm sure you can go ten rounds with the electro-whip and not flinch, too. Can you please shelve your pride for two seconds? I'm trying to get us out of here."

"Fine." He leans his head back, pretending to sleep. After a moment, he opens one eye. "I can see up your nose."

The corners of my lips tug. "Be quiet. You're dead, re-member?"

We turn down three more corridors and take the trans-port elevator to the seventh floor. Along the way, we pass half a dozen FuMA employees, but just as I hoped, they do nothing more than nod and salute.

Once we reach the dispensary, I scan my retinas and fingerprints and then guide Ryder inside. Rows of floor-to-ceiling racks line one side of the long, narrow room. Each revolving rack is ten deep and holds trays stocked with tubes in every shade of the rainbow. The chilly air makes the goose bumps pop out on my arm. At least this time, I know why I'm cold.

I move to the com terminal at the front of the room, pulling up the location codes for Callie's antibiotic…and the anesthetic I don't want Ryder to know about.

When I turn, my heart jumps into my throat. Ryder's gotten out of the chair, and he's peering into the racks.

"What are you doing?"

He emits a low whistle. "Take a look at this. What's this formula used for?"

I walk over to stand next to him, and my eyes widen. Row after row of trays are filled with tubes of amber-colored formula. Why, fully half of the dispensary must be stocked with that medicine alone.

I swallow hard. Why do we need so much of that formula? Could the confused victims of future memory require such a large supply? The image of my mother's bruised stomach flashes through my mind. Maybe, especially if the other victims need as many injections as my mother.

"People have been having these weird symptoms lately," I say. "Walking into walls, holding conversations with someone who isn't there. This formula's used to treat whatever's going on."

His brows knit together. "Really? That sounds an awful lot like the way Callie's been acting."

It's my turn to frown. "I thought you said she has an infection from a cut on her palm."

"She does. I think." He shakes his head. "Maybe we don't really know."

A crash sounds outside the dispensary, and then I hear excited murmurs and footsteps running. Limbo. We're taking too much time. We should've been out of here minutes ago.

I try to push him back toward the chair. "Please. Go sit back down."

"Why?"

"You're still weak. I need to retrieve the syringes, and I don't want to worry about you falling." I lick my lips. "Besides, you make me nervous."

He arches an eyebrow and steps closer. "I make you nervous? Is that why you drop the ends of your sentences?"

I freeze. Here it comes. The mocking, the ridicule, the shame. No one typically throws my speech patterns in my face—I am, after all, the chairwoman's daughter—but I've heard the whispers. I've imagined the jeers.

"It's nothing to be embarrassed about," Ryder continues. "I used to skip words in my sentences, too."

My mouth falls open. I can't imagine it. He's such a big guy, but more than that, he emits this air of easygoing confidence, the kind you have when you know your place in the world. I'd never guess he had any annoying speech tics. "You?"

"Oh sure. Back when I was a kid. Jessa was so grateful I put up with her not talking, but really, her silence made my few meager words look like a lot." He moves his shoulders. "It never seemed like a big deal, 'cause Jessa always understood what I was saying."

Ah. Maybe that's why Jessa's never commented on my habit; maybe that's why she's never had a problem picking up the threads of our conversations. She's had practice.

A surge of warmth moves through me, because of Jessa's friendship and also, inexplicably, because of this guy in front of me. Another surprise. I never thought I would have such soft feelings for such a hard boy.

We look at each other for an infinitesimal moment, during which my stomach sprouts wings and flits around my insides, and then I put my hands on his chest and push him again. Only this time, I'm acutely aware of my bare skin touching his, of the frantic beating of his heart a few inches from my fingers. "Have a seat," I say. "Please."

"Fine." He holds my eyes for another moment and then lurches to the gliding chair and sits down. It's a small concession, but I'm beginning to suspect just how much it costs him to give even this much.

I can't let that affect what I need to do next.

My movements jerky, I move down the aisle, passing a small section of tubes with clear formula. I shudder. The clear liquid stands out against the bright, brilliant hues of the rest of the vials in the room, sinister in its absence of color. Ever since I was a child, my mother's instilled in me a deep suspicion of a vial with clear liquid. Disguised with the same appearance as the most innocuous substance in the world, water, this formula has one function alone: to kill.

I should know. This is the very same formula Ryder injected me with in his future memory. I can't forget that. No matter how nicely he's acting, this boy is going to kill me. Soon. In twenty days, to be precise.

Squaring my shoulders, I retrieve the tubes I'm looking for—a grass-green formula and an ocean-teal. I even take the amber-colored one, just in case.

I stick the tubes into a calibration machine on the wall, and it dispenses the proper dosage into syringes.

Pocketing the syringes, I walk back to Ryder and bend down so that our faces are level. He smiles. *Oh Fates, don't notice how the smile transforms his face. Don't think how that curve of his lips makes your pulse run wild.*

Quickly, before I lose my courage, I plunge the teal

syringe into his neck and depress the barrel.

His hands shoot out, gripping my neck and yanking me forward. I stumble and land awkwardly in his lap.

"What…did you…do…to me?" he rasps, his voice already fading. His grip already loosening.

"I'm sorry," I say helplessly. "This was the only pathway I found."

His hands drop from my neck, fluttering down my arms like falling leaves. "Never…trust you…again."

"Forgive me," I whisper. But it's too late.

He's already passed out.

8

Ten minutes later I'm tugging Ryder's unconscious body from the gliding chair into a coffin that I've situated on the conveyor belt. I already lowered the belt all the way to the floor and tilted the seat of the chair. With any luck, gravity will help me move his muscular body...

Oomph. I've moved him into the coffin all right. There's only one problem. I fell in first, and he's landed right on top of me.

For a moment, all I can feel is the hard planes of his chest and thighs pushing into my body. My ears, my neck, even my toes heat. This should be uncomfortable—Limbo, it *is* uncomfortable—but for some reason, I wish we could stay like this, if not forever, then at least for a few long minutes.

Ridiculous. Clearly, the crush of his weight is making me delirious. I grit my teeth and begin to wiggle out from underneath him. Maybe I should've asked Jessa and Tanner to meet me here, in the Cadaver Transfer Unit, instead of outside by the dumping grounds. This is where the bodies go when they've outlived their usefulness in the Dream Lab, the place where scientists study the brain activity of people in a coma.

I catch a whiff of formaldehyde, and my stomach turns. *Don't freak out,* I order myself sternly. *Now is not the time for a panic attack.* For all practical purposes, these people have been dead for years. Besides, they donated their brains to science. They knew their bodies would eventually end up here.

At least the corpses are kept in cabinets built into the walls before they're transferred to their coffins—although I suppose "coffin" is too fancy a word. They're really just rectangular plastic crates designed to minimize the diseases associated with disposing large quantities of bodies.

A few muscle-aching minutes later, I manage to extract myself. My clothes are now soaked in sweat, but at least Ryder is resting in peace on his back.

Now comes the hard part. I have to take off his pants.

The conveyor belt takes the coffins via a lengthy tunnel to a dumping ground on the outskirts of the FuMA property, where they're collected once a day. From there, the coffins are either dropped in the middle of the ocean or ejected into space. So long as the scanner doesn't detect any metal or large movement, the corpse inside the coffin is allowed to exit without an identity scan. That's what I'm counting on. The teal formula has put Ryder's body into an anesthetized state, and the slight rise and fall of his chest should fall short of setting off the scanner.

I just have to get rid of the metal.

Taking a deep breath, I grab a pair of laser shears from the work table and attack his pants. Most pants these days are attached by magnets or patented molding technology, but Ryder wears the pre-Boom kind with zippers. It would take too much time to remove them the normal way...and oh my. The heat climbs my face. His legs are sculpted like one of those statues displayed in the Museum of Artifacts. Muscular, lean, and hard.

I swallow. Not that I'm noticing. Really.

I pull the fabric from underneath his legs, giving his underwear a wide berth. Surely there's nothing in *there* that the scanner will pick up. Right?

Grabbing a medic gown from a stack on the table, I throw one over his lower body. Better.

I force my gaze away—and it snags on his face. He looks younger with his eyes closed. More innocent. His eyelashes brush against his cheek, and everything about him appears soft. His lips, his skin—Limbo, even the sharp lines of his jaw.

Something twinges in my heart. Regret, maybe? Longing? What would our friendship have been like if our circumstances had been different? If I had been a normal girl who met him in the T-minus school system, would I still feel this same draw to him? Would I gravitate toward his warmth, drink up all his features, the way I'm doing now?

I'll never know.

"You're ready." I would've guessed it would be easier to talk to him when he's not conscious to hear me—but it's not. Strangely, my speech is just as fluid whether he's awake or asleep. "I'm sorry I had to anesthetize you, but it's a long tunnel. I couldn't be sure that you wouldn't move. But you're safe, I promise. I'll see you soon."

At least, in seventy percent of the pathways, I will. This is the only way out of here. The branch with the highest percentage of success. He's going to be mad, but he'll thank me later. Maybe.

I lower the magnetized lid onto the coffin and activate the conveyor belt with a voice command. The coffin containing Ryder's body moves up the ramp...and disappears into the tunnel.

...

Hundreds of coffins are stacked around the dumping grounds. As soon as a coffin clears the conveyor belt, bots transfer it to one of a dozen pallets lining the fence. In the short time it took me to run out here, Ryder's coffin has already been removed and stacked among the others.

"What is this place?" Jessa whispers beside me. She and Tanner have met me here, just like they promised.

"It's the dumping ground for the morgue," Tanner says, approaching a stack of coffins and peering at the numbered labels displayed on one side. "Remember those bodies you saw in the hallway outside the Dream Lab? This is where they end up."

She nods, sadness etched into her features. "Oh. I always wondered where they went. Don't tell me Ryder's...here?"

"He's in A-307. But it's not what you think." I smooth my hand over one coffin. Oh Fates, there are *people* inside each box. Stacked on top of one another like trays of assembled meals.

Quickly, I push the image away and explain everything that happened after they left, from my decision to torture my mom to the anesthesia that I injected into Ryder's neck.

Jessa's eyes widen. "Holy Time. You made your mom live through the phobias?"

I nod slowly. "Twenty of them."

"Wow. She's not going to be happy with you."

The understatement of the year. I can no longer see into her future—and as a result, any part of my future that involves her is also blank—but I'd guess there's a fifty-fifty chance she tosses me straight into detainment when she finds me.

Whatever the consequences, I'll just have to live with them. Because this was the right thing to do.

I lift my chin. "She'll have to catch me first."

"Oh hey," Tanner calls from the third pallet. "Lookee here. Found him."

I trip over my feet moving to the pallet and help Tanner wrestle the coffin down. Once we break the seal with a demagnification wand, Ryder's square jaw peeks out at me, along with his muscled torso. My shoulders sag. Thank the Fates he's safe.

Jessa rushes to her best friend, her hands hovering like moths over his body. "Oh, Olivia, thank you." Her voice trembles. "You saved him. You got him out of there, without any pain."

"But I tortured him," I say. "With a memory of being drowned alive. And then, I stabbed him. With a syringe that knocked him…"

…*out.*

"Under the circumstances, I think he'll forgive you."

"Like he's forgiven you?" The words slip out before I can stop myself. Problem is, I know exactly where they came from. From the place deep inside my rib cage, in a spot behind my heart, where I shove all of my guilt and disgust. "Sorry. I shouldn't have said…"

…*that.*

"Don't apologize." She bites her lip, and color floods into the flesh. "This war is making us all do things we'd rather not."

"People will be saved." Tanner puts his hand at the nape of her neck. "That's what we have to remember."

She nods. "That's the only thing keeping me going."

"I thought *I* was the reason you got out of bed every morning," he says, tickling her. "Your every breath, your every action—all because of me."

Jessa snorts, and I laugh. Tanner Callahan is the most arrogant guy I've ever met, but he's certainly one of a kind.

Crouching down, he fastens together six hoverboards of his own invention. Jessa and Tanner had brought the hoverboards to the dumping grounds, along with a couple backpacks of supplies.

This is why I messaged them. I could barely get Ryder into the coffin. There's no way I could've carted him off to safety without assistance.

Tanner stands by Ryder's head and gestures for Jessa and me to each take a leg. "On three. One…two…three…"

Oof. With a gigantic effort, we heave him onto the hoverboards. After a bit of arranging, he's situated as comfortably as we can make him.

"That should do it," Tanner says. "These boards are similar to the ones we use in the hover park. However, they're powered from the sun, and they utilize the magnets deep in the Earth's surface. Put the boards on auto-mode, at the lowest speed, and you should be able to get him where you need to go."

"Thank you. I couldn't have done it without *you*." I wince. In my determination to say the last word of my sentence, it came out too loudly.

I glance at the metal and glass spires of the FuMA building. I don't hear an alarm—yet. But that doesn't mean the guards aren't searching for me. "If anyone asks, I acted alone. You have no idea where I went, what my intentions *are*."

Father of Time. *Again.* But neither Tanner nor Jessa bats an eye.

"Livvy, are you sure?" my old playmate asks instead. "We can send Ryder on the hoverboards by himself. He'll have the antibiotics, and when he wakes up, he'll find his way back to his family. Alone."

"I have to go with him." I tell them about the overlapping bruises along my mother's waist. About Ryder's claim that Callie is exhibiting the same symptoms. "If Callie has the same illness as my mom, she's going to need more than one amber syringe. I either have to bring her back here or figure out how to get her more syringes."

"I should go," Jessa bursts out. "She's my sister. If anyone's going to risk themselves to save her, it should be me."

I place a hand on her arm. "True. But the chairwoman's already after me. There's no reason to jeopardize her trust in both of us. Besides, the genocide's coming soon, Jessa. In less than a month, my mother will start executing the kids who receive mediocre memories. At least, that's what my vision predicts. You need to stay here so that you can stop her.

"I know I'm asking a lot." I lick my lips. "I'm asking you to put Callie's safety in the hands of someone who's better suited for the sidelines. Maybe I shouldn't even be…"

…*suggesting this*.

She seizes my hand. "I trust you, Olivia," she says fiercely. "You can do this. I have full faith that you will save my sister."

Is she right? Jessa's baby precognition means that she can only see a few minutes into the future, so she has even less knowledge than me. But if her certainty stems from her belief in me…I'll take it.

9

A few hours later, the unconscious Ryder and I squeeze through a thicket of bushes and come upon a cabin next to a fenced-in area full of bloodhounds. Trees surround the property on all four sides, and every log, every window, looks the same. They probably are. The outside world may change, technology may evolve, cities of metal and glass may shoot into the sky—but here, in these woods, I can almost believe that this cabin will endure for the rest of time.

I want to weep. "We're here, Ryder." I wipe a hand across the dried sweat and dirt caked on my forehead. "We finally made it."

He doesn't respond, of course. In fact, the floating platform of hoverboards continues forward at the same even pace, and I have to rush to catch up with it.

"Olivia, is that you?" A figure steps outside the chain link fence.

Shading my eyes, I see a hefty man with white whiskers and ruddy cheeks. He wears his usual uniform of water-resistant pants and a black mesh shirt. Potts.

I command the hover platform to stop, and run straight into his arms. He lifts me up and spins me around, the way he's been greeting me for the last ten years.

"It's been too long, girl," he says gruffly. "Where have you been?"

"I'm no longer in my cabin in the woods, Potts. Went back to FuMA about six months ago. I'm living out in the open now."

"Your mother okay with that?"

"It was her idea." I drop my eyes to the ground, even though I've never had a problem looking at or talking to this man. "She, um, wanted me to shadow her new assistant. Said it was about time I got re-acclimated to society." There's more to it, of course. Such as the fact that I agreed because the terrifying blank wall of my precognition is looming closer and closer. Because the number of weeks remaining until genocide can be counted on one hand. For my own reasons, I want to live—just a little bit—before I have to die.

He grunts. It's a simple sound that could mean nothing or anything. It's one of the things I love most about him. He's one of the very few people I might consider a friend.

A few months after I went into isolation, I got lost during one of my forays into the woods and stumbled onto this lonely cabin with the kennel of bloodhounds.

From the beginning, I was drawn to Potts. He's not like anyone I've ever met. First, because he has no interest in the Committee of Agencies, or ComA, the governing entity that oversees our nation. Although he may supply them with his bloodhounds, he stays resolutely out of politics. And second, because he has so few pathways in his future. Whereas most people still have hundreds of branches stemming from a handful of major arteries remaining when they hit middle age, Potts has fewer than ten. His days are exactly the same. He wears the same clothes, eats the same meals. Takes care of his dogs. When I'm around other people, millions of pathways constantly bombard me. Not true with him.

And so, I would sneak away to visit Potts every few months, to play with his hounds or to curl up in front of his fire. To collect the three acorns he always left for me on his sill.

A bloodhound with a reddish-brown and black coat bounds over to me. "Hi Betsy!" I say enthusiastically. She's probably not the same dog I played with six months ago, but it doesn't matter. Potts's bloodhounds are constantly changing, but they're all named Betsy.

He raises his eyebrows at the platform of boards hovering next to me. "What do we have here?"

"Oh, um. It's complicated." I rack my brain, trying to find the easiest way to explain. "We just need a place to hide until he wakes up. And then we'll be on our way."

He scrutinizes my forehead, my brows, my eyes. "You're a good girl, Olivia. You always have been. Are you quite certain you're not in over your head?"

"I probably am," I say, and a part of me yearns to run to my hiding spot behind his glider, the place where I cowered if I happened to hear a loud noise or if even Potts's meager world turned out to be too much. "In fact, I'm sure of it. But what else was I supposed to do? I couldn't just leave him."

I glance down at Ryder's sleeping form, but Potts continues to stare at me, so long I wonder if he can read my mind. But he's never admitted to having any kind of psychic ability—not that he would in this political climate.

"Fine," he finally says. "You can stay here." He snaps his fingers, and the bloodhound that's been sniffing around me trots to him. "Me and Betsy, we've been planning a little camp-out. Maybe do some fishing, a little hunting." His eyes sharpen. "Given what you don't want to tell me about this boy, maybe we should go ahead and take that trip now."

"Maybe so," I say.

He nods. "Got it. Just remember, if it ever comes to it, I never gave you permission to crash in my cabin."

I widen my eyes. "I never even saw you."

He pats my hand and walks away, whistling a tune. Betsy lopes after him. As I watch their retreating backs, an old yearning rises in me—one that I don't fully understand. Potts has always been kind to me, and he listens to me. Maybe that explains my feelings. Fates knows, simple appreciation has been hard to come by in my life.

Doesn't mean I have to get nostalgic. Doesn't mean I have to let my mind wander to the chairwoman, to whether she's recovered from the torture.

Turning, I command the hover platform to bring Ryder into the cabin.

I have a mission to accomplish.

10

Ryder bolts upright and gasps, hungrily sucking in air as if it's his first breath in hours. Day has turned to night outside the cabin, and it's about time he woke up.

"Where in Fates am I?" he rasps. His eyes roam the room, skipping from me to the rickety shelf that holds actual books, to the fire flickering behind the grate. "What did you do to me?"

My heart bounces around my chest like the racquetball I used to play with as a kid, but I calmly carry over a cup of water and a plate of sandwiches. "You must be thirsty. And hungry. Potts has only the most basic Meal Assembler. I wasn't sure how you like your turkey sandwiches, so I ordered up the works. Lettuce, cheese, mayo, pickles."

He stares at me like I just proposed eating the same meal for the rest of the year. Which is probably what Potts does.

"You were sitting on my lap. You had one hand on my chest, and the other hand…" His brow creases. "Your other hand had just stabbed something into my neck." His fingers drift to the puncture site. "And now I'm here. What happened?"

I begin to rip his sandwich into tiny pieces, to give my hands something to do. "I injected you with an anesthetic, and you passed out. And then you exited the building through the conveyor belt that takes out the corpses." I move my shoulders helplessly. "It was the only way. You'd never have been able to get past the identity scans."

He gapes. "You drugged me?"

"I guess." His dinner is now inedible—unless he likes sandwich confetti.

He looks down at his body, at the unfamiliar sweats and T-shirt. The question hangs in the air between us.

"Um, Potts got you dressed before he left on his hunting trip." The blush flames up my cheeks. I'm not sure when would be a good time to tell him I cut off his pants. Maybe never.

"You should've asked before injecting me," he says.

"You would've refused. Look how difficult you were when I asked you to play dead! No way you would've trusted me enough to let me inject you with anything."

His jaw clenches. "That should've been your first clue not to do it."

"I had to! Every other pathway gave us an almost nonexistent chance of escape."

"So you know everything, don't you?" He leaps to his feet. "You can foresee my every move."

"That's not the way it works." I fight to keep my voice even. "I can't tell the future. What I see are possible pathways. The only predictions I give are based on percentages."

"Oh yeah?" His eyebrows climb his forehead. "Well, predict this."

He strides to the door of the cabin, flings it open, and disappears into the night.

My mouth drops open. Aw, Limbo. He's right—I did see

this particular branch in his future. But it had only a thirty percent chance of occurring. And it's cold out there…and he's barefoot… Fike. I can't believe this is happening.

Grabbing a pair of Potts's shoes and an overcoat, I run into the dark. The world outside has turned into fog and shadows, with only a sliver of light emanating from the half-moon nestled above the trees. I can just make out Ryder's shoulders bobbing in the distance.

"Wait, Ryder, you need shoes! Your feet are going to get totally ripped up if you go out like that."

I put on a burst of speed and catch up with him. He doesn't even break his stride.

"You betrayed me," he says, training his eyes straight ahead. "You don't know me, but you'll figure out soon enough. I don't give second chances."

I puff out a breath. "I'm not asking for your life, Ryder. It's *just* a pair of shoes."

He stops walking abruptly and turns to me, his eyes narrowed. "You got some kind of tracking device in there?"

"Of course not," I say, indignant.

"You think you're going to bribe your way into coming with me, then? Not a chance."

I take a rattling breath and try to pretend it's just from running. Try to pretend it's not because I'm unreasonably hurt. "Maybe I'm just being nice. You ever consider that? Father of Time, Ryder, I'm not the enemy here. I tortured my own mother. I hauled your ass onto a platform of six hoverboards and then guided you through miles of bramble and trees. I even cut off your pants." Oops. So much for keeping that a secret. "What more do you want from me? How else can I prove that I'm trustworthy?"

He sets his jaw. "I trusted someone before. And look what happened."

"Are you talking about Jessa?" I take a step forward, so he has no choice but to look at me. "She didn't do it to hurt you. In fact, turning your family in was the hardest thing she's ever done. I should know. We share an apartment in the scientific residences, and she still wakes up crying every night."

I reach out my hand—but I don't touch him. Because I don't know how he would react. Fates, I don't know how *I* would react. "Nothing's more important to Jessa than her family, and yet, she betrayed them anyway. She did it so she could gain the chairwoman's trust, Ryder. So she could fight this war from within. So we can stop genocide once and for all."

He goes still, and for a moment, all I can hear is the sound of his ragged breathing. "If that's true, why didn't she tell me? She could've just explained. I would've played along."

"Would you have?" I ask. "Somehow, I doubt that. You would've argued, Mikey would've refused. Logan would've thought it was too dangerous."

"Maybe," he admits. "But ultimately, I would've listened. She knows exactly how difficult it is for me to give my trust, and after all we've been through, she should've confided in me. It kills me that she didn't."

"I know," I say helplessly, even as my mind spins. How hard *is* it for him to give his trust? What could've happened to etch that pain across his face? "I'm sorry. She was busy. Busy with saving her sister and busy with…"

I trail off deliberately this time, not wanting to say my old playmate's name, not knowing if Ryder's just an old friend…or a rival for Jessa's affections.

"You mean Tanner?" Ryder says harshly. Anger and more than a tinge of jealousy color his words.

Well. I guess that answers my question. I close my eyes, fighting the wave of disappointment that sweeps over me. It's silly to feel this way. Ridiculous. Even if he weren't my future executioner, I have no business noticing his looks or reacting to his nearness. I'm the chairwoman's daughter, and he…he's in love with his former best friend.

We stand there for a moment, the wind cutting through my thin clothes, the ground shooting icicles through my sneakers.

"You owe me," I say, pulling out my trump card. "Nineteen days from now, you will execute me. That's the ultimate betrayal there is. Don't you think that at least warrants me the benefit of the doubt?"

He pushes his hand dismissively through the air. "I told you before. I'm not going to let that happen."

"You don't know what your circumstances will be in nineteen days. You don't know what might compel you to make that decision." I draw a full breath. "But what it comes down to is you're asking me to trust you. With my life. You're really not going to give me the same courtesy in return?"

He eyes Potts's shoes warily. They're the old-school kind, the ones without the cooling gel and automatic venting. They won't even help you stay on a hoverboard, as the only magnets they contain are the ones keeping the clasps closed. "You really want to waste your second chance on a pair of shoes?"

"That and a night for you to rest, here at Potts's." I hold up a hand as he begins to protest. "Just hear me out. It's dark now. And cold. You just woke up, figuratively, from the dead. You need to drink and eat and sleep." I attempt a smile. "I can virtually guarantee—in over ninety percent of the pathways—that you're better off having spent the night."

As if to punctuate my words, a sudden gust pelts us with water droplets. He squints first at the dark sky and then at me. "Fine," he says reluctantly. It's just a single word, but it makes all the air expel from my chest. He agreed. He's staying. "But let me make one thing clear. This is the last chance you get. Understood?"

"Absolutely."

"Just don't expect me to change my mind in the morning and let you tag along with me."

I don't say anything. I don't have to. Because I've seen his future pathways, and that's exactly what I'm hoping for.

11

dream.

Disjointed images. A dirt road that shifts and crumbles beneath my feet. My mother, with her arms crossed and a sneer upon her face. People in my peripheral vision pulsing in and out of this realm. One moment I see them; the next, I don't.

A feeling rises within me, washing over me, threatening to pull me under. An underlying edge of fear. A vague sense of things ending. I can't quite grasp what it means. I reach for it. I stretch my mind for some kind of understanding, for even a handful of words.

It's big. Bigger than me, bigger than my life. A decision point. The weight of the world resting on the fragile point of a pin. Like a house of playing cards, like a long line of dominoes. Something that took a person a lifetime to set up.

I reach my hand toward her, my mother, my entire world. Carefully, cautiously. One false move, one wrong action, and it could all come crashing down. And yet, my motion is too sudden, too fast. Because then I hear it: the silence that rings in your ears before the crash of an entire time stream.

It's over. She's gone. This is the end…the end…the end…

...

"Olivia! Wake up!" A low and familiar voice yanks me out of the dream.

I blink into the dark. The sheets are twisted around my legs, and I'm drenched with sweat. My heart thunders in my ears, and for a moment, all I can breathe is utter and complete despair.

And then the nightmare fades, like the turrets of a sand castle built too close to the ocean. Real life settles in, fact by concrete fact. Ryder. Potts's cabin. The two of us crashed in the living area on couches opposite each other. It must still be the middle of the night, as the room is illuminated only by the moonbeams slinking through the skylight.

It was a dream. Only a dream. Nothing but a dream.

I turn to Ryder to tell him I'm fine. And realize I'm not the one who needs comforting.

His eyes are wide, and he's gulping at the air. He looks like he's seen a ghost. No, not a ghost, because that would imply something that was living and is now dead. He looks like he's seen the future—our future.

"Ryder, you're shaking," I venture.

"You were talking in your sleep," he whispers. "You cried: don't leave me. You screamed: please, Mom, I'm begging you. And then you moaned like your heart would break. Like no matter what you said or did, she left you anyway."

I freeze. I've never revealed so much of myself to anyone. Not MK, who was my child-minder for the first six years of my life. Not Jessa, who I've lived with for the last six months. Certainly not my mother.

"You don't have any right," he gasps. "These are my dreams. This is my past. Stay out of my head."

For a moment, all I can do is blink. And then, comprehension crashes over me. Holy Fates. He thinks this was *his* nightmare. Not mine.

"I'm a precognitive," I say carefully. "I can't climb into your mind and read your thoughts. I don't steal dreams."

He stares. And then snaps his mouth closed, as though realizing how much *he's* revealed.

"Oh," he mumbles. "I, uh… Forget I said anything."

His muscles tense like he's about to bolt, and I don't want him to bolt. More than that, I want to erase the miserable look on his face.

"I've had this nightmare ever since I was a kid," I say slowly. Conversationally. As if we were just two people who met at the virtual theater. "Sometimes the details change. Eden City might be burning behind me, or I might get sucked into the concrete sidewalk like I'm standing in quicksand. But one thing is always the same." I swallow. "I make the wrong decision. My mother leaves me irrevocably. I feel hollowed out, a shell of a person, and then…the world ends."

"The apocalypse," he says, drawn in despite himself.

"Maybe." Overheated, all of a sudden, I toss off my quilt. Limbo. The oversized shirt I borrowed from Potts has ridden up, and I'm showing way too much of my bare legs. Not that Ryder notices. His eyes are practically magnetized to my face. I tug my shirt down. "I mean, it's just a dream, but I'm also a precognitive. I can't just discount my dreams like most people. Especially now that the timing's ripe for a disaster.

"My mother's risen in power. She's Chairwoman of the entire Committee of Agencies, not just FuMA. The people are getting agitated. Ever since Mikey left civilization, taking with him his controlled and peaceful leadership of the Underground, there have been more skirmishes. More open defiance of ComA." I shake my head. "These small rebellions have been quelled, quickly, but I foresee riots in our future. I foresee chaos and destruction. The pathways our world will take are still too varied for me to predict, but the end is coming. Even if I can't visualize it, I feel it in my bones."

"Is that why you chose to defy your mother now?" he asks.

I start. Is it? I've always known about the end of the world, and I've always thought I would sit on the sidelines and watch it happen. I assumed I pushed my mother into the reclining chair because I finally saw her for who she really was. Because I wanted to save Callie, because I couldn't bear for this boy to be tortured.

But maybe there's more to it than that. Maybe I also want to avoid that wrong decision.

"I don't know," I say honestly.

He eases back. The couch squeaks, and the air between us is solid. Heavy with an expectation that I don't want him to feel but that I'd like him to fulfill anyway. I told him about my dream, something I've never shared with anyone before. I'm curious—no, dying—to hear about his. Because it seems like his mother abandoned him, too. It appears he knows how it feels to be lost and unloved, too. Maybe, like me, he's even questioned his worth. When your own parent doesn't see your value, then who will?

"You don't have to tell me," I say into the silence. "I mean, dreams... They're really personal even if they aren't real. But, um...I think I might understand how you feel. I think I might even feel the same way. Because the chairwoman doesn't love me. Not in any meaningful way."

He looks at me with heartbreak in his eyes. "I wish

my dream wasn't real. But this recurring nightmare is something that happened when I was six years old."

"Do you want to talk about it?"

"In all this time, I've told this story to three people. Jessa, Mikey, and Angela. You'll be the fourth." He pulls my blanket onto his legs and digs his fingers into the fabric. Takes a deep breath. I can't believe he's actually going to tell me.

"My brother, Damian, had a psychic ability. All he had to do was touch you, and he could tell what you were thinking. It was pretty awesome, but it was embarrassing, too. Like, he would grab my hand and then tell my teacher I thought she was pretty. Or he would sneak into my dreams at night and then recount them to my parents over breakfast the next day." He ducks his head. "I guess that's why I assumed you had gotten in my dreams earlier. Sorry."

"No problem," I say softly, not wanting to interrupt him.

"Anyhow, I always knew that Damian was their favorite son. He was older than me and smarter. And well, he was their *first*, you know? I think my parents gave him so much of themselves that there wasn't any left for me. And that didn't bother me too much. It was just the way life was.

"Back then, ComA was locking up psychics so they could study them, and my parents were terrified they were going to find out about Damian. They got in touch with Melie, the leader of the Underground back then, and she told them about Harmony, the community in the wilderness where psychics and their families could go to escape persecution." He stops, rubs his forehead. "Only my mom didn't want to run away from civilization and give up all the luxuries associated with it. She thought they should change their identities instead and hide out in a smaller town, one far away from the capitol of North Amerie."

He traces his fingers along a pattern in the quilt. His pinky brushes the back of my hand, accidentally, and for a moment, I feel like I can't breathe. "Of course, I didn't find out any of this until I woke up one night, and there they were, my parents and Damian, all packed and ready to go. Without me." He looks up, his lips thin and something very close to shame etched into his features. "That's the moment I dream about. I begged them to take me with them. I promised I would be a good boy, that I wouldn't ask so many questions, that I would eat my meals faster, but they didn't care. You see, they knew ComA would be looking for a family with two boys, and the best way to throw them off track was to turn into a family of three."

"You mean they abandoned you?" The horror is too large for my words, too large for my body. I was sent away at six years old, too. But at least I saw my mom once in a while. She may not have loved me. But she was there.

"Yes," he says to his fingers. Or maybe, *our* fingers, since they're side by side now. "They took off in the middle of the night, and I was in that house by myself for three days before Melie came by and found me."

"Oh, Ryder." I can't help it. I take his hand and weave it through mine. No wonder he has such a difficult time trusting people. No wonder he took Jessa's betrayal so personally. He was betrayed as a child by the people he trusted most.

He grips my fingers, as though he never wants to let go. "Yeah. Well, I was lucky, in a sense. Melie shipped me off to Harmony, even though I didn't have a psychic ability or a future memory I was running from. She told everyone that my parents were locked up by FuMA, rather than reveal the truth." He drops his head. "That my folks left me. That they didn't want me. But it's okay, because I found the best parents in the world, Mikey and Angela. They adopted me a few months after I arrived, even though they were barely more than kids themselves." He sets his jaw, the lost little boy vanishing. "They are everything to me, my wilderness family. And I will do anything to protect them."

"Yes." I nod. "I can see that."

"I'm not one for silver linings, but at least my parents' betrayal taught me an important lesson," he continues in a low voice.

"What's that?"

"People aren't what they seem," he says. "Trust is something that's earned over years of knowledge and familiarity, with countless actions that prove a person's loyalty." His jaw hardens, and he pulls his hand away. "Even then, there's no guarantee that person won't eventually betray you. So, the fewer chances you take on people, the better."

His words ring through the night, and my heart plummets to my feet. Because with this speech, the chances of him taking me to his family in the morning have dropped to zero.

12

We go back to sleep on our respective couches. Or at least, I pretend to. I'm pretty sure Ryder's pretending, too, even though it's still nighttime and we could both use the rest.

He's planning to sneak out before dawn. Gather his supplies, leave the cabin. Ditch me. I could've guessed this even if I didn't have precognition. But I do, and in eighty percent of the pathways, this is precisely what he does.

Which means I need to be ready for him.

So I lay on the beat-up sofa, forcing myself to breathe lightly and evenly. Ryder's doing the same thing. Never have I been more aware of his every move. The way his chest rises and falls. The little inhalations through his nose. Even the slight squeak of his skin against the cushions as he tries to find a more comfortable position.

An hour before dawn, he eases off the couch and makes his way soundlessly to the front hall, where I've left the hoverboards along with a couple of backpacks filled with gear. A few minutes later, the door beeps, signaling that it's been opened, and then closes once again.

I make myself count to ten. And another ten for good measure. And then I spring to my feet. In record time, I change my clothes and bound into the hall. He's taken most of the provisions from my backpack, leaving me only a couple bottles of water and a little food. The grass-green syringe—the antiseptic—is also gone, although he's left the amber syringe in the side pocket. He must not have seen me dispense it, so he didn't know to look for it.

A flurry of futures rushes through my mind, but I don't have time to pick through them. I have to go now if I don't want to lose him. Grabbing my own hoverboard and backpack, I shoot through the door.

There! Just disappearing around a bend in the trees is the tail of a board. Lucky for me, Ryder chose one of Tanner's showier boards, one that's painted fluorescent yellow and decorated with a three-legged mouse.

I shove the helmet on my head and hop onto my board, thankful that Tanner insisted on giving me lessons these last six months. It never would've occurred to me to try hovering, but a board showed up at my cabin right before I moved out. That's how it was the entire ten years I was in isolation: every couple weeks, a present would magically appear on my doorstep. Sometimes, it was a delicacy from a fancy Meal Assembler—crispy taro chips with aioli dip or roasted bone marrow. Other times, it was a color-changing ribbon or a holo-vid. I never knew who sent me these presents...but I always secretly hoped it was my mother.

The hoverboard was my biggest present yet, and I didn't have a clue what to do with it. And then, one day, shortly after I reentered society, Tanner invited me to tag along with him and Jessa to the hover park. In all the years I'd known him, this was the first time he invited me anywhere. I jumped at the chance.

I may not have his or Jessa's natural grace, but I'm fast. And I can stick a landing like my feet are fused to the board. Tanner always said that hovering was a good skill to have in your repertoire. Limbo, maybe he has a touch of precognition, too.

I aim the board in the direction where I last saw the fluorescent yellow board. I've never hovered outside of a park before, but how different can it be? Ah! There's Ryder now, an expertly weaving figure in the distance. The wind blows the hair that's sticking out underneath my helmet. It snags on a few passing branches, and I yank it back and stuff it inside my shirt.

Where are we going? Unless my sense of direction is completely off, we've looped around the cabin a couple times. The trees, the rocks, the ever-brightening sky flash by at a dizzying pace. Does he know I'm tailing him? I'm too far away for him to hear the soft whirr of my hoverboard. I reach forward to his futures, but they're no help. There are too many possibilities to make an educated guess. I lower my body to a crouch and urge my board even faster.

After circling the woods a few more times, Ryder heads toward the cliffs that form the eastern boundary of Eden City. I hear the roar of the river as we approach. I don't have to see it to remember the majestic sight of white foam crashing over rocks, the turbulent water rushing past a craggy land. The sun's climbed past the tree line now, and it shines a spotlight on Ryder as he zooms right up to the cliff, where crumbling earth meets sky.

He hovers for an infinitesimal second on the edge, and for a moment, I think he's going to swoop right down the side of the cliff like it's just another bowl at the hover park.

My stomach clenches. There's no way I can follow him. Not with six months of lessons.

Thankfully, he veers to the right, finding a more gradual slope down the cliff. I follow at a safe distance, picking my way along the rocks.

Eventually, he reaches river level and skims the top of the water to the land on the other side. I wait until he is safely ensconced in the trees before I attempt my own river hover.

A smile splits my face. Oh wow. There's nothing quite like this. The current rushes underneath me, spraying droplets on my skin and glistening like diamonds under the sun. The board vibrates beneath my feet, the hair blows out of my shirt, and I feel like I'm riding the wind.

Without warning, the river dips. My board jerks underneath me, and I'm not ready. I didn't move into the proper stance. All of a sudden, my body is flailing backward against gravity. Oh Limbo, oh Limbo. I rock back and forth on the board, trying desperately to regain my balance. I'm falling, I'm falling, there's no way… But then, by some miracle, the board doesn't shoot out from underneath me. I hang on, literally by the edge of my feet…

…and then, I touch down on land. Not a moment too soon. I tumble off my board and collapse on the ground, more shaken than I realized.

Seconds or maybe even minutes later, when I feel like I can see straight again, I sit up. Fate fike it. How much time did I waste? Ryder must be long gone by now. Should've pulled myself together a little faster.

Sighing, I climb back onto my hoverboard and point it into the trees.

Immediately, at the edge of my vision, I catch a flash of fluorescent yellow zipping around a trunk. Hot Limbo, he's still here. Did he take a break, too? And it just happened to be at the same time as mine?

No way. I've seen enough futures to know that coincidences *do* happen. But more often than not, there's a reason behind those coincidences—and not necessarily an innocent one.

The hair stands at the back of my neck. I get the feeling I'm playing a game...but I don't understand the rules. Like my nightmare, however, one wrong move and the pieces will come crashing down.

I don't have time to dwell on my uneasiness. Ryder's flying through the air at top speed, and it takes all my concentration to keep him in my sights.

For the rest of the morning, we push hard through the woods. The sun penetrates the cover of the trees and beats against the black fabric of my mesh shirt, thank goodness, since the boards are powered by solar energy. Underneath my helmet, my hair is plastered to my forehead. Just when I feel like I can't continue, Ryder stops for a break. I hide behind a tree, gulp down my water—careful to ration the two bottles—and gather my strength to hop back on the board. And so it continues for three more cycles.

Finally, we arrive at a clearing. Ryder lands his hoverboard and steps off. A safe distance behind him, I do the same. My mouth dries, despite the water I just swigged. What is this place? The only structure still standing is a sturdy log building in the center of the clearing. Rows of rubble flank three sides of the square. If I squint and reach backward in time, I can imagine that these piles of wood were once livable huts.

Something's not right. If his family is staying here, then where are they? Shouldn't Mikey or Angela be rushing out to greet him? Shouldn't there be some sign of life? A fire recently lit or leftover scraps of food? Instead, there's just a stillness in the air...along with a few vultures feeding on the bloody remains of a deer.

A bird squawks. I duck, covering my head in case the vultures mistake me for a dead feast. When I straighten, Ryder's gone.

Great. Invisible fingers creep up my spine. Where did he go? A person can't just disappear. Maybe he stepped into one of the structures. The log building is too far away, but there's a hut at the end of the row that's only three-quarters dilapidated.

Alarm bells scream in my head. The futures flip through my mind like a deck of playing cards, too quickly for me to see each one. But I'm able to glean the overall gist of the pathways: not good.

Not good, not good, not good.

Forget Ryder! my instincts scream. *Run!* But my feet walk toward the dilapidated hut, and I'm incapable of making them stop. Incapable of turning around.

There's a gaping hole in the crisscross of sticks that might've been a door. My heart is in my throat, and I dig my nails into my palms. Saying a prayer to the Fates, I step inside.

I stumble over a rut, and a pair of hands grab me on my way to the ground. Before I can shout or kick or jab, the hands whirl me around and press me into the dirt. I look up into a pair of very pretty, very enraged eyes. Ryder's eyes.

"Exactly how long were you planning to follow me?" he demands.

13

gulp the air, but there's not enough oxygen, even though the collapsing hut is completely open to the wind. It's hot, too hot, and his body is pressing into mine, his legs on my legs, his torso on my torso. I can't move, I can't breathe. There's no way I can think.

"How long have you known I was following you?" I croak.

He smiles tightly, although I can tell from his eyes that he's not happy. Far from it. "Oh, I don't know. Maybe from the moment you first stepped outside the cabin."

I gape. "You knew this entire time?"

"I sure did." He eases his body to the side, although he keeps my hands pinned above my head. "Why do you think I waited for you all those times, when you would've lost me? I've been hovering for years, Olivia. How long have you been on the board? A few weeks?"

"Six months," I snap. "And I would've taken it up sooner. I always wanted to. I just didn't…have the chance."

Something moves across his face, something that looks very close to sympathy, but then he sets his jaw, and the expression disappears.

"You've been boarding for six months? What in Fates would you have done if I had gone down that cliff? I hope to Time you weren't planning on following me. You would've broken your neck."

"I can stick any landing," I insist.

"It would've been suicide," he counters. It's hard to tell if he's more disgusted with me or my skills. "Even skimming across the water, you were vibrating so much I thought I was going to have to dive in and save you."

Oh. This somehow makes me feel even more foolish. "You were watching?"

"I thought we already established that."

He lets go of my hands and sits up, obviously deciding I'm no longer a flight risk. I push myself up shakily. The rotting skeleton of the hut curves over our heads. Through the crisscross structure, I glimpse patches of blue sky, wispy clouds, and even a bird or two. I don't have an ability to reach into the past, but I can almost imagine what it was like to live in this hut once upon a time.

When I glance back down, Ryder's eyes are fixed on my face.

"Just look at you." His voice is softer now, much less angry. "You're filthy, and you look like you're about to come apart any moment. I left you two bottles of water. Have you been drinking them?"

I wet my lips. Or at least, I try to. 'Cause he's right. My lips, tongue, mouth are as dry as sandpaper. "I've, uh, been rationing them. I didn't know how long I'd be chasing you, and I didn't want to run out."

"I never would've let it get that far!" Groaning, he riffles in his backpack and shoves a bottle of water at me. "Here, drink this. All of it. I would've left you more, but I didn't want to make you carry it."

I take the water, oddly touched. "That's why you took all of my supplies?"

"Well, yeah." Those deep, black eyes bore into mine. "I don't know if I can trust you, but I don't want you to suffer. Not if there's something I can do about it."

I look away. I have to. His voice is like a feather brushing up my spine, leaving me both shivery and warm. I'm not sure how I'm supposed to feel when it comes to Ryder—but it's not this. Unscrewing the bottle of water, I take a long gulp, both to hydrate my body and to give me time to think.

"So, you want to tell me why we just spent an entire day hovering through the forest, only to end up here, at this abandoned campsite?" I finally ask.

"I was testing you." He lifts his chin, as if he's determined not to look guilty, but the way his eyes shift gives him away. "As much as I'd like to take you at your word, I can't. So I led you to the river, knowing that the sudden dip in the water would rattle you—literally. I thought there was no way you'd be able to keep your board, and the moment you started wobbling all over the place, whoever was trailing you—trailing *us*—would come out and rescue you." He pauses. "Well, that didn't happen. And when you collapsed to the ground, no one came to your aid, either."

"Because there wasn't anybody!" I shove my hands through my matted hair.

He swallows. "I gathered that."

"What if I had fallen in the water? Would you have let me drown, just to play out your precious test?"

"Of course not." He has the gall to sound offended, even though we both know what he'll be capable of nineteen days from now.

"Why didn't you approach me after it was clear no one was following us?" I persist.

"I had to be sure. You might not have had an ally present, but maybe you were in communication with someone. So I came here." He stares through the bones of the former hut to the piles of rubble, the open clearing, the sturdy log cabin. "This is the original Harmony, my first home after I left civilization. Of course, back then, we had dozens of 'spiders' projecting holographic illusions around the camp, so that no one could find us." He stops. "If you pretending to torture your mom was all a ruse that the two of you designed, the second you saw signs of a fugitive camp, you would've reported the coordinates to FuMA. Well, we've been here ten minutes now. If they're coming, they should be here any second."

He looks at me searchingly. It's so quiet we'd be able to hear the nearly inaudible whisper-whirr of the stealth copter. But we don't. Seconds pass, and then a minute. Nobody bursts in to arrest Ryder. For one good reason.

"I didn't call anyone," I say quietly. "I'm the chairwoman's daughter, but my loyalty to her ends with my name alone." An image of her flailing body flashes across my mind, and I wince. I may have severed ties with my mother the moment I tortured her, but that doesn't mean I'll ever enjoy that memory. "I don't agree with what she's doing. I hope it goes without saying that I don't support genocide. In fact, Jessa and I are doing everything we can to try to stop her." I take a breath. "In the meantime, Jessa's asked me to help her sister. But I can't do that if you don't take me to your family."

There. I've said my piece. Now I'm balanced at the juncture of two major branches. Either he'll lead me to Callie—or he won't. Clearly, I won't be able to follow without him knowing.

"I have the antibiotic," he says. "Why do you need to be there?"

I blink. "She's exhibiting the same symptoms as my mother and a bunch of other recipients of future memory. I'm not at all sure she's got a simple infection from a knife wound. And if she doesn't, well...we'll need to figure out how to get her the amber formula she needs."

"And that's all?" he asks skeptically.

I open my mouth and then snap it shut again. Damn the Fates, that's not all. I just met this guy. How can he know me so well?

The truth is, I've wanted to meet Callie all my life, first because she seemed so loving when she picked up Jessa from school. And then, because of the action she took that rocked the world.

Ten years ago, Callie received a future memory, which showed that her future self would inject a syringe into Jessa's chest—and kill her. Instead of fulfilling that memory, she chose to stab the needle into her own heart, sending herself into a decade-long coma. Callie's name became a rallying cry for the Underground, the people who were rebelling against ComA and their persecution of individuals with psychic gifts. To them, her action proved that the future could be changed.

But that's not precisely accurate.

When a future memory is sent to the past, all it does is lop off the majority of a person's branches, leaving only a few possible pathways. So, sending a memory is an attempt to "fix" the future—but it doesn't guarantee it.

In Callie's case, the path she followed existed in fewer than one percent of her futures. It was her extreme love for her sister that allowed her to find this path and take it.

And so, Callie is extraordinary not because she did the impossible, but because she took an action all of us are capable of. We just have to be strong enough and brave enough to seek out the right path.

She inspired everyone around her—especially me. She made me feel like I could be more than just my name, more than what everyone else perceived. And now, I need her example more than ever. Especially if the chairwoman fulfills her future of genocide. Especially if my dreams of the apocalypse come true.

"I didn't plan on torturing my mother," I say in a low voice. "But I did, and that changed everything. It changed me. You see, all my life, I've been loyal to the chairwoman's *potential*, to who she could be if she would only make the right decision. But in that moment, I realized I couldn't do that anymore. I had to see who she really is. Here. In this timeline. Despite all the futures I can see—" My voice hitches. I stop and try again. "Maybe *because* of the futures I can see, I don't know who I am anymore. If I ever knew. Like me, Callie also chose a pathway that changed everything. Now, I'm not equating my action to hers. But I'm hoping being around her will help me figure out my place in this world."

I close my eyes. Maybe all this angst is pointless, since I won't be here much longer. But before I die, I'd like to understand the life I'm leaving behind.

Two seconds pass. And then four. I peek up at Ryder to see if he's even listening, and he's nodding. "Okay," he says.

"Okay?" I repeat, hope bubbling in my chest.

"Yes. Okay." He gets to his feet and offers me his hand. "If this was the final test, then you passed. We all worship Callie, although when you meet her, you'll see she's more like an annoying big sister than any kind of saint." He wraps his fingers around my wrist. "But anyone who looks up to her as much as I do has got to be okay."

I can't help it. I make a face. "Gee, are you sure? There have got to be some other tests you can put me through. Like, you can make me go swimming with the sharks during dinnertime. Or jump out of a stealth copter without a parachute. Or—"

He laughs, a deep and low rumble in his chest. "Come on. Let's go find my family."

He tugs, and I try to stand. Only, I must've stepped on a weak part of the ground. Because, all of sudden, the dirt is crumbling, and I'm falling, slipping, sliding, as the earth opens up from underneath me.

14

*T*hud.

I hit the ground with my shoulder, and the impact spreads through my body. *Ow, ow, ow.*

"Olivia, are you okay?" I hear Ryder's panicked voice above me. "Oh Fates. Please tell me you aren't hurt."

Slowly, I sit up, coughing from the dust that's been stirred up. I shake out my arms and legs, wiggle and twist my back and torso. At least I can move everything.

"I'm fine," I croak out. It's dark all around me. The only illumination comes from the meager amount of sunshine creeping through the hole, but Ryder's head blocks most of it. "What is this place?"

"No clue," he says. "The floor must've given out. This was Mikey's hut back in the day. Maybe he had a hideaway dug out underneath. If so, he never shared it with me." He inhales sharply. "Okay. Move over."

"What?"

"I'm coming in." He dangles his legs through the opening. "If this is my dad's secret hideout, then I want to see."

"Are you serious?" I ask incredulously. "What if we both

get stuck in here?"

"We're not going to get stuck." I can almost hear the
eyes rolling in his head. "The floor's at most a foot above
your head. At worst, I'll hoist you onto my shoulders, and
you'll climb right out. But probably, there's a way into and
out of that room."

His legs disappear from the hole, and I hear rustling,
as though he's digging through his backpack. And then he
drops headgear with a light attached through the hole. "Put
that on and tell me what you see."

I slip on the headgear, and a thin beam of light slices
through the darkness. I turn in a small circle. "It's a smallish
room. Maybe five feet by five feet. Smooth stone walls like
a cave. How in Fates did Mikey dig a cave under his hut?"

"More likely, he had his hut built *over* the cave. He
was the founder of Harmony, you know. He could've done
anything he wanted. Keep going."

"There's writing all over the walls. Crammed into every
available space." I twist my head, and the light swings with
me. "Aha! Some kind of handle on the ceiling. A ladder
leads up to it."

"Perfect. Make some room." A moment later, he jumps
down beside me. The cave, all of a sudden, seems a whole
lot smaller.

I'm staring right at his chest. He's at most six—no,
maybe four—inches away from me, and my mouth goes dry.
The scent of evergreens wraps around me. We both took
long showers at Potts's cabin, but he shouldn't smell so
good after a long day of hovering. It isn't right.

I feel like a bat with echolocation, sending out waves
to determine where every inch of his body is in relation to
mine. His thighs to my thighs, his biceps to my shoulders,
and his mouth... Oh Fates, if I looked up, there would be a

direct line running from his lips to mine.

"Olivia," he says. My name. Just like that. Four distinct syllables, in his low, caressing voice.

My eyes flutter up, snagging on every ridged part of him. The perfectly sculpted chest, the sharp lines of his jaw. He looks almost unreal, like he's a statue carved out of warm, living stone. Jessa talked about him all the time—but other than a quick aside about how the girls at school would set his image to run across their holo-screens, she never mentioned his looks. Is it possible that she never noticed?

I realize, all of a sudden, that he's gone perfectly, utterly still. His breath thunders in my ears, ragged and uneven. "Olivia," he says again, in a strained voice. "You're standing too close to me."

I blink. Huh? As the meaning of his words seep in, my cheeks burn. Oh Fates. He doesn't want me this close. He thinks I'm invading his personal space.

I scramble backward so quickly I stumble over my own feet. I keep going until my back is pressed against the cave wall, and that still isn't far enough.

"I told you to make room for me," he says, as if this makes everything better. It *doesn't*. This rational explanation just makes things *worse*.

Clearly, he doesn't think of me like that—whatever *that* is. I'm just a girl to him, someone he's going to execute in three weeks. Fates, I practically had to pry out the miniscule amount of trust he's deigned to give me. Even then, it's cautious and grudging. And it's in danger of evaporating if I accidentally look at him the wrong way. *Of course* he doesn't want me close. Why would he?

It's not like I'm Jessa. Not his childhood friend, not someone with whom he had years and years to build up respect. I'm sure he wouldn't tell her to back up. But then,

I'm not as brave as her, not as pretty, not as smart.

And I'm absolutely not going to do this right now.

With a forced casualness, as though he didn't just reject me, I hand him the headgear. Automatically, he reaches up to his head, his fingers moving as if he's adjusting something.

Except nothing's there.

"What are you doing?" I ask.

"Oh." He drops his hand, looking startled and then sheepish. "Um, habit, I guess. I usually wear these magnifying goggles, but Mikey persuaded me to leave them off for my trip. Of course, we didn't expect for me to be arrested."

The gesture triggers something inside me. I'm reminded...of Danni Lee, the girl who earnestly explained her metaphor for life to someone who wasn't there. Ryder couldn't be getting sick, could he?

Nah. It's probably just what he said. An old habit.

And yet, I can't quite stifle the chill that runs down my spine.

Pushing my uneasiness away, I squat in front of the wall in front of a patch of writing, where Ryder's flashlight is pointing. The letters lack the clear, crisp edges produced by our auto-writers; instead, they appear to have been produced by hand. Moreover, the ink's not the black I'm used to, but a warm, toasty brown, almost like the color of...

"Walnut ink," Ryder says, as though he's reading my mind. He crouches beside me, his shoulder brushing mine. "That's what we had to use out here in the wilderness."

I refuse to notice his touch and wrench my attention back to the wall. The writing appears to be a series of equations. Other than "$e = mc^2$," they all look like gibberish. But then, my education was unconventional at best. My mother's former assistant, MK, gave me a few lessons over

the years, but the chairwoman didn't want a whole stream
of tutors visiting me in isolation. So my schooling basically
consisted of me meandering through whatever interested
me at the time—usually the literature of the ages. Of course,
the hundreds of books I've inhaled don't help me now.

"Do you recognize any of these symbols?" I ask.

"A few." He pauses. "I couldn't tell you what they mean,
but these equations look a whole lot like the ones we
studied in my Advanced Physics Core. In the Time Travel
unit, to be precise."

"Was Mikey building a time machine?" I squint at
the scribbles again. And I thought T.S. Eliot was hard to
decipher. "A machine no one knows about. Is that why he
needed this hideaway?"

"Maybe," Ryder says. "I wouldn't put it past Mikey to
build a secret contraption. Except…a time machine already
exists. It was invented over twenty years ago, when Preston
used it to travel to our future." He tenses, as though he's
said something he shouldn't.

"Jessa told me," I say quietly. "She told me everything.
How she discovered Preston is her father. How she and
Tanner time-traveled to the past. How you all woke Callie
from her coma."

He nods stiffly. Great. Now, he's mad that an outsider
knows so much about his tight-knit community.

Sighing, I retreat to a corner and stare at another
meaningless scribble of letters and numbers. What am
I'm looking for? If something's important, will I be able
to recognize it? No clue. Still, I methodically scan first one
row and then another. I turn to a section of the wall—and
my breath catches in my throat.

The equations give way to a set of drawings. A stick
figure stands on one side, with a series of lines emanating

from him. No, not just lines. Branches. Branches of potential futures. When I was a kid, I would sketch out exactly these diagrams, again and again, as I tried to explain to the scientists how my precognition worked.

But this drawing differs from my sketches in a major way. A section of the branches is boxed off. Next to the box is another diagram, showing the enclosed area in greater detail. A sort of window is rendered in between two of the branches. An arrow is drawn through the window, with a smattering of stick figures walking through the opening.

I frown and then frown again. The typical depiction of a timeline moves horizontally from left to right—past, then present, and then future. This enlarged diagram shows a line that moves *vertically* between branches. It doesn't make any sense. Unless…unless…

The line represents people traveling from one branch to the other.

My blood runs cold, each individual drop freezing and falling from my veins. "Oh dear Fates," I whisper.

Ryder is at my side in an instance. "What is it, Olivia?"

"It looks like Mikey's building something, all right, but it's not a time machine," I say, not sure how I'm forming the words. "I think he's building a…a…*realm* machine." I glance back at the drawing, at the line of people walking through the window. "Something that allows you to travel from one parallel world to another."

15

My mind whirls, the thoughts so loud I can't hear anything else. The implications so glaring I can't see anything else. Mikey...a realm machine...but oh Fates, one like we've never seen...one that could change our world forever.

"Breathe," Ryder says gruffly. He pushes my head down. "Between your knees, Olivia. I can't have you hyperventilating on me."

That's when I realize my breath is keeping time with my thoughts. Huff and huff and huff some more. Faster and faster like an engine revving to life. My heart's trying to drill a hole through my chest, and I can't feel my fingers. Any of them. Not my pinky, not my thumb. Even my palms have gone numb.

Yep, the classic signs of a panic attack. And one of the reasons I retreated into isolation to begin with: so that I could learn to stop such attacks before they begin.

Deliberately, I sit up and try to slow my breathing. Ryder takes my hands and rubs them between his fingers. A warm, tingly sensation begins to seep back in.

"Count with me," he says. "Don't take another breath until we get to five."

We count to five. And then again. And again. The feeling in my hands returns all the way, and I'm acutely aware of the calluses of his palms brushing against my skin.

"...three...four...five." I lift my head as we finish counting the last set. Our lips move at the exact same time, saying the exact same words. It's unnerving as Limbo, but nice, too.

"You, um...you're good at this," I say. If we weren't already in a hole in the ground, I'd want to dig one.

"Angela used to have panic attacks," he says, completely unfazed. "Especially when she would relive her future memory of watching her baby girl crawl off a cliff. From the time I was six and came to live with her and Mikey in Harmony, I would hold her hands and count just like that. She said I was her lifeline."

"You probably were," I murmur. I can just imagine him. A little boy with skinny arms and an oversized head, vigilantly counting with his adoptive mother. And it makes my heart feel too large for my chest.

"You want to tell me what you're thinking?" he asks.

I take a deep breath. I'm not used to this. Confiding my thoughts to someone. I don't know what to say. I don't know how much detail I can go into before I lose his attention.

"I've always had a window into these parallel worlds," I begin haltingly. "I don't get to live them, I don't get to try them out, and neither does anyone else. Because that's all it's ever been: a window. A glimpse into all these possible futures. We have access to only one world, to one timeline, and that's this one." I lick my lips. "Do you understand how dangerous a realm machine is? If Mikey has actually invented one, we could cross between worlds. You wouldn't have to go back in time to fix your mistakes; you could jump to a new time stream altogether. Can you imagine what would happen if people started jumping between worlds? It would destroy our time stream and render it meaningless. Render *us* meaningless."

He rubs a hand over his head. "Yeah, I see what you mean. But it hasn't happened yet. Maybe it won't ever happen. These are just preliminary calculations. Maybe Mikey's abandoned the project. Maybe he found it was impossible in practice. We can't worry about what we don't know."

Inexplicably, I think of Danni Lee and her theory on living. Like a moth to a flame, she said. In other words, focus on today. Live for what is real and actual and true—not for something that might never come to pass.

Such as the realm machine. My precognition cuts off too early. I can't accurately assign a probability for whether such a machine will ever be invented. So I can't let its possible consequences run me into the ground.

Wordlessly we climb the ladder and exit through the trap door. Ryder plops a helmet onto his head, looking impossibly cute.

"Have you...changed your mind about me coming with you?" I venture.

"Why would I change my mind?"

Because I'm not the kind of girl he's used to. The kind who makes big moves and saves people. I'm better suited to the shadows, and I'm a few quick breaths away from a panic attack at any moment. As he witnessed.

I open my mouth to tell him precisely this when something in his eyes stops me. He looks at me like I'm fully capable of attacking any obstacle head on. He looks at me like I'm…like I'm…Jessa. And Fate help me, that makes me want to try.

"No reason." I try to smile. "Just making sure."

We climb onto our hoverboards, and Ryder rattles off a set of instructions. Follow him closely. Blink my headgear twice if I need to rest. If I lose him, stay where I am. He'll double back and find me.

"We've got a few hours before sunset," he says, squinting at the sky. "If we push hard, I think we can make it before dark."

He reaches out and fastens my helmet strap. I freeze as his knuckles brush against my cheek. All too soon, he moves away, and I'm left wondering if I imagined the touch.

"You ready?" he asks, his voice husky.

I drag my words from where they're hiding underneath my heart. "Ready."

We hover back to the river, and Ryder stops at the base of two tree trunks twisted together. He reaches under one of the exposed roots and comes up with nothing. "Our rendezvous point." He brushes the dirt off his palm. "If they moved camp, they would leave me a message here. Otherwise, I'd never find them again."

We continue on our way. Three hard hours later, during which I meekly blink my light only once for a rest, Ryder slows his hoverboard and hops off. "We're here," he pronounces.

The sun is caressing the treetops with its last fingers of light, and this patch of the forest looks no different than the woods through which we've been traveling: dense clumps of trees, a smattering of boulders, moss battling dirt on the ground.

"Let me guess," I say. "Holographic 'spiders'?"

He grins like I've said something clever. "You got it. Of

course, these spiders are even more advanced than the ones we used at Harmony, 'cause they also absorb sound and heat waves. That's why the chairwoman hasn't been able to find us. No doubt she'd send in her troops if she could figure out our location."

I sag against a boulder and gulp the air. I'm no weakling—there was ample time in isolation to train—but I feel like I've taken a shower in my own sweat. "Aren't you going to ask how I'm doing?"

"Nah." He grins. "I don't need to ask. You're a fighter, Olivia."

Am I? I take a swig of water. Maybe I am. Or, at least, I could pretend to be.

He hoists both of our hoverboards over his shoulders. "Enough rest. Let's go."

I push myself off the boulder and follow him, keeping my eyes glued to his solidly muscled back. There's still enough sunlight to see, but if these spiders work the way I've heard, he's going to disappear any moment.

Three…two…one…

Poof.

As if on cue, he's gone. My steps falter, but I force myself to continue walking. I brace myself for some kind of *zing*, but there's nothing. One moment, I'm surrounded by woods, and the next, I see a handful of tents, pitched in a half-circle around a flaming fire.

A wail wrenches the air.

"Oh. Is that Remi? Do you think she's hungry?" I rifle through my backpack for the food rations, but Ryder puts his hand out, stopping me.

I meet his stricken, horror-filled eyes—and that's when I realize that the cries are unmistakably adult. Unmistakably female. And they sound just like Jessa.

But it's not Jessa, clearly. She's back in Eden City.

My stomach drops. Oh dear Fate. It could be only one other person. Callie Stone—my idol, the girl who's inspired me to keep going all these years—is screaming like her fingers are being sliced off, one by one.

16

The screams seem to come from everywhere at once. Ryder starts running from one tent to the next as he tries to locate the origin. Just as he approaches the largest tent in the center of the half circle, a woman steps out.

My breath catches. The woman's skin is as dark as Ryder's, and, even in the fading light, her eyes pierce into me. She wears her shoulder-length hair in a million tiny braids, and a long piece of fabric is wrapped around her upper body. She exudes a potent combination of strength and gentleness: firm shoulders, relaxed lips, erect posture, soft movements. Even though they have no blood relation, I know in an instant that this is Angela, Ryder's mom.

He runs straight into her arms.

"Oh, dear boy, you're back. You're back." Even though he towers over her by a foot, she embraces him like a child. In the tight hold of her arms, I can almost see the scrawny six-year-old he must've been when she adopted him. "I thought for sure they captured you."

"They did." He buries his face, briefly, in the crook of her neck, his hands dislodging the strips of fabric on her back.

I finally figure out what the contraption is: a baby carrier. Her daughter, Remi, must be sleeping in a tent somewhere, not too far away. Jessa's told me stories of Angela's overprotectiveness, and who can blame her? I'd be a stealth-copter parent, too, if I had Angela's future memory of her baby crawling off a cliff. Jessa said it took ages for Mikey to persuade Angela to risk even having a child—and she agreed only after Callie proved that the future could be changed. Still, Angela watches Remi like a surveillance bot. According to Jessa, she'd have her daughter surgically fused to her if she could.

"That's not important now," Ryder continues. "How's Callie? Not good, I guess. I have antibiotics." He fumbles with the backpack, his hands large and clumsy. After he grapples with the clasps for the third time, Angela gently takes the pack from him.

"I wish I could say it's worse than it sounds," she says. "But Callie's deteriorating, fast. She has these episodes where she thinks she's somewhere else. They're not nightmares or night terrors. She's not asleep. She's simply... not here."

"But we had time!" Ryder cries. "She wasn't supposed to succumb to the infection for days, weeks even. That's why I didn't come straight here." His voice breaks on the last word.

Angela pats his arm. "You couldn't have known. This isn't a regular infection, and both her brain and body are reeling from it." She pauses, as if not sure she should continue. "Zed, Laurel, and Brayden left yesterday, to search for you and to procure the antibiotics. We had no idea where you were, or if you'd ever be coming back. Logan would've gone himself, but he can't bring himself to leave Callie's side, not when..."

She cuts off, but the words might as well be projected in the air. *Not when he might lose her again.*

I swallow, pushing down fear—and a selfish sliver of relief. Six months ago, Zed kidnapped me and almost beat me. In fact, a future version of him did...and sent that memory to his younger self. Because of Jessa, he was able to stop himself before he fulfilled his memory.

They returned me to isolation, unharmed. But not undamaged. I never felt safe in my cabin again, and it was almost a relief when my mother pulled me out to integrate me back into society.

To this day, I'm not sure how I feel about Zed. But at least I won't have to see him.

Angela peers over Ryder's shoulder. "Who do we have here?"

"She's a ComA employee," he says. "She helped me escape."

A ComA employee, I remind myself. Not friend, not ally. That's how he thinks of me. That's what I can't forget.

I could assert that I'm also the girl he's going to kill in a little over two weeks, but I don't. It won't help either my feelings or the situation.

His adoptive mom lifts the flap of the tent, ushering us inside. "I'm Angela," she says as I approach. "What's your name?"

"Livvy," Ryder interjects quickly. "Her name is Livvy."

So, he doesn't want her to know who I am. At least not yet. It shouldn't matter. When I was in isolation, no one called me by any name. That I have a name at all is what's important.

Except..."Livvy" isn't just a name. It's Tanner's nickname for me, the only semi-affectionate nickname I've ever had. And hearing it on Ryder's lips—when he's using it only for artifice—strangely deflates me.

"Go ahead, Livvy," Angela says warmly. "I'll wait out here—too many people."

We duck inside. In the center of the tent, Callie lies on a thin inflatable mattress, the kind that has air conditioning and massaging vibrations built in. Her eyes are open, and she thrashes around, alternating between screams and nonsensical mumbling.

I haven't seen her in a decade, but I'd recognize her anywhere. She looks just like Jessa, after all, albeit thinner and older. They were formed from the same egg, although Jessa's embryo was removed and re-implanted eleven years later.

Pop-up tables surround the bed, and a woman in her fifties, along with three men in their late twenties or early thirties, crowd around Callie.

I recognize all of them immediately. The woman with the silver hair must be Callie's mother, Phoebe, which means the man with black hair and the familiar teardrop eyes is her time-traveling father, Preston. The other two men, with their dark blond hair and muscular builds, have to be the Russell brothers, Mikey and Logan.

"Thank the Fates you're back," one of the Russell brothers—presumably Logan, since he's holding Callie's hand—says. "She's burning up, and we can't get her fever to break. Do you have the antibiotics?"

"Right here." Ryder takes the syringe out of the now unlatched backpack.

Automatically, I step back until I fade into the shadows of the tent. There's no available furniture to hide behind, but at least I can try to blend with the navy nylon.

"Sorry it took me so long to get back." Ryder hands Logan the syringe with the grass-green liquid flowing through the barrel. "I ran into trouble."

The man I assume is Mikey, Ryder's adoptive dad, stiffens. "What kind of trouble?"

"Not yet. Callie first." Logan zaps the inside of Callie's elbow with an antiseptic laser. When he finishes, the laser floats away and lands on the table. I blink—and then I remember I'm in the company of a group of people persecuted for their psychic abilities. Logan must have telekinesis.

In one smooth motion, he pushes the syringe into her arm and depresses the barrel. "There you go, dear heart," he mutters. A cloth levitates into his hand, and he dabs her forehead. "You've got your meds now. You'll be better soon."

"How long?" Phoebe asks, wringing her hands.

Everyone looks at Ryder, who in turn looks at me.

My face burns. "I got the fast-acting…"

…*antidote*. Limbo, Limbo, Limbo. I was doing so well. During my entire day with Ryder, I didn't drop my words once. Gritting my teeth, I try again. "If her symptoms are from the infection, we should see improvement in ten, fifteen *minutes*."

Too loud. It figures. At least I got the word out.

"Who's this?" Mikey barks. If I had any doubts about his identity as the leader of the Underground, they evaporate like dew in the morning sun.

"Livvy. A ComA employee. The chairwoman captured me. She broke me out." Ryder's words are short and staccato, as though Mikey might overlook them if they're sufficiently brief. No such luck.

"Livvy?" He arches an eyebrow. "Do you have a last name, Livvy?"

I dart my eyes to Ryder. What does he want me to do?

Should I lie or—

"Your last name wouldn't happen to be Dresden, would it?" Mikey continues. "And Livvy. Would that happen to be short for Olivia? As in, Olivia Dresden, the chairwoman's daughter?"

The question hangs in the air. Not for the first time, I wish that I could say "no." That I could be someone else, someone they would accept. Someone to whom Ryder would give a nickname—and actually mean it.

But there's only one answer, and with Mikey staring me in the face, I have to give it. "Yes."

Mikey slams his hand against the internal structure of the tent, and the nylon wobbles violently. "Seriously, Ryder? How could you bring an enemy into our camp? What were you thinking?"

"She's on our side, Mikey." Ryder runs a hand across the back of his neck. "She tortured her own mother to rescue me. And then she broke into the dispensary to get us the antibiotics."

"Doesn't mean a damn thing," Mikey says, and I know—I know—where Ryder got his lack of trust. The roots may have started with his parents' betrayal, but it flourished with his adoptive father's influence. "She could have her own agenda."

"I tested her," Ryder says. Briefly, he describes our trip to Harmony and how no FuMA authorities ever showed up.

Mikey softens, just a tad. "Fine. But we're clearing out as soon as Callie improves. And then I want her gone." He points a finger at me, and it feels like more than a simple gesture. It feels like I've been charged, tried, and convicted.

At that moment, Callie's entire body jerks, and she lets out a cry that splits the air.

"I'm disappearing!" She launches herself up and shoves

her hands in front of her. "Look! My hands are fading away. Do you see?" She wiggles her fingers. "Look!"

We focus on those waving fingers. It's difficult to see, on account of her rapid movement, but her fingers are all there, every last one of them.

"No, my red leaf," Logan says gently. "Your fingers are here. Let me count them for you." He touches her fingers, one by one. "You see, all ten of them are present and accounted for."

"No!" Her voice rises hysterically. "Can't you see? My hands aren't solid anymore. I can pass right through them."

She jams her pointer finger against the palm of her other hand. Bam. Bam. Bam. Each time, the finger connects with solid flesh and bounces off.

And then…during one particularly strong jab…for just a few seconds…her entire hand turns transparent, as though a finger *could* pass through them. As though it's a bad transmission of a hologram.

As though she might disappear right before our very eyes.

17

blink. And blink again. Did I just see what I thought I saw? Impossible. Is this…is this a psychic ability? If so, it's not like any I've ever seen.

"What just happened?" Logan asks, his voice equal parts wonder and fear. "Did she just become translucent for a moment?"

Phoebe's mouth forms an *O*, Ryder's eyes take up half his face, and Preston's forehead glistens with sweat. Slowly, each one of them nods. They saw the same thing. They saw the impossible.

"What in Limbo is going on?" Mikey rounds on Preston, as though he somehow has the answers. "Does she have a spider? Small mirrors to bend the light?"

"You know she doesn't have any such technology," Preston says quietly. Something passes between them, the two scientists in the room. Something deep and resonant and fearful. Something lost to everyone else.

"I'm not hallucinating, you know," Callie says, her voice clear and lucid. "This is real."

It certainly feels real. She looks from one person to

the next, her eyes focusing on each one. Wherever she was before, she's here now.

And then, her gaze lands on me. And stays there.

"You," she says. "Olivia Dresden. I'd remember you anywhere. You're the only true precognitive of our time. I know you can see what I'm talking about. Come here."

I stand rooted to the spot. This isn't the way it's supposed to be. I'm not supposed to be the center of attention.

Ryder puts his hand on my shoulder. "Do it," he murmurs. "If it will help Callie, please do what she says."

That's why I came here, isn't it? To help Callie. Swallowing hard, I walk forward and kneel by her side.

She reaches out to me. "Take my hand."

I don't want to. What if I touch her palm...and I feel nothing?

A shudder moves through me, and the inflatable mattress, the makeshift tables, and the nylon walls ripple in my vision. This is ridiculous. I shouldn't be scared. I've seen much freakier things in the future pathways. But maybe that's precisely why my blood's frosted over. I've seen what's possible. And I'm afraid to live it.

Someone steps up behind me. Even though he doesn't touch me, I know it's Ryder. I know how important Callie is to him, to all of them. And although she's reentered my life only a few minutes ago, to me, as well.

I take her hand. Slowly, I run my fingers over her wrist, her palm, each of her digits. Everything seems solid, intact. No holographic transparency.

My shoulders slump, but before I can take a full breath, Callie grabs my wrist.

"You can see this," she insists. "Maybe not now in the present, but in the future. Go ahead. Reach into my future, and you'll see me turn transparent, for longer and longer periods of time. I'll become harder and harder to see. And then I'll disappear altogether."

I don't want to. I don't want to. I don't want to.

But this is my purpose in this life. The reason, as the chairwoman liked to say, I was put on this earth. The only way I am any good to my mother or anyone else.

Taking a deep breath, I reach into her future — all her futures, all the different pathways that her life might lead until it dead-ends abruptly on May Fourth, like all my visions.

I flip through the thousands of pathways that still remain, and she's right. In some of her futures, her body remains intact. But in others, she slowly disappears. The extremities first, and then the rest of her body. Flickering in and out of this world, first for a few seconds, then minutes, then hours. And then, at some point, she never comes back at all. Where does she go? I don't know. Scientifically, physiologically, it doesn't make any sense. But this isn't my field; I don't have any specialized knowledge. All I know is: she's right.

"Do you see me?" she asks. "Do you see me fading away?"

Reluctantly, I nod.

"So, help me, then. You're the only one who can see. Explain it to them so that they understand. Please," she whispers. Sweat breaks out on her forehead, on her neck, on her arms. Her lips are the color of parchment paper, and her limbs shake like leaves dancing in the wind. "I don't want to leave Logan again. Not when I've just come back to him."

Her eyes flutter closed as she says the last word. And then she passes out.

The room erupts, with Phoebe crying, Logan moaning, and Preston shouting instructions. But Mikey's attention is on me.

He strides forward and rips my hand out of Callie's. "What did you do to her? Tell me. Now!"

Spinning me around, he grips me by the shoulders. With him so close, I can barely think, let alone talk. And then Ryder wrenches his father away, putting his bulk between us.

"Don't touch her," he says, his voice low. "You may be the leader of the Underground, but I won't let you treat her this way. She didn't do anything, okay? Callie passed out on her own. Anyone can see that."

"He's right," Logan says tiredly. "I was standing right here, and that's what I saw, too."

Mikey looks from his adopted son to his brother. And then, as though recognizing he is outnumbered, he nods. "Fine." He pushes himself away from Ryder. "I'm not accusing you—yet," he says to me.

Gee, thanks, I want to say, but don't—mostly because Ryder has shifted to stand protectively next to me, and I don't want to make the situation worse.

Behind us, Phoebe runs a damp cloth over Callie's limbs. "She's burning up. What's her temperature, Logan?"

He aims a laser at her forehead and reads the results on a digital display. "One hundred and two degrees." He turns to Preston. "How soon can we expect results?"

He rubs his forehead. "Her fever should've gone down by now. If the antibiotic's not working, then Callie doesn't have an infection."

"What does she have, then?" Logan asks despairingly.

All of a sudden, it clicks. Images flash through my mind. People walking into walls that aren't there. Mikey's realm machine to a different world. Callie's transparent hand.

My knees buckle, and Ryder's hand shoots out, catching me. I'm gasping, gasping, gasping—but whether it's for air or the truth, I couldn't say.

"What is it, Olivia?" Ryder asks. "What are you thinking?"

I straighten, willing my mind to focus, to work through the tangled threads of my thoughts. "I think I know why Callie is…"

…*disappearing*.

I grit my teeth and try again. "I think Callie is being deleted from our time *stream*."

Everyone starts talking at once.

"What?" Logan's eyes bulge.

"That can't be true," Phoebe cries.

"Is it possible?" Mikey asks his colleague, Preston — softly, so softly — and yet…I can hear every word as though they were imprinted on my brain.

Preston nods. "It's possible. But I want to know more about Olivia's theory. Go on."

I take a deep breath. "Callie has the same symptoms as my mother, as many other recent recipients of future…"

…*memory*. Fate fike it, this isn't going to work. I can't get through this explanation without dropping words all over the place. Or shouting them out and breaking everyone's eardrums. I can't. I'm the Shadow. I'm not —

Ryder squeezes my hand and brings his mouth so close to my ear that his lips brush against my earlobe. "You're a fighter, Olivia."

I let all the air leak out of my lungs until my mind is quiet. He's right. I am.

"My mother and the other patients get confused, walk into walls, have conversations with people who aren't there." My words are even. The rhythm of my speech is steady. "Callie's symptoms are the most severe I've seen, but that may be because she's not being treated." I sum up everything I know about the amber formula: how my mom's been injecting herself for the last decade, how the formula's being mass produced, how the newest victims are receiving doses. And I don't drop a single word.

Next comes the unbelievable part, the part I'm not sure I even fully believe. "I think Callie and the others waver in and out of this time. They walk into furniture because where they are, those objects don't exist. They talk to people we can't see, because those people reside there and not here." I lick my lips. "What I'm saying is: for long moments, Callie goes to a different world—a parallel world in a different time stream."

I peek at the faces around me. Ryder looks stunned, Angela's eyes are glazed. But Preston is nodding.

"Yes," he says, rubbing his chin. I detect fine lines by his eyes and mouth, which make him appear older than his years. As old as his wife, Phoebe. It doesn't surprise me. He might be the same physical age as Mikey, but he's a traveler from the past. When he leaped over twenty years into the future—and got stuck here—he suffered hardships the rest of us could only imagine. He left behind the love of his life. He missed out on Callie's childhood and didn't even learn about Jessa's existence until she was a teenager. He has since been reunited with his wife and Callie, but those heartaches leave traces you can never erase.

"I theorized that a deterioration of the time stream was possible," he says. "In fact, the team and I researched the issue thoroughly before I attempted to travel forward in time. We concluded that a single jump might cause a ripple in the stream, but the impact was so slight as to be negligible. However, a thousand ripples, on a daily basis, no matter how small, would add up. With enough repetition, these ripples would rip and tear at the fabric of time."

Logan gasps. "Future memory. Every day, a whole new

group of seventeen-year-olds receives a memory from the future."

"Exactly," Preston says. "It's not time travel in the traditional sense of sending an object into the past. But memories can also alter a person's actions, which in turn, create tension on the time stream."

I massage my temples. "That's why these symptoms slowed down during the ten years that future memory was delayed. That's also why these cases reappeared and escalated after Tanner discovered future memory once again."

"That's not all," Preston says grimly. "It gets worse."

Phoebe plucks at the sheets twisted around her daughter's legs. "What could be worse than Callie disappearing from our world?" she asks, tears roughing up her voice.

"If we're right, then it's not just going to affect Callie." Preston stops, gives himself a shake, and then starts again. "Think of it as a virus of sorts. Not like a cold because it's not contagious. We're not talking about an infectious agent here. Rather, this condition is like a computer virus that slowly eats away at the program. Sooner or later, the virus will affect our entire time stream. Which means that Callie might be the first to go. But the rest of us will follow, one by one."

18

Phoebe's hands go wild, tugging and pulling at the sheet, as if that will somehow bring her daughter closer to her. As if that will somehow keep Callie and the rest of us safe. "Is it true?" she asks me, but it's not a question, not really. She doesn't actually want an honest answer. "You can see into the future. Is this what's in store for us?"

"I don't know," I answer truthfully. And I don't. Because I can't see past the blank wall in my vision. After my own demise, I have no idea what will happen to everyone else.

"What do we do?" She hugs herself, rocking back and forth.

"We live," Logan says. Mikey might be more muscular, Ryder's definitely taller, but at this moment, Logan is the biggest presence in the tent. "We continue to live, day by day, the best way we know how. Because Callie showed us that the future is not given. She showed us that there's always a way. And if there is, we'll find it. We're not going to give up when we don't have all the information. And even if we did, even if all hope were lost, we still wouldn't give up. Whether we have two weeks or two centuries remaining, we're going to live for today. For each other and for this moment.

"And I'm going to start by helping Callie." He takes a deep breath. "Well? Now that we have a new diagnosis, what should we do?"

Mikey blinks as though he's returning from a long journey. The energy inside the tent shifts, as though the rest of them, too, are shaking off the future.

"If we're to believe Olivia, it seems like they've developed an antidote," Mikey says, authority snapping back into his voice. "Which means we need the amber formula. What do you say, Ryder? Ready for another mission?"

"Anytime, sir," Ryder answers immediately.

The others discuss who should go and when they should leave. I feel as…ephemeral as ever. Like I might disappear any moment, like I'm Callie's hand. The rest of them are freaking out over Callie's transparency. What they don't know is that I've always felt transparent. This is their world, their life. I'm merely a visitor, someone who passes through and observes, but who has no lasting impact one way or the other.

Not anymore. Not since I tortured my mother. Not since I took a definitive action, for the first time in my life.

"You don't have to go on a mission," I say faintly. "I have the formula. Right here with me."

They all gape at me, even Ryder. Especially Ryder.

"I took an extra syringe when we were in the dispensary," I say to him, my voice still fragile, still flimsy. "One that was filled with amber-colored liquid. I didn't know for sure if Callie needed it. But I took it, just in case." I rummage in my backpack, praying that the glass barrel didn't break during our travels.

It didn't, thank the Fates. I hold up the syringe for everyone to see. The amber-colored liquid looks remarkably close to urine, but we all stare as if it is a thing of beauty.

I move toward Callie's unconscious form and am about to uncap the syringe when Mikey lifts his hand. "Wait a minute. I don't want her injecting unidentified substances into Callie. How do we know the formula is what she says?"

Logan tightens his hands on Callie, who is still out cold. "You're the one who just told us we need to get ahold of the formula!"

"*If* it's the right formula. What if it's not? Maybe it contains a tracking device. Maybe it will stop Callie's heart instantly. We don't know."

"I know it's hard for you to trust," Ryder bursts out. "It's hard for me, too. But you don't have to trust her. You can trust me." He lowers his voice. "I'll…I'll stand in for her."

Mikey freezes. They all freeze. The tent is so still we could be a single frame of a holo-vid. I don't know what just happened. I don't know what Ryder means, other than that he's vouching for me.

"Are you sure, Ryder?" Mikey asks. The anger and tension has left his face, replaced by a rawness and vulnerability I don't understand.

Ryder straightens his shoulders. "As sure as I've ever been in my life."

"The last girl you were willing to stand in for was Jessa," his dad says quietly.

Ryder's jaw clenches. "That should tell you how seriously I take my statement. I wouldn't give it lightly."

Incredibly and unbelievably, Mikey nods. "In front of my very eyes, my son grows from a boy to a man. Let's do this."

My head spins. I still don't understand the dynamics,

and I doubt reaching into the future would help me. But I know one thing: I've been given permission to inject Callie with the syringe.

I walk to Callie's limp body. Once upon a time, in a different world, she approached her six-year-old sister this way, with the barrel of a needle rolling in her hand, with the beat of fear in her heart. But I'm not trying to kill the person in front of me. I'm trying to save her.

Oh dear Fate, I hope I'm right.

I let all the air flow out of my body. And I plunge the syringe right into her chest.

19

A couple hours later, I'm lying on an inflatable mattress, and the cool fabric presses against the flushed heat of my skin. As night falls and my body temperature drops, the fabric will turn warm to provide me with maximum comfort. Since there's only one mattress inside our tent, and Ryder insisted I take it, he's making do with a bed of hastily gathered pine needles and a couple of animal skins. I'm not used to sleeping so low to the ground, and the scent of the earth is almost overpowering.

At least Callie's better. Fifteen tense minutes after the injection, her fever broke. She even woke, smiled wanly, and took sips of the vitamin water that Logan spoon-fed her. There was no more talk of transparent hands. When Ryder and I left, she was resting peacefully, her fingers intertwined with Logan's.

I roll over and stare at the nylon material of Ryder's tent. Angela offered to let me stay with her and Mikey, but I didn't want to sleep under the same tent as a man who would like nothing more than for me to disappear—at least from his campsite. Ryder had room, and although the idea of us sharing made Angela raise her eyebrows, in the end, she was too tired to argue. I don't know what the etiquette of a teenage boy and girl sleeping together would be back in Eden City, but we're not in civilization. I suppose, in a way, I never really was.

Antsy, I flip over again. This time, however, I look right into Ryder's deep, black eyes.

"Oh." I stifle a gasp. "I thought you were asleep."

"With all the acrobatics going on over there? Not a chance."

I blush. "I...uh, couldn't settle my mind."

"Really?" he says dryly. "And here I thought you were practicing your routine for gold-star gymnastics."

"I wish. Not many opportunities for lessons when you're in isolation."

"Not many out in the wilderness, either."

We stare at each other. The lines of his face are illuminated by the moonlight sliding in through the mesh window, and a bird calls in the distance. Here's another reason why our childhoods weren't so very different. The similarities are beginning to pile up so quickly I'm not sure I can count them all.

"What did you mean when you said that you would stand in for me?" I blurt and then cringe. I'm quite sure I wouldn't have asked in the daylight, but the darkness surrounds us like a cozy blanket, lulling me into safety.

He rolls onto his back. "It meant I was giving you my support."

"I got that much." I hesitate, not sure how far to push him. "But it seemed like your words had more significance to Mikey."

He doesn't say anything. The bird outside continues to call...and sing...and screech like a cricket. Must be a mockingbird. Potts didn't spend all those hours teaching me about bird calls for nothing.

I turn back to the nylon wall. "Never mind. Forget I asked."

"No, I want to tell you. I'm just trying to figure out how." His nails scrape against the mattress, like he might've reached for me and encountered the bedding.

And that might just be my painfully wishful thinking.

"I don't trust very many people," he begins, his words as slow and sticky as molasses.

"No, really?" I joke. "And here I thought you went around buying knock-off gadgets and handing out credits to everyone you meet."

He doesn't laugh. Limbo, the corners of his lips don't even twitch. "Sorry," I say. "I'll be quiet now. Please go on."

"Seriously, I could count on one hand the number of people I've ever been able to rely on." He holds up his hand to demonstrate. "Mikey. Angela. Once upon a time, Jessa. And more and more, Phoebe and Preston. So, I don't give my trust easily, but once I do, there's nothing I wouldn't do for that person."

He raises himself onto an elbow. "Jessa and I were the only two kids in Harmony, so it was natural we became friends. But I think we would've been friends no matter where we met. We had an instant connection, like we'd known each other from a former life."

I swallow hard. The instant connection, the lifelong friendship. How could I ever hope to compete with that?

"One day, Jessa and I were climbing trees, even though Angela had told us not to. We attached a rope made of animal sinew to one of the branches and swung from it. Well, the branch broke, and Jessa dislocated her shoulder."

He breathes faster. "All the adults became frantic, as

they were with every injury out in the wilderness. I heard lots of shouting about how Mikey was going to have to hurt her, to get her shoulder back into place."

"'I'll do it,' I stood up and shouted. 'I'll stand in for her. Don't hurt Jessa. Hurt *me*.' You see, I didn't understand. In all of my misplaced nobleness, I thought I was offering to take her punishment." He rolls his eyes. "Ridiculous, wasn't I? The adults got a good chuckle out of it, Mikey popped Jessa's shoulder back into place, and that's how the term 'standing in' was born."

I blink and blink again. My heart feels like the air a moment before it bursts into rain. Because of the little boy who offered to sacrifice for Jessa, and more importantly, because of the grown-up guy who offered to stand in for *me*. "You...you must've cared about her very much."

"Yeah. Well." He studies his knuckles. "I guess that's why I took her betrayal so hard."

I shouldn't ask. It's none of my business, truly. But for some reason, I have to say the words. For some reason, I need confirmation of my suspicions.

"Do you...are you...in love with her?"

He snaps up his head. "Fates no. I mean, I loved her, of course, and maybe everyone in Harmony expected us to end up together. But she was always like a sister to me." He rubs his forehead. "No, that's not accurate. She wasn't just a sister. You see, for a long time, Jessa and I were the most important people in the world to each other. Callie was gone; she wasn't close to her mother. Angela and Mikey loved me, I never doubted that. I still don't. But they had each other. An entire community to lead. And then little Remi was born, and she was the center of all our worlds. So, Jessa and I, we were a team, you know? The two of us against everybody else.

"Then she met Tanner, and everything changed. I was grounded from seeing her, but I don't think she missed me as much as I missed her. Even before the betrayal, something...shifted between us. I was no longer first in her life." He grimaces. "Fates, I sound like such a baby, don't I?"

I lick my lips. "Not at all. I know how you feel. I'm not first in anyone's life, either. The difference is, I never was. It makes me feel so..."

...*alone.*

I usually never repeat a missing word. Once it's dropped, the moment has passed. The conversation has moved on. But this time, I want to. Because if I hold it inside, I'll only feel more isolated.

"I feel so alone, Ryder. So terribly, horribly alone."

An expression I can't read crosses his face. Aw, Limbo. Did I say too much? Does he feel sorry for me?

He turns his head, avoiding me. Father of Time, even his ear is perfect, a nice shape and lying flatly against his head. That, somehow, makes me feel even more foolish.

I rack my brain for another subject. Anything that will take his mind off my confession. Anything to make him stop pitying me. "You told Mikey you'd stand in for me," I blurt. "Does that mean that you trust me?"

"No." The answer is immediate and unapologetic. "I said that only so Mikey would let you inject Callie with the syringe. I was confident, at least, that you were telling the truth about the formula. Beyond that..." He shakes his head. "No offense, Olivia, but we just met. I barely know you."

Oh. I expected his response. That's why I asked the question. So that he could get all righteous and indignant. So that he would forget about my admission of loneliness. Doesn't mean I like his answer. Doesn't mean I agree. We haven't known each other very long, but I'm starting to have a very good idea exactly who Ryder Russell is.

Suddenly, I'm tired. So tired. I feel the exhaustion all the way to my bones. Figuring our conversation is finished—because, really, what more is there to say?—I roll onto my side to go to sleep.

I'm just beginning to drift off when I feel a hand on my shoulder. I look up, and Ryder's hovering above me, his dark eyes piercing all the way through me.

"I may not know you, and I can't make any promises about the future," he says gruffly, placing his finger on my lips. "But I don't want you to feel alone anymore."

20

I go perfectly still. Ryder's touched me before, but always by accident or happenstance. But this touch is precise; this touch is deliberate. This touch is centered squarely on my lips.

I don't dare exhale, for fear of huffing hot air onto his fingers. And even if I wanted to, I don't think I could. The atmosphere has turned thick, like steamy soup, and it's all I can do to take quick, tiny sips of the air.

He moves his hand, tracing his finger over my cheek, along my jaw, and back to my lips. I almost burst.

Maybe he means this to be a kind gesture, a flick of the finger to show compassion and connection. But the electricity snaps between us, and I'm acutely aware of every sensation: the nylon sleeping bag sticking to my skin; his subtle, almost spicy scent of evergreens; the sound of his labored breathing.

Wait…is his breathing labored? Or is that just my own heart pounding in my ears?

Automatically, I reach into the future. The pathways rush in on me, the hundreds of different ways the next few

SEIZE TODAY   124

minutes could unfold, some of them disappointing, but
most of them…very, very good.

"Are you sifting through my possible pathways?" he
asks, his voice husky.

I freeze. But if I'm a block of ice, his fingers do their job,
tracing my lips again and again until I melt. "How…how do
you know?" Not easy, talking with someone's hand on your
lips.

"Your eyes," he says. "They dilate when you're reaching
into the future. I'm starting to learn when you're not here."

I blink. Nobody's ever told me that before. Limbo, I
didn't even know that was true.

"You…noticed?" I ask.

"I notice everything about you," he says easily. "So, tell
me. What did you see in our possible futures?" His voice is
low and liquid, and it reaches inside me and caresses parts
I didn't know existed. "What did I do? More importantly,
what did you like?"

Heat floods my face. "What, exactly, are we talking
about?"

"I don't know." His eyes gleam wickedly. "What do you
think we're talking about?"

"Future pathways," I snap. If I have to electro-whip my
attention back on track, I'll do it, damn the Fates. "I see
everything from me slapping you to…" I trail off, and my
cheeks flame even hotter. Oh my. I can't possibly put into
words the images flying through my head like a hailstorm.

"Now I'm really intrigued." He moves his hand to my
hair, tugging slightly. I feel the tension all the way to my
toes. "Are you really not going to tell me? Because, you
know, then I'll have to guess."

"I'm not going to tell you," I whisper.

His lips curve in a mischievous grin that makes me want

to tuck him in my pocket and keep him forever. And then, while I'm still reeling from his cuteness, he leans in.

I'm not ready. My mouth is partway open, and I'm in the middle of a breath. He kisses me anyway. His warm breath rushes over my tongue, and his lips move over mine. I shut my mouth in a hurry. And then my nerve endings explode.

Lips, so soft. His back and shoulders, so hard. Holy Fates, that was his tongue. His *tongue*, slipping between my teeth. His fingers caress my waist, my hips. Lingering. Sliding under my shirt. Sparks. So many sparks, igniting in the air around us.

"How's this?" he whispers against my mouth. He's so close, I can't tell if my ears are hearing the words or if my lips are interpreting their shape. "Did you see this in our future?"

I nod helplessly.

He moves closer, scooping me up and shifting me on the mattress so that he can lie next to me. Our foreheads touch; so do our knees. "And this? Was this in some of our pathways?"

I nod again, but that doesn't seem to satisfy him anymore. His eyes intent on mine, he catches my lower lip between his teeth. "Do you like it?"

Do I like it? What kind of question is that?

I've tasted every emotion in our world. I know the sorrow a mother feels when she clasps her deceased baby to her chest. I know the pride of a gold-star athlete when he stands on a podium and accepts North Amerie's highest honor. I know the rage that silences the heart of a murderer as he cuts short another's life.

I even know kisses—hot, frenzied, passionate, fumbling, sweet, aching, innocent kisses. I've seen them all in other people's futures, thousands of kisses, millions of kisses, as varied as the pathways themselves.

And yet...and yet...I've felt nothing like kissing Ryder. Even the vision of this moment itself.

So, yeah, I like it. It scares me how much I like it.

Instead of answering, I raise myself on my hands so that I'm towering over him. So that I'm looking down on him. So that, when I lower my mouth, *I'm* kissing *him*.

And that is a whole different sensation altogether.

21

We lie on the mattress, staring up at the underside of the tent. My elbow sticks over the edge, as this mattress was designed for one, but I'm not complaining. Not when my head is pillowed on Ryder's shoulder, and both our hands are intertwined. His chest moves up and down in an even rhythm. If he's not already asleep, he's on his way there. That's what I want, too, more than anything.

Don't think, don't think. Don't let the future come crashing in. I want to keep the pathways at bay. I want, with every cell in my body, to live in the here and now. I want, for once in my life, to be happy. It may have just been kissing, but, for a girl like me, with no experience, a few kisses are a big deal.

Brick by brick, I build my walls, as quickly as my mental hands can move. But the bricks dissolve as soon as they hit ground, and the future laps with higher and higher waves.

I should be better at this by now. Damn the Fates, I *am* good at this. But the wall is always harder to build, harder to keep intact in times of emotional turmoil.

Sure enough, one particularly powerful wave knocks

the wall over. My defenses crumble, and the futures come roaring in.

I bolt straight up, covering my ears, squeezing my eyes shut, but of course, that can't block what I already know.

"Olivia! What's wrong?" Ryder sits up next to me, his eyes wild. I guess he must've been asleep, after all.

"This isn't going to work," I manage.

He's still blinking, still trying to fight through the webs of his sleep. "What?"

"Us. You and me. Together." I shove my hand into the air between us.

For a moment, he doesn't say anything. And then he lies back down, covering his eyes with his arm. "Never said it would," he drawls in a couldn't-care-less voice.

But he doesn't fool me. Not anymore. Not when he's shared his heart with me. Not when I know how deeply he cares—not about me, but about the people who matter in his life.

"Listen." I owe him an explanation. "You said so yourself, we don't know each other. A short time from now, you're going to kill me. This was…" I pause, trying to find the right words. "A diversion. A chance for us to connect when we were both feeling low. But it doesn't need to be any more than that."

"A diversion, huh?" I don't have to see his brows to know that they're climbing toward his scalp. "Is that what this was?"

"You said it, Ryder. You said you didn't trust me. You said you couldn't make any promises about the future."

Silence.

I chew on the inside of my cheek. "I've reached into our futures, and this ends only one way: in the execution room."

"We've had this conversation." He moves his arm so that

I can see his eyes, dark and fathomless. "Not. Happening."

"It's not something you can change," I say. "Callie was different. The future that she changed? The one where she sacrificed herself in order to save Jessa? That pathway actually existed. It was a single future in maybe a thousand, but she found it. She took it. I'm telling you right now. The pathway where you *don't* execute me doesn't exist. This is our Fixed."

"But maybe—"

"There is no maybe. All of my futures lead to one moment. You plunge a syringe full of poison into my chest. And then my vision ends. Not just in my life." I press his hand, willing him to understand. "My vision cuts out at the exact same moment in everyone's futures." I move my shoulders helplessly. "I've known this, even before I saw your vision. Ever since I was a little girl. I've known the exact date that I'm going to die. May Fourth. Eighteen days from now."

He sets his jaw; his temple throbs. "There has to be another explanation."

"I've accepted this, Ryder," I say quietly. "Not at first. But I do now. You have to accept it, too."

"I don't want to."

I can't help it. He sounds so much like a little kid that I laugh through the moisture lining my throat. I wish…I wish I had known him earlier. I wish our Fate was anything but this. But it's not. And I'm not going to waste any more seconds wanting the impossible.

Not when my seconds are limited as it is.

"When it comes to our relationship, there are two major branches ahead of us," I say, hoping my voice sounds as sensible as my words. "In one branch, we continue… whatever this is. This game of pretend, this foolish distraction, whatever you want to call it."

I touch him again, this time lightly on the wrist. Fates, I need to stop. I can tell myself that I'm emphasizing a point, but the physical contact isn't helping anyone. I start to withdraw my hand, and he grabs my fingers.

"How about we're just two people intrigued by each other?" he asks. "Did you ever think of that? What if we just want to get to know each other better?"

I drop my gaze. "You…feel sorry for me."

"I feel a lot of things for you," he growls. "Sorry isn't one of them. And I'm pretty sure you felt the same way."

"It was my first kiss! How did you expect me to react?"

His hand tightens around my fingertips. "I was your first kiss?"

Limbo. I hadn't meant to tell him that. "Well, yeah. I've been in isolation for ten years. Who did you want me to kiss? The chipmunk outside my window?"

He groans, tugging me forward so that I fall against him. "You do know that just makes me want to kiss you again."

His lips move over mine, practiced and now familiar. And not a bit less searing. An ache builds inside me, sharp and yearning. It would be so easy to lose myself in this kiss, to lose myself in Ryder. I could spend my last two weeks on this world kissing him, and then, at least, I'd die happy. Right?

Wrong. I've seen my future pathways, and I've got about a two percent chance of that happening.

I wrench my lips away, and it's like ripping them from an electric outlet. "I'm not finished," I gasp. "If we continue down this path, one or both of us will get confused. We'll trick ourselves into thinking what we're feeling is real." I swallow around the lump that's magically appeared in my throat. "Can you imagine how excruciating that will be, for you to kill me, believing you have real feelings for me? Or for me to die at your hands, feeling the same way?" I shake my head. "I won't put you through that, Ryder. It's better if we travel down the other branch, so that my execution is as painless as possible, for both of us."

"Stop being so noble."

"I'm not noble!" I yell, a lot louder than I intend. In the past, I've blamed my lack of practice with voice modulation, but now? Now, I'm just mad. "That's what you don't understand. I'm not Callie. I'm not even Jessa. I don't have this all-encompassing love for others. I don't sacrifice everything dear to me to do what's right." I stop, my breath coming faster. I don't want to tell him this. This isn't how I want him to see me. But it's the truth.

"All my life, I've chosen to do the selfish thing. The thing that will help *me* the most. That's why I locked myself away for ten years. That's right: me. Not my mom, even though that's what everyone thought. It was *my* decision. It was what *I* wanted to do." My voice breaks. I've always felt sorry for myself, for having to bear the burden of everyone's futures. But now, I'm beginning to understand that the past is equally heavy.

"I was six years old when I first saw the nightmare." The words scrape and tear out of my throat. "Myself, in detainment. With a cell full of other Mediocres. My own mother condemned me to death for not being good enough. I didn't fully understand what I was seeing, but it rattled me to the core. I suppose that's why I showed the vision to Callie."

His fingers creep toward mine on top of the mattress. But he doesn't pick up my hand; he doesn't even touch me. That kind of easy, casual affection is behind us now.

"Once I saw that vision, I couldn't unsee it." I snatch

my hand away. It was either that or grab his hand, because the in-between stage was destroying me. "And I couldn't handle it. I'd handled everything else up to that point, but this...this was too much for me. I begged my mom to hide me from the world, giving her some line about building walls and learning how to shield myself. Even then, you see, I could predict which arguments would work and which wouldn't. But the truth was, I didn't care about controlling my powers. I just couldn't exist in the world any longer.

"So there you have it." I swallow hard. "Now you know who I really am. I'm selfish. I'm weak. I've spent my entire life hiding. I'm a shadow, 'cause that's the only thing I'm good for. Always watching, never acting."

"That's not the story I heard." He sits up, so that his eyes are level with mine. "I heard about a girl who has the weight of the world's futures on her shoulders. That's too much for an entire society to bear, much less a single person. I heard about a six-year-old who was shown, in clear and distinct images, the scene of her own death, instigated by her mother.

"And that's not the person I see. I see someone who offered to punish me, not because she's cruel but because she wanted to help out a friend. Someone who tortured her own mother to help me escape. Someone who chased after me on a hoverboard and stood up to Mikey." His words grab me through the dimness, holding me as tightly as any physical embrace. "You're not selfish, Olivia. Far from it. You just don't understand your own heart. And you're not an observer. In fact, all I've seen you do is take action after action. The opposite of a shadow."

I squeeze my eyes shut. Nobody's ever said these things to me before—for one good reason. Ryder's the only person who's ever seen me this way. Ever since I've met him, somehow, I've been inspired to act this way. Maybe that's why I went down this path with him. Maybe that's why I kissed him. So that, for once in my life, I can know how it feels to be respected. To be valued.

"Thank you," I say quietly. "I mean that more than I can say. But I stand by my decision. From this point on, I'm cutting myself off from you. Completely."

And then I turn and face the nylon tent wall.

It's past time I got some sleep.

22

jerk awake. What? Where am I? An inflatable mattress. A pile of animal skins. Nylon tent. No Ryder.

No Ryder.

Right. Deliberately, I take a deep breath, count to five. I'm camping with the fugitives, and Callie got a dose of the amber formula last night. Ryder and I kissed—and then we fell asleep on opposite sides of the tent.

The emotions flow over me. I could spend the rest of the day tucked into this sleeping bag, atop this thin mattress, wallowing.

Instead, I force myself to get up and duck outside. The sun is high in the sky, so I must've slept later than I thought. A fire is smoldering in the wooden pit, embers glowing bright amid a pile of ash. All that's left of the other tents are squares of nylon folded on the ground.

Guess Mikey wasn't kidding about clearing out today. I set my teeth. With all the excitement last night, I didn't have a chance to tell them the implications of Callie's symptoms. If she has the same sickness as my mother, then she'll need repeated doses of the formula. Which means they aren't going anywhere—except back to civilization.

Somehow, I don't think anyone's going to take that well, least of all Mikey.

Sighing, I pick up a bar of lye soap and a jug of water, which Angela pointed out to me last night. I'm not sure where everyone is, but I might as well get clean in the meantime. Adding a washcloth to my stash, I retreat behind a clump of trees to freshen up. When I return, Ryder's standing next to our tent, his head tilted to the sky, mumbling something under his breath.

My steps falter. Okay. I can do this. I mean, I'm the one who set the parameters. I said I was cutting myself off from him, but surely, we can still exchange polite civilities.

I walk up behind him, not trying to be quiet. The leaves rustle, and the twigs crack. But he doesn't turn around.

I clear my throat. "Listen, Ryder, about last night…"

He doesn't react. Instead, he just continues mumbling.

Okay, so that's how he's going to be. That's fair. Can't expect him to greet me with one of his brilliant smiles when I rejected him last night.

"I meant what I said," I continue. "We can't keep up a… um, romance. But we still have to be around each other, at least for the time being. I hope we can be…well, not friends, exactly, but acquaintances, maybe? Yes, acquaintances who like and respect each other. Because I do respect you. A lot. And I like you, as well. Too much. That's part of the problem."

My face burns. Oh dear Fate. Could I ramble any more? Apparently, Ryder is the only one who can transform me from a girl who doesn't talk enough to one who talks *too* much. Still, all I've said is the truth, and, after last night, that's what he deserves.

Not that it matters. I doubt that Ryder is even listening,

much less worried about what I think he deserves.

"Come on, Ryder," I plead to his broad shoulders and nicely muscled back. "Don't be like this. Don't make this any more difficult than it already is."

At long last, he turns. Finally. I tighten my stomach, bracing myself for his glare. But he doesn't frown. His features aren't even hard like granite. Instead, he's laughing, his eyes crinkled at the corners, like I've just told the best joke in this time.

"Good one, Brayden," he says approvingly, staring at a spot over my head. "But I'll see your crab traps and double down on my fishing lures. Bet I get a bigger haul than you in half a day."

Huh? Is this his version of giving me the silent treatment?

"I'm trying to apologize, if that wasn't clear," I venture. "I wish the situation didn't have to be like this. But it is."

He snorts. "You scared, man? Wouldn't blame you. Last week, I caught a dozen fish in a couple hours. Tell you what. I'll give you a ninety-minute head start. What do you say?"

The prickles start at my scalp, but in a moment, my neck is tingling, my spine is shaking, and my skin seems to be shooting out sparks. I've heard this back-and-forth before— or, if not exactly this one, then one very much like it. Three days ago, Jessa crouched in front of Danni Lee, and they held two simultaneous but distinct conversations. Just like Ryder and I are now.

Oh dear Fate. Ryder couldn't be sick. Could he?

No way. I refuse. He's probably just mad at me. That has to be it. "Ryder, if you're mad at me, just say so." My tone exits pleading and borders on desperate. "Please just tell me you're mad. Oh, please…"

The words die in my throat as he turns away and plows

straight into the tent. He falls, his arms and legs twisting in the nylon.

"Ryder!" I rush over to him. "Are you okay?"

He blinks, gazing at the nylon, the smoldering fire, the rods that are now sticking straight up in the air, as though seeing them for the first time. And maybe he is.

I sit down, too, my bottom thumping onto the hard-packed dirt. "Ryder, are you here? Can you hear my voice? It's me, Olivia."

He continues to look around, dazed, for a few moments. And then his eyes focus on my face. My shoulders slump forward. Thank the Fates. He *sees* me. He's back.

"Olivia?" he asks, recognition snapping into his voice. "What's going on? Why am I sitting on the ground?"

23

wrap my arms around myself, suddenly cold, despite the sun beating down on us. "You couldn't see me," I tell Ryder. "You were talking to Brayden about fish traps. You weren't here."

He shakes his head, as though expecting to find some loose thoughts rattling around. "I remember that. He was right there, climbing that oak tree, gathering acorns." He points at the open patch of sky, where there are obviously no trees, and shakes his head again. "Clearly, there's nothing there. I don't understand."

"You have the same sickness as Callie," I say in a low voice. "The virus that Preston was talking about. Whatever it is, it's afflicting you, too."

He gets to his feet and makes his way over the nylon, almost losing his balance as different parts of the tent pop out underneath him. He stumbles next to me—and I shoot out a hand to steady him.

We both freeze. My fingers landed on his very muscular, very sculpted bicep—the bicep I was very happily caressing last night. Something moves across his face, something both regretful and heated.

At that moment, I hear a light humming and the distinct fall of footsteps. I hastily withdraw my fingers just as Callie appears from behind the trees. Baby Remi is strapped to her chest via long strips of fabric.

Her hair appears freshly washed, streaks of gold shining amid the deep brown strands like bits of sunshine got stuck there. A warm yellow-brown glow has returned to her skin, and she looks healthy, vital, alive—so unlike the wan figure who insisted her hand was disappearing last night.

"You're so beautiful," I blurt out. Limbo. Could I sound any more like a groupie?

But I can't help it. This is *the* Callie Stone, the girl I've looked up to most of my life. Sure, I spoke to her last night, but that was different. She was caught in the throes of her illness, hardly lucid. Now, here she is in front of me, completely and unequivocally herself.

"Don't mind her," Ryder says to Callie. "She's been in isolation for the last ten years. She would think a tree stump is attractive."

"Which might explain why I kissed you," I mutter, loud enough for only him to hear.

Callie laughs, bright and sparkly, not at all offended. And why should she be? Ryder's teasing tone is threaded with relief, and all you have to do is look at his face to know he thinks she's a goddess.

She unwraps the sling and sits on the ground, plunking Remi between her legs and offering the toddler a handful of nuts. As soon as Remi spies Ryder, she holds her arms out to him.

"Ry Ry!" she cries.

He crosses to her in a few long strides and scoops her up. "I missed you, too, puffin."

He tosses her into the air, and she shrieks with delight.

"Angela's heart would stop if she saw this," Callie says, grinning. "But there's no thwarting these two. And thanks for the compliment. I feel great. Better than I have for weeks. Whatever was in that formula, it certainly did the trick."

We both watch as Ryder gently settles Remi on the ground and rolls a couple of nuts toward her. As soon as she picks one up, it turns into a brightly colored rattle.

My mouth drops open, and Callie laughs. "It's my psychic ability. I didn't come into it until I woke from my coma, but I have the power to manipulate perception, so that people see what I want them to see."

"That's amazing." Now that she says it, I all of a sudden remember. This ability is precisely why my mother was so obsessed with Callie for ten years. Since Callie has the ability to manipulate images in her visions, the chairwoman hoped that studying her brain would lead to a way to manufacture future memories. The scientists' research, however, was interrupted when Callie escaped into the wilderness with the rest of her family.

Callie turns to Ryder. "My mom and dad went ahead to the rendezvous spot, so that they could leave a message for Zed, Brayden, and Laurel. The others are at the lake, trying to catch enough food for the trip. Which leaves me with child-minding. They're afraid I'll accidentally fall in the water or get bitten by a creature." She sighs and ruffles Remi's curls. "Don't get me wrong. I love watching Remi. She's a dear heart, but I could do without all of this overprotection."

"Logan's not hovering." Ryder glances up from his game with Remi. "At least, he's trying not to be suffocating. He's just worried about you. Especially with your condition."

"What condition?" I ask.

"Oh." If possible, Callie's glow brightens a notch. "I guess you wouldn't know. I'm pregnant."

I suck in a breath. That's right. Ryder had mentioned it when he was talking to Jessa. I completely forgot. I stare at Callie's belly. It's nicely rounded, but I never would've guessed.

"Congratulations," I say.

"Thank you," she says quietly. "Logan and I got married shortly after we left civilization. My parents are both thrilled. And Logan, well…" She blushes. "I never thought I could be more in love. But when he places his hand on my belly and whispers to our child, I know it was worth battling time and Fate for him. The only person missing is Jessa. She should be here, too."

Remi turns and pats Callie's belly with her small hand.

"That's right, my love." Callie plants a kiss on her head. "Your little cousin will be born in six months. And then you'll have a playmate! You'd like that, wouldn't you?"

I swallow. There's a lump in my throat, formed from someone else's emotion, through someone else's tears. But I feel it, anyway. "You're right. Jessa would want to be here."

Ryder picks up a leaf, spinning the stem with his fingers. "Olivia told me Jessa didn't want to betray us. It was the only way she could gain the chairwoman's trust, so that she could try to stop our future of genocide."

Callie smiles indulgently. "That's what I've been telling you all along." She turns to me. "I've managed to convince my parents and the others. They've forgiven her, but Mikey and Ryder didn't want to listen."

"Why am I not surprised?" I mutter.

Ryder doesn't say anything. He doesn't have to. I can read his response in the firm planes of his face: *I don't give second chances. Once you break my trust, it's broken forever.*

In the silence, Callie takes his arm and turns it over, displaying the purplish bruise forming over his elbow. "How did you get this?"

I glance at Ryder, and he nods, as if giving me permission to continue. "He walked into a tent," I say. Briefly, I explain what I suspect about his affliction. It's only when I finish that I realize I didn't drop a single word.

Callie sighs. "It was only a matter of time. All the others have had episodes, as well." She taps Ryder on the shoulder. "You doing okay, squirt?"

I struggle to keep a straight face. Squirt? When he towers her by nearly a foot?

"I'm fine. It was the weirdest thing. I just got really disoriented for a moment."

"You take care of yourself," she says in a low voice. "I worry about you, you know?"

"I know." He squeezes her hand briefly, and genuine feeling flows between them.

Ping. There goes my heart. It's funny. I never feel this way around my mom or the other FuMA employees. Not much love flowing in that building. But with Jessa or the rest of her family, my heart's constantly pinging and panging all over the place.

Not that it does me any good.

Sighing, I hone in on something Callie said. "Everyone here has had an episode?"

"Everyone who's received a future memory or traveled through time," Callie says. "Which means…not Mikey. And not Ryder, until you just told me otherwise."

"I received my future memory a few days ago," he says. "When I was under FuMA's custody."

She pauses. "Should I ask about your vision?"

He squeezes his eyes shut. "Maybe later."

She nods, not pushing him further. Of all people, Callie knows what it's like to receive a bad memory, one you can't imagine, much less talk about. "The episodes have been coming more frequently, especially in the last few days since Ryder's been gone."

Alarm bells ring in my head. "But this is awful. Don't you see? The episodes aren't going to go away, and they're not going to get any better. If all of you are sick, then you *all* need the formula. What's more, one dose won't be enough. My mom injects herself daily, so the effects must wear off." I take a deep breath. "You all have to go back to civilization. Or, at least, get close enough so that I can provide you with a steady supply of syringes."

"I know," Callie says softly.

Remi rolls her rattle away, and her little face scrunches up. Before she can wail, Callie gives her another handful of nuts. They transform into a set of animal finger puppets.

"We discussed it this morning by the lake," she continues. "I wasn't being entirely truthful, before. The others didn't send me back to camp just to watch Remi. They also wanted me to give you a message."

She puts her hand on my arm, her eyes kind, even as her smile is sorrowful. "I appreciate everything you've done for us. I can't even begin to tell you how much better I feel. But…Mikey's decided. From this point forward, we'll proceed on our own."

I stare. "But how will you access the formula? You can't just pick it up from a pharm bot, you know. The formula's available only at FuMA."

"We'll figure something out." She presses her lips together. "I'm sorry, Olivia, but Mikey's made up his mind. He says he doesn't trust you." She glances at the boy behind me. "Ryder standing in for you only goes so far."

Her hand falls away. "This will sound harsh. But you need to leave before the others get back. I'm sorry to say this is good-bye."

24

Ryder leads me away from the campsite. The hoverboards trail behind us like loyal pets, one of them loaded with my rations for my day-long trip home, the other ready for me to hop on and zoom away. We don't say much—either because there's nothing to say or because everything's already been said. The only sound, as we hop over tree roots and squeeze between branches, is the low hum of the boards.

"You need to make the most of your trip while the sun is out," Ryder finally says. "It's not as direct, but if you head north, eventually you'll hit the river, which you can follow all the way back to the FuMA building."

He doesn't say "home," even though I've lived there all my life. I'm not surprised. "Home" is where your family is; it's the place you feel safe and secure. I don't have that. I'm not sure I ever have.

Anger surges inside me. For the first time in my life, I was *doing* something. I was working toward a cause instead of sitting on the sidelines, observing. And now, my mission has been summarily dismissed. Just like that. Because

Mikey said so. And I couldn't even argue or plead my case because the message was relayed through Callie.

"Do you always do what Mikey tells you to do?" I blurt out.

Ryder holds a branch back, so that I can pass through without getting scratched. "He's my father. And our leader."

"Does that mean he gets to do all your thinking?"

"That's not fair." He scuttles down a sharp incline of rocks and then offers his hand to me, which I ignore. "When we've disagreed with him, all of us—myself, Jessa, Callie, Logan—have gone our own ways. But it has to be something important, something we feel really strongly about. Because the truth is, Mikey's a good leader. We've made it this far because of him. He's proven, again and again, that he has our best interests at heart. We respect him, and that's why we respect his decisions."

Okay, then. I have my answer. Ryder's willing to disobey his father when the cause is important—and I'm just not important enough.

My feet suddenly feel like tree stumps, and I'm dragging so low, I'm not sure a hoverboard could get me off the ground. "This is far enough," I manage to get out. "You can leave me now."

He spins around, so abruptly I have to throw out my hands to avoid stumbling. They land squarely on his chest, and my mouth ends up inches from his.

"Did you know?" His tone is low and urgent. "When you said you didn't want to have anything to do with me, ever again, did you know you'd be leaving in a few hours' time?"

I sigh. "I was aware it was a possibility. But since it appeared in under half of the branches, I was hoping your offer to stand in for me would sway Mikey more than it did."

He shifts closer, so that my hands feel less like a barrier between us — and more like a caress. "It's nice to know that in some worlds, he values my opinion."

"He always values you, in every branch, in every world," I say, on the verge of tears and not sure why. "And so do Angela, Logan, and Callie. You are so loved. I don't have to tell you that, but you should hear it anyway."

His fingers hover in the air, and then they swoop down, tucking a strand of hair behind my ear. "And what about you? Are you loved?"

I laugh, and the sound scrapes against my throat. "You don't have to see into the future to know the answer to that question."

"Olivia…" My name is both a plea and a question. His hand pauses at the patch of skin under my earlobe, waiting.

I back away, one big step and then another. It shouldn't hurt, not in any physical way, but I feel like my skin's being ripped apart. "I was right, you know. This makes it easier to say good-bye."

"Does it?" he asks. "Because where I'm standing, it's not easy. It's not easy at all."

We stare at each other for a long moment, a moment where — in other worlds — anything could happen. A kiss, a hug, a slap, a shove. More words, meaningful words, hurtful words.

But in this moment, in this world, he turns and walks away. Weaving around the hoverboards, he stops and places a device on the end of one. No, *two* devices with square bodies and a plethora of outstretched legs. "Here are two spiders. If you attach one to yourself and the other to the end of a hoverboard, you'll be rendered invisible." He meets my eyes for one searing moment. "In case you ever need to follow anyone unseen."

He leaves without another backward glance.

I pick up one of the spiders, rubbing the "legs" against my chin. Huh. It's just possible I'm not so unimportant, after all.

25

For the next three days, I follow the group of four adults, one teenager, and one toddler, thankful that the fugitive crew has split up, so that there's fewer of them to track. Mikey always leads the way, with Angela following closely behind, little Remi strapped to her chest. Logan and Callie hike in the middle of the pack, and Ryder brings up the rear.

He can't see me or hear me—I know that. And yet, he looks over his shoulder at least once every ten minutes, shooting a smile out into the wilderness. Sometimes, he's staring right at me; other times, he's off by a few yards. But I know the gesture is meant for me, and that makes my own lips curve.

It's strange. I never smiled much in isolation. There was no point, since no one was around, and back then, I thought smiles served an entirely social function. But now, I know sometimes you smile just because you want to. Sometimes you smile because you can't help yourself.

I do my best to stretch my rations, but I quickly run out. I'm not concerned. I used to go for days without food while I was in isolation. Since only a select few people knew my location, my mother herself would bring me a day's worth of food every morning. Invariably, there were days—and one time, even a week—when she would get busy and forget. So, I've gone hungry before, and I can go hungry now.

Turns out, my stomach doesn't growl once. At every meal, Ryder surreptitiously divides his portion in half—and leaves me the fried meat and scoop of rice on a broad leaf. I tried to give the food back at first, but after a heated game of pushing the rabbit's leg back and forth, and Angela glancing up and asking Ryder what he was doing, I relented.

Of course, this means Ryder is eating only half of his rations. With every bite that goes into my belly instead of his, I forgive him a little more for killing me in fifteen days.

I don't know what my next move is. I'm not sure how I'm going to persuade Mikey to bring his family back to civilization. The pathways unfurl before me, but so much depends on other people's decisions, I can't predict how—and if—I'll be successful.

What makes it more difficult is that I no longer have access to Callie's future. Lately, her pathways have been blurry. Huge chunks of the branches are missing, as though I'm hitting a partial blank wall. In turn, her presence in my traveling companions' futures is also cloudy, so it's hard to get a complete picture.

I don't know what to make of it. Maybe the deteriorating time stream is affecting me, too. Or maybe, this close to my death, I'm beginning to lose key components of my abilities.

In the middle of the third day, the group stops for the night—ostensibly, to replenish their food supply. But even from the rear of the pack, I can see Logan watching Callie with increasing concern. Sweat gleams on her skin, and her breath, while steady and strong the previous two days, now comes quickly and shallowly.

It isn't any wonder. It's been over sixty hours since she was injected with the formula. She's due for another dose—and soon.

At least we're getting closer to civilization. We hit the river last night, and for the past couple hours, we've been traveling up, up, up into the mountains. Now, we've stopped at a wide-open ledge, overlooking the roaring river, and the gang is dumping their gear on the field.

If I didn't know better, I'd think we were at the grassy area behind the FuMA building, the one open to the public for picnicking and sight-seeing. My mom never took me there, of course. But before I went into isolation, MK took Tanner and me a few times. Once, when I accidentally let go of my sandwich and watched it fall into the cascading white foam, Tanner even gave me half of his. It's my favorite memory from childhood.

Smiling at the recollection, I retreat farther up the gradual slope. I settle upon a rocky overhang, where I have a good view of everyone, and remove the spider that hangs on the headgear around my forehead.

Below me, the gang divvies up the equipment and splits—Logan, Callie, and Ryder to hunt and Mikey and Angela to gather berries.

I close my eyes, tilting my face to the sky. The sun sinks into my bones, and a slight breeze lifts the hair off my sweat-soaked skin. I take the moment to just be. No visions of the future, blurry or otherwise, no thoughts of the past. Just here, now. Crumbling rocks jab into my thighs, and the scent of dust and bird fike surrounds me.

Alive. For fifteen more days.

My stomach churns at the thought. I don't want to die. I *don't*. I may not have had much as a life, as sheltered as

I am, but it's *my* life. And I want it to continue. There's so much I haven't experienced, so many emotions I haven't felt. So much life left to live.

Presently, I hear singing below me and open my eyes. It's Angela, with a roughly woven bag filled with what I assume are berries. She drops the bag and loosens the wrap around her torso, letting Remi onto the ground. Mikey's nowhere to be seen.

Angela settles herself next to Remi, and my eyes start to close again, lulled by her singing.

All of a sudden, they pop back open. Faint bells ring in my head. Something's...not right. This scene is somehow... wrong. But how?

I dart my eyes from the mother-daughter pair to the open clearing that dead-ends in a cliff. Father of Time. That's the problem. Angela's let Remi down too close to the cliff. According to Jessa, she's way too protective to ever do that, especially since her daughter crawling over a cliff is precisely the future memory she's trying to avoid. She'd slit her own wrists first.

What's going on? Is Angela just tired? Not thinking clearly?

I look back at the pair. Remi's tracing her fingers through the dirt, and Angela's hands are manipulating something. What? Squinting, I lean forward, trying to see. She's pulling, twisting, stuffing...nothing at all.

I shake my head, trying to clear it. Either Angela is fiddling with an invisible juice box, or...or...

Oh Fates. She must be lost in an episode from another time. She must think she's put Remi down in a safe, enclosed space, far, far, away from any cliffs. That's the only thing that explains her carelessness.

I should do something. What? I'm thirty feet above

them. If I shout something, I'll give away my presence.

Oh, Remi, please keep playing in the dirt. Please have no interest in the wide open spaces beyond.

As soon as I have the thought, a moth flutters through the air and lands on Remi's nose. She bats at the winged insect and laughs delightedly.

Angela doesn't turn, but of course she wouldn't. She's somewhere else. She doesn't hear her child. Alarms aren't sounding in her brain.

The little girl waves her hands in the air, trying to catch the moth and just missing. The moth flits around her, as though inviting her to play, and then flies away…in the direction of the cliff.

Remi starts crawling after the moth.

Oh Fates, oh Fates, oh Fates. I can't just hope for the best anymore.

"Angela!" I cup my hands around my mouth. "Remi's on the move. She's heading toward the cliff. Angela!" I yell so loudly my throat's scraped raw. She has to hear me. She's got to.

But her hands continue moving the invisible straw, and the little girl is now twenty feet from the edge of the cliff.

Limbo. There's no way I'll be able to scamper down there in time. I grab a rock and throw it at Angela. She can't hear me, but she should be able to feel, right?

Wrong. The rock hits her squarely in the back. She doesn't turn; she doesn't even flinch.

Ten feet. Sweat pours down my face. I don't flash forward to the future; I don't have time. I look wildly around, and my gaze lands on the hoverboard. Of course. I jump on and as soon as I'm positioned, I zoom down the slope to the open field. Five feet.

"Remi!" Angela screams, her voice so shrill it winds into

my heart and shatters it. "Stop! What are you doing? Remi!"

She takes off running, but she'll never make it. Remi's already at the edge. In slow motion, I watch as the little girl puts one hand into empty space and then the other. And then…she tumbles over.

It's too late. It's too late.

"Noooooo!!!!!" Angela's cry splits my body, splits my world. Splits my very soul. "No, Remi, no! Noooooo!!!"

I charge forward, straight off the side of the cliff, without pause, without hesitation. Ryder said I would break my neck. Ryder said going down this cliff was suicide. I don't care. All I care about is a little girl falling through space.

Down, down, down, I plunge. The wind blasts me head on, my skin rippling under its force like bedsheets. My stomach falls along with my feet, and it's all I can do to grit my teeth and stay on.

The river rushes up at me at an alarming rate. I ignore it and search for Remi. There! Her limbs flail in the air, so tiny, so helpless. I barrel toward her, my arms outstretched. Almost there, almost there. I grasp at her and get a corner of her shirt, which immediately slides out of my grip.

Fate fike it, Olivia. You can do this. So do it.

I try again. The wind whistles over my arms, but my hands close around a bigger swatch of her shirt…and then her warm, solid torso. I bring the little girl to my chest, hugging her tight, just as I pull up the board at the last second.

The front of the board skids along the water, and the platform trembles violently. I rock wildly, about to fall off.

I can stick any landing, remember? Tanner used to say I had adhesive on my feet. I can stick any landing. I can stick any landing…

The board skims the river, more surf than hover, and finally, I reach the shore.

I touch down and stumble off. My knees have turned as boneless as sea anemone, and my heart's about to punch a hole through my chest. But I have the little girl. I have Remi.

Spent, I collapse on the ground. Remi climbs on top of me, her little hands pounding on my chest. I open my eyes, and she's smiling, shrieking. And safe.

That's all that matters. She's safe.

26

I don't know how long I lie there, minutes or seconds. Probably seconds, since I don't think Remi's patience would last that long. When I sit up, I see small figures on the cliff above us, watching me, watching Remi. They must've all come running when they heard Angela's screams. I wouldn't be surprised if they heard her cries all the way back in Eden City.

Giving them a wave, I get to my feet, hauling Remi up with me. My movements are shaky, and my bones feel like they're made of gelatin—and not the firm kind, either. I can't quite catch a full breath, no matter how deeply I inhale. Before I can relax, however, I need to get Remi back to her parents.

I mount my board, tucking the little girl inside my zippered jacket. It's not quite as secure as a baby sling, but it'll have to do. Carefully, I make my way back across the river and find a gradual slope to follow up to the ledge. After everything we've been through, it would be a shame to drop Remi now.

After a winding and arduous ten minutes, I finally reach

the top, and the fugitives converge on me.

"Oh, my darling." Angela snatches her daughter from me, her voice as tear-stained as her cheeks. "Oh, my dear, sweet baby. You're safe. You're okay."

With a wary glance at the cliff's edge, she retreats ten feet, twenty feet, thirty feet before collapsing to her knees. The rest of us follow, and Mikey drops to the ground beside his wife and daughter.

"I'm so sorry, dear heart. So sorry," Angela whispers against Remi's hair. "I should've known better. I've spent my life dreading this moment, preparing for it, doing everything in my power to prevent it. And still, I failed you. If it weren't for Olivia…I would've…you would've…" She trails off and rocks Remi back and forth.

Mikey wraps his arms around both his wife and daughter. "This wasn't your fault, Ange."

"But it was," she says despairingly. "I was in another time. I could've sworn we were in the eating area of a residential unit. I set her down in a playpen while I fiddled with her juice box. That's what I thought. That's what I saw."

He strokes her hair. "So, you see? You couldn't have known."

"It didn't make any sense. Why didn't I wonder why we were in a unit? Why didn't I ask myself how we got there from the middle of the woods?" She's not asking us, but berating herself. Which means these questions won't go away. No matter what answer we give, they'll chase her until the end of time.

"That's the nature of these episodes," Callie says. "When you're in the middle of one, you have no idea. You don't think to question it. You just feel like you're living your life."

"I should've known," Angela repeats woodenly.

"What's important is that she's safe. You're safe. We're

all together." Mikey drops kisses on both of their heads, tears streaming openly down his face.

I stare. I've never see him like this. More than that, in all his futures, he's this emotional in only one particular pathway. This one.

He looks up and gestures for Ryder to join them, and Callie and Logan, too. Pretty soon, they're all laughing and hugging and crying, this family that I'm not a part of, related by blood and bonds and love.

Quietly, I set the hoverboard down and lean against the rock wall of the slope. I don't feel excluded, exactly. I don't feel anything. I mean, sure, there's this thickness in my throat; there's this pressure at the pit of my stomach. But those things don't mean anything. How can they?

I've always been the outsider. I've always been the observer. Angela and Mikey and the rest don't mean to exclude me. They simply don't remember me. To feel anything, now, would be like a mouse bemoaning the fact that it scurries on all fours, like a fire lamenting the heat of its flame.

There's nothing to feel. It simply is. I simply am.

And then Ryder looks up, glances around, and finds me. He detaches himself from the group and crosses to me, taking both my hands into the warm cavern of his palms.

"Thank you." The words are low, his voice rumbling. "Thank you for saving my sister's life. It was way too risky. You could've splintered every bone in your body. But I'm so glad you did."

He kisses my forehead, one cheek, the other cheek… and then his lips hover inches above mine. "I don't want to ignore your wishes," he says huskily. "I heard every word, loud and clear. You don't want anything to do with me. I get that. I'll honor that. But I want…I need…" He dips his head, which brings his mouth even closer.

Somewhere between the kisses and his words, my brain short-circuits, because my head nods of its own volition. And then his lips brush against mine.

His mouth moves over my mouth, my tongue, my teeth. But it also reaches further inside me, soothing aches I didn't know existed, smoothing out hurts I'd buried long ago. In his kiss, I feel the only thing I've ever wanted. I feel like I'm not alone.

Too soon, he pulls back, searching for something inside my eyes. His mouth opens, that perfect, beautiful mouth I'd love to sketch, if I'd taken the pathway of an artist. Before he can say anything, however, a pair of soft arms encircles me.

Ryder lets go, and I'm looking into Angela's eyes, Remi squeezed in between us.

"Thank you," she says quietly. "From the depth of my heart, from the bottom of my soul. You are my angel."

From there, I'm passed on to Callie's fierce hug and to Logan's heartfelt one. And then, to Mikey. To my utter shock, he embraces me, too.

"I owe you," he says gruffly. "Even though I don't know why you're here."

He glances at the spider still attached to my hoverboard, useless without its twin on my forehead. "I have a pretty good idea, though. Care to explain?"

"Mikey." Angela's voice slices through the air. "She risked her own life in order to save your daughter. You will not interrogate her, do you hear me? I don't care why she's here. I would give my life a thousand times over for her to be here."

She stops, her breath coming faster than her words. "She's given me...everything. Every gulp of air I take, every drop of blood in my veins. So whatever she says, whatever she wants, I'll do it. I'll go back to civilization with her. Do you understand?"

She crosses over to stand next to me, with Remi pulling at her hair.

"Me, too." Callie winks at me, as though she's been waiting for just the right moment to defy Mikey.

Logan slings an arm around her shoulder. "Me, three."

Mikey turns to Ryder. "What about you?"

"I told you I'd stand in for her." Ryder's voice is quiet, but his gaze is directed at me, questioning…and something else. Something I don't understand.

Mikey studies his family members, one by one. By the time his scrutiny reaches me, he's smiling. "I'm surprised you could think that I would feel any differently. Prepare yourself, everyone. Guess we're going back to civilization."

27

I'm back where I started a week ago. Potts's cabin. The same log building, the same chain link kennel. The grass grows in random patches here and there, like the hair of a balding man, and the musty smell of wet dog surrounds me.

I don't know why I expected the property to look any different. Only seven days have passed. And yet, I'm different, and not just because the pathways have gotten blurry. Not just because I have only thirteen days left to live. In ways I can't precisely define, the girl whose feet are sinking into the mud now is not the same person who trudged through this muck a week ago.

There's no sign of Potts or the bloodhounds. No excited barking at the sound of our footsteps, no clinking of the chains as a nose or two pokes through the fence. Weird. Potts doesn't stray far from his cabin, other than his two annual camping trips. He just went on one last week. Would he be on another already? And would he take all his dogs?

I reach into his future…and I hit a blank wall. The same wall I crash into when I reach into my mother's future, the same wall that I encounter on any pathway after

May Fourth. Not just partially blank this time—but fully, completely, entirely blank.

My mouth dries. The hair on the back of my neck prickles. First, the partial block on Callie's future; now, the total block on Potts's. What's going on? Have I lost my precognition altogether?

Testing, I reach into Angela's future and see her nursing Remi. I reach into Ryder's future and see him brushing the hair off my forehead. In fact, every pathway that doesn't involve Callie is still perfectly clear. So, no. My ability's still here. It's just the futures of certain people that are blocked.

I don't get it. Potts should be the last person in this world affected by the time stream virus. He has no contact with the outside world. He has next to no technology. He's never mentioned receiving a future memory, and the chances of him time traveling are low to nil. I mean, he doesn't even *like* the ComA. So, he wouldn't have had any exposure to any scientists. Why is his future closed off to me? Will he die, too? No, that can't be right. I haven't been able to reach into my mother's futures for years, and she's still very much alive.

I let out a slow breath. I suppose it doesn't matter. Not at this precise moment. I don't need Potts to get inside. He doesn't use a biometric scanner, and I've known that he hides a pre-Boom key under the front doormat ever since my second visit.

Pushing my uneasiness away, I retrieve the key and open the front door. "Here we are," I say to the gang. "Make yourselves comfortable."

Mikey leads the way, taking slow, exaggerated steps like he's navigating a minefield. I don't blame him. He may have agreed to trust me, but they haven't set foot in a residential structure of any sort for the last six months. I brought them here only because Callie's getting worse by the day. We need a place where they can be safe while I go back to FuMA and retrieve a batch of formula.

Once Mikey is inside and no alarms go off, he gestures for the others to follow him.

Angela sinks onto the living area floor, loosening the sling to let Remi down so that she can nurse her. As previously discussed, Ryder sits cross-legged next to his mom. Shortly after the little girl's near-fatal accident, Angela announced the two-adult rule: while they are having these episodes, two adults must be close by Remi at any time.

Callie and Logan walk into the cabin last, their eyes wide and their breathing shallow.

"Is something wrong?" I ask.

Callie licks her lips. "Who did you say the owner was?"

"His name is Potts."

She and Logan exchange a look, and then he trails his fingers over the old-fashioned glider, the sofa with the triangular cushions, the utilitarian end tables. "Unbelievable," he says under his breath. "This place looks exactly the same, and it's been over ten years."

I frown. "You've been here before?"

"Yes." His gaze crawls back to Callie, and she nods, once. "The day before Callie injected the syringe into her heart," he continues. "She sprained her ankle as we were coming back to civilization, and Potts helped us out."

"He was so kind to me," she says. "He put this magic salve on my ankle. Made it better right away."

Logan tangles his fingers in her hair and tugs her close, as if remembering the fateful day that resulted in him losing her to a coma for a decade.

She leans back against his chest. "Potts talked about a

mountain community. Remember that? A group of people who wanted nothing to do with technology, who had been living together, in their way of life, even before the Boom. Whatever happened to them?"

"They're still there, I guess," I say. "I don't hear about them much. ComA's never been interested in them." I gnaw on my cheek. But why not? Sure, the mountain people don't bother anybody, but ComA is interested in *everybody*.

"I've always wondered about them," Callie murmurs. "Wondered if Potts was one of them." She and Logan drift to the sofa, the one they must've sat on all those years ago. They settle in, holding hands and whispering, lost in memories of yesterday.

I frown. Is she right? I never considered the idea before, but it would make sense if Potts is one of the mountain people. It would explain his disinterest in technology.

Ryder joins me, his eyes trained on his sister. Angela's laid Remi in her inflatable crib and is rocking it and humming. Behind them, Mikey's fiddling with a panel on the wall.

"She wouldn't nurse," Ryder says, rubbing his eyes. "Angela says it's gotten worse since the accident. She won't eat any of our rations, either. Yesterday, when I was changing her, I could see every one of her ribs."

"I'll look in Potts's pantry," I say. "He has only that basic Meal Assembler, but maybe I can find something Remi will like."

"No rush. Angela wants her to nap before we try feeding her again."

We lapse into silence. I rack my mind, trying to think of something to say.

The problem, I suppose, is that I can still feel the sweet ache of his kiss. True to his word, the kiss was confined to that moment alone. He hasn't touched me since. He's barely even spoken to me. I'm not sure why he's here now.

"You look...disturbed," he says, angling forward.

"Oh." I flush. Like Limbo I'm going to admit I was thinking about our kiss. "It's, um, Potts's absence," I say, reaching for the first thing on my mind. "He hardly ever leaves his cabin, so I'm not sure why he isn't here now." I take a deep breath. "I don't know. I have a funny feeling about it."

"We should tell Mikey," he says immediately.

"It's nothing concrete," I protest. "Just a feeling."

"You're a precognitive, Olivia. I would never dismiss any of your feelings." He turns to look for Mikey, but he's not there anymore.

All of a sudden, I realize that the panel has been moved from the wall. Behind it is an entryway into a small room. I blink. A secret door to a secret room. Potts is the simplest person I know. What could he possibly be hiding?

At the same moment, Mikey appears in the entry to the room, where he has apparently ducked inside. "We have to leave."

Angela's hand stops mid-rock. "What? Remi just went to sleep."

"I don't care." Mikey rakes his fingers through his hair. "It's not safe here."

"Potts is neutral. No one will think to look for you in his cabin." I stop. At least, I *thought* he was. In the pathways I could see, we were safe here. But I didn't see all of them. I have several blank spots in my vision now. Maybe I didn't pay enough attention to those holes. Maybe, for the first time I can remember, I am dead wrong.

Mikey is studying me carefully. "Potts is neutral, is he? Then why was your mom here?"

"What?" I gape.

"Come see." Abruptly, he turns on his heel and walks back into the room. I follow him in—and gasp.

The room is small, but it is better outfitted than most labs in the Technology Research Agency, or TechRA. Panels of instruments cover each wall, and four com terminals are crowded together in the center of the room. Mikey moves directly to the keyball and runs his hands over the spherical surface. A moment later, a holo-doc pops into the air. "This is the security log. Says right here the chairwoman's biometrics were scanned two days ago."

My knees go weak. "That can't be right. Potts doesn't even have a biometric scanner. This is a simple log cabin."

Mikey looks pointedly around the room. "He doesn't have a scanner you know about. But it doesn't seem like you know him very well, do you? Why was your mother here, Olivia?"

"Maybe she trailed us last week," Ryder suggests. "Maybe she came back later to interrogate Potts."

"But no one followed us," I protest. "I made sure of it." I grab my temples as something occurs to me. "Oh Fates. That's why Potts is gone. My mom arrested him—and all of his dogs, too. Because he helped us. What have I done?"

Mikey shakes his head slowly. The lights from the machines blink behind him, mocking me. "Hate to break it to you, but that wasn't the chairwoman's first visit. She's logged over a dozen trips here in the last ten years."

"No way." I push past Mikey so that I can get a closer look at the holo-doc.

I rub my eyes. And rub them again. But there's no denying what's in the air. In regular intervals over the last decade, my mother's biometrics have been scanned at Potts's over a dozen times. The visits were less frequent in the beginning, but lately, she's been coming every month. Did she know I was sneaking here? Or did she visit Potts for another reason entirely? One that has nothing to do with me?

I let out a shaky breath. "I know how this looks. But I promise you, I'm not betraying you. I had no idea my mother even knew Potts."

Mikey sighs. "You know what? I actually believe you. But we still have to get out of here."

All of a sudden, the room darkens, as though a large object is passing over the skylight in the living area. I dash out of the secret room into the living area and look straight up into a panel of black metal.

My stomach drops. We didn't hear a sound, and it isn't any wonder. A stealth copter.

Limbo, Limbo, Limbo.

"It's too late," I say faintly. "ComA's already here."

28

As if on cue, Remi lets out a shriek. For a moment, we freeze, the cry wrapping around us and keeping us in place.

"What do we do?" Callie asks.

But she's not looking at Mikey. She's looking at *me*. In fact, they're all turned toward me, even the leader of the Underground himself.

"Hide," I blurt out. "There's a cellar underneath the sink in the eating area. Potts said it was the only place he could find to put it." Even as the words leave my mouth, I realize how unlikely this is. He has a hidden room behind a wall. How many other secret places do I not know about? I can't believe I was so gullible, taking everything he said and did at face value.

The others spring into action, unconcerned about my naïveté. Ryder is barely able to fold his tall frame into the cabinet, where the entrance to the cellar is located, but he manages. I hear a clatter against wood, as if someone has just fallen down the stairs, and wince. But at least they're inside.

I walk back into the living area and have just folded my hands demurely when the door flies open.

My mother strides into the room, flanked by four guards, her icicle heels leading the way. It's been a week since I've seen her. A week since I shoved her into the reclining chair, since I pressed the button that strapped her arms and thighs into place. A week since I made her relive the memory reel of humankind's worst phobias. And yet, I swear the fine lines along her eyes have multiplied. The hair pulled so tightly into a chignon is more gray than silver, more tired than sophisticated.

We regard each other. Correction. She circles me like I'm the newest iteration of a bot on sale to the highest bidder. I do my best to keep my expression placid. Not blinking, not flinching, and especially not cowering.

"That will be all," my mother says to the guards, her tone as crisp as autumn apples. "You may return to the copter."

The guards exchange a glance.

"With all due respect, Chairwoman, it wouldn't be prudent for us to leave you in such a high-risk security situation," the one with the three metal bars across his shoulders says. A scar snakes down the side of his face.

A shiver runs through me. Could this be...Scar Face, the guard who harassed Callie all those years ago? Jessa tried to track him down, but without a real name, she didn't have any luck.

Now I know why. If Scar Face became captain of the guards, then his underlings would never admit to recognizing the description of his scar.

"This is not a security situation," my mother snaps. "This is my daughter."

"A daughter who tortured you," Scar Face returns smoothly. "By the time we found you, your clothes looked like they had been dunked in a swimming pool. You didn't stop twitching for days. I would strongly advise that you let us remain."

My mother draws herself to her full height, pulling the cloak of authority around her. Uh-oh. Bad move, Scar Face, throwing her physical deficiencies in her face. The guard's chances of convincing her have evaporated.

"You have five seconds to leave before I relieve you of your stations," she says calmly.

The guards start, confer with their eyes, and then scurry out of the cabin with one second to spare.

"That's better." She gestures to the couch, ever the mistress even in someone else's home. "Sit down," she says grandly. "And then, you may apologize to me."

"Limbo, no," I say. "You deserved to suffer. After all those people you killed, after the little kids you tortured, I should've trapped you in that machine for an entire day."

Her head rears back like I've slapped her. And no wonder. I've never spoken to her this way, ever. No matter how cruel she was, I always reminded myself of her alternate futures, the pathways where there was a reason for her madness, where a red heart beats underneath her cruelty. I was always convinced that she was a good person underneath all her complicated layers.

No more. She no longer gets a free pass for her actions in *this* life, in *this* time stream.

"What was your worst phobia?" I ask. "You know, the one that made you scream the loudest. The one that the com detected and made you live over and over until you collapsed." The words pour out of me. Now that I started telling my mother how I really feel, I can't seem to stop. "For Tanner, it was heights. Remember when you did that, Mother? When you took a six-year-old boy who had just mysteriously 'lost' his parents and made him feel like he was falling to his death, again and again, for six long months. Was that one of your finest moments, Mom?"

She pushes herself off the couch and stalks up and down the living area. "Do you think I wanted to torture them? That I was doing it for my own pleasure?"

"You needed information," I say mockingly. "You had to do whatever it took to get it."

"Exactly. The ends justify the means." Her voice rises. "None of this is random; none of it is senseless. Everything I do is with an ultimate goal in mind. With all of your vast knowledge of the future, how can you not see that?"

"There are some lines you don't cross," I whisper. "You don't torture children. And you don't kill innocent people."

"*You* crossed that line. *You* tortured me."

I stop, her words cementing me in place. I did cross that line. So if she's a monster, what does that make me?

She sits and takes both my hands in her perpetually chilly ones. Bad circulation, she's always told me. But now, I wonder if my mother really does have freshly melted icicles running through her veins.

"I'm not angry at you, Olivia," she says softly. "You wanted to help Ryder escape. You wanted to save Callie. You did what you had to do, for what you believed was right. How can I hold that against you?"

I stare at our interlocking hands. Once upon a time, this was all I wanted. To sit on a couch with my mother. To have her absolve me of my sins because she loved me. But now that a twisted version of that scenario has arrived, it's all I can do to push the bile back down my throat. "I tortured you," I say. "How can you have no feelings about that whatsoever?"

"I have feelings. They're just not angry." She chews

her lip. It's a testament to our technology that the red tint doesn't fade. "I only hope, when the time comes, that you'll judge me by the same standard."

I pull my hands away. "I don't agree with you. The end doesn't always justify the means."

"When the end is big enough, it does," she says wearily. "When it involves the very existence of our time stream? I'll do just about anything to save our world."

I go still. Every molecule in my body, every molecule in the air stops dancing. "So, it's true? Our entire time stream is deteriorating? Our very existence, our very world, is in danger of disappearing?"

She nods, once. But once is all it takes.

Numbly, I fall against the couch. But I'm not surprised. Not really. Deep down, I knew it was more than just a theory. I knew it was actually happening, in the here and now.

"How much time do we have?" I mumble. "How much time until we all evaporate?"

"A month, six weeks if we're lucky. The time stream is already ripping, and once it hits a critical mass, the deterioration will move quickly. Fortunately we've developed a formula to treat the sickness." She leans forward. "That's the good news: there's hope. We all need to come together now. Everyone in Eden City, North Amerie, the entire planet. The top government officials from around the world have been working closely together toward a solution. But in order to take the final step, I need my top scientists, Olivia. I need Mikey and Preston. Where are they?"

"I'm not giving them up," I say automatically.

"I checked the dispensary records," she says. "One of the tubes of amber formula was missing. Did you steal it to give to Callie?"

I nod. Nothing to gain by lying now.

"Good. She'll need more, every single day. Of all the people who will come apart, she'll be the first because of her Asynchronicity."

I suck in a breath. Of course. That's why her symptoms were more severe than any of the others. For the ten long years that she was in her coma, she suffered from a condition where her mind was detached from her body. She realigned her mental and physical time only six months ago. It wouldn't take much to knock it off-balance again.

"Give me the formula," I say. "An entire month's supply, with provisions for the others, too, because they're all having episodes. I'll deliver it to them."

Her face splits into a smile. "That's not how negotia-tions work, Olivia. I have something you want, you have something I want. Hand over Preston and Mikey, and I'll give you all the formula you need."

Ryder's laugh sounds in my mind, short and harsh. *That's what you'll never understand, Chairwoman,* he said right before she forced me to torture him. *We're a family. That means we stick together.*

He didn't take my mother's offer then, and I can't take it now.

"It's not my bargain to accept," I whisper. "It's not my decision to make."

She looks at me for a long moment. "Use your precog-nition, Olivia. Reach into the future and tell me what will happen if you *don't* turn your friends in. And then tell me if that's a future you want to live with. A future you want to be responsible for."

"I…can't see clearly into the future anymore," I admit. "The pathways that involve Callie are blurry, and I'm not sure why."

She nods sagely. "Another effect of the time stream deterioration. But go ahead. Look anyway. Even if you get a partial image of the pathways, you'll see what I'm talking about."

I take a shuddering breath. And then another. I have a bad feeling about what's coming. But I have no other choice.

The futures crash down on me, blurred branch after blurred branch. Partial pictures and singed-off scenes, and yet the pathways all depict variations of the same future. Callie getting sicker and sicker. Turning transparent for minutes, and then hours. Logan beside himself with despair. Mikey and Angela, distracted. Tempers flaring, words flinging. Too many episodes, not enough adults. Remi having one accident after another. Falling down a hole, wading too deeply into water, cutting herself on a sharp rock.

And Ryder. Oh Ryder. Blaming himself for his family's ailments. Embarking on riskier and riskier missions. Inevitably, getting caught. Being punished. Lashed a hundred times with the electro-whip, forced to endure thousands of hours of the phobia reel.

Sometimes, I'm able to get them a round of formula. Maybe even two or three rounds. But what I can bring is never enough. They always need more.

Can I really subject my friends to this future? No. But I can't break my word to them, either. They trusted me. Even Mikey. They all trusted me to keep them safe. If I turn them in now, Ryder will… He'll never forgive me. He already gave me a second chance. No way he'll give me a third.

I squeeze my eyes shut. What do I do? My brain is pushing me one way, but my heart is pulling another. I feel like I'm about to explode, my body ripped apart by this decision. In a choice between two evils, there's no "lesser than." Both options are unthinkable. Both are unbearable.

"Listen, I know this is hard for you," my mother says gently. "But I promise your friends will be treated well. I'll pardon them of all their crimes. They can even return to their homes in the Underground compound and live there, if they like. They'll have the formula, Olivia. Food and shelter, all the comforts our technology has to offer."

I massage my temples, as much to relieve the pressure as to hold my brain together. What do I do? What do I do? What would Callie do? What would Jessa?

My mother is watching me carefully, with an expression that makes a chill creep up my spine. It's an expression that says she knows my heart, she sees my soul. An expression that suggests she knows me better than I know myself.

"I don't know if you're aware of this, Olivia, but your cabin was equipped with state-of-the-art surveillance equipment." She tosses her head haughtily, as if to fend off any accusations before they come. "After all, you were six years old when you went into isolation. I couldn't have you living in the woods by yourself, unsupervised. At any rate, I heard some of the things you yelled during your nightmares." She reaches out and brushes a strand of hair from my face. "And I know how you wish you were as brave and unselfish as your friends. As Callie and Jessa."

I freeze, every lash, every limb. Even my breath is shuttered in my throat. She was spying on me? What did she hear? What did I say?

"This is your opportunity, Olivia. Would you subject your friends to that nightmare mockery of a life, just so you can keep your word? Just so you can know that someone was thinking fondly of you? They might hate you if you turn them in, but at least they'll be safe. At least they'll get the treatment they need. If you truly cared about these people, if you truly cared about that boy, Ryder, you would do what's best for them. Not what's best for you. For once in your life, Olivia, you have the chance to be unselfish. Do it."

I know the answer now. It came to me at some point during my mother's speech. Even as my stomach revolts, even as my soul mourns, even as my heart withstands the jabs of a thousand swords. There's only. One. Decision.

I open my eyes. And pray to the Father of Time to forgive me. Because Fates know, no one else will.

I tell my mother about the rendezvous point, describing its approximate location and the twisted-together tree trunks. She'll find Preston and some of the fugitives there, I say. And if not, the directions to the next campsite will be found underneath the roots.

"Perfect," my mother says, tapping the information into her wrist com. "And the others? Mikey? Where are they?"

I take a deep breath. "They're hiding in a cellar in this very cabin."

29

When I crouch in front of the cabinet and open the trap door to the cellar, Ryder's the first one up the stairs. Limbo. He's the last person I want to see.

The smile spreads widely, automatically, across his face, and everything inside me shrinks into a little ball.

"Are they gone?" he asks. "Is it safe?"

I don't respond. I don't have to.

I know the moment he glimpses the guards' heavy black boots over my shoulder. The smile evaporates in an instant, and confusion clouds his eyes.

Ow, that hurts. That single moment when he's not sure what happened, when he still wants to believe the best, despite the evidence stacked against me. I feel it like a dagger piercing my throat.

"Olivia?" he asks quietly. "What's going on?"

Tears leap into my eyes. The situation is obvious, and yet, he's still asking. He's still hoping he's wrong. "I'm sorry, Ryder. I messed up. I shouldn't have brought you guys here, but I did. And now, I have no choice."

His mouth tightens. "You always have a choice."

"Yes," I say. "But it's not always the one you want to make. Don't worry, though. You'll be safe. Pardoned from your crimes. All the formula you need—"

I break off mid-sentence as Scar Face shoves me roughly away. "Come out, now, before I drag you out," he growls, jabbing the electro-whip directly in Ryder's chest.

"What are you doing?" I shriek. "He's not a criminal. Get that thing away from him." In response, Scar Face just pushes the electro-whip deeper.

I whirl to my mother, who is standing with her arms folded casually across her chest. "Mom! Tell him to back off!"

"I'm sorry, Olivia," she says, and there's not a single note of regret in her voice. "As I said, when the ends are big enough, any means will justify them. I can't let your friends loose in society. They're too big a risk. I said what I had to say to get what I want."

I inhale sharply, and my heart drops like an anchor in my chest. I can't believe it…and yet, I should've known. The chairwoman thinks nothing of torturing small children. She would have no qualms about lying to me.

Oh Fates. I'm sorry. I'm so sorry.

I try desperately to catch Ryder's eyes, but he won't look at me as he maneuvers his body through the open cabinet door, his movements stiff. The rest of them crawl out after him. Angela, with Remi clasped to her chest. Mikey, his eyes narrowed and glaring. Logan, who keeps his gaze down, as though he's afraid of what his eyes might reveal, as though the monster he keeps tethered so tightly will come roaring out. And finally, Callie.

She trips on the bottom frame of the cabinet, and her body launches into Scar Face. Their eyes lock, and something moves over his features, something dark and disturbing.

"So…Callie Stone. We meet again." The vicious smile

pulls and yanks at his scar. He taps the electro-whip against his palm. "It's been ten years, and I still haven't forgotten what you did to me."

She returns his smile, just as cruel, just as brutal. Before any of us can react, she brings her knee up, straight into his groin. "And you won't forget me today."

He doubles over, moaning. A second guard rushes forward. He's much younger than Scar Face, much newer and more inexperienced. Not good. That will mean he has something to prove.

He flicks his finger, and the electro-whip in his hand hums to life.

Father of Time. He can't actually mean to whip Callie.

I dart a glance at my mom, and she's leaning against the wall now. Her face is pained, but she's not doing a damn thing to stop the guard.

Logan steps between Callie and the ray of electricity.

"Out of my way," the second guard growls. Scar Face has limped to the side and watches with a mixture of pride and glee. The other guards are slipping electro-cuffs on the wrists and ankles of Mikey, Angela, and Ryder, rendering them immobile.

Logan spreads his legs, blocking Callie with his body. "You will not touch her. You will not hurt my family."

The two men size each other up. They appear equally matched with lean, muscular builds. But the guard has a distinct advantage. He has a weapon—and Logan doesn't.

"Last warning." The guard spits on the ground. "Move, or I'll take out my extreme displeasure on your girlfriend."

Logan bares his teeth. "She's my *wife*. And you'll have to get through me first."

I grab the guard's sleeve. "Please, I'm begging you. You don't have to do this. We'll find another way to punish them."

He flicks my hand away, the energy roiling through his body. Limbo. Before I can blink, he snaps his wrist, and the whip lashes Logan directly across the chest. I feel—rather than see—the electricity sizzle through his body, and he collapses to the floor.

Callie cries out and drops next to him, pulling his head onto her lap.

"Stand up," the guard barks. "You're next."

"Wait!" I say. "She's pregnant. If you whip her, you'll endanger the baby."

The hand holding the electro-whip stills, as the guard looks from me to Callie.

"What are you waiting for?" Scar Face snaps. "Finish her off."

"But Captain." The hand lowers completely. "She's a lady carrying a baby."

"Then she should've behaved more like a lady." Scar Face strides forward and grabs the electro-whip from his assistant. "If you can't get the job done, I'll do it myself."

I start forward, but my mother grabs my shoulders. "Don't, Olivia. We have to give the guards autonomy to act."

I look directly into her opaque eyes. The chairwoman never shows any emotion, never gives anything away. Is that because she's the consummate actress? Or because she has no soul? "You're a mother, too. You know how this feels." *Or at least you should.*

The chairwoman's fingers dig in to my bones. "The child doesn't matter, Olivia. Callie won't live long enough for it to be born."

Sorrow arrows into my heart. This is my fault. I made this decision. I set us on this path.

I used to think the burden of precognition was seeing tragedy in the future and being helpless to stop it. Now, I know the real pain: seeing tragedy—and choosing it anyway.

"I won't live that long, either," I whisper.

Callie's still sitting on the floor. Scar Face whips back his entire arm, and the electricity arcs toward her torso. Toward Logan's head on her lap.

I leap in front of the electricity. And it sears me instead.

30

drift. Not quite awake but not quite asleep. Not quite dreaming but not quite aware. I'm jostled, moved from one surface to another. I hear the chatter of indistinct voices. Hands poke and prod me, injecting me with this and wrapping me with that.

At one point, I feel a soft kiss on my forehead. "I love you," a voice says. "More than you'll ever know. More than you can even begin to fathom."

It sounds…a whole lot like…my mom.

But that can't be right. The chairwoman doesn't love me. She never has. Am I dreaming, after all? Or remembering one of my mother's alternate pathways?

Minutes or hours later, I return to myself enough to wrench open my eyes. Red digits blink on the ceiling above me, denoting the time and date. Twelve days. I have twelve more days left to live. A wave of sadness hits me, and I feel like I'll drown in its tide. Oh Fates, that's not enough time! I need so many more hours, more days, more years.

"You're awake," a voice says.

That's when I realize I'm lying in a bed, and somebody's

sitting next to me. But it's not my mother. It's Jessa.

She picks up my hand. "Thank the Fates. Logan woke hours ago. He's a lot bigger than you, but still, we were beginning to worry. Scar Face had his electro-whip dialed to the maximum setting."

"So that *was* Scar Face?" I ask. "The one you've been looking for this entire time?"

She nods. "I already broke into the database and cut his credits in half. Made sure the uniforms he ordered are a size too small. Put laxatives in the Drinks Assembler in his office. I only wish I'd found him sooner."

I manage a smile, even though any petty revenge Jessa takes will never be enough. Will never take away the soul-deep pain he inflicted on both Callie and me.

I sit up, wincing. Every part of my body feels like a self-driving pod has run it over, repeatedly. "You mentioned a 'we,'" I say hesitantly. "Who's 'we'? You…and my mom?"

"I meant Tanner." She bites her lip. "I haven't seen the chairwoman. I don't think she's been by to visit. Yet," she adds awkwardly.

So. There's my answer. That wasn't my mother telling me she loved me. Doesn't matter. Once upon a time, I may have indulged in daydreams about my mother's love, but I'm not a kid anymore. Not by a long shot.

"How's Logan?" I ask, changing the subject.

Jessa grimaces. "The medics let him stay in the recovery area for an hour after he woke up. And then, they shipped him to the detainment cells with the others."

I jerk. "They're in detainment? Callie, Ryder…everyone?"

"They're criminals, Olivia. They've committed treason against ComA. I know they got injected with a round of the formula, but after that, they went straight to detainment." Her words are slow, as though each one has to be individually pried from her mouth. I don't know what's more painful: her saying the words—or me hearing them. I knew my mother had lied to me—but I didn't know the extent of her betrayal.

I throw myself back against the pillows. So many pillows—and so soft. What are the others sleeping on? The hard concrete floor? A mat thinner than a strand of my hair?

With a sweep of my arm, I send my pillows to the floor. I thought it would make me feel better. It doesn't.

This is my fault. All of it. I should never have led them to Potts's cabin. I should never have turned them in. I made the decision based on my mother's words, based on my vision—but my precognition is faulty! Blurred pathways, missing branches. I shouldn't trust it.

Just like I shouldn't trust me.

I close my eyes, disgust swirling in my stomach. When am I going to learn? I'm better off on the sidelines, following the lead of others. I have no business making decisions, especially when they affect other people.

At least I'm back at FuMA now, with Jessa. And it doesn't look like I'll be joining the others in detainment. I can go back to playing the role I was meant to fill. Jessa's shadow.

"They told me how you got lashed," she says, her voice thick with emotion. "Because you jumped in front of Callie—and her unborn baby." She stops and gulps at the air. "The chairwoman stopped the guards after that, even though she wasn't willing to do it before. Thank you. You didn't have to sacrifice yourself. I'm so grateful."

"Don't thank me," I say, my voice—and my heart—overflowing with disgust. "Don't ever thank me, for anything, ever again. I don't deserve it."

I squeeze my eyes shut, and when I'm done stuffing my

self-loathing into a corner of my soul, I open them again. "Have you seen them?"

"I was waiting for you." A sound scratches out of her throat. "Silly, isn't it? They're only my family. I've dreamed about seeing them every day for the last six months. And yet…" She licks her lips. "I wanted to talk to you first. Find out if you explained. Find out…if they've forgiven me."

I sigh. And wish there was another answer I could give. "I did explain, and Callie said they'd all forgiven you, except for Mikey and Ryder. But I can't tell you how they feel anymore, about either of us, since I betrayed them. They may think we were working together." I clench my stomach, bracing myself for her anger—or worse, her disappointment. "I'm sorry, Jessa. I really believed I had to do it. I saw into their future, and I thought the alternative was so much worse. I thought this was the only way to protect them. My mother lied to me. I didn't know she would throw them in detainment, but I should've guessed."

"I believe you." She doesn't push me further. I suppose she, of all people, would understand. She did the same thing, after all.

"I've gotten permission to bring my family their evening meals," she says. "Will you come with me?"

Does she even need to ask? That's my job. To be her trusty shadow. Her loyal ally. There's no shame in that. Even the most courageous people need a little help now and then. If this is my fate, I'll embrace it.

I was just…confused for a little while. I liked viewing myself through Ryder's eyes. I liked feeling like I was in charge of my own fate. But that's over now. He doesn't see me like that anymore.

And neither do I.

"Sure," I say to Jessa. "When do we leave?"

...

Half an hour later, we're guiding a metal cart filled with Meal Assembler trays toward detainment. The handle is lower than is comfortable, as it's meant for bots, and the cart hovers a few inches above the tile. The thin, bland odor of the food winds into the air, smelling like sawdust and defeat.

"Talk to me," Jessa mutters. Perspiration dots her upper lip, and the hand that's not wrapped around the handle is noticeably shaking.

"You know I'm not one for chitchat," I say.

"True. But you've been talking a lot more, and you haven't dropped a single word since you came back from the wilderness. Have you noticed that?"

I pause. Is that right? I suppose. My words flowed so easily around Ryder. It was just like talking to Potts or to the old Tanner before I left civilization. I haven't been that comfortable around anyone for ages. I guess my comfort slowly extended to everyone else.

Too soon, we arrive at a metal door equipped with four types of identity scans — voice, retina, fingerprint, and blood. Jessa takes a deep breath. And then another.

Quickly, I scan all four of my biometrics before we run out of oxygen.

We walk inside. A long, narrow corridor unfurls before us. The concrete is bare, and the light is dim — not because of faulty bulbs but because ComA programmed it to be so. The air pushes down on my shoulders, hot and heavy and dense, and already, the smells of sweat and urine cling to each molecule.

Angela and Remi are in the first cell. The little girl looks up as we approach and lets loose a bone-vibrating shriek. She toddles over to the bars, holding her arms open wide.

"She remembers me?" Jessa's eyes are wide with wonder and shock. "Oh Fates. She's gotten so big. And she's walking! When did she learn to walk?" She falls to her knees in front of the cell, reaching a hand through the bars to touch Remi's hair. "I knew you wouldn't lose your curl when your hair grew out. I just knew it!"

"She does that with everyone," Angela says flatly, scooping Remi up and out of Jessa's reach. "Total strangers. Poisonous snakes. She was six months old when you betrayed us. Of course she doesn't remember you."

"Oh." Jessa folds her hands in front of her, clearly at a loss for words.

Hurriedly, I pick up two trays of gruel and slide them through a slot into the cell. But it doesn't break the tension. Jessa and Angela continue to stare at each other. I might as well be in another time.

"Where's, um, where's Callie?" Jessa asks finally. "And Mikey?"

"ComA took them." Angela hugs Remi, pressing the little girl's face against the coarse material of her dull gray jumpsuit. Remi cries out and pulls away. "They have Callie under surveillance in the medical wing, and they needed Mikey on some super-secret project. They wanted Preston, too, but he's not here. Yet. The chairwoman took great pleasure in telling me that a team was being sent to the rendezvous point. So no doubt, the others will be joining us shortly."

The words are spoken to Jessa, but she turns her accusing, angry glare on me.

"That was me," I say quietly. "I told my mom about the rendezvous point. I didn't know how else to get you the formula, and she promised me you would be treated well. Obviously, she lied." I move my shoulders helplessly. "I'm sorry. You'll never know how sorry."

Angela blinks, her eyes big and brilliant. "You saved my daughter, Olivia. I won't ever forget that," she says slowly, as though puzzling out her feelings. "But now, because of you, we're here, behind bars. I believe you meant well, but that's the problem with breaking someone's trust. You have no control over the consequences."

"Remi's safer here," I say miserably. "You should've seen what was in store for her in the other futures."

But Angela's already turned away, trying to find a comfortable patch on her shoulder for her daughter to lie on. Closing her eyes, she strokes Remi's hair and croons softly. Jessa and I exchange a deep, sorrowful look, but there's nothing else we can say or do, so we push the wobbly cart down the hall.

We pass Logan, asleep on a mat in his cell. The mat's thicker than a strand of my hair—but not much. I slide a tray of gruel into his cell, and we keep going.

Ryder's waiting for us by the bars. "Don't talk to me," he says darkly. "Just give me the food and go."

His eyes skim over Jessa, as though she doesn't exist, but they latch onto me, the rage burning more brightly than anything else in this corridor.

"Ryder, I—" I start to say.

"I said, *don't talk to me*," he thunders. "I gave you a second chance. Against my instinct, against my nature, I trusted you. And this is how you repay me?" He shakes his head, his chest vibrating with anger.

My skin should be thicker by now. I should've expected nothing less. But his anger cuts me off at the knees, and I stumble, gasping for breath.

Jessa leaps forward, catching my elbow. "Olivia! Are you okay?"

I manage to nod, and Jessa rounds on her former best friend. "I'm ashamed of you," she says. "You can be mad at me all you want. I'll be the first to say I deserve it. But what has Olivia done? She owes the lot of you nothing, and yet, she dove in front of an electro-lash to protect Callie and her unborn baby."

He sets his jaw. "She was the reason we were in that situation to begin with."

"She was trying to save you, damn the Fates! She did what she thought was right. Just like I did." Jessa steps forward until the only things separating them are the metal bars and a few inches of air. "I know it's hard for you to see things from my perspective. And probably, you'll never agree with me. But I hope one day you'll understand that I never wanted to hurt you. I'm the same girl I always was. I love you just as much now as I always did." She takes a deep breath. "If you can't trust me today, then you were wrong to ever trust me. Then our friendship, from the mud puddles to the acorn graves, from the hover parks to the ten-foot wall, was false. Can you tell me you honestly believe that?"

"I..." Right before my eyes, Ryder's hard and impenetrable features begin to melt. "I don't know what to do. How to feel." His voice is low and anguished. "I've been betrayed all my life, Jessa. You know that. It's the only thing I've come to expect. I don't know how to take a leap of faith. I wouldn't even know where to start."

"How about your heart?" Jessa puts her hand on the bars, over his fingers. "That's never steered you wrong before. And it won't lead you wrong now."

I hold my breath, waiting for the improbable. Will

Ryder forgive Jessa? Will he forgive *me*?

Before he can respond, the door swings open and Tanner bursts into the corridor. He runs too fast and crashes into the metal cart, sending a couple of trays flying to the ground.

"Jessa! Livvy!" He scrambles to his feet, tries to pick up the trays, but then stumbles again. I've never seen him so frantic. "You have to come! Now!"

"What is it, Tanner?" Jessa asks.

His eyes focus on her, dark and scared. "It's Callie. They're withholding the formula from her, and she's fading away."

31

All the color disappears from Jessa's face, until it looks like she, too, might vanish.

I also feel faint but for an entirely different reason. I've seen this pathway before, over a decade ago. It didn't make sense at the time. It was ripped out of context. But it contained one dominant image that's been seared into my mind for the last ten years: Jessa and me, fighting side by side.

I drift over to her and grasp her hand. "I've seen this, Jessa, all those years ago. This is the scene I told you about, when you traveled ten years into the past and talked to my six-year-old self. The two of us, fighting together to save your sister. We can do this. We can get her the formula. We can make sure she doesn't disappear."

My words seem to bring Jessa back to herself. A hint of color flows into her cheeks, and she nods resolutely.

Ryder rattles the bars. "Take me with you. I can help."

Tanner swivels his head from us to the detainee. "I could break into the com terminal at the guard's station. Open his cell door. But then, the chairwoman will know we're not on her side."

"Won't she already know that?" Jessa asks, a muscle throbbing at her temple. "We're going to defy all her orders and get the formula to Callie. I think the jig is up."

"You wanted me to trust you." Ryder reaches through the bars and touches Jessa's shoulder. "Well, then, you have to trust me, too. Let me help. Callie's like a sister to me. I can't just sit here and do nothing. Please."

Jessa turns to me. "What do you think, Olivia? What does the future show?"

"Very little," I say slowly. "I've had big holes in my precognition lately. My mom says it's just part of the time stream deterioration. I can't see enough to get a full picture."

Energy snaps into her body, and it's clear she's made a decision. "Fine. Do it," she says to Tanner. "We don't know what we're up against, and an extra body won't hurt."

Tanner dashes into the glass-walled office. Less than a minute later, the gate slides open. Ryder bounds out, rubbing his wrists where the electro-cuffs must've pinched.

"Let's go," Tanner calls from the guards' station.

We sprint past a drowsy Logan who's beginning to wake. Past the identical gaping mouths of Angela and Remi. Out of detainment and down the corridor, as fast as I've ever run in my entire life.

"The chairwoman's put out a news alert," Tanner pants as we run. "It's been flashing across all the holo-screens at fifteen-minute intervals. That's how I found out about Callie."

We take the elevator capsules to the ground floor and step out. The sheer number of people causes me to stumble backward. Civilians are packed so tightly in the open atrium there's hardly room to breathe, let alone move. Not just the seventeen-year-olds I'm used to seeing in the FuMA lobby,

SEIZE TODAY   192

either. There are people here of every age, from babies younger than Remi to the elderly who have mechanical braces on their legs. They push and bump, elbows flying, as FuMA guards attempt — badly — to organize them into lines.

"What in Limbo are they all doing here?" Ryder asks.

"That's what I was telling you," Tanner says. "They're here because of the chairwoman's news alert."

He drapes his arm around Jessa, in an attempt to shield her from the errant elbows, and pushes into the crowd.

After a moment's hesitation, Ryder does the same with me. My lips part. A few minutes ago, he glared at me with hatred in his eyes. But I suppose we need to work together if we're going to save Callie. I close my mouth — my acknowledgment of our uneasy truce — and we follow Jessa and Tanner.

We haven't traveled ten feet when the holo-screen on the three-story atrium wall flashes. An instant later, an image of my mother appears.

Ryder's hand tightens on my shoulder. "I think we're about to find out what's happening," he mutters, so close to me that his lips brush against my earlobe. "Whether we like the answer or not."

Involuntarily, my stomach flips, but I push the fluttery sensation away. I have no business feeling *this*, for this boy, under these circumstances.

The holo-image of the chairwoman smiles, the picture of serenity. She could be advertising a lake vacation at a virtual theater.

"Citizens of North Amerie," she begins. "We find ourselves once again in the middle of a crisis. But like every other challenge our nation has faced, I am confident if we come together as a people, we will vanquish this problem.

"Some of you may have noticed some strange symptoms

of late. Walking into walls, when your eyes are laser-
corrected. Holding conversations with people who don't
exist, when you've never been accused of daydreaming in
your life. Perhaps you've simply been dizzy or confused.
Maybe, all of a sudden, you've found yourself in a different
place, a different time."

All around us, the mob murmurs its agreement. A few
even yell at the holo-screen, although the newsfeed isn't
live.

"I thought I was kissing my wife, and it turned out to be
my dog!" a man with moving tattoos shouts. The red rose
transforms from bud to bloom to dust—and starts all over
again.

"I tried to do the butterfly stroke in my bed," a kid with
a swim cap offers.

"I told my boss I loved her," the woman next to us says.
And then she smirks. "Although I wasn't actually confused."

The crowd snickers and hoots. Oblivious, my mother
leans forward, as if she's sharing a secret with the entire
nation. "These symptoms are the result of what we're
calling a virus of sorts that's spreading rapidly across North
Amerie and the entire world. This time stream virus causes
us to waver in and out of our time. In those moments of
dizziness and confusion, you aren't imagining things that
don't exist. You are literally in a different time stream, on a
parallel world similar to but not quite this one."

The chairwoman pauses, as if to make sure the audience
understands her point. Even through a holo-screen, she
makes me want to shrink under Ryder's arm.

"The bad news is: if left unabated, this virus will affect
us all, every man, woman, and child. The good news is that
we have an antidote. A formula our scientists have been
hard at work developing for months. Sector by sector, we

will ask all of you to proceed to your local FuMA office, where you will receive a dose, courtesy of ComA."

The people in the atrium clap and cheer, but that's to be expected. After all, they're already inside, which means they were the first sector called.

"Now, some of you may feel like you're too busy," the chairwoman says. "You may think a little dizziness here and there is no big deal. I assure you it is. But you don't have to take my word for it. Take a look at this."

The holo-screen divides in half, and a vid of Callie lying on a medical bed appears on the right. At first, I think it is a bad transmission, but then, I realize that Callie is flickering in and out of this world. One moment we can see her ghostly outline, and the next moment, we don't. Tears stream down her face, and she's holding her hand up in front of her. It is a replay of the scene inside the tent — except for one thing. Whereas before, her hand simply turned transparent, this time, the flesh above her wrist is simply...gone.

I gasp, and Jessa cries out, clinging to Tanner.

"What's happening to her? Will she get her hand back?" she sobs.

Tanner told us Callie was fading away. Intellectually, I knew what this meant. But none of it prepared me for the sight of a hand that's simply been...erased. I flash back to the futures I saw for Callie, before her pathways were blocked to me. The virus affects the extremities first. What's next? Her entire arm? The rest of her body?

"Advanced symptoms include parts of your body fading from this time stream," the chairwoman says. "We have reason to believe that as the sickness progresses, your entire body will disappear altogether."

The murmurs increase in volume, and Jessa buries her

face deeper in Tanner's shoulder.

"Luckily, we have access to the patient with the most advanced condition. Our First Victim, if you will. By studying her symptoms, we hope to stay ahead of the virus and develop formulas to treat each stage. But we need your help, too." My mother folds her hands in front of her. "The Adam sector, please proceed to your local FuMA office as quickly as possible. Everyone else, please sit tight. I promise you will all have a turn."

The newsfeed flicks off, and the pushing commences.

Tanner turns to us, and between his and Ryder's broad shoulders, we're shielded from the swarm.

"Poor Callie," Jessa moans. "We have to find her. We have to get her the formula."

I frown. "I can't believe even my mother is this cruel."

"She wants to study the progression of the disease," Tanner says, his voice grim. "She can't do that unless one of the victims…progresses."

Of course. That kind of cold thinking fits perfectly with my mom's philosophy. Sacrifice the individual for the greater good.

"Well, we're not going to let them." Jessa straightens, pushing away her despair. "Do you know where Callie is?" she asks Tanner.

He nods. "B-273. The medic floor. I looked up her location in the patient portal."

"Good." She surveys the throng. "There." She points, and I notice for the first time that the people are semi-organized into a blobby, winding line, leading to a conference room. "The line flows that way. That's probably where they're getting their injections."

"Okay." Tanner nods rapidly. "We'll go into the room. I'll distract the technicians with my extraordinarily good looks—and you girls and Ryder will grab the syringes."

"Hey, what am I?" Ryder protests. "Day-old gruel?"

Tanner runs his eyes over Ryder's body. "You're not bad. But don't forget, I'm famous, too. Combine my looks with my status as the Father of Future Memory, and they don't stand a chance."

Jessa rolls her eyes. "At least we know some things never change. Can you see into the future, Olivia? Is Tanner as charming as he thinks he is?"

"I'll try," I mumble. Taking a deep breath, I reach forward to Tanner's futures. The branches are filled with blurry images and missing pathways, but I see enough to hazard a guess. "In roughly one-third of the pathways, the technicians are female, and they find Tanner absolutely adorable." I pause. "In another third, the technicians are male, and they also find Tanner absolutely adorable."

His chest puffs out. "What can I say? I have what they call 'universal appeal.'"

"In the final third, the technicians, male and female, seem to find him about as appealing as lab mice. Not only do we fail miserably in filching the syringes, but they also report us to the chairwoman."

Tanner's mouth opens and closes. "But I like lab mice," he protests. "And so does Jessa." He fiddles with her collar. "You think lab mice are cute, don't you, Jess?"

She slaps his hand away. "Only on Tuesdays and Thursdays." She turns to me. "Are those odds...good?"

I shrug. "About as good as we're going to get."

She releases a long breath. "Let's do it. I just hope we get a syringe before Callie's entire arm disappears."

32

We tunnel our way through the crowd. Again and again, people turn, mouths open and eyes slit, ready to condemn us for cutting. But then, they see our uniforms—at least mine and Tanner's and Jessa's, since Ryder's still wearing his gray jumpsuit—and they face forward once again. No one wants to risk being pulled out of line by a FuMA official when they're so close to the front.

Still, it takes us nearly fifteen minutes to reach the first conference room. Along the way, we decide that, instead of accompanying us inside, Ryder should procure us some weapons—just in case. He peels off as we reach the conference room, and I say a quick prayer to the Fates for both our successes.

We walk into an open area that's been divided into twenty cubicles. A female FuMA employee stands at the front, directing traffic, while technicians sit at wide tables holding disinfectant guns and covered racks of what I assume are needles. The last round of patients has just emptied out of the room, and the scent of blood and alcohol envelops me.

Tanner gives the FuMA employee his best smile. "I'm Tanner Callahan." His tone is as warm and decadent as melted caramel. "You might know me as the scientist who discovered future memory."

"Of course!" the lady coos. She may have zapped the wrinkles from her skin and tinted her eyelids a cloudless sky blue, but she still gives off a distinct grandmotherly vibe. "I'm Elsa. I've been hoping to catch a glimpse of you ever since I started working here." She runs her gaze over him, from his floppy black hair to the high-top hover shoes, in a survey that is anything but maternal. "I must say. I didn't expect you to be quite so…young."

"That's the great thing about scientists who play with time travel. I can be any age you want me to be," he says with a wink.

Elsa giggles. "Aren't you adorable? Tell me, do they make Tanner Assemblers? I could eat you for breakfast, lunch, and dinner."

Jessa makes a gagging sound in her throat. I step on her foot, and she turns it into a cough. This is good. Elsa's use of the word "adorable" cues me that we're on one of the successful pathways.

"Listen, can you do me a favor?" Tanner leans forward conspiratorially. "As you know, I work closely with the chairwoman." He gestures at us. "These ladies are her personal assistant and her daughter. She sent us down to grab a few syringes from each batch, so that she can test them for quality control. You know how important this project is to her, and she wants to ensure personally that the formula is effective."

Elsa doesn't hesitate. "Of course, of course." She turns and claps her hands above her head. "Listen up, techies!

This is Tanner Callahan, the Father of Future Memory. He's here to retrieve a few needles from each station, under Chairwoman Dresden's orders. Got that?"

She faces forward again, muttering under her breath, "The Father of Future Memory? Limbo, he can father my babies."

I blink. Did she actually say that? I turn toward Jessa, and she nods, as if reading my mind. *Yes, she certainly did.*

Wow. Either Elsa's suffering from an episode, or Tanner's more charming than I thought.

Jessa and I head to the cubicles. This is almost too easy. We don't have to resort to physical subterfuge or sleight of hand. They're just *handing* us the syringes.

I walk down the row, collecting three amber-colored syringes from each table. When I reach the final station, however, a prickling on my scalp makes me turn around. Elsa's no longer flirting with Tanner. Instead, she's speaking into her wrist com, a crease between her eyebrows.

My stomach sloshes uneasily, and I reach into her future. Three things happen at once. Her pathways flip through my mind, fully intact for once. A couple of burly FuMA guards burst into the room. And Tanner cups a hand around his mouth and yells, "Run, Jessa! Run, Livvy! Run!"

Run? Aw, Limbo. I should've reached into the future sooner. Because Elsa's approaching me now, flanked by two guards carrying electro-whips, not looking remotely grandmotherly.

I grab Jessa's arm. "A technician's about to lurch up and barrel right into Elsa's path. She'll shriek, throw up her hands, and smack both of the guards in the face. That's our opening."

We head toward them, and sure enough, in three

seconds, the scene plays out just as I foresaw. I duck right and Jessa ducks left. Half a minute later, we join Ryder and Tanner in the atrium.

"Now what?" I pant.

In response, Ryder places an electro-whip directly in my hands.

33

We start sprinting.

Shouts lob over our heads like frantic volleyballs, and there's a blur of motion in my peripheral vision.

"Where did you get this?" I yell at Ryder, holding the weapon as gingerly as possible, given that I'm running. I don't think I've touched an electro-whip in my life, much less used one. And I really don't want to start now.

"I raided the artillery cage while you were in the conference room," Ryder says.

That's when I notice they all have electro-whips, and their hands are wrapped much more confidently around the shafts than mine.

"Set it to low," Jessa pants. "You'll immobilize the guards for a few minutes, but you won't hurt them."

I nod, trying to focus my thoughts. This is it. The scene I foresaw as a child: Jessa and me, fighting side by side. In some pathways, we used electro-whips. In others, we wielded stun guns or employed force-field walls. In none of them did we sit around and drink tea.

We make our way through the atrium, moving against

the current of people. As difficult as it is to trip over feet and bump into shoulders, there's a certain security in the crowd. Once we emerge into the corridor, just the four of us and a long empty stretch of tile, my heart shoots into hyperdrive. Our protective shield is gone, and we need to make it down the arena-length space before we can get off this floor.

"Keep the weapons hidden," Tanner says, perspiration dotting his lip. "We don't want to use them unless we have to."

He doesn't have to tell me twice.

We walk down the hall, as quickly and casually as we can. Our footsteps slap noisily against the tile, and the fumes of grease and short-circuited wiring scent the air. A couple of bot service techs emerge out of a doorway. But because the electro-whips are ensconced inside our jackets and Ryder's jumpsuit, they merely salute us and continue on their way.

Once we reach the double doors, we hit our first decision point.

"The moving ladder is not as fast, but the elevator capsule gives them a chance to ambush us." Jessa flicks the hair out of her face. "Olivia? I know your precognition's blurry, but any insight?"

I bite my lip. "I don't want to give you the wrong information.'"

She raises her eyebrows. "The guards are hunting us down as we speak. We have to get to Callie before they capture us."

"Okay." I close my eyes, concentrating. "Moving ladders. That's my best guess. But take out your electro-whips. Just in case."

We pull out our weapons and exit through the double

doors into the ladder well. Two mechanical ladders are strung in the center of the well, one rolling up, the other rolling down. Every rung is equipped with hand grips and a small ledge. A pre-Boom staircase winds around the ladders, although it is primarily used by the mechanics for repairs.

First Jessa and then Tanner leap onto the moving ladder, slipping their hands into the leather grips. The double doors fly open and a swarm of FuMA guards bursts inside.

Limbo, Limbo, Limbo. I guessed wrong, once again.

"They're here! They're here!" Ryder shouts up to Tanner and Jessa.

"On the next floor, too," Jessa calls down. "They've got us surrounded."

"Electro-whips on!" Tanner commands.

I switch on my weapon, and for a moment, that low hum of electricity paralyzes me.

"Start swinging, Olivia," Ryder yells, his wrist already snapping and retracting. "Now, while we still have the chance."

He's right. The guards didn't expect to see us in the ladder well, and they're fumbling at their waists for weapons. The next few seconds will be determinative.

Above me, slashes of electricity crackle and flash as Jessa and Tanner battle with the guards on the next level. Without giving myself a chance to think, I snap my wrist. The electricity arcs through the air and strikes a guard in the chest. He crumples to the floor. My stomach twists, but I can't dwell on it. I can't.

I crack my wrist again. And again. Beside me, the wave of lightning above Ryder's head goes wild. More guards fall.

And then, a meaty guy emerges into my focus, his mouth set and his features stern. Instinct has me reaching into his pathways. The futures rush through my mind, sharp and clear. I have no idea why I can see some pathways and not others—but I don't have time to dwell on it. I foresee a ray of electricity whipping through the air and winding around my ankle. One sharp tug, and I'm falling, falling. Wrenched from the ladder and dropped into the seemingly bottomless well below.

No. Not if I have anything to do with it.

I jump as the lightning flashes through the air, and the electro-whip just misses my ankle. Father of Time, it misses. I want to weep, but when my feet land back on the rungs, they slip, and I'm sliding along the ladder, falling anyway.

"Ryyyyydderrrrrrrr!" I grasp at the metal, trying desperately to stop my descent. But instead of kicking Ryder in the head and knocking him off, I'm slammed against the ladder. The rungs strike me across the chest and stomach, but I've stopped falling.

I hug the rungs to me, panting. And then I realize that the hard wall of Ryder's chest is pressed against my back. How he caught me, I don't know. And I don't really care.

I glance up, and Ryder's dark eyes peer at me. "Are you okay?" he asks, his tone laced with concern.

A level flashes by. The ladder we're clinging to is still moving, oblivious to the battle taking place. Above us, I can make out Jessa's strong calves. Tanner looks down and shoots us a thumbs-up sign. Below, the bodies of the guards lie prone on the platforms of two separate levels. One or two of them begin stirring, but it's too late. The ladder has already carried the four of us out of reach.

This battle is over.

A smile splits my cheeks. "I'm perfect," I say to Ryder.

34

few minutes later, we barge into room B-273. Medical equipment lines the walls, and a see-through Callie is convulsing on a bed in the middle of the room. Two medics in scrubs, with masks over their noses and mouths, stand around her, but they're not doing anything to help her. Instead, they're tapping notes into their wrist coms, while Callie's body arches off the mattress.

She's gasping, and her eyes roll wildly in her head. Her arm below her elbow is gone, and she's writhing as if each of her cells is being chiseled off, one by one.

I suck in a breath, bringing my hand to my chest. Somehow, I never imagined this. Somehow, I never considered that it would be painful to vanish from this time stream, bit by bit.

As though preplanned, Tanner and Ryder each approach a medic, shoving them away from the bed.

"Hey, you can't be in here!" one of them shouts. "This is a restricted area—" He falls silent as Ryder presses the handle of the electro-whip into his chest.

Jessa runs to her sister, lines of determination etched

into her forehead. Ignoring the seizing and the pants, she stabilizes Callie's good arm and injects the amber-colored syringe into the inner side of her elbow.

For a moment, Callie stiffens, and then her body goes limp—her legs, her whole arm, even the arm that's half gone. She moans, but it is a sound of relief, as though the pain has finally lifted.

Jessa crawls onto the bed beside her sister, cradling her torso. "Oh Callie," she sobs. "I'm here, Callie. I'm here. You're going to be okay."

"Jessa?" Callie looks up at her sister, her eyes glazed. "Is that really you?"

"We're never going to be apart, ever again," Jessa says fiercely.

And then, I hear the distinct sounds of heels clicking against the tile. As it has my entire life, my stomach drops.

Before I can shout a warning, the door whooshes open, and the chairwoman stalks into the room.

Ryder and Tanner are otherwise preoccupied, so I switch on my electro-whip and advance toward my mother.

"Don't, Olivia," she says softly. Her chignon, which is normally so tight, wobbles dangerously. Any moment now, the entire up-do will come down. Her jacket is off; her shirt is untucked. This is my mother like I've never seen her. "A battalion of guards waits outside this room, ready to move in at my signal. I have even more guards on standby. You're not going to be able to fight your way out of this one."

Through the window, I see dozens of guards standing at the ready, hands clasped behind their backs. More than the number in the ladder well. More than the four of us will be able to take on, especially now that we have an injured party to protect.

She's right. The electro-whip droops in my hand. As she

likes to tell me, the chairwoman is always and unequivocally right.

She sweeps around the room, looking at her personal assistant, Jessa, and one of her head scientists, Tanner. But she ends up in front of me. Whatever she wants to say, she intends to address *me*.

"Why must you fight me every step of the way, Olivia?" she asks. "This is my life's work. I've been building toward this goal for years. Every action I took, every thought I had, was for this. I've sacrificed my family, I've sacrificed my morality—" She stares at Callie's missing hand, shuddering. The harsh light exaggerates every wrinkle, every crease in her face. "And yet, you continue to thwart me."

"We had a deal," I say coldly. "I turn in my friends, in exchange for their pardon and access to all the formula they need. Instead, you decided to throw them in detainment and withhold the medicine from Callie for no good reason."

She slaps her hand on an end table, and the glass vibrates violently. "There *is* a good reason. If you were listening to the newsfeed, you would know that. The truth is, the situation's even more dire than I presented. But that's the problem with you precogs," she says, which is wholly unfair, since I'm the only true precognitive of our time. "You discount something just because you can't foretell it. But don't you see, Olivia? That was intentional, too. I wanted to protect you from the truth."

"Protect me?" I scoff. "Mom, I've known ever since I was six years old that you were going to commit genocide one day."

"And look what happened after you saw that vision." She reaches out her hand, as if to touch my cheek, but more than space separates us. "You isolated yourself, closed yourself off from society. You screamed and screamed whenever anyone was present—even MK, even Tanner. The only company you would tolerate was the animals.'"

She slides a glance at Tanner, who has an unreadable expression on his face. "You know, I used to have Tanner catch chipmunks in the woods, so that we could let them loose outside your window. Even squirrels made you skittish, but you thought chipmunks were the perfect size. You'd get this big, delighted smile every time you glimpsed one." She stops. "There was a time when I would've done anything to see that smile," she says, almost to herself.

My head feels off-balance, like it doesn't belong on my body. I look between my mom and my old playmate, not sure whom I'm seeing more differently. I had no idea. I always thought my slice of the woods had a lot of chipmunks, but I never dreamed my mother put them there. Or that she'd ordered Tanner to catch them.

The thought is mind-blowing. Not impossible, of course. In a universe of nearly infinite worlds, anything is possible. Doesn't mean it's likely.

"You did that?" I ask Tanner.

"Yes." A sorrow I don't understand laces his voice. "But not because she made me. Because I wanted to."

My mother steps between us, as though she won't tolerate the attention moving off her. "Enough talking. I hope the four of you have been enjoying one another's company. Because you're about to get a lot more of it. You will be escorted to your detainment cells. As for Callie…" She sets her jaw. "She'll be staying right here. You may have managed to give her one more dose. But all you've done is delay the inevitable."

For a moment, nobody speaks. The barely audible hum of the medical equipment roars in my ears. An overeager guard knocks his head against the window. All around this world, people make decisions that lop off branches of their possible pathways. And still, I'm struggling to comprehend my mother's words.

We can't be going to detainment. This can't be the end of our fight.

And it's not.

Jessa eases out from behind her sister and lays Callie gently on the bed. Hopping onto the floor, she faces my mother. "Not so fast, Chairwoman."

35

gape at Jessa. Around the room, varying degrees of surprise show on Tanner's, Ryder's, and the medics' faces. But no one's eyes are wider than my mother's.

"You dare to contradict me, Jessa?" the chairwoman asks. "Haven't you caused enough trouble?"

"As your assistant, I have access to all your security clearances," Jessa says, her voice thick with the future — or the lack thereof. "I was curious about the amber formula, so I did a little research. Guess what I found?"

My mother doesn't respond.

"What?" Tanner supplies helpfully, even as he keeps his electro-whip trained on the guard.

"Contrary to what people think, the formula doesn't cure the time stream virus." Jessa moves from her sister's bedside, until she's standing in the middle of the room. "It merely delays the symptoms. Those who have gotten a dose will need more injections on a regular basis, and there's not nearly enough formula." She scans our faces. "Think about it. The math doesn't work. If we have to provide everyone in this world with an injection every single day — or even ebout the time stream deterioration for years," she says wearily. "And we've been stockpiling formula ever since. But Jessa's right. Our supply's already halved. If any part of the human race is to have a fighting chance, we need to cut down our population. By a lot." She takes a shaky breath and looks at her assistant. "What are you going to do with these documents?"

"It's simple, really," Jessa says. "Unless I enter a security code—one that only I know—every six hours, my files will be sent to every major media outlet in North Amerie. It won't take long for the people to figure out what it means. Can you imagine the riots that will take place then?"

The chairwoman's breathing comes out in jerky pants, as though she is trying—and failing—to control it. "Don't try me, Jessa. I can have you tortured until you give up the security code."

Jessa glances at the red digital numbers on the ceiling. "In the next four hours? I don't think so. I lasted way longer than that, even when I was a child."

The chairwoman bites her lip, considering. I don't think a single one of us breathes—especially Ryder, as he stares at the girl who was his best friend. As if sensing the weight of his gaze, Jessa turns. *You see?* her face seems to say.

*Doesn't this prove that I didn't betray you after all? I would
never betray you.*

An expression crosses Ryder's face, and try as I might, I
can't read it.

"What do you want?" my mother asks.

Jessa tears her eyes from Ryder. "What you should've
given us to begin with. An unlimited supply of the formula.
Callie discharged from this so-called 'medic wing.' My
entire family pardoned. Apartments in the scientific
residences for all of them. And Tanner, Olivia, and I will
all retain our positions and clearance, without any penalty
whatsoever."

The chairwoman regards her evenly. "Fine. But in
exchange, you not only keep the documents to yourself, but
you also make sure Preston and Mikey cooperate with the
solution."

"There's a solution?" Ryder blurts out.

"Oh yes." My mother's lips don't quite curve, but a
flame leaps into her face, the kind that continues to burn
through the darkest hour. "The problem's been kept highly
classified, but the world's leaders joined forces long ago
to form an International Council dedicated to finding a
solution. And we're close now. Very close."

"Here's what I don't understand," Tanner interjects. "If
future memory was the cause of the deterioration, then
why were you so fixated on me inventing it? Callie already
delayed the discovery of future memory. If we'd ignored it,
maybe the technology would've just disappeared. Maybe
our time stream would've remained intact."

"Because the deterioration didn't stop." The chairwoman
shoves her hands through her hair, and the already loose
chignon falls apart. "Even in the ten years when we didn't
have future memory, new victims continued to come down

with symptoms. You just didn't hear about it because I buried the cases. I personally still experienced the time displacement every day. Once future memory was invented in *any* part of our timeline, I think we were doomed. It happened. We couldn't make it unhappen. I hoped that by inventing future memory, the way we were supposed to, and keeping a tight rein over the recipients' actions, we could control the ripping and tearing." She moves her shoulders. "Instead, the opposite happened. The moment future memory was reintroduced to society, the symptoms blew up."

She takes a deep breath. "Our solution is twofold. First, we need to increase supply and decrease demand. But in case we're not successful, we're also building a machine — something we call a 'realm machine.' Not one that travels backward or forward on our timeline. But a machine that will be large enough and powerful enough to take a segment of our population into a parallel world." Her eyes shine. "We're starting over, and we're crossing our very realm in order to do it."

36

The warehouse is the size of an airplane hangar, tucked in the middle of the woods. But instead of airplanes, it houses a machine—an enormous, metal-plated machine comprised of two podiums connected by an arch the length of a football field. An electric fence surrounds the entire contraption, and the only entrance into the arch is through a long tunnel.

More guards than I can count patrol the perimeter of the machine, electro-whips in hand, and scientists in white lab coats bustle around—conversing at com terminals, attaching the metal plates of the tunnel, even hanging from a sling at the center of the arch. I stand at the front of the hangar, trying to take it all in—and failing miserably.

It's been four days since my mother told us the truth. Four days in which I assume Jessa and Tanner got her family settled at the scientific residences. I wouldn't actually know. I've spent the last four days back in my cabin. Isolated.

After hearing my mother's news, I couldn't bear to be around anybody. As nice as Jessa is, as much as I yearn for Ryder's company, being around them just reminded me how I failed. Even now, I feel weights pressing down on my shoulders. Not just sand-filled duffel bags, but a lead hammer pounding me deeper and deeper into the ground.

I thought I could make a difference. I had so much advance notice of my mother's goals. I thought, with Jessa by my side, we could prevent the majority of the world from dying. But we can't.

Oh sure, large portions of the population are still being injected with the amber syringes—for now. Their symptoms have stabilized—for the time being. But sooner or later, the vast majority of them will succumb to the literal ravages of time. Those who aren't lucky enough to walk through this realm machine and travel to a parallel world will eventually disappear.

And there's not a damn thing I can do about it.

"Impressive, isn't it?" a voice says from behind me.

I jump. It's Mikey. He's wearing a white lab coat over his regular clothes, and his blond hair is pulled back with a piece of rawhide. His eyes are as intense as ever, but there's a strain to his mouth that suggests he, too, has been mourning for the last four days.

I didn't expect to see him. I didn't expect to see anyone, really. I just wanted to glimpse the realm machine for myself, to convince myself once and for all that this is real and happening and not some hideous nightmare from which I can't wake.

But now that Mikey's here, in front of me, I can't help but think about Ryder. How does he feel, now that he's able to sleep in a real bed once again? Is he able to eat his favorite foods? What *are* his favorite foods? What does he think about this turn of events?

The questions flash in my mind, fast and furious, threatening to overwhelm me. Threatening to break down the meager shields that remain. "My mom only told me a few days ago," I blurt to Mikey, shoving away thoughts of his adopted son. "I had no idea there wasn't enough formula. No clue this machine even existed. I wasn't hiding the information from you. I really didn't know."

"I believe you." He puts his hand on my shoulder, moving me aside to make room for two people carrying what looks like a large circuit board. "I didn't know, either. I can't believe they've accomplished so much in such a short time."

We both contemplate the machine. It's so large I can't see all of it at once. I can catch only a patch of metal here, a curve of the arch there.

"How does it work?" I ask.

"Once the machine's activated, an energy field will form underneath the arch. That's the window. The people will walk into the window and hopefully into another world." He points at the metal-plated tunnel. "See that entrance? Only a couple people can walk through at a time, so the tunnel regulates traffic." He pulls a metal wristband imprinted with an intricate design out of his pocket. "Every approved walker gets one of these. A scanner at the front reads the code on these bracelets. You won't be granted access without one."

"It must be surreal seeing your plans come to life," I venture.

"For sure," he says. "You know, in my years back in civilization, the chairwoman always encouraged me to pursue my pet project, the realm machine, in addition to my official research. I've always been fascinated by the idea of travel to parallel worlds, and I thought she was just humoring me. I had no idea she was actually paying attention. That my wildly theoretical plans would have a very real and practical purpose."

"That's why she was so fixated on finding you and Preston," I say in a flash of clarity. "I thought she just couldn't handle any of her former scientists defecting."

"She wanted us to lead the project, since we're the world's foremost experts on realm-travel," he says, without an ounce of arrogance. Probably because his statement is true. "They found Preston, you know, as well as the others. At the rendezvous point, just like you said. Jessa and Callie are relieved, at least, that their parents are safe, and we're all living together at the scientific residences now."

I swallow hard. I shouldn't feel guilty. If I left them in the wilderness, Preston and the others would've come apart in the deteriorating time stream. Here, at least, they have a chance to survive. A shot to cross to another world. And yet my stomach churns anyway.

I ignore the feeling. "So, does this thing actually work?"

"It should. I worked for years on the blueprints, and every detail has been tested. I was missing only one thing in my plans: the anchor."

"Anchor?" I echo.

"It's like when you travel back in time. You know how you need an anchor to focus your journey so that you don't get stuck in outer space?"

I nod.

"Well, it's the same concept, except a little more complicated. For travel within the same timeline, you need an anchor who's resided in the same physical location during the time you want to travel. So when Jessa and Tanner traveled ten years to the past, they were able to use her mom, Phoebe, as an anchor, since she lived in the same house for all those years.

"For travel to a parallel world, however, it's not the

physical place that needs to remain the same, but the person himself or herself." He pauses to see if I'm following.

I shake my head, lift my eyebrows, crease my forehead. Overkill, maybe, but he seems to get the message.

"Let me explain," he says. "In order to travel from one parallel world to another, you need a connection between those two worlds. Such a connection is created when those two worlds are perfectly aligned—in other words, at that precise moment in time, those worlds are exactly the same. It can be for one second; it can be for ten minutes. The connection stays open as long as this alignment holds.

"Now, clearly, it would be impossible to find a moment when *everything* in both worlds is the same. That's why we use an anchor. So long as a moment is fixed, from one world to the next, in that anchor's life, then we get our connection. Make sense?"

"I think so," I say doubtfully.

Mikey barrels on. "Now, the tricky part is finding an anchor whose worlds are aligned for longer than a few seconds. Long enough to get a good number of people through that window. The chairwoman thinks she's found someone, and he's staying in that shed over there." He points to a square structure in the corner of the warehouse, no bigger than ten feet by ten feet.

"He's eating his meals at the exact same time, going to the bathroom at regular intervals, meditating for long swatches the rest of the day. Apparently, he's been doing this for years. Trying to live in the exact same way, so that when the moment comes, he's able to keep the window open for as long as possible." He lowers his voice. "So that as many people as possible can travel to a different world— and be saved."

For a moment, neither of us says anything. An inkling

of an idea forms at the back of my head. There's only one person I know who lives his life so regularly. One person whom my mom visited a dozen times over the years. One person who is suddenly missing from his normal life.

Potts. All of a sudden, I'm positive he's the anchor. There's too much coincidence, otherwise. But how did my mom find him? And when?

My mind whirls with questions, but before I can even attempt to propose an answer, a heavy piece of sheeting is dropped at the other end of the warehouse, followed by excited shouts.

I shake my head, pulling myself back to the present. "How will they determine who gets to walk through the window?"

"Based on who they consider to be, uh, superlative, I guess."

"What?" My mouth drops, but as his words sink in, the puzzle pieces begin to fall into place. When I was six years old, I had a vision where the chairwoman used future memory to determine who was mediocre and who was superlative. This is the reason why. This is her rationale for executing ninety-nine percent of the population. They wouldn't be walking through the window, anyhow, and this way, the small portion of the human race left behind will have a fighting chance. Her words, not mine.

"Why are the Superlatives any more deserving of being saved?" I croak out. "Why not a lottery where we all have an equal chance?"

"I don't know," Mikey says. I can tell by the quiet anguish in his voice that these questions have haunted his days and nights. "That's what the International Council decided. They said we won't know what state we'll find the parallel world in. To have the best chance of survival, they said, we need to send our best and brightest."

"And how do they define such a thing?"

He opens his mouth, stops, and then makes a choking sound in his throat. Shaking his head rapidly, he snaps his mouth closed. "I'm sorry. I..." But he can't even finish the sentence. Instead, he spins on his heel and runs out of the warehouse.

I gape. Mikey Russell doesn't run from questions, and he certainly doesn't run from me.

Which means my pathways for this decision tree just narrowed down to one: I take off after him.

37

Mikey sprints into the woods. Normally, he's athletic and graceful, but today, his stride is sloppy. He slides on the pine-needle-covered ground, and given the way he's flailing about, he's more accurately lurching than running.

I catch up with him within a minute. "Mikey, what's going on? Why did you leave like that?"

Giving up, he falls to the ground. It's not the best place to stop. The weeds are overgrown here and taller than Mikey's kneeling form. Plant stalks poke me in my neck, waist, arms, ankles, basically anywhere I'm showing skin. But I don't think Mikey cares—or even notices.

"Are you okay?" I say, my concern growing. "Should I call a medic?"

His shoulders start shaking. Oh Limbo, he's having a seizure! But, no—upon closer examination, I realize he's not spasming at all. Instead, he's crying but without any tears. Double Limbo.

I sink to my knees, ignoring the weeds even as they're taunting me. "Mikey, is this about the criteria for the best and brightest?"

"The International Council put together a committee to determine who qualifies," he mumbles, his chin tucked into his chest, his words so muffled I can barely understand him. "They've released an initial list of the people who will march through the window first. Leaders in the scientific and medical fields, from all over the world. Academics recognized in math, literature, philosophy. Musicians. Artists. Gold-star athletes. In the next week, they'll all travel here, so that they can walk through the realm machine. There's only one, you know. All of the countries in the world have pooled their resources to get this one built." He lifts his head, and I suck in a breath. He looks… destroyed. As though his soul was plucked out of his body and fed through the shredder. Twice. "Preston and I are both on the list, as is your mother. We can each choose one person to bring with us. Only one, Olivia. Only one."

Oh. *Oh.* Preston and Mikey each have a wife and two children. I'm beginning to understand the problem.

"Who will…you choose?" I ask.

His eyes brim with tears, but they don't spill out, not a single drop. Somehow, this makes the moment even worse. "Your mother, at least, has only one child. For the rest of us, it's a heart-wrenching decision. But Preston has it easier. Tanner also qualifies, as he's the Father of Future Memory, and he's assured Preston that he'll bring Jessa."

He begins to rip out the weeds, one by one, but it will take hours of work before he makes a dent in this field. "The gold-star national swim meet is next week. Logan is eligible to compete, based on his old qualification. Every waking moment now, he's in the swimming pool, trying to make up for the training he lost while we were on the run. We all pray…" He raises his eyes to a blue sky that is mockingly cloudless. He blinks, as though he can't

understand how that wide expanse can look so serene—
when it covers a world that's coming apart at the seams.

He lets out a long breath. "If he wins, of course he'll
take Callie. Which will leave Preston able to bring his wife,
Phoebe, and his entire family will be intact.

"As for me…as for me…" Mikey's face crumples, and
the tears stream out now, fast and unstoppable. "My world
is made up of Angela, Ryder, and Remi. And I have to
leave someone behind, no matter what I do."

"Oh, Mikey." Acting on pure instinct, I pull him into an
embrace. I'm terrible at comforting people. At times over
the past couple weeks, he might have even hated me. But
none of that matters right now. All that matters is that my
heart is cracking, right along with his.

"I'd give up my spot altogether, you know," he says
quietly. "But that's not allowed. If I don't go, none of my
family goes. So I have to make a decision."

He pulls back, attempts to wipe his face, but succeeds
merely in smearing the tears. "There's only one decision
that makes sense, really. The International Council says if a
child can be carried, she can walk through with her mother.
Since it won't take any extra time, she doesn't count as an
additional person. Which means, if I choose Angela, then
she and Remi can both go."

I swallow hard. I agree. It's the only decision that makes
sense. But…but… "Does Ryder know?"

"He insisted," Mikey says, his lower lip trembling. "Even
before he knew about the loophole, he took himself out
of the running. To him, it was a foregone conclusion that
I would pick Remi, and if not Remi, then Angela. He's
always felt second-best in our hearts, even though it's not
true. Has never been true. But I have to wonder what I've
done to make him feel that way." He looks away, as though

he can't bear to see himself reflected in my eyes.

"No. Stop." I resort to patting his back helplessly. The more ineffectual I feel, the faster I pat. "He doesn't think that at all. He told me himself he was blessed to have the best parents in the world."

He shakes his head. "But don't you see? That's just like Ryder. He thinks he needs to feel grateful for any crumbs of our affection, because we adopted him. Because his biological parents foolishly abandoned him. When the truth is, I'm the one who's been blessed with the honor of being his father." He squeezes his eyes shut. "I've wished all my life that he could see that. That his biological parents choosing his brother and leaving him behind was *their* shortcoming, and not his. That he is the most wonderful, generous, lovable boy in the world. But now, he'll die believing the opposite, and I won't even blame him. Because I'm making the same decision his other parents did. To take Angela and Remi. And leave him behind."

He breaks down completely then, and it's all I can do to pat-pat-pat. And then pat some more, until my hand feels like the wings of a hummingbird.

My throat locks up, barricading an avalanche of tears, and my chest aches like there's a pump filling it with more and more pressure. There's nothing right about this situation. Nothing right or redeemable or fair. The world is ending, and we're all being forced to make decisions we abhor. I feel every emotion that ever existed in any pathway in the world—but more than anything else, I just feel sorry for us all.

38

The corridor is dark and still. Little wonder. It's the middle of the night, and everyone in the scientific residences appears to be asleep.

My shoes squeak against the floor, and the only illumination comes from the light of the emergency exit. I probably should've come in the morning. That would've been the wise thing to do, the sensible thing. But I couldn't sleep. And ever since Mikey told me Ryder will die believing he's second best...well, I just don't feel like being wise or sensible anymore.

I scan my biometrics and tiptoe into my living unit. There weren't enough units for all the fugitives, so Jessa offered Ryder my room, since I wasn't staying there anyway.

At least her family seems to have forgiven her, even if they didn't automatically resume their previous relationships. A six-month rift is much too large for *that*. But day by day, they're slowly rebuilding the bonds.

I pad to my sleeping area and push the door open. It creaks, and I stop breathing, waiting to see if the noise woke anyone, but the night remains still. I ease inside.

Moonlight spills through the window, and Ryder's lying on the floor, hands folded on his chest. No pillow, no blanket—although there's a perfectly good bed beside him.

A mixture of sadness and regret rises inside me. Why is he sleeping on the floor? Is he still so angry that he doesn't want to touch my things? Or does he just not want to impose? Either reason is ridiculous. I doubt I'll ever sleep in that bed again, and the world is ending in exactly eight days—if not for everyone else, then at least for me. He should spend his last days here in comfort.

For a fleeting moment, I want to wake him and whisk him away from here. That's what Jessa told me Logan did for Callie all those years ago, when she was running from her future. But there's nowhere for us to go. No safe haven in the middle of the wilderness, no Harmony to welcome us and keep us safe. No matter how far we run, no matter how deeply we hide, we won't be able to escape this evil.

I approach his sleeping form. Now what? Somehow, I hadn't gotten this far in my planning, and Ryder's pathways are blurry to me now. Should I make more noise? Nah. Don't want to wake Jessa in the next room. Instead, I kneel by him and shake his shoulders.

His hands shoot out, grab me, and yank me forward. I fall against his chest.

"Olivia?" he asks, his eyes wide, his breathing hard. He looks wildly around the room, as if trying to place where we are. "What are you doing here?"

"I, um…wanted to talk." His heart thunders against my fingertips, and his lips are inches from mine. His familiar scent of evergreens assaults me, and it's been too long since I've experienced that smell. I can't think. I need to move away. Put some distance between us.

Come on, Olivia. You can do it. On the count of three.

One…two…

I start to draw back, but he sits up with me, his hands locking behind me. Surprised, I stop pulling.

With a groan, he tugs me into the best hug I've ever had. His chest is warm; his arms are firm. He envelops me completely, his body around my torso, his presence around my heart. I feel a shield building in front of us, one that even Fate and Time can't penetrate. I close my eyes and sink into his embrace. If this feeling means I'm drowning, then I never want to be saved.

And then, the hug ends. Ryder shifts away, running a hand over his head. Cool, unsatisfying air rushes in to take his place.

"Sorry about that," he says, his voice low and gravelly. "I guess I needed a hug after the recent news."

"Does that mean you've forgiven me?" I ask, studying my fingers even though I can hardly see them in the dim light.

On top of everything else, that question has been tormenting me over the last few days. He shielded me from the crowd. He fought by my side. He caught me before I fell down the ladder well. And yet, I still don't know how he feels about me.

"I don't know," he says quietly. "It's difficult for me to recover from a betrayal. I haven't had much practice with it. But I've been thinking about what Jessa said—a lot. And in light of everything that's going down in the world, it seems silly to hold a grudge. It's just…can you promise me that you'll never betray me again?"

"I don't think you'll have much chance to test me," I choke out. "The world's ending in a matter of days."

"I know that." He looks down, and all I can see is his Adam's apple moving. "But you've broken my trust twice now. I just need some assurance that you won't do it a third time. Otherwise, I…I don't know what I'll do. It'll make me feel like the biggest fool in the world. Like I haven't learned anything from my parents' betrayal. Like I'm still that little boy, skipping through life, without a clue that his parents never loved him."

I swallow hard. I didn't think my heart could crack any more, but his matter-of-fact tone splits it right open.

He lifts his head. "If another situation comes up, just talk to me first, okay? That's what you didn't do. That's what Jessa never did. I promise you, I'm a reasonable guy. If there really is a good reason, I'll see it. But if you don't consult me at all…" He lifts his shoulders. "Then I guess I was never very important."

"You have my word, Ryder."

Tentatively, he picks up my hand and brings it to his lips. "Thank you."

"You, uh, should sleep in my bed," I say. "You'd be more comfortable that way."

He regards me steadily. "Is that why you came here in the middle of the night? To assess my level of comfort?"

"No." I rack my brain, trying to think of an excuse I can give him. A message from Mikey, an order from the chairwoman. Anything. But the only thing I can think of is the truth, because that's all there is left. "I wanted to see you."

Even in the moonlight, I can see his eyes flash. "What about staying away from each other?" he asks. "What about it being unbearable when the inevitable comes?"

I lick my lips. I've never done this before: live for the present without any thought to the future. "It's unbearable now," I whisper. "I want to be with you today. And I don't care what tomorrow brings."

He closes the distance between us, sweeping me into his arms. "For the record?" he murmurs. "I'm not in your bed because it smells just like you. Like the grass after a heavy rain. It was damn distracting, and I couldn't sleep."

He lowers his lips to mine. If his embrace a few minutes ago was the best hug ever, then this is the best kiss. Because there's no longer any pretense between us, no longer any artifice. There's just him and me. Ryder and Olivia. And that's it. That's enough.

But the kiss doesn't turn passionate, as I half expect. Instead, he presses his face into my neck, and my hair next to his eyes turns inexplicably wet.

"Ryder?" I ask questioningly.

He holds me tighter. "I don't want to talk about it. Not here, not now."

"Is it Mikey?" I didn't ask before, but if not now, then when? It's not like we have copious amounts of time left. "I talked to him, you know. He told me about...the decision he has to make."

"Yeah." Ryder's voice is thick with emotion. "It really tore him up. I wish it wouldn't. He shouldn't feel guilty. I would've made the same decision."

"He loves you."

"He loves them more."

"Damn the Fates, it's not about that. It's—"

"Hey." He lifts his head and traces his finger over my cheeks, my lips, my jaw. "It's okay. You don't have to comfort me. Not when I have two parents who love me. And you don't have any."

My throat moves. With all the futures I've ever seen, I never would've predicted this turn in our conversation. "My mother...is a unique person. That's for sure."

"She's a monster," he says heatedly. "No one would

argue with that. I've got a thousand reasons to hate her, but the one that stands out most is the way she treats you, Olivia. For most of your life, you've done nothing but help her, and she doesn't value you the way she should—" He cuts off abruptly.

I straighten. This isn't idle raving. He has something specific in mind, I can tell. "What do you mean by that?"

"It's nothing." He drops his head.

I lift his chin. "It's something. You wouldn't look away from me if it were nothing."

"I don't know how to tell you this, Olivia." His eyes blaze trails across my soul. "I wouldn't have even known myself, but Mikey let the information slip."

"What is it? Trust me, there's not much you can say that will shock me." I attempt to laugh, but it dies in my throat. "I've seen it all. Literally."

"I'm not walking through the window of the realm machine," he says slowly. "But you're not, either."

I stare. "Yes, I know. I told you, I'm going to die before then."

"That's debatable. And that's not what I'm talking about. You're not walking through the window because you're not on the prequalified list."

"So?" My voice rises. I'm probably waking Jessa, but I can't seem to lower it. "The chairwoman is. And she might be the worst mother in this timeline, but she's not going to bring someone else as her 'plus one.' I'm her only daughter. She doesn't even have a spouse. Even if she doesn't love me, she'd still choose me, in order to save face."

He weaves both his hands through mine, in what I'm beginning to think of as his signature move. Last time, it made me feel like a flame was burning inside me. But not now.

I brace myself. The gesture can mean only one thing. He's trying to soften the blow of his words.

"Olivia, she's waiving her option of a 'plus one' altogether. So you're right. She's not taking someone in place of you. She's not taking anybody at all."

39

A few hours later, I stalk down a hallway toward a tucked-away lab in a tucked-away wing in the half of the building that belongs to TechRA. I don't think my shoulders have ever been so stiff. I don't think my spine has ever been so straight. In the last few hours, shock has turned to anger, and I've never been more ready to confront my mother. I would've gone to her sleeping unit hours ago, but she sleeps in a chamber with the tightest security, one that doesn't allow unannounced visitors. Not even me.

At least I had more time in Ryder's arms. The boiling in my blood recedes as I think of last night. After he told me the truth, we lay on my bed, with my head on his chest and his fingers in my hair. After a minute or ten, he started telling me about his childhood in the wilderness. The first time he caught a fish. The day he and Jessa spent an entire afternoon in the trees, pretending they were monkeys. How he would watch the clouds move in the sky and wonder if somehow, somewhere, his brother was watching the same clouds.

For two hours, we whispered to each other, his heart a rhythmic beat against my chin. We didn't talk about my mom or the future or both of our looming deaths. I think, for a moment, we both just wanted something normal.

Seven more days. I'm not sure why or how, but in seven more days, this same boy will stick a needle into my chest and kill me.

I burst into a bustling lab stuffed with com terminals. Everywhere I look, techs are spinning in their chairs, running from one keyball to another, gesturing excitedly at holo-docs projected in the air.

I stumble on the threshold. This…this isn't what I expected. When Jessa accessed the geo-locator on the chairwoman's wrist com, and a glowing dot appeared in a hardly used wing of TechRA, I assumed my mother was meeting with a solitary scientist. I had no idea she'd be in this hub of activity.

But there she is, her navy suit as crisp as ever, pulling a helmetlike contraption off her head and handing it to a nameless tech. "I can see the seams in this one," she says. "The memory jerks as you transition from one image to the next. Fix it."

She moves to the next terminal, slipping on another helmet for a few seconds before removing it again. "Sharpen the color," she snaps. "The blues and greens are completely washed out. Come on, people!" She swivels on her heels, so that she's addressing the lab at large. "No one's going to be fooled by this fike. I feel like I'm looking at a pre-Boom television! This needed to be fixed yesterday."

She shakes her head in disgust and looks up—right into my eyes. She opens her mouth—to do what? Stop me in my tracks? Try to explain the unexplainable?—but it's too late. I dive to the closest terminal and shove a helmet on my head.

"Hey," the tech protests. "I'm working here."

But I'm already sinking into the memory.

•••

I'm standing on a slick gymnasium floor, gleaming with varnish. The crowd in the bleachers stamps and cheers, the noise rattling the rafters and vibrating my teeth. A line of sweat drips down the forehead of my opponent, a large man with hands like mitts. In what feels like slow motion, I palm a basketball and jump into the air. The image jerks. When it resettles, I'm still jumping, two feet, three feet, and then I swing my arm and dunk the ball right into the hoop.

•••

I claw at the helmet, throwing it off my head. The pure athletic prowess in the memory reminds me of Ryder, but that's not why a cold sweat springs out on my neck. Dear Fate. My mother's done it. She's figured out how to manufacture a memory. She took a regular memory of someone jumping—and added a couple feet of air. Sure, there's still that jerk in the image—that seam she was complaining about—but she's nearly there.

My stomach rocks back and forth, and nausea climbs my throat. I can't stop my fingers from shaking, and yet, I grab the helmet from the next terminal and put it on my head. I have to see. I have to be sure.

•••

I'm balancing a violin under my chin, one hand cradling the neck of the instrument, the other moving a bow with strong, controlled strokes. Silk whispers against my thighs, and the violin emits notes that are high, beautiful, and heart-wrenching.

But I'm doing more than just playing. The perspective

zooms out. A few pauses and jumps later, I'm standing on a hoverboard, flying around the track even as I produce stunning music.

...

Shakily, I open my eyes. Again, I think of Ryder and his skills on the hoverboard. And again, it's a spliced-together memory. Jessa warned me. She told me about Callie's ability to manipulate images, about my mom's keen interest in this power. But nothing ever came of it, and we were so occupied by the prospect of genocide I'd mostly forgotten about her preoccupation.

My mother crosses the lab and takes the helmet from my head. "Well?" she asks, as though I'm just another tech. "If you're not looking for them, I'd say the pauses and jerks are barely noticeable, don't you think?"

"What are you doing, Mother?" I ask, the fury barely contained in my voice.

She smiles and strokes my hair like the mother she never was. "If you're going to question me, darling girl, you know better than to do it in public," she murmurs under her breath.

Sure enough, all the techs have stopped working and are staring at us. Without taking her eyes off me, she raises her hand in the air and snaps twice. "Back to work, everyone. Nothing to see here." She lowers her hand and inclines her head. "Come along now."

Like mice, the techs scurry to obey. Also like a mouse, I follow her—but for the last time.

Never again, I vow to myself. This is the last time I fall in line like a good employee, like a good daughter. She has no hold over me anymore. Why did I try so hard these last seventeen years? What was I hoping to earn? Her respect?

Ha. Her love and esteem? Even more laughable.

We walk into the next room, which is also a lab. Unlike the first one, however, this lab's been outfitted as my mom's personal office. Her favorite Drinks Assembler is perched on the counter, and the hard, white sofa looks strange against the tiles embedded with com screens.

The Drinks Assembler switches on as soon as we enter, preparing my mother's favorite chrysanthemum tea. A few seconds later, a bot brings the cup into the chairwoman's waiting hands.

She settles on the hard cushions as though sinking into a bubble bath. "What would you like to drink?"

"Don't do that, Mother. Don't pull the gracious hostess routine on me. Not when you waived your right to take a *plus one*. Not when you threw away your chance to save me." My voice cracks on the last word.

She purses her lips. "Jumping to conclusions again, Olivia. What do you think I'm doing in that lab?"

"Manufacturing future memories," I mumble. "That much is obvious."

"Yes," she persists. "But why?"

Without waiting for an answer, she barrels on. "You've heard about the list of Superlatives the International Council released? That's how you know about the 'plus one'?"

I nod.

"Well, the list is far from complete. The committee will admit any gold-star winners from this week's competition. They're also combing through the archives, searching for superlative memories."

"That's why you're manufacturing memories?" I bite out. "So you can help people cheat?"

"Not just people, darling." She leans forward. "*You*. In

two days, you see, the International Council will go public with the realm machine, as well as the list of approved walkers. We won't reveal the severity of the time stream situation. We'll simply spin the trip as a mission to explore a parallel world. Still, there'll be a lot of accusations of bias and partiality, as people jostle for a position on the list. The other leaders and I must demonstrate our commitment to a fair selection process. We can't be seen to show any favoritism whatsoever. That's why we're waiving our *plus ones*." She takes a deep breath. "But you have to believe me, Olivia. I never would've done it if I didn't have a back door to get you in."

"But then it won't be fair. It's all a lie." I sag against the sofa. If my mother is to be believed—and that's a big if— then she didn't forsake me. But it's hard to bring myself to feel any relief—to feel anything, really—in light of this fraud.

"That's the nature of life, Olivia."

"I won't do it. I won't take away someone else's spot by using a fake memory."

She sighs. "For Fate's sake, don't be so juvenile. For once in your life, try to understand." She leans gingerly against the cushion. "We world leaders are in a difficult position. We need to pacify billions, even as their very lives, their very bodies, are fading away. And yet, if we want to save the human race, we must keep the truth from them. Think of the realm machine as a lifeboat. If too many people rush on, then the whole boat sinks, and everybody dies. Do you get that? We're trying to save the people who stay behind, but if we don't get off this time stream, there's a big chance that every single person living on this planet will be gone. The human race, extinguished. Is that what you want?"

"I don't want any of this," I say fiercely.

"You think I do?" She raises her voice. "What do you think I've been working to prevent my entire life? I gave up everything for this. I gave up who I am, the woman I wanted to be." She stops, and for a moment, the only sound I hear is her ragged breathing. "I relinquished the love of my life," she continues, this time, her voice quiet. "I couldn't be the mother you yearned for, the one who you deserved. I was...I am...ruthless." She closes her eyes, as though she can't bear to see this truth. But the moment passes, and then she opens them again. The chairwoman didn't become who she was by hiding from the unpleasant.

"I've done...terrible things, Olivia. I suppose I don't have to tell you that. Limbo, an entire movement rose up against me, the Underground, founded by my very own sister, Melie. Did you know she never spoke to me again, after our argument twenty years ago? She passed away without ever forgiving me, and now, it's too late." Her words are both sorrowful and angry, full of despair and rage. "I endured it. I endured it all, in the hopes of preventing this moment." She moves her shoulders. "And still, I failed."

I stare at her. "You killed people, Mother. All those people in detainment. You made them fulfill their future crimes, and then you killed them."

"I was trying to preserve the time stream!" She lurches to her feet, knocking over the teacup. "Every time a future memory was sent to the past, it created ripples. I was trying to repair the largest ones."

She sinks back down, her shoulders rolled forward so that she appears smaller than she is. "I was just trying to restore the balance," she says in a softer voice. "I suppose, once I hardened my heart, it was difficult to let any bit of kindness, any semblance of mercy, seep in. I suppose I did some things that weren't entirely necessary. That some people would consider to be...cruel." She presses her lips together. "But I *had* to. Don't you see? If I didn't cut myself off from feeling altogether, I never would've been able to make the decisions I thought were necessary to try to save the world."

I breathe deeply, feeling the tightness of my chest, the expansion of my abdomen. It's a lot to take in, and yet... and yet...somehow, it doesn't surprise me. Because this is the person I believed in all along. This is the woman I knew she could be, if she would only take a different path. If she had only been able to show me.

Oh Fates, this explanation doesn't excuse her. She isn't redeemed. She chose to kill those people. She chose to torture those children. She has a million sins on her soul, and her justification doesn't lighten the weight of a single one.

But, at least now, I'm beginning to understand her.

Which might be the only reason I decide to push my luck.

"You mentioned the love of your life. So, once upon a time, you did feel something." I pause, licking my lips. "Are you talking about my father?"

40

The lab is so quiet I can hear the gurgle of the Drinks Assembler. Ten seconds pass, and then twenty. I shift against the cushions. Despite the revelations my mom just shared, I wouldn't be surprised if she ordered me out of her sight now.

We don't talk about my dad—ever. I don't know his name; I don't even know what he looked like. Limbo, maybe my mother doesn't even know. I'm not a betting girl. I've never had to be, when all the pathways were laid out before me. But if I were, I'd say there's a fifty-fifty chance my mom got his sperm from a conception bank.

"Yes," she says finally. "I'm talking about your father."

My jaw drops. Yes. Just like that, with a single word, I've learned more about my father than I have in a lifetime.

She walks to the window of the lab, striking the pose I normally see when she's leaning against the floor-to-ceiling glass wall in her office. But we're not in her office. She's not looking out over the raging river and the majestic cliffs. Instead, we're in an old lab in an out-of-the-way wing, and the only thing outside her window is a dusty and low-trafficked corridor. She continues staring out anyway. That's when I understand she just doesn't want to look at me.

"I never talked about him for a reason, you know. I thought if I said too much, the events wouldn't unfold the way we wanted. The way we hoped and planned, before you were even born. But I suppose now, it doesn't matter." She laughs, but it is short and abrupt—and sadder than I ever thought a laugh could be. "Things will play out the way they're going to play out, and there's nothing I can do to change it."

"Tell me *something*, please," I say, getting off the couch and walking toward her, hoping against hope that this time, her response will be different. That this time, she'll actually tell me. "His favorite food, an annoying tic. I'd be happy to hear any of it."

"He was a scientist." Her tone is tinged with a mixture of wonder and relief, as though she can't believe she's finally saying the words. I can't believe it, either. I don't know what's changed. I don't know if the time stream deterioration is so advanced she thinks her explanation won't make any difference. I don't know if the dam holding back her words finally broke. But I'm not about to question her sudden willingness to share.

"I was a scientist, too, back in the day," she continues. "Back before I became the chairwoman. It was such an exciting time, an exhilarating time. Your father and I, along with Preston, were playing with time travel, as giddy as kids at the virtual theater. Oh, nothing like the realm machine we're building now. We wouldn't have the foundation for that kind of scale until much later."

"Wait a minute," I interrupt. "Preston. Are you talking about Callie and Jessa's father? You knew him?"

"Of course I did." Her lips curve, like she's remembering

the past. "Who do you think he came to the moment he arrived in the future? Who do you think gave him the job overseeing the research into Callie's mind? Those things didn't happen by coincidence, you know."

"You were his friend," I say, the gears in my head turning, recalibrating, recasting the events of the past. "And yet, you would've let Callie die."

"Yes. And he will probably never forgive me for it. His friendship is one of the many things I've had to sacrifice." She looks at me, pure sorrow shining in her eyes.

I swallow hard. "Go on."

"Preston has the psychic ability of physical displacement, meaning he could pop his body into a space across the room just by willing it there. By studying his power, we were able to extrapolate a way to move his body into a different time." She wanders to the next window, even though it looks out onto the same view. "So there we were, popping him backward and forward in time in tiny increments, five minutes, then ten minutes, and then an hour. We were ecstatic about our discoveries. And then, everything started to go wrong. Preston insisted on going into the future—*far* into the future—and we couldn't talk him out of it. As you know, he got stuck there—or rather, here. Your father and I tried desperately to get him back, and during one of our experiments, I was accidentally displaced into a parallel world."

I gape at her. "What?"

"Oh, I was there for only a few minutes, before your father found a way to haul me back. But the damage was already done." She crosses over to me and picks up my hands with her cold, cold fingers. "You see, I was pregnant with you. And so, your developing fetus traveled to a parallel world and then back again. More importantly, you moved through the realm in between worlds." She stops. Takes a breath. "To our knowledge, no fetus has ever done this before. And that is why your father and I believe you are the only true precognitive of our time."

I drop her hands and stumble backward, until my knees hit the couch and I fall onto the hard cushion. Oh dear Fate, it makes total sense. That's why I've been able to see other pathways, other worlds. Because I existed in the realm between those worlds. I wasn't a genetic accident or a twist of Fate. I was the direct result of my mother's actions.

I lift my chin, realization dawning. "And Jessa...?"

My mother nods. "Yes. For a similar reason, we think that's why Jessa can see a couple minutes into the future. The sperm that conceived her had traveled through time."

My mind whirls, as I try to work through everything she's saying. "But what about Callie? They're identical twins, at least genetically. Why isn't she a near-future precog, too?"

"I don't have a good answer for you, because the truth is, we don't know." She shakes her head. "The research on precognitives is murky at best. There aren't too many of you around, you know."

I look down at my hands. At the cuticles that need to be lasered off, at the half-moon nails that are devoid of tints. Nothing's changed—I know that. I'm still the same person I was when I charged into the lab, ready to confront my mom. Yet I feel completely different.

A thought flashes through my mind. I can't wait to tell Ryder about this conversation. I can't wait to see what he thinks about my origins as a precog. Will he be surprised—or will he grab my hands and say he knew all along that I was an original? And yet, I haven't even heard the whole story.

"So what happened to my father?" I ask.

She sits down next to me, running her hands over the cushions as though she's trying to gather the threads of her story.

"I began having symptoms as soon as I returned from the parallel world, and your father quickly diagnosed it as a type of Asynchronicity. My mind and my body had come back intact, but I guess you could say that the bonds tying my mind to this time had loosened." She wets her lips. "There were moments when my mind would drift to a different world—the parallel world where I had gone, to be precise. We developed a formula to keep me in this time, and in those early days, I had to inject myself only once a month.

"Then you were born." Her lips curve, and an expression I've never seen crosses her face. It is at once gentle and intense, tender and fierce. Maternal love.

Jealousy sprouts in my stomach. She's never looked at me that way in my entire life. And then, I realize that the expression *is* about me, albeit a much younger version.

"Those were the happiest days of my life," she says dreamily. "I used to stare at you for hours while you were sleeping. The curve of your cheeks. Your perfect lips. Your father and I spent our days researching travel to parallel worlds, trying to understand the meaning of the universe. When, the entire time, the meaning of our lives was right there in front of us. With you."

A softness rounds her face, and the years seem to melt away. I can almost believe I'm looking at the woman she used to be.

"It didn't take us long to realize that you weren't like other babies," she continues. "Every time I walked into the room, you were standing at the edge of your crib, already waiting for me. You'd start crying *before* I put the hot baby bottle into your mouth, and you'd scream and fuss when I pressed the button for the spinach purée, instead of sweet potato, even though you were in the other room.

"But we didn't understand the true extent of your powers until you started talking." Her shoulders begin to tremble, ever so slightly. "It was your father's idea to search your mind for the possible outcomes of my disease. I'd all but forgotten about my Asynchronicity, as the formula made me completely functional. But he feared the worst." She swallows hard. "It turned out, he was right.

"You won't remember this, of course. Fates, you were only a toddler at the time. But we showed you the amber syringe and asked you to show us the futures surrounding this formula. Your father had just invented the machine that translated a vision across five senses, so we were able to see the images directly from your mind. It was horrifying."

Her voice drops to a whisper. "In roughly half the futures, under an extremely tight regime, we were able to keep the time stream intact. But in the other half…our entire world blinked out of existence. Like it's happening now. There was only one scenario where we could save a portion of the population, and that was to build a realm machine and move them to a parallel world. We knew all about realm machines, of course, because even back then, your father and Preston had theorized the conditions that would need to be fulfilled. It would take Mikey's research later to fill in the details. There was only one problem. We didn't have an anchor."

She starts panting, faster and faster, until I'm afraid she's going to hyperventilate. I'm afraid I won't hear the end of her story.

"What happened then, Mom?" I grab her arm, digging my nails in, hoping to make her return to herself. "Tell me. *Tell me.*"

"Your father volunteered," she gasps. "In order to save that small fraction of the human race, he left us, he left his work, he left everything he loved. He withdrew into the woods to raise his bloodhounds and live a plain life, a simple life, one where every day was the same as the previous one.'"

My mouth drops. "You mean to say…"

"Yes, Olivia." The look in her eyes is more than just crushed. It's like Fate swept up her soul and pulverized it, and all that's left is a few floating specks of dust. "Your father is the anchor. And the anchor is Potts."

41

Potts is my father. Potts is my father. Potts is my father.

It's been an entire day now, and the words won't stop playing in a loop through my head. They accompany me on my walk into the woods, up to the warehouse containing the realm machine. They keep time with my footsteps as I dodge the technicians carrying heavy equipment, as I skirt around the scientists huddled around a com terminal. And they follow me right up to the shed in the corner, where one person resides, living his life the exact same way, every day, every minute.

Our anchor.

Potts.

My father.

My throat convulses as I look at the crimson paint on the shed. Did my mom choose that color deliberately? As a warning for others to stay away? In case the message isn't clear, a holographic phrase runs around the walls of the shed. *Keep out,* it says. *Keep out. Keep out.*

At least it doesn't echo that loop in my brain, *Potts is my father.*

A young technician approaches, a good-looking guy with jet black hair and laser-sharp eyes. "You want to see inside?" he asks with a rakish grin.

My mouth parts. "Are we allowed?"'

"We're not supposed to talk to the anchor, of course. Or bother him in any way. But there's a window up there, so that he can get some natural light." He gestures, and I notice a skylight in the roof. The window is a small square, no wider than my forearm.

"Yes," I say. "I would like to see."

I'd like to do so much. I'd like to introduce him to Ryder, I'd like to brush the dog hair off his clothes, I'd like to fall into silence as we both get lost in the crackle of the fire, and know, in those moments, that he is my father. We wouldn't even have to talk. We wouldn't need to have some big, long conversation acknowledging our relationship. That's not our way—has never been our way.

That would be enough for me. Just one more moment to be with him, to be in the quiet, steady presence that's been my core my entire life. To let him know that I've found someone who takes away my loneliness. Potts would like that, I think. It's what he's always wanted for me.

But I can't have that final good-bye. Not unless I want to jeopardize the mission for which he's sacrificed his entire life.

The tech pulls out a portable revolving ladder. He sets it against the side of the shed, and then, he smiles at me. Waiting.

"Ladies first," he says with a flourish.

Out of politeness, I wrench up the corners of my lips. He's cute, I guess, if you like the type. But he's not as tall as Ryder, and he's not as broad. He doesn't have that flash of kindness in his eyes, or that magnetic energy that infuses each of Ryder's movements.

Because, in short, he's not Ryder.

I hop onto the ladder and stick my hand through the leather hold. The revolution takes me to the top of the shed. I peer into the skylight. And look straight down onto Potts's thinning hair. He's walking, back and forth, head down, hands clasped behind his back. Probably meditating.

"I've never met anyone so simple in my entire life," the tech says below me. "He doesn't want anything; he doesn't need anything. He's perfectly content just walking, back and forth, and back and forth. Doing absolutely nothing."

I grit my teeth. *He wasn't always like that!* I want to yell. *He made himself that way. Stripped himself of his desires, stripped himself of his family. In order to save you. To save a vestige of the human race.*

But I don't yell, of course, because the tech didn't mean anything by it. He was just trying to make conversation. Just trying to flirt—and doing a terrible job.

I should probably hit the button so that the revolution takes me back down. Should probably say good-bye and leave my father, for maybe forever. But I can't rip my eyes from his pacing form.

Unbidden, a memory flashes across my mind.

• • •

"You don't have as many chipmunks here as I do back home," *my eight-year-old self says.*

"Is that right?" Potts kneels inside the kennel, brushing a bloodhound with a black and tan coat. Ten or so more hounds roam the fenced-in area, waiting their turn, and the smell of wet dog and dusty feed fills my nose.

"Oh yes." With a rag, I wipe the slobber off the jowls of a dog. "Every morning, I wake up to dozens of them outside

my window. My cabin is like a chipmunk magnet. They're probably attracted to my scent—"

I break off. Does Potts think I'm bragging? I wasn't trying to brag, but before I was in isolation, if I said something like that at school, the girls would link their arms together, so that not even a fly could buzz through, and whisper, whisper, whisper.

Will Potts turn away, too? Maybe he'll take the rag out of my hands and tell me I'm not allowed to come back. Maybe he'll say I can't help him take care of his hounds anymore.

"I don't know about that. I doubt they'd be able to smell you through the house." Gently, he slips a finger under my chin and tilts it up. He's got loose dog fur on his hands. He's probably getting it on me, too, but I don't care. "You know, you look like a chipmunk. Maybe that's why they come to your house. 'Cause they know they're in the presence of their own kind."

"You think so?" I grin.

"Oh sure." He drops my chin. "Those chubby cheeks? Those big round eyes? They certainly scream chipmunk to me. Tell me something. Do you like acorns?"

"I do," I say solemnly, although I'm not sure I've ever tasted an acorn. It's not a nut my Meal Assembler dispenses, but as soon as possible, I swear to the Fates I'll get ahold of one.

"That settles it, then. You're definitely descended from the chipmunks. Didn't you say you didn't know your pop? Maybe he's the king of the chipmunks. And you're the princess."

"I think so!" I clap my hands. It makes a soft, thudding noise, since I'm still holding the slobber rag.

Grinning, Potts attacks the bloodhound's coat. I return to my work, too, but as I clean the saliva from the dogs' droopy lips, I'm dreaming of acorn tiaras and chipmunks, of living in a hollowed-out tree trunk with my father.

*Potts doesn't mention my ancestry again, but he doesn't
need to. Because at the end of that visit, and every visit
thereafter, I find three perfect acorns on the windowsill. And
that's all the mention I'll ever need.*

• • •

I blink. I'm on the ladder once again, looking through
the skylight at Potts, who is still pacing. Only now do I
remember the way his hands lingered on my chin an instant
longer than necessary. The sheen of moisture in his eyes
before he turned back to the dogs. Details my eight-year-
old brain must've picked up and filed away, even if I didn't
register them at the time.

Or maybe that's not what happened at all. Maybe those
details were never there, and I'm just remembering the
scene the way I want it to have happened.

"Hey, are you going to come down from there?" the
tech calls. He glances nervously over his shoulder. "The
chairwoman's not going to be happy if she catches me
letting civilians peek at the anchor."

So he doesn't recognize me. No surprise there, since I
don't have on my FuMA uniform. But if he assumes I'm a
civilian, what does he think I'm doing inside a top-secret
warehouse? I guess it doesn't matter.

"Coming," I say. But as I start to push the button, I catch
a flash of something through the skylight. No. It can't be. I
plaster myself against the window.

I can't believe it. Maybe I'm not imagining details, after
all. Maybe Potts—my father—feels every emotion I've
attributed to him.

Because there, on a table inside the shed, lay three
perfect acorns.

42

"The chairwoman's set the date. You're due to show your future memory to the committee tomorrow morning," Jessa tells me three days later, as we board a pod on our way to the gold-star swim meet. My mom gave Jessa the afternoon off to watch the meet, as well as the use of one of FuMA's self-driving vehicles. She must've mellowed since she struck that bargain with Jessa, or maybe she just feels guilty.

She gave Tanner the same time off, but he refused to go after learning that we were taking a pod. Can't fault the poor guy. His parents died in a suspicious pod "accident," after all. But if the chairwoman wanted to kill us, there are far easier methods.

I'm dying to know where Ryder is, to know if he's going to the swim meet, too. I haven't seen much of him these past few days. I stopped by my living unit a couple times, but he wasn't there, and I can't ask Jessa, lest I seem too eager.

"Then the committee's going to be disappointed," I say instead, as we settle into our curved eggshell seats. "Precognitives don't *receive* future memories because we can already see it all."

Seat belts fasten over us, and the hatch door seals closed. The pod walls turn transparent, and I can see the glass and metal spires of the FuMA building.

"I know that," Jessa says as the pod shoots into the sky and finds a lane with more clouds than traffic. Pods zip past us, above and below our lane, so quickly that the passengers are a blur. "But the committee doesn't. And I think the chairwoman's still hoping you'll use a manufactured memory. In fact, she's scheduled an appointment in the Memory Lab for you this afternoon."

"I'm not doing it, Jessa. Sorry." I press my lips together. Three more days. Three more days until my life is over. A lot of good a memory—manufactured or not—will do me then.

But Jessa has no idea about my impending death. She saw Ryder's future memory, but she doesn't know about the blank wall in my vision. She doesn't know I've been counting down to May Fourth my entire life.

Exhaling, she looks around the pod as though she hopes to catch sight of a bird. But no winged creature can fly at our speed. "I understand why. But I think you might be looking at this the wrong way."

The pod dives and swoops over the majestic river, nearly as exhilarating as a ride on a hoverboard, but she doesn't even blink. "You and I both know that future memories aren't always an accurate measure of someone's worth. Take Callie, for example. Her memory showed her as nothing more than a common criminal, and yet, she's the strongest person I know. You can't tell me we don't need someone like Callie in our new world. And yet, she's dependent on Logan winning today to get on this so-called list."

The pod tilts again, and I grab the armrests to keep from crushing into Jessa. "What's so special about this new world that they need all these people with superlative abilities?"

She narrows her eyes. "You mean your mom didn't tell you?"

"I'm not her assistant, Jessa. She doesn't tell me everything. Besides, she's too busy upending everything I know about my life." I sound so bitter my words taste bad in my mouth.

"Mikey said they don't know what world they're walking into," I continue. "They don't know what challenges they'll face, so they need to be prepared for everything."

"It's a little more complicated than that." She braces herself as the pod takes another dip. "You see, Livvy, we're going to a parallel world. Do you understand what that means? Our parallel selves will already be living there! So, we can't just march into society when we arrive, because then, there would be two of each of us."

I gasp. She's right. Two of Callie, two of Jessa, two of Tanner. I can't believe I didn't think of it before.

Two Ryders. Two of his nicely sculpted chest. Two of his powerful physique. Now *that's* an appealing thought.

"That's dangerous!" I say. "What if someone in the parallel world catches sight of the duplicates? They might be killed or locked up on sight!"

"Correct. So we won't be able to live in the existing society," she says, "which means we'll need to carve out our own physical space. A place where we can live as a self-contained society. Where the parallel government might know about us—but has no reason to bother us."

Something clicks in my mind. "You mean, kind of like the mountain community we have here."

"*Exactly* like the mountain community." She looks at me expectantly, but I don't get the significance of her word.

She leans forward. "The chairwoman told me that at the very highest levels of the government, there's been a tacit agreement to not expand into the mountains, so that a community can set roots there, should it want to. To not have any contact with such a community, should one spring up. In essence, to let the mountains function as a safe haven for any refugees from a parallel world."

I stare. The pod drops to the landing pad on the roof of the gymnasium. The vehicle glides to a stop, the seat belts retract, and the walls turn opaque again. And I continue staring at Jessa.

"But who's to say that a parallel world would make the same agreement?" I frown. "Wait—unless you're saying the top officials from the International Council have actually had *contact* with people from a parallel world? How is that possible when we hadn't even invented the realm machine yet?" My voice rises. "Are you saying if we go into the mountains right now, we'll find doubles of ourselves living there?"

A smile tugs at her lips. "Don't sound so freaked out, Livvy. We're not talking about aliens from outer space, you know. This is just *us*, from a different world."

"I can't wrap my mind around it."

She sobers. "To answer your questions, I don't know. Your mom doesn't know, either. We don't know if realm machines have already been invented in other worlds—and if so, *when* they were invented. We also don't know if there was actual contact from a parallel world or if this is just a wishful hope that's been flung out into the universe. That could work, you know. In fact, Tanner's obsessed with the idea of communicating with our parallel selves by taking action in our present world. There's a bunch of experiments he wants to do, but…" She moves her shoulders. "That will have to wait."

I know what she means. A lot of things have had to be put on hold. And once they're on that shelf, most will never be taken down, ever again.

I let out a long breath. I can't think about that right now. I can't worry that three days from now, my visions will come to a complete and abrupt stop. I can't stress about whether everyone I care about will make it through that window—or if they'll be left behind to fade away. I can't even untangle the very layered knots of my mother's culpability.

Now, more than ever, I just want to seize the day. Because the present may be all I have left.

The hatch of the pod automatically lifts, as it does when we've been sitting inside too long. Outside, the sun glares off the concrete roof, as other pods land around us.

"Come on," I say to Jessa. "Let's go watch Logan win a gold star."

43

The swim center reverberates with noise, and the smell of sweat and chlorine clings to the air. A large banner with the words Gold-Star National Meet hangs on the far wall, while swimmers wearing navy caps with gold stars warm up in the pool. The bleachers are bursting with people—waving flags, stomping feet, and chatting with neighbors in ever-increasing voices to be heard above the din.

In the exact center of the stands, in the chairwoman's personal box, a bunch of FuMA guards sit, along with Jessa's family—Mikey, Angela, and Remi; Preston and Phoebe; Callie, with her hand solid and intact; and last but certainly not least, Ryder. My knees go weak at the sight of him, and I have to stop myself from running to his side.

I wrench my mind to the spectacle of all these people. Wow. Giving Jessa the afternoon off was uncharacteristic of my mom. But now, she's given the fugitives the use of a personal box? And provided them with her guards? Why?

Guilt. That's the only reason I can come up with, and yet, even I don't completely buy that answer.

Beside me, Jessa quickens her steps. She's made up with

each of her family individually, but that can't be the same as seeing them all at once. With a final leap, she's in the box—hugging her parents, laughing with Mikey, kissing Angela on the cheek, and tossing Remi into the air. And then, she faces Callie. For a moment, the two sisters just stare. Then, they crash their arms around each other with so much emotion that it takes my breath away.

"They look so much alike, don't they?" a voice asks behind me. "Same hair, same eyes, even that same brilliant smile."

I turn, and it's Ryder. Of course it's Ryder, with a hint of laughter behind his solemn eyes, with a ready smirk behind his relaxed lips.

I smile hesitantly. I want to leap into his arms, but the truth is, I'm still not sure where we stand. I can't help but remember the conditions he's placed on our relationship.

Can you promise me that you'll never betray me again? he asked. *Otherwise, I don't know what I'll do. It'll make me feel like the biggest fool in the world.*

My future pathways are blocked now when it comes to Ryder. In fact, there are so many holes in all my visions I'm catching only patches of futures here and there. Doesn't matter, I suppose. I have three days remaining. What could possibly happen in three days?

And yet…and yet…I have this terrible foreboding. I feel like I'll do exactly as he fears and betray him.

Limbo, it's not like I'm *planning* to break his trust. Fates no. He's been hurt so much in his life—by his biological parents, by Jessa, by Mikey.

By me.

I'd give so much to keep from hurting him, ever again. But I didn't plan on betraying him the first two times, either. Those actions came about because I felt like I had no choice.

What will happen if I'm faced with a similar situation? Will I decide, once again, to go against this boy who's become so dear to me?

"I saved you a seat." Ryder gestures at the velvet chairs, pulling me from my thoughts.

"You mean, you saved us a seat," I correct. "Jessa and me."

"No," he says. "I was thinking specifically of you."

Our eyes meet, and something moves between us. Something that is at once intangible and concrete. Something indecipherable, and yet something that makes the bond between us flare brighter than ever.

My heart throbs. Oh Fates, it's these moments that reach inside my heart and squeeze. These moments that make me feel like I'll do *anything* to preserve what we have—even if it's only for three more days.

I swallow hard, and we sit down. That's when I notice he's wearing electro-cuffs on both his ankles. I look around, and the rest of Jessa's family is wearing them, too, with the exception of Remi, probably because they don't make electro-cuffs that small. Ropes of electricity surround the box, effectively trapping the cuffed people inside. Quickly, I count the number of FuMA guards. One for each fugitive. It can't be a coincidence.

"The chairwoman may have released us to live in the scientific residences," Ryder says, seeing my glance. "But that doesn't mean she trusts us to roam free in society. She said letting us loose would be akin to releasing the documents—and there was nothing Jessa could do to change her mind."

So much for my mother being generous. But if security is such an issue, why let them come to the swim meet at all?

The hair prickles at the back of my neck, and every nerve shouts at me to *run!* But Ryder drops his hand onto my arm, smoothing away the goose bumps.

I roll my shoulders. "You seem...relaxed," I say to Ryder, studying the long length of his body. His leg isn't jiggling, his hands aren't fidgeting. He's been in motion ever since I've met him, and now he's finally still. "No, not just relaxed. You seem at peace."

"I am." He picks up my hand, brushing his lips across my knuckles. I shiver. Even in this crowded natatorium, with people screaming from every direction, he makes me feel like the only girl in this time.

"Jessa told me about the manufactured memories," he says. "And I'm happy for two reasons. First, because Mikey's going to ask the chairwoman about letting me use one—"

"And you'd do it?" I interrupt. "Even if it means you'd be cheating to gain a spot on the list?"

His eyes flash. "Right and wrong became blurred for me the moment my biological parents abandoned me. Using a manufactured memory would mean I could be with the people I love. It would mean I could live. That's good enough for me."

"You know what?" I say, realizing something. "That would be good enough for me, too. If you could live—I wouldn't even care if you cheated. Because right and wrong isn't a rigid line. It's about what you feel in your heart."

"The people I love are what's in my heart," he says. "That's how I live my life—how I've always lived my life. I put my trust in my family, and they put their trust in me. I don't know what will happen if I don't walk through that window. I don't know how it feels for my body to vanish, bit by bit. I don't know...death."

There's a finality to his words. A resoluteness that I can't argue with—that I don't *want* to argue with. When we look death in the face, we peel back the layers of our heart to the core of who we are. Who am I to judge the choices that are made? Maybe, in that moment, there is no morality. Maybe there are just the choices we can bear on our souls—and the ones that we can't.

I lick my lips. "You said there were two reasons why you're happy. What's the second?"

"They know how to manufacture memories." He turns to me, his eyes bright. "Don't you see what this means? That vision of me injecting you with the syringe. It's not going to happen after all. Because it's not a real memory. They made up the entire thing."

He is so hopeful, so relieved. It's as though a weight was strapped to each of his nerves, and now, they've all been released.

I can't bear to tell him he's wrong. Because I lived his memory seventeen days ago, and it was pristine. Seamless. Not a jerk or a jostle to be found. As of a couple mornings ago, TechRA was still ironing out those final wrinkles.

My mother may have figured out how to manufacture future memories...but Ryder's memory isn't one of them.

"Yeah." I hope I sound more convincing than I feel. "Maybe so."

All of a sudden, the crowd begins yelling Logan's name. He's standing on the hard concrete next to the starting line, water dripping from his body as though he's just pulled himself out of the pool. He's been gone six months, but Logan's still the local favorite, still Eden City's big hope for a gold star.

He rips the swim cap off his head, and his eyes roam the bleachers, skimming, skimming, skimming. He's looking for one person, and one person alone, and I know exactly who it is.

Sure enough, his eyes fasten on Callie. I don't know what she says or does—there are too many people sitting between us—but whatever it is makes Logan straighten his shoulders and stand tall. A power exudes from him, further fueled by the cheers of the crowd. He doesn't just look like a gold-star swimmer. He looks damn near invincible.

A buzzer sounds, signaling the swimmers to take their starting positions. Logan moves to the third of nine stalls. This is it. The final meet. The most important swim of Logan's life. Whoever wins this race will be crowned the gold-star winner of North Amerie. More than that, he—and his plus one—will be granted the opportunity to leave this deteriorating time stream and walk through a window into another world. He is literally swimming for his—and his wife's and unborn baby's—lives.

I stop clapping abruptly. If the fetus travels through the realm between times, it may become a precognitive like me. Will her life be as difficult as mine? Will she feel as isolated, will she feel as alone? For a moment, the worry buries inside me, sinking into my stomach. And then, I do my best to push the niggling aside. Better a precog than dead, I suppose.

A hush falls over the crowd. Around the box, Jessa's family joins hands, first Callie and Jessa with their parents, and then Mikey, Angela, Ryder—and me.

I stare uncomprehendingly at my hand clutched in Ryder's. We've held hands before, but never like this. Never when it connects me so intimately with his family.

The buzzer goes off, and the swimmers dive into the water. One of them edges in front of the others. Could it be? First—second—third stall—yes! It's Logan!

"You can do it!" Jessa screams. "Go, Logan! Go!"

Everyone in the box starts chanting his name, even the FuMA guards, and Ryder's on his feet, waving his hands, yelling at the top of his lungs.

I reach into Logan's future. As blurry as it is, one outcome seems to dominate the rest. And still, and still, I hold my breath for the next one minute and fifty-four seconds, until Logan's hand slaps against the concrete, until he heaves his powerful body out of the water, until the referee grabs his hand and stabs it into the air and declares him the official gold-star winner.

He did it, he did it. Around me, Phoebe bursts into tears, and Callie and Jessa hold each other as though they'll never let go. Mikey jumps to his feet, giving Logan a standing ovation, and if there were a prouder brother in any time stream, I've never seen him, in all the billions of pathways that have crossed my mind.

Ryder sweeps me up, and I somehow find myself in the middle of them, this celebrating, happy clan. Callie kisses me on both cheeks, and Jessa swings me around. Even Mikey encloses me in a hard, fierce hug. Bubbles like this have never fizzed up inside me—big and inclusive and unbreakable. I've never felt my lungs burn with this much happiness; I've never felt my skin stretch and stretch until it covers not just myself but all of us. An entire community. An entire family.

And then, the lights dim. The national anthem cuts off, not cleanly as befitting our advanced technology, but with a screech that could only be deliberate in order to grab our attention.

An enormous, three-dimensional hologram appears above the swimming pool. It is my mother, blown up to ten times her normal size.

All jubilation and cheer drain out of the natatorium.

44

"Greetings, citizens of North Amerie," the chairwoman begins. The hologram shows her from the shoulders up, but I can imagine her legs crossed demurely. "Thank you for interrupting your daily routines, whether they be work or school, virtual theaters or swim meets." Her left eye twitches as she says the final words. The movement is subtle, but it's there.

My core turns ice cold. She knows we're here, trapped in her personal box by rays of electricity. Of course she knows. She orchestrated the entire thing. Whatever this announcement, she wants all of us in one place and under the custody of her FuMA guards.

Why? my mind screams. *Why? Why? Why?*

Automatically, I reach into her future, even though I know I don't have access. Once again, there's nothing. A blankness so gaping it rivals the blankness of all my visions after May Fourth.

"I am pleased to inform you we have decided to switch up the order of those who receive the antidote. So many of you have expressed concern over your children that we have decided to treat our youngest citizens first," my mother continues. "Thus, we will no longer proceed by sector but by age."

The hologram switches to a vid, showing a row of babies being injected by techs in scrubs and face masks. But the syringes don't have amber-colored liquid swishing in their barrels. Instead, the formula is clear.

My mind whirls so quickly and so chaotically, it might fall right out of this dimension.

Clear.

Clear like the formula that Callie plunged into her own heart, causing it to stop. Clear like the syringe that Ryder will inject into me in three days' time.

Sinister in its absence of color. A liquid that stands out against the bright, brilliant colors of the rest of the vials.

From the time I was a child, my mother has taught me one thing about a syringe with clear liquid swimming in the barrel.

Clear is bad. Clear means poison. Clear tells you to run, run, run.

But I don't run. I can't even move, as the thoughts circle my body like creeping vines, fixing me in place.

Why? Why is the chairwoman injecting kids with the clear formula?

My mother's words echo in my mind. *We have to increase supply and decrease demand*, she said. *We need to cut down our population. By a lot.*

The International Council's solution was always two-fold. They built a realm machine to take a miniscule portion of the human race to a parallel world. And for everyone else? In order to give them a fighting chance, they would have to get the number of people in line with the meager supply of formula.

My thoughts spiral and tighten, spiral and tighten until they come down to one inevitable conclusion. Oh dear Fate. The council's decided to cut down the population. Starting with society's youngest, most defenseless citizens.

While I'm still reeling from the horror, the chairwoman continues. "Please bring children under the age of five to your nearest FuMA office, so that they may be injected with the antidote. This is not a request, nor is it voluntary. In order to eradicate this virus from our world, we will need one hundred percent participation. What does this mean?" The chairwoman smiles, the picture of all things kind and good. "This means if you don't bring in your child to receive his or her injection…" Her eyes flash. "We will."

My toes go numb, my knees knock together, and my teeth would chatter if I weren't clenching them so tightly. My mother just issued a death sentence for all the children under five in North Amerie.

That's why she wanted all of us in one place. So that she could keep us contained and under her control when she broke this news to the public.

The hologram shuts off, and the pool hall erupts in shouts and cheers. But I hardly hear any of it. I'm too busy staring at one person, and she's currently gnawing on her mother's collarbone, completely unaware.

Remi.

45

For an infinitesimal moment, I am frozen. And then one of the FuMA guards stands up casually and begins to walk toward Remi, his hand caressing the electro-whip at his belt.

No. His future pours into my mind, patchy and crumbling. But one thing is clear. He's going to grab Remi. He'll take her to a center to be injected with the "antidote." And she'll die.

Not if I have anything to do with it.

I don't think. Lunging forward, I snatch Remi out of Angela's arms. Angela blinks, too shocked to react, and the baby shrieks, pummeling me with her little fists.

"Olivia," Ryder barks. "What in Limbo are you doing? Give her back to her mother."

"You don't understand," I say, my eyes darting to the guards, who are advancing on me.

Limbo. Limbo. Limbo. The others didn't notice the clear formula. They don't comprehend its significance. But there's no time. No time to explain. No time for reassurances. No time to feel the little nails biting across my skin.

If Remi and I are going to get out of here, we have to leave *now*.

The guards pull out their weapons, and the electro-rays surrounding the box hum to life, ready to electrocute any cuffed person who crosses its boundary.

But I don't have on electro-cuffs, and neither does Remi. Holding the baby close, I duck underneath the rays and lose myself in the crowd.

"O-liv-i-a!" I hear Ryder's angry scream over the din. "Get back here right now!"

I grit my teeth and continue weaving, even as sorrow lances through my heart. *I'm sorry, Ryder. I'm sorry. I knew I was going to lose your trust. I knew it. But if it comes down to your good opinion or Remi's life, I will always choose Remi.*

The people no longer sit in orderly rows. They're on their feet, tossing pennants in the air, shouting at friends six seats over. They return to celebrating Logan's win, unaware of the ramifications of what just happened. Unaware their children are about to die.

He hates me. He hates me. He hates me. The thought repeats in my mind, but I don't have time to mourn. I don't have time for anything other than to keep moving. The guards are right at my heels, but luckily, I have the advantage of foresight. Short-term physical movements, devoid of complex human decision. Even Jessa or any baby precog could predict these moves.

The guards look left, and I duck under a beefy guy's arm. They charge straight ahead, and I double back and head for the rear exit. After a complicated five minutes of mouse-and-maze, I exit onto the roof of the building, where the self-driving pods are parked.

Good. I need to get far from here, fast. And a vehicle's

the only way to do it.

Remi's still crying, still ramming her head against my shoulder. It's like she's completely forgotten I already rescued her once. I push forward through the crowd. *Come on, kid. Help me out here.*

We're almost at my pod before I think to reach into my future. And it stops me in my tracks.

Limbo, Limbo, Limbo. My precognition's half useless now, but on all the pathways I can see, if I get into that vehicle, they'll catch us. I could gamble that the pathways I *can't* see yield a better result—but I'd rather not.

The pod is an official FuMA vehicle, one that's equipped with a tracking device. That's probably why my mother so "generously" loaned it to us in the first place. She may have confessed to having feelings once upon a time, but that doesn't mean the chairwoman's changed. She's still the woman she always was. Every action she takes is for an ultimate end goal. Just because that goal happens to be saving our world doesn't make her any less hard.

I charge back toward the entrance but stop short of crossing the threshold. Now what? I can't go back inside. They'll just lock down the building, and then it'll be a matter of time before they find us. Jessa told me once that Logan and Callie jumped off a building into the river to escape, but that's not an option. For one thing, I have a squirming baby in my arms. For another, there's no river nearby.

I squint at the blue, blue sky, and a pathway unfurls before me. Calmer now, Remi lays her head on my shoulder and stuffs her thumb in her mouth.

Yes. It just might work. We may not be able to use the vehicle I arrived in, but maybe we can hitch a ride in another pod.

The doors of the elevator capsule open, and a trio of FuMA guards spills out, with Scar Face leading the way.

Oh Fates. He wasn't sitting with us in the box. He must've been stationed somewhere else. My heart thudding in my throat, I swing back around. Poor Remi's probably getting whiplash. People stream past me. Big, bulky guys and lean, angular women. Young girls with rainbow hair and elderly men with mechanically straightened spines. There are so many of them, and they're all walking so fast. No way do I have time to search all their futures, not with Scar Face breathing down my back. I just have to pick one and hope for the best.

There! A woman with shoulder-length brown hair, flipped up at the ends like a question mark, is ushering a boy toward a silver-gray pod. She's a mom. Surely she'll be sympathetic to my and Remi's plight.

I rush toward them as the boy climbs inside.

"Excuse me, ma'am!" I pant. Coming up behind the woman, I put my hand on her slim shoulder. "I have an emergency. Could you please give me and my little girl a ride?"

The woman turns, and I look right into the eyes of my mother's former assistant and my long ago child-minder. It's been over ten years, but she hasn't changed one bit.

MK Rivers.

46

MK gapes at me, and then her eyes dart over my shoulder. Does she see Scar Face? Are the guards barreling toward us? I don't dare turn around.

"Well, don't just stand there," she says. "Get in!"

Oh, bless the Fates that led me to MK. Action first, questions later. That's the only way we'll get out of here.

I clamor into the pod, one hand supporting Remi's bottom and the other cradling her head. The boy jumps into the back row of seats. MK's son, I'm assuming. He's about eight years old and has the same red hair with golden tips as his dad. If I ever knew his name, though, I no longer remember it.

MK slams down the locks and engages the engine. The walls shimmer and start to turn transparent. I grab her arm, and Remi falls into my lap.

"Should we leave the walls opaque?" I ask.

Her fingers hover over the controls. "I don't think so." Sweat dots her upper lip, and she's not even the one running away. "If we stay opaque, they'll notice our pod in an instant. Better to turn transparent and hope they don't see us. Do you agree?"

I flash forward to the future. My pathways are more riddled with holes than Swiss cheese. I have no idea if she's right, just like I have no idea if Ryder will ever forgive me, but we have to make a decision. "Transparent. Do it."

The pod rises. By the time we're ten feet off the ground, the walls are completely clear. It's like we're sitting inside a glass bubble. A sea of heads appears under our feet, creating undulating waves with their varying heights. Black hair, silver hair, red hair, pink—and some shiny scalps with no hair at all. I can almost feel the wind that's knocking around these precisely designed hairstyles.

"No sudden movements," MK says. "Keep as still as possible and chances are, they'll scan right past us."

It's good advice—except I have a one-year-old in my lap. If they notice her, they'll take a second look, no matter how still I sit.

"There now, Remi," I murmur. What can I say? How do I keep her still? Ryder would know. He's so good with his little sister. So good with everything, really. "Let's pretend you're a stuffed animal, sitting quietly on my lap," I say quickly. "Can you do that?"

"Bun-bun!" She bounces on my lap, doing a rather good imitation of a rabbit.

"A sleeping bunny," I say quickly. "A tired bunny, with no more energy. A bunny that's, you know, tranquilized."

MK snorts, and I wince at my choice of words. But at least they seem to work. Remi sags against me, her arms dangling limply.

Thank the Fates. And not a second too soon. The pod passes over Scar Face's head, which is easily recognizable, since it towers over the rest of the crowd. He's got deep scratches on his scalp that match the ones on his cheeks.

Most people laser away such imperfections, but he kept his. Why? Simply to be intimidating? Or is there another reason? I hope I never find out.

Just as we're about to leave his field of vision, he looks up. I freeze. Does he see us? I can't tell. He doesn't move. He doesn't spin around and bark orders. Maybe it'll be okay. Maybe we're safe after all.

Tentatively, I reach into the future, more out of habit than any belief that I'll find anything useful. The paths I can see seem evenly split between him seeing us and not, between a battalion of guards waiting for us wherever we land…and not. All I can do is fling a prayer to the Fates and wait.

The pod finds an available lane in the sky and shoots away.

"Where do you want to go?" MK's hands move rapidly over a palm-sized keyball on the control panel.

Limbo, I hadn't thought that far ahead. Is there anywhere I can go that will keep Remi safe? My timeline ends three days from now. If I don't get Remi back to her parents, if she doesn't walk through that window, she has no shot at life. How do I ensure her safety in the short time I have left? Despair drags at me, threatening to pull me under.

And then, the toddler pops up, bored of being an exhausted bunny. She puts her little hand on my nose, and then the little fingers slip down to my mouth. "Vee," she says. "Vee."

Oh. She's saying my name. In just the same way she says Ryder's. My heart doesn't stand a chance, a flimsy shard of ice next to the blazing fire of her sun. "Good girl, Remi. You're a good, sweet, precious girl."

I can't let her down. I won't. I'll find a way. Any way.

"Take me to the woods." I name a forest miles away from the FuMA building and Potts's cabin. They'll search for me at both spots. If I land far enough away, maybe I'll have time to figure out what to do.

MK keys in the location without question.

"Thanks, MK," I say. "About the emergency…"

"Stop." She puts her hand in the air. "Don't say any more. Whatever it is, I'm sure you have a good reason. I'm just minding my own business. Giving my old charge a ride."

I nod, understanding. The less she knows, the less trouble she'll get into later, if it ever comes to that. "Thank you." I pack as much gratitude as possible into those two words.

"Not at all." She glances over her shoulder. "I took my son Cameron to watch the gold-star meet, because he dreams of competing himself one day. Isn't that right, Cam?"

"Did you see Logan shooting through that water?" The words burst out of the boy like an electro-ray. "Man oh man! He must've had solar-propellers on his feet!"

"He sure did." She reaches behind her and ruffles his hair.

"Do you think I'll ever swim like that, Mom?" he asks.

"I'm sure you will, dear heart," she says, her voice thick.

Remi peers over my shoulder and gurgles, pointing at his hair.

"Yep." Cam grins, shaking his head. "It's red. You like it? If you want, you can touch it."

Remi claps her hands and holds out her arms. She may have a limited vocabulary, but she certainly knows how to communicate.

Carefully, I move her to the back row, and the harness fastens over her. Remi grabs a fistful of Cam's hair, and I return to my seat.

"He likes peanut butter, banana, and honey sandwiches, too," MK says casually.

The air catches in my lungs. When I was a little girl, that was what I ate for lunch. Every day. "You remember?"

"How could I forget?" She smiles, revealing deep grooves in her cheeks. And all of a sudden, I'm sure those lines weren't formed from the passage of time, but from something else entirely. From too much knowledge about too tragic events.

"You know, don't you?" I ask. "You know everything."

She looks at the kids. Cam has now engaged Remi in a game of peek-a-boo, and the toddler is shrieking with laughter. Neither of them pays attention to a word we're saying.

"Everything. That's such an imprecise, all-consuming word. But in this case, it's perfectly appropriate. Yes, I know. I know about the time stream apocalypse." She attempts to keep her voice light, but regret lines her words like well-fitted bedsheets. "I know my son won't live long enough to succeed—or even fail—at his dream. There's value in that, too, you know: failing. Because if he fails, then at least he will have lived long enough to try."

I swallow, but the lump won't go away. Just as nothing I say will ever erase the cracks in MK's soul. "Is that why you left your position as my mother's assistant? Because you learned the truth?"

"I've always known the truth," she says wearily. "Ever since you had that vision of genocide when you were six years old. Oh, we kept it quiet. Very few people other than myself ever saw your vision or even heard about it. But I was the chairwoman's assistant. In order to do my job effectively, I had to know everything she did. I demanded answers, and…she gave them to me." She shakes her head, as lost as the girl she must've been when she first heard the truth.

I know exactly how she feels. That was me, a few days ago. But the difference is, I've lived with the knowledge of the world ending for a matter of days. She's endured these fears for the last decade.

"Why did you stay with her for so long?" I ask. "Why didn't you leave, raise your family, enjoy life?"

"That's what William wanted me to do. But the chairwoman tricked me. She showed me the extended version of your vision, the same one she showed Jessa. I saw an assistant with brown hair curved at the ends. Just like mine." She shudders. "The chairwoman said it was me, and I believed her. I thought I was complicit in the genocide, so I stayed to try to stop the atrocity. I felt like I owed my people, my world, that much." She takes a deep breath. "It wasn't until Jessa betrayed her family that the chairwoman revealed the rest of the vision. The birthmark on the assistant's waist proved that it was Jessa all along. Never me. So when your mother offered me the opportunity to be with my family for these last six months, I took it."

She lifts her eyes to mine. All the resoluteness in the world can't erase the guilt that lingers there.

"No one would fault you, MK," I say softly. "It's time for you to think about your family." Remi's high-pitched laugh and Cam's equally spirited cackle wind through the air. I wish I could wrap those sounds around me forever. "It's time for all of us to think about family."

Soon after that, the pod touches down in the woods. I gather Remi from the back row. She comes willingly enough, wrapping her arms around my neck, but her eyes stay in the back, on her new playmate, Cam. In a different place, a different time, maybe their camaraderie would

PINTIP DUNN

have developed into a real friendship. That's something I would've liked to see.

I turn to MK. I doubt I'll ever see her again, and maybe that shouldn't be important. I haven't seen her for ten years. Three days from now, I won't see many, many people ever again. But this is my first good-bye—the first of many.

"I appreciate the ride," I say awkwardly.

"Anytime," she says.

"Thanks for ordering that Meal Assembler," I blurt out. "The one that made those sandwiches. I know my mom didn't want it. I know you had to pretend that you really liked peanut butter, banana, and honey sandwiches. I probably didn't say it at the time, but it meant a lot to me."

She touches my cheek, the way she used to do when I was a little girl. Did she ever want to see me again, after I went into isolation? Did she ever ask my mom about me?

I don't voice either question. I don't want to know the answer. Or rather, I'm afraid I won't get the answer I want.

"The taste grew on me," she says. "These days, I even find myself putting honey on my banana pudding."

The tears gather behind my eyes and I push them back before they can spill out. I hop onto the ground, with Remi on my hip. Clumps of trees surround us, their leaves swaying in the breeze, and the sun's climbed to the very center of the sky. It's only midday, although it feels much later.

The pod lifts into the sky, and the opaque walls turn clear as glass. Remi waves both hands at the pod; Cam, with his nose pressed to the wall, returns the gesture. It's silly, but their obvious yearning for each other sparks something inside me. That's exactly how I feel about Ryder. But too bad for me, the feeling isn't mutual. We watch the pod until it is out of sight.

"Well, kiddo, I guess it's just us now," I say to Remi.

"Afraid not," a booming voice says behind me.

My stomach drops. Limbo. I was so distracted by the good-bye that I forgot to look out for Scar Face.

I turn slowly. Just as I expected, the captain of the guards is smiling at me, the gash of his cheek shining under the hot sun. He stands in front of a group of four men and women, all holding electro-whips.

47

stumble backward, my shoes scuffing against the complex growth of weeds and grass. Sweat springs onto my forehead, and the air feels as thick and unbreathable as the peanut butter I like so much. Just because I knew this outcome was a possibility doesn't make it any easier. Doesn't make the reality any less crushing.

"You didn't think you would actually get away, did you?" Scar Face asks, his lips bisecting his cheeks—again. He's always smiling when he talks to me. There's no way he's this happy all the time. He has to know smiling makes the scar gape horrifyingly on his face. "I saw you in MK's pod. Hard to miss, when you flew right over our heads. You think you're so smart, Miss I-Can-See-Into-Everyone's-Future. Guess you didn't know the chairwoman had a tracking device placed in her former assistant's pod without MK's knowledge."

Remi slips on my hip, and I hoist her higher. I don't respond. I refuse to give him the satisfaction.

"Go with them." He jerks his thumb over his shoulder. "As the chairwoman ordered, we'll leave your punishment to her. This little angel is a different story. Give her here."

SEIZE TODAY   280

Not while there's an ounce of breath left in my body.

"No." If possible, I pull Remi even closer to my chest. I didn't incur Ryder's rage just to give her up now. "You can't have her."

He lifts a bushy eyebrow. Clearly, he hasn't made use of the laser treatment for hair removal, either. "No? You heard, just as clearly as I did, the chairwoman's edict concerning the children in North Amerie. I'm taking her. And you can't stop me."

"I can." My mind whirls, considering and discarding possibilities as quickly as the partial pathways that flip through my mind. "Remi is one of the props I need for my manufactured memory."

Yes. This excuse will work. I pull my spine straight. "If you're so concerned about the chairwoman's edicts, then you should know that I'm due in the Memory Lab right about now. And my mother has issued strict instructions that I'm to have whatever prop I want. Well, this is want I want. Remi."

One of the guards scans through his wrist com. "She's right," he says a few moments later. "Olivia Dresden is scheduled in the Memory Lab at 1600, and she's to have whatever she wants."

Scar Face's temple throbs, but he can't argue, not anymore. "Fine," he growls. "Escort them both to the Memory Lab."

Light-headed, I turn. Before I can leave, however, Scar Face grabs my wrist. "You think you've won, Olivia. But I assure you, this isn't the end."

He's wrong. But I can't muster up the energy to tell him how very wrong he is. Because for me, this *is* the end.

Or at least, it will be in exactly three days.

...

A few hours later, I set Remi down, and she claps her hands, probably anxious to walk, to explore, to do anything after being held in my arms for so long. I give her a handful of cotton balls, the safest items I can find in the lab, and wish I had Callie's ability to change them into something more interesting.

"Are you absolutely sure this is the memory you want?" the tech, Kanya, asks me. She's got slashing cheekbones and straight black hair, and she's been assigned to help me manufacture the memory I'll be showing to the selection committee tomorrow.

Sometime before my arrival at the lab, I remembered my long-ago vision of genocide.

In my vision, I had been locked in a detainment cell full of Mediocres. My mother had been furious at me for sending the wrong memory, one where I held my newborn baby in my arms and felt at peace with the world.

"Why did you send this one?" she had demanded.

"Maybe my future self thought it wasn't right to execute ninety-nine percent of the population on the basis of their memories," I'd answered. "Maybe she knew this was the only way to get you to listen. To show you there's more to humanity than pure talent. There's also happiness. And love."

I remembered these words a future version of me spoke on a particular pathway. And as I awkwardly cradled Remi (who's not exactly a newborn anymore), I felt the pure and utter truth of my words.

That's the memory I asked Kanya to manufacture. And yet, and yet...I'm not sure it's the right one. Because

I already sent myself that memory, once upon a time. It didn't convince my mom to change her mind then, and it's not going to convince her now.

I don't want to repeat the mistakes of a doomed vision, the one I've been trying to avoid for ten years. Unlike people not blessed with precognition, I know I can choose a different path.

"Are you sure you don't want a memory that shows off your skills as a musician?" Kanya persists. "We could give you the one that you saw in the lab, the one where the girl plays violin on a hoverboard. The truth is, Olivia..." She stops, licking her lips. "The truth is, the memory you chose isn't superlative in the slightest."

"Does it matter?" I ask absently. Her mention of the manufactured memory makes me think of Ryder once again, and a sharp pain lances through my heart. I know the pain will only increase once I actually have the time to process what he perceived as my betrayal.

It's not important, I tell myself. *I have only a little over two days remaining. It shouldn't make a difference what Ryder thinks of me now.*

Tell that to my aching heart.

"Of course the memory matters." Kanya's cheeks turn ruddy red. "The chairwoman will be here in a few minutes, and she's not going to like this mediocre memory we just made. I'd like to still have a job tomorrow."

"Why? It's not like anybody's going to have a job in a few days," I say without thinking.

She swivels in her chair. "What?"

Aw, fike. That's what I get for thinking about Ryder instead of our conversation. "Nothing. I don't know what I'm talking about," I say quickly. Perhaps too quickly, since the eyebrows rise even higher on her forehead. Limbo,

Limbo, Limbo.

I catch a patchy glimpse of Kanya's futures. And I see her worrying late into the night because of my careless words.

Part of me wants to shout the truth. *These might be our last days in this world. Go. Be with your family. Ask for forgiveness for your sins. Make the most of this final time.*

But I can't. While it's not fair for Kanya to be stressing about a job that will soon be irrelevant, it's also not right to destroy a segment of the population's hope for survival. That's what will happen if word gets out. I flash forward to the future and see horrifying visions: mobs storming the warehouse, lobbing rocks at the realm machine, dragging Potts out of the shed. Not good. Not good at all.

And so, I paste on a ditzy smile and send a prayer to the Fates that Kanya assumes I'm as strange and out-of-touch as the rest of the world believes. That she dismisses my words as the nonsensical ravings of a girl who's been in isolation for the past ten years.

And in sixty percent of the pathways, she actually does.

"I changed my mind. I'm not satisfied with the memory, after all," I say. "There's one very important change I want to make."

48

I takes Kanya forty minutes to make the alterations I want. Forty minutes that bring me that much closer to my impending death. Forty minutes when thoughts of Ryder sneak through my defenses. Forty minutes when I change Remi's diaper and feed her the hummus and pita strips I ordered from the Snack Assembler. She may not like solids much, but she must be hungry because she scarfs down the food. Forty minutes when I turn to the door at the slightest squeak in anticipation of my mother's arrival.

Not two seconds after Kanya finishes, I hear the clink of my mother's icicle heels along the corridor's tiles. She, too, has learned from my childhood vision of genocide, and she's here to approve my manufactured memory before I show it to the selection committee.

The chairwoman strides inside, wasting no time shaking her head. "What were you thinking, Olivia, running away like that? How do you think that made me look? My edict was never meant to apply to Remi. She's on the list to walk through the window. You know that."

"The guards in the box certainly weren't aware of that,"

I counter. "Neither was Scar Face. They were ready to snatch Remi right out of my arms."

She startles, as if this is news to her. "Well, they would've caught the mistake before Remi was injected."

I raise my eyebrows. "Would they have? That's a risk I wasn't about to take." Even at the expense of Ryder's good opinion.

She waves her hand in the air, as if the subject no longer has any consequence. "Devon told me you wanted to use the baby as a prop."

Devon? Who's Devon? Ah, she must be talking about Scar Face. He has an actual name? Imagine that.

"I pray to the Fates you're not going to send yourself the same memory that got you into trouble in that vision!"

I lift my chin. "So what if I did?" I gesture at Remi, who is stacking the cotton balls on top of each other and giggling when they topple over. "If little Remi doesn't represent everything that's important and precious in this world, then what does?"

She clicks her tongue in disgust. "Have you learned nothing from being my daughter? The memories from the future are here to guide you, but they also serve as a warning, damn it. If you don't like the future you're shown, then you choose a different pathway. End of story. And the memory of you holding a baby doesn't end well for anyone."

"Least of all me," I murmur.

"I am trying to save your life, Olivia." She blows the hair off her forehead, exasperated. "Please tell me you didn't manufacture that same pointless memory. Please."

"Why don't you see for yourself?" I hold out the helmet.

Huffing out a breath, she grabs the contraption and slaps it on her head. With trembling fingers, I pick up a second helmet and slip it on, so that we can live the memory together.

Kanya cues up the vision.

I'm standing in the middle of a riot. All around me, people are shoving one another, breaking biometric scanners with blunt weapons, yanking metal statues of trees out of the ground. Smoke billows out of gaping holes in buildings where holo-screens used to reside, and the smell of fire and ash burns my nostrils.

But I hardly even notice. I've created my own vacuum, here in the middle of this riot, and no one can touch me. I hold my baby in the air, my elbows straight, and spin in a slow circle. My heart swells, larger than my body, larger than this safe space I created. Larger even than the mob.

The baby reaches out a hand, trying to swipe my nose, which is just out of her reach. Her dimpled thighs kick and squirm, right in front of my face. She laughs, and I laugh, because I know without a doubt this is the most important thing in the world: this love that flows between us.

But the baby is not Remi. She doesn't have Remi's dark skin or her curly hair. Instead, the baby looks like a younger version of me, of Olivia Dresden. Brown hair, olive skin, big solemn eyes.

I gasp, my head whipping up just as two bulky men pass, carrying a holo-screen between them. The screen is off, but the black surface reflects my image back to me. I don't have gleaming silver hair. I don't have a web of lines around my eyes and mouth. And yet, my features are unmistakable.

I'm Marigold Dresden. The chairwoman.

· · ·

My mother shrieks, falling out of the vision. Calmly, I slip off the headset and wait.

She gasps at the air like her lungs have transformed to the gills of a fish. "Why...why did you do that?" she whispers.

The two of us and Kanya may be the only ones who will ever know. The chairwoman will never let this vid get out, so no one will ever see this woman and baby. I took the faces directly from one of the few holo-images I have of me and my mother, one where our cheeks are pressed close, laughing at an unknown joke.

"I'm reminding you, Mother," I say. "I'm reminding you how you felt, once upon a time, when you looked at me. Remi's safety is not enough. I'm asking you to call off the systematic execution of the children in North Amerie."

She shakes her head, as though she can rattle the memory loose from her mind.

"You may have buried it long ago," I say softly. "You may have banished such emotions in favor of duty to your nation, in favor of saving the world. But you remember feeling this way. You *told* me how much you loved me when I was a baby." I take a deep breath, letting the air stretch my body to its full height. "And now that you did, I remember it, too. I remember that you loved me more than anything in this time. That's why I believed in you for so long. That's why I was convinced you still had goodness left in you. I thought it was because I saw your alternate pathways. But that's not the reason at all. It's because I remember how your heart feels, beating next to mine."

My mother's face crumples, and she covers it with her palms before I can see. Before she has to admit her feelings to herself. A full minute passes, when her shoulders heave but no sound comes out.

"We have to give the people who don't walk a fighting chance," she whispers. "The only way to do that is to reduce the population, sooner rather than later. I'm not executing children, Olivia. They're going to die anyway. One of the leaders proposed that the approved walkers each carry a baby through the window, in order to save more people, but the International Council voted it down. There aren't nearly enough walkers for the number of babies, and if the children aren't with their parents, they're more likely to scream and wail and cry. The Council felt like it would create too much chaos and ultimately lead to fewer people crossing the threshold." She moves her shoulders. "I'm just…trying to make sure the few people who remain on this world survive. That's it."

"Not like this," I say. "You don't know what the future holds. Give them *all* a fighting chance. Please. Remember the mother you used to be. Remember how much you loved me. Back then, wouldn't you want to give your baby a few more days of life? In case something changes. In case a solution is found. Just…in case. Because some hope is better than none at all."

She closes her eyes, her chest heaving, as though she's raging a battle with herself.

I hold my breath. I've done my best. The rest is up to her. She opens her eyes and looks directly at Kanya, whose mouth fell open at the beginning of our confrontation and hasn't closed since.

"Call the guards. Return this baby to her mother, Angela Russell." She swallows hard. "Pull the, uh, 'antidote' from the FuMA centers. Tell them there's been a recall. We need to study the formula further before we inject anybody else. As for Olivia…" She winces, as though my very name pains her. "Send her to detainment. The International Council is watching, and her subpar memory will not pass their exacting standards." She turns to me. "The injection of the children was only one way that we were beginning to cull the population. We've also started eliminating the Mediocres. You'll be executed along with them."

I step forward, my hands outstretched. But my mom's already moved away, so the only thing I touch is air. "Mom. You can't do this. You love me, remember? I'm your daughter. Your daughter!"

"Yes," she says. "And it's because I remember the love a mother has for her baby that I'm recalling the formula against my best judgment. But I can't save you, Olivia. Not anymore. I told you I can't show favoritism, and you doomed yourself by choosing a mediocre memory."

Before I can respond, even before the guards pounding down the corridor can enter the lab, my mom spins on her heel and strides out of the room.

49

shouldn't have fought the guards. It was pointless and futile. I don't even need the pathways to tell me I'm no match for their electro-whips. But still, I kicked and clawed and thrashed. Because you don't go quietly to your own death. Even if it's been predicted for the last seventeen years.

As a result, thick, bloody scratches travel up my arms. The smell of urine chokes the air, and teenage girls in dirty school uniforms press all around me.

At one end of the detainment cell, a brunette roars and leaps onto a redhead's back, grabbing her hair and yanking until it detaches in clumps. Another girl in the corner sings at the top of her lungs. Her head lolls around in a pile of feces, streaking her once blond hair with brown.

Just a few days ago, these girls were probably so hopeful, so excited. Ready to receive the memories that would shape the rest of their lives. And now, just because Fate has handed them a vision that was deemed mediocre, their days are as numbered as mine.

Two days. Two more days left to live and breathe this

stagnant air. Two more days to replay Ryder's anger over and over in my head. As miserable as I am now, I'll be sorry to leave this life.

Suddenly I hear short, staccato raps against the concrete floor. We all fall silent, even the singing girl. Two people appear at the end of the hallway, my mother and her personal assistant. Jessa's shoulder-length hair is flipped up at the ends, just like MK's. Just like my vision. They converse briefly, and then the chairwoman walks toward us, resplendent in her navy uniform.

I stand on wobbly legs and grab the metal bars of the detainment cell. "Mom. You have to call off the execution." The words spill from my mouth automatically, almost without thought.

The hand of Fate is strong. I've said these words before. In all my possible pathways, this is the moment that's lived the most strongly. Perhaps this was why Fate sent this vision to my six-year-old self. Perhaps this is why she continues to push us toward this exact path.

My mother scans past me a few times, and then she finally meets my gaze and smiles sadly, as though she, too, knows that we've been here before. "I told you, Olivia. You knew the price of receiving a mediocre memory, but you wouldn't listen, would you?"

My mouth opens to give her the automatic response, the words my brain has formed without me realizing it.

No. I clamp my mouth shut. I won't go down this path again. I can resist Fate's pull, I can wrench our world onto a different path...but we both have to try.

"You don't have to do this, Mom," I say softly. "Give these girls a chance, too, like you gave the children. They won't walk through the window. They're too mediocre for that." Bitterness laces my tone, and I push it away. "Let them live and stay in this time stream, for as long as they can."

A muscle ticks at the corner of her mouth. "I would if I could, Olivia. But you have to understand, the order's not coming from me. It originates from the highest levels of the International Council. They're not happy with me for pulling the 'antidote' for the children, and their instructions were clear. If I interfere with any more population culling procedures, they'll pull their resources, resources we need if the realm machine is going to work."

She touches my hand through the bars, but even her cold fingertips do nothing to pierce through my haze. "Most of these girls will never get a single dose of the formula, so it is a kindness to end their life now, without torture, without pain, rather than make them face what's to come."

"A kindness?" My eyebrows have never climbed higher on my forehead. "Come on, Mom. If you're going to murder masses of people, at least call it what it is."

Her eyes flash. "What would you have me do, Olivia? There's not enough formula. We can't all walk through that window. The bodies of the people who are left will slowly deteriorate, day by day. You think seeing Callie's missing hand was bad?" She shudders. "We hope that once the major organs disappear, the entire body will go, too, but we're not sure. Time deterioration doesn't follow the same rules as physical degeneration. How would it feel to exist without lungs, without intestines?

"That's not even the worst of it." Her lips turn so white I think she might faint. "Riots are going to break out. Stealing, fighting. Mayhem like you've never seen. What happens when people realize the world is ending? Civilization breaks down. Laws will be ignored, courtesy rendered meaningless. It will be survival of the fittest at its most violent. Except even the fittest won't survive."

She stops, breathing hard. "I'm doing what I have to do, for the greatest good of the people. But if you don't buy that argument, all you have to know is the International Council is here, monitoring our every move. Watching us even now."

I freeze. Her eyes are wide and laser-sharp. She's trying to tell me something, something important. I just don't know what.

"Especially now, they want us to follow their orders to the letter," she says. Her eyes don't waver from mine, not by an inch, not by a centimeter.

I lick my lips. "What do you mean, especially now?"

"The word's gotten out, which is to be expected," she says, her lips hardly moving. I have to lean forward in order to hear her. "You can't start executing Mediocres and expect it to stay a secret. But it's more than that. We took Kanya into custody immediately, but she must've released the vid of your memory while we were talking. It's out now, that memory of me looking into your baby face. The vid's gone viral. The people are holding you up as an example of someone the Council executes, and they're screaming for your release. In a matter of hours, you've become a symbol to them, about what this world means, about what this world needs."

She wraps her hands over mine on the bars. "The Council wants to put an end to this uprising, so they're offering free entry through the window to anyone who's willing to kill you. This is their way of wrenching back control. By showing the people that everything has a price. That greed and self-interest will always trump love and goodness."

"No one's going to take them up on it," I say, horrified.

Her fingers fall away. "They already have. In the first hour alone, hundreds of offers poured in. But one person in particular put in his name, and the Council selected him, based on his relationship with you. The execution has been set. You will serve your sentence two days from now."

She looks at me, her eyes caressing every curve and angle of my face, and then she turns and walks away, her heels clicking against the floor.

"Mom! Tell me!" I call after her, even though I already know. Even though there's only one answer that makes sense. I just can't bring myself to believe it. "Who is it? Who did the Council select to kill me?"

"I'm sure you can guess." Her voice carries down the long hallway, and I can't see her face anymore. The only thing I can make out is her navy uniform. "Mikey approached me too late about getting his son a manufactured memory. The Memory Lab was booked solid. And so, he had to find a different way. You may not want to admit it, but you've known for eighteen days, when you lived his future memory along with a room full of people, who is going to kill you. Ryder Russell."

50

My mind is numb. A solid, frigid cage that keeps out every thought, every feeling. It stays frozen when the redhead shoves the brunette in the chest, resuming their fight. When the streaky-haired blonde picks up her song mid-lyric, exactly where she'd left off. It continues to be rigid when the slim detainment guard comes to our cell, motioning me out and leading me down the corridor.

"You're getting your own cell," she says. "By order of the International Council."

How…nice. Should I send them a thank-you note? Tell them how grateful I am for this courtesy? I start laughing, hysterically, the sounds bubbling out of me like champagne foam. We arrive at my cell, and abruptly, I shut it off.

I stumble inside, collapsing on the threadbare blanket and pillow on the concrete floor. When you're executing masses of people, I guess you have to forgo such luxuries as comfy beds and last meals.

"You get a final good-bye," the guard says, as though reading my mind. "A final visit with the person of your choice. Who would you like to see?"

Who would I like to see? The laughter comes back full force. It spews out wildly, and even slapping my hand over my mouth doesn't stem the flow. My mother threw me at the Council's nonexistent mercy. Ryder couldn't volunteer fast enough to end my life. The emotions surge, but I shut them down. I reinforce the steel cage around my mind. Around my heart. I can't bring myself to feel anything. Not yet.

My mother and Ryder are the only two people who *might* have cared about me. If they've already forsaken me, then who's left? Jessa? Callie? They're nice enough to visit if I ask, but I don't need any pity good-byes.

"I don't care," I say dully. "Whoever wants to, I guess. Or nobody, if it comes to that."

The guard nods. Her eyes catch the light, and I glimpse a sheen of moisture. Wonderful. It's the end of my life, and the closest thing I get to tears is from a stranger who's known me for two minutes.

Maybe I'm better off returning to the numbness after all.

The hours pass. As the lights come on for my last full day on Earth, I'm kicking the metal bars over and over again, fully knowing they won't move, and then adding my fists when the pain isn't enough. When they bring me my midday meal, I'm sobbing into my blanket, an ocean's worth of tears for myself and the other Mediocres, for the lives we won't live, for the moments we'll never have.

For Ryder.

Oh, I shouldn't be surprised he volunteered to execute me. I can still hear the anger in his voice at the pool hall. He warned me, clearly and concisely. He didn't know what he would do if I broke his trust again.

Well, I did it. I snatched his sister from his mother's

arms and ran away. And I didn't consult him, I didn't explain. Not a single word. What choice did he have but to conclude that I betrayed him once again?

One way or another, he was going to walk through that window—either through a manufactured memory or through the murder of a girl who, in the end, is nothing more than his enemy's daughter. The chairwoman turned down his request for a manufactured memory, so what else was he supposed to do?

I know all this, rationally. But oh Fates, how my heart aches. I feel like it's been locked in a vise, one that squeezes in every direction, so that there's no room, no outlet. So, the pressure builds and builds, until I think it might pop into a trillion pieces, one for every pathway I've ever seen, and Father of Time, I want it to pop because then it won't ache anymore. Then it won't hurt anymore. Then I won't live anymore.

When the lights blink off again, signaling night, I pick myself up, wipe the tears on my pillow because my blanket's soaked through, and give myself a stern lecture.

I knew this was how it would all turn out. I knew it. Oh, not the end of the world. Not the wholesale destruction of our time stream. But the fact that my life would end tomorrow, on May Fourth—and at Ryder's hands? That was all foretold to me. It didn't *have* to unfold this way, but there was a high probability that it would. If I chose not to believe it, then that was my own damn fault.

If I could strip away the layers of my subjectivity, if I could yank all the pain from my heart, I might even agree that Ryder made the right decision. I'm going to die, regardless, if not by his hands then by another's. Might as well save the life of someone I care about in the process.

Because I do care about him. The thought is sobering,

but I'm at the end of my life, and there's no more time for lies. No point in protecting a heart that's about to stop beating, anyway. I care about him more than I could've imagined. More than I want to admit.

I squeeze my eyes shut, fighting my feelings. I should hate him. I should recoil at the thought of his name. And yet...and yet...a small part of me wants him to walk through my cell door, to give me my final good-bye. That part wants to get lost in his deep, dark eyes once again. Feel the scrape of his jaw against my cheek, his hot breath against my ear. One. Last. Time.

Ridiculous, I know. And yet, there it is.

By the time the morning of my execution comes, I've given up hope that anyone's coming for a final visit, much less Ryder. And that's okay. Better to exit my life knowing the stark truth rather than indulge in any last-minute hope.

I'm rearranging my blanket, trying to make a softer cushion, when I hear footsteps in the corridor. *Two* sets of footsteps, presumably an official and a visitor, heading right for my cell.

My breath catches. Someone's coming to see me after all. Perhaps someone young and male and handsome...

He appears in front of my cell, next to a detainment guard. I was right. He is young and handsome. But I was also wrong. He's not Ryder.

"Tanner?" I gape. "What are you doing here?"

shake my head, attempting to clear it. Have my long hours of solitude evoked this hallucination? But no. Even after repeated jiggles, my childhood companion is still here, still standing before me.

The guard waves a wand in front of the sensor, and the gate slides open. "Ten minutes."

Tanner nods and steps over the threshold, his black hair brushing against his straight brows. I haven't seen him look this solemn since he was six years old. For a moment, we both listen to the heavy tread of the guard's departing footsteps.

"Why are you here?" I ask again. Awkwardly. To fill the silence. And also, because I really want to know.

"Why do you think? I'm here to give you a couple messages. And to say good-bye."

I laugh harshly. "I guess nobody else wanted to do it, huh? Sorry you got stuck with it."

"Actually, I had to fight for this visit," he says, his eyes black coals in his face. "Jessa, Angela, even Mikey—they all wanted to come. But when I made my case, they backed down. They all recognized I should be the one here."

I pinch the bridge of my nose. He didn't mention Ryder, and that's fine. That's expected. "Why? Because you've tormented me the longest?"

"No," he says slowly. "Because I've cared about you the longest."

I blink. And blink again. Is that what they're doing these days during the Final Good-byes? Make stuff up to make the detainee feel good? I have no idea. I never studied that particular etiquette book.

Swallowing hard, I order myself not to read too much into his words. "What are your messages?"

He shuffles his feet, clasping and unclasping his hands, as though he's grown extra limbs and doesn't know what to do with them. "Jessa wanted me to tell you not to worry about the Mediocres. She broke into the database, put in an order to improve their living conditions. She also pushed back their execution dates by a year." He pauses, the implication hanging between us. A year from now, this time stream will no longer exist, so it doesn't much matter what the date is. But at least the girls will be safe, for the time being.

I hug myself. So, Jessa did it, in a way. She stopped the execution of the Mediocres. Of course, we didn't know the world would be ending. We didn't know the people will blink out of existence, anyway, a short time from now. But she accomplished her mission, the mission I set her on.

There's satisfaction in that. There has to be.

"The chairwoman and the rest of the International Council are so busy with preparations for the window, they won't even notice," he continues. "The deterioration has accelerated. Even the formula's not doing its job anymore, and people are fading away, fast. Callie, Jessa, everyone.

The pain comes and goes. One minute we're fine, and the next, we're gasping at the air. It's a good thing Logan already won his gold star. He's so weak now I doubt he'd be able to swim the length of a pool. You need muscles for that, and lungs, and his are...faded."

He stops. Swallows. For the first time, I notice he's not quite as solid as he used to be. If I stare, really stare, I can almost see through him to the other side. "We're scheduled to walk through the window tomorrow," he says.

"Good," I say softly. "I'm glad. You need to get out of here before you disappear altogether."

Silence descends between us, for seconds, maybe even minutes. What do you say to someone when you're about to die? When the world is crumbling around you? Nothing I can think of feels appropriate. Nothing feels sufficiently weighty.

"What was the other message?" I ask finally.

"That one's from me." He rubs the back of his neck, the one that's beginning to turn transparent. I half expect his fingers to dip inside his skin and disappear. "I never had a family, you know. Just my parents, and they were taken from me when I was a kid. You...you were the only constant in my life." He licks his lips. "Sure, we bickered. Sometimes, I wasn't even sure if you liked me. But you looked out for me, too. Over and over again, when I made a mess in the lab or was late for a meal, you'd make an excuse for me or take the blame yourself.

"When the scientists tortured me, and I was so broken afterward I couldn't do anything but lie in bed, you would read me your ridiculous chipmunk stories for hours."

I stare. "You hated those stories."

"Nah," he says. "I *pretended* to hate them. Secretly, I couldn't believe anyone cared enough to try to make me feel better." He walks across the cell, his feet getting tangled with the blanket on the floor. For a moment, he stares at the lone blanket and pillow, and his face crumples. And then, he takes a deep breath and irons out his features once again. "I tried to look out for you, too. When you went to isolation, I sent you those care packages, the ones filled with all the things you liked to eat. And the foods I thought you might like to try, as you grew older and your taste changed."

My mouth drops. "That was you?'"

"Who did you think it was?"

"I wasn't sure," I admit. "My mom, maybe MK. A kind tech who serviced the Meal Assemblers. I think I considered everyone except for you. I mean, those few moments aside, I was a total brat to you."

"Sisters are supposed to be bratty; it doesn't mean we love them any less."

I can't speak. Not because my mind is numb, but because of the opposite. I have too many thoughts, too many feelings. They crowd together, pushing and jostling, and I can't grasp ahold of any particular one.

"We're the same, you know," he continues haltingly. "We don't have family the way other people do. We had only each other. And I always thought…" He stops, glances down at his fingers. Swallows. Turns his fingers over. Swallows again. "I always thought if I had anything close to resembling a family, you were it. And…" He breaks off. "If I had the choice, if I could go back to the beginning of my life and choose a different pathway, I wouldn't want to. I would choose you as my sister. Every time."

He looks straight at me. "That's my message. I just wanted to let you know."

The tears fall down his cheeks, and they gather in my

own eyes. I...I can't believe this. In all the pathways I ever yearned for, on all the stars I ever wished, I never imagined I would have a brother, after all. And that it would turn out to be Tanner.

Awkwardly, we embrace, and he drops a kiss on my forehead. And then, we back up shyly.

"I'm so proud of you," he says. "I've watched you over the years, and I'm so proud of the way you grew up."

"Thank you." The words feel like rocks in my mouth, dry and clunky. "I always wondered what it would be like to have a sibling."

"I'm sorry," he whispers. The tears shine on his cheeks, but he doesn't bother wiping them away. He doesn't need to. He's already given me his heart, and he has nothing else to hide. "I'm sorry I didn't tell you earlier. I'm sorry I'm letting you down now. Jessa and I traveled to the past to do what we thought was impossible. We saved her sister. I'm so very, very sorry that we can't save mine."

He breaks down then, his hands covering his face, sobs racking his entire body.

"What are you talking about?" I pull him into a hard, fierce hug, no longer shy. No longer awkward. "You *have* saved me. You've given me the only thing I've always wanted: love."

I pull back and look into his face, the one that's been so familiar to me my entire life. And I speak the full and utter truth. "Now that I have that, I can leave this life with peace in my heart. That's all I can ask for. That's all any of us can ask for."

52

Two hours later, I'm not so sure. My heart's trying to hammer its way out of my chest, and the back of my shirt is drenched with sweat. Cold air blasts into the room, mixing the smells of lemony air freshener and leftover blood.

I'm chained to a throne-like chair, one made with cold silver metal and hollow glass legs. An arena of seats surrounds me, although the spots are only partially filled. My mother, front and center, as the Chairwoman of the Future Memory Agency. Two officials from the International Council. And Callie. That's it.

They all look...insubstantial. As if they're made up of a ray of light and a wish. As though they might evaporate in a matter of hours. And they very well might. One of the officials flickers in and out of this world, and my mother looks like a hologram. A particularly realistic one, but a hologram nonetheless. Callie appears to be solid, but under her shirt, her formerly round belly seems...deflated.

For a moment, I'm seized with fear. What if time makes her fetus vanish before she can walk through that window?

What if Callie travels to the new world no longer pregnant?

I take a steadying breath. Worrying won't do either of us any good. Why is Callie here, anyhow? Was I allowed to have one person present for my death? If so, they never asked me. Maybe they assumed I wouldn't have an opinion on this, either.

Still, I'm glad it's not Tanner. We already said our good-byes, and I'm thankful to spare him the sight of my execution. But why Callie? I just met her. I've known Jessa longer. In fact, I even thought she was beginning to care about me.

A surge of disappointment rises in me, and I push it down. I can't waste my final moments feeling hurt. Tanner told me Jessa fought him for the final visit. He told me he loves me like a sister. That has to be enough.

My mother's wrist com beeps, and they all rise. It's time to start.

The side door opens, and Ryder enters the room. He's dressed entirely in black. Not the light gray jumpsuits of the detainees, but not the uniforms of the FuMA employees, either. This must be the official garb of the assassin.

He stands, his spine perfectly rigid, his hands clasped behind his back. He, too, appears transparent, like I might be able to pass my fingers right through his body.

He doesn't look at me. He doesn't grimace or flinch. In fact, he gives no indication whatsoever that this is personal.

As I watch him, my last, secret hope that I'll make it through this hour alive melts away. He's no longer Ryder Russell, the boy who kissed me and made me feel like I was the heroine in my own story. He's no longer the person who saw me as an active force, rather than a passive observer. Now, he's simply a soldier, waiting for his next orders. Ensuring his safe passage through the window.

Callie steps around him and approaches me. Her nose, her mouth, her eyes look so much like Jessa's that my heart wrenches. She stops in front of me, placing her cool, soft hand on my cheeks.

"Be brave," she says simply.

The tears I've kept dammed up spring to my eyes. But I don't let them fall out. Callie's been here, too. She marched right up to Death's face, and she didn't waver, she didn't crack. She did what she had to do. She did what she believed was right.

"How?" I whisper. "I'm not like you, Callie. I'm not brave."

"Oh, but you are, Olivia. You've always been brave, but no one's given you credit for it, least of all yourself."

With one last smile, one last touch, she steps aside.

My mother clears her throat. Her eyes are wet and glossy, but she doesn't budge from her spot in the stands. "On this fourth day of May, do you have any final words?" she intones.

So this is what they've decided to give me. No final night in a comfy bed. No last meal. But a ceremonial execution with a final speech, instead of being marched through a slaughter room like the others. I'll take it.

I exhale shakily. These are among the last words I'll ever say, and the light blinking in the dome above lets me know they're recording this, so that they can stream my execution onto the wall screens for all of North Amerie to see. I hope this moment counts.

Straightening my shoulders, I look right at the officials and say the words I rehearsed in my cell. "I stand before you today about to die for the crime of being mediocre. In your eyes, I have no place in the new world. You don't even think I should be spared to find my own pathway in this crumbling time stream. And that's not right. I stand by my memory."

I swallow, gathering my thoughts. "Do you want to know the truly superlative thing about humanity? It's not selfishness and greed. It's not self-interest. Those drives have been ingrained in us since the beginning of time. There's something much more important than the instinct for survival, and that's love. Love is what defines human life and makes it special. Love is the only emotion powerful enough to make people decide against self-interest, against survival."

I take a deep breath, feeling my stomach expand with air. "The men and women you've chosen as superlative truly are remarkable in their talents. But I hope, for your sakes, that they have love in their hearts, as well. Because you're never going to thrive without it."

I stop. Both the officials are blinking. I can't tell if they've heard my words. I don't know if they'll have any capacity to make decisions in the new world. But at least there's the chance the right people will hear what I said. And maybe, just maybe, some small part of me will make it through the window.

I look at my mother. Pain as well as regret line her face. She never wears her emotions so openly, but she's dropped her shields now. Maybe, so that I can see, in the last moments of my life, how she really feels. The choices she's made today are consistent with the way she's always lived her life. She's doing what she has to do for the greatest good of her people. I don't agree with her decisions. But…I can understand them. Maybe.

Ryder steps forward. As much as he refused to look at me before, his eyes are devouring me now. Deep. Dark. Unfathomable.

Once upon a time, I thought I was beginning to know him. I thought I could look into his face and see his past, present, and future all rolled into one. But now, unlike my mother, his mask is firmly in place, and he's as unreadable to me as he was the first time I saw him, twenty days ago.

Callie holds up a clear rectangular case, which contains a single syringe. Ryder removes the needle and lifts it to the light, so that the officials can see the clear liquid inside.

This is it. The final moments of my life.

My pulse races, and the breath exits my body in quick, hard pants. My peripheral vision blurs, and the only thing that remains in focus is Ryder's face. His square jaw, his full lips. His eyes. For a moment, the mask slips, and what I see is so unbearably sad that my heart breaks. But that's okay, because my heart's about to crumble into a million pieces anyhow.

"Forgive me," Ryder whispers. And then he stabs the syringe right into the middle of my chest.

The formula enters my bloodstream, and then it flows through my veins, touching every cell and converting it.

Oh Fates. My limbs begin to convulse, my arms, my legs, my knees, my elbows—all with a life of their own. I didn't know death was supposed to hurt this much. My blood is fire, and my nerves explode like popcorn held too close to the flame. The poison attacks every cell in my body, jabbing each one with increasingly sharp barbs.

"What's going on?" Callie whispers. "She's not supposed to react like this."

"The formula," Ryder says furiously. "It's the formula."

I fall to my knees, my hands outstretched. What are they talking about? How else am I supposed to react? I'm supposed to die. And that's what I'm doing now: dying.

Panic flashes across both Ryder's and Callie's faces, and they rush forward, catching me before I collapse.

I know rather than feel that Ryder's hands are cradling

my head. His mouth opens, an *O* of horror, and I want to reassure him. I want to tell him that I understand, that I forgive him. My last living act is to forgive him.

I reach out to touch his face…

And then everything goes black.

53

A brilliant light burns the backs of my lids. I crack my eyes open and immediately close them again. So bright, so glaring. It would be so easy to retreat back into the darkness, to retreat back into sleep. But I've been sleeping for a long time now. Something calls me from the edge of my consciousness. A thought that wants to get in. I can't quite comprehend the meaning, but it makes me want to try again.

I flutter my lids. More light, but also more sensation. I'm lying on a cot, the mattress hard and thin. Barely more comfortable than the concrete of my detainment cell. With each blink, I catch glimpses of a wall, one with bends and grooves. Perhaps a partition. The groaning and clanking of a machine fills my ears, along with loud indistinguishable chatter, the kind that a stadium full of people would produce. There's also a thudding sound, as though a battering ram is being driven against a wall. And I smell… evergreens.

My eyes fly open. "Where am I?" The words rasp from my throat. I try to swallow, but my mouth is too dry.

Someone holds a tin cup of water in front of me. Taking the cup, I turn and look straight into the eyes of an angel.

"Ryder," I breathe. Oh dear Fate, he's here. He's here. The sharp edge of his jaw catches the light, and his startling deep eyes pierce into me. His soft lips part—the softest lips I've ever seen—and I pick up his hand and press it against my heart. "Are you dead, too?"

"You're not dead. If you were dead, could you feel this?" In one smooth motion, he slides forward and presses his mouth against mine, at once strong and gentle, sweet and burning. I want to weep. I feel it all in sharp hyper-focus. His lips, rubbing against mine like electric-charged silk. The little flicks of his tongue that make me want to curl into myself. The mint flavor of his toothpaste. This is nothing like the hazy fog-like film that I imagine shrouds the afterlife. Nothing like the imprecise, ungraspable quality of a dream.

This must be real. I must be…alive.

He pulls back, too soon, and tangles his fingers in my hair. "I should've done that more," he says gruffly. "Before. When we had the chance. I should've been doing that, every second of every day. I shouldn't have let you up for air. When I thought we'd lost you…" He brings my hand to his lips like he wants to imprint my skin onto his taste buds, forever.

Above the din, I hear the squeak of a sneaker against the concrete, as though someone's shifting her weight from one foot to the other. I lift my head and glance around the small, walled-off area. Oh. We're not alone. Jessa's here, and so is Callie.

"Oh Olivia. I'm so glad you're okay." Jessa kneels by my cot.

More information assaults my brain. Finally, I remember where I've heard the groan and clank of the machines before. Still can't figure out the thudding noise, though.

"We're in the warehouse," I say. "Sectioned off in a corner away from the realm machine. And the rumble of the voices outside? Those must be the Superlatives, waiting to walk through the window."

"Yes," Jessa says. "The window will open in a few minutes. You woke up just in time."

Just in time for answers. Just in time for another round of good-byes, when I thought I was done with them, forever.

I swallow the sorrow. At least I'm still alive to feel the sadness. That's what's important.

I focus on the girl in front of me. Her eyes are alert, her cheeks flushed with red. Her hair still looks like MK's, with the ends flipped up like a question mark.

"I never got the chance to ask: why are you wearing your hair like that?"

"Oh." Jessa touches the ends of her hair self-consciously. "It was Remi. Your ride in the pod made quite the impression on her. She wouldn't stop babbling about Cam and MK and crying because she couldn't see them. Me wearing my hair like this was the only thing that could appease her."

Ah. I see. The laughter tickles against my throat. Such a simple reason for such a long misunderstanding. "It looks good on you," I say.

She takes the hand that Ryder's not holding, and her fingers feel...substantial. Nothing like the paper-thin fragility I saw in all the people in the arena earlier.

"You're so solid," I say wonderingly. "How are you so solid? Or did you not start fading away like the others?"

"I did. Just as transparent as the rest of them." She glances at Ryder and her sister, and I realize they're all more solid, more fixed in this time than before. I can't see through any of them, but more than that, I just feel their presence more strongly.

"As soon as Ryder injected you with the syringe, we felt this…this jolt," Jessa says. "Like the universe was shifting in some indescribable way. All of us—even me, although I wasn't in the room with you." She ducks, and the lighter hair at her scalp reflects the overhead beams.

"Can you ever forgive me for not coming to see you?" she asks in a low voice. "I wanted to so much. I didn't want you to think that I had forgotten about you. That I was able to brush aside our friendship so easily. But both Tanner and Callie had more compelling reasons than me to be with you."

I pull my hands from both of their grips. I can't be touching either of them right now, or I'll come apart at the seams. Instead, I pick up the tin cup and take a swallow of water. I drink half the damn thing before I feel like I can talk again.

"There's nothing to forgive," I say scratchily. "But I still don't understand." I shift my gaze to Ryder. "What happened back in the arena? Why am I still alive?"

He lowers his head. "You have to believe me. I never, ever meant to hurt you. From the moment I volunteered to be your executioner, I had a plan in mind. Not for a second did I contemplate letting poison anywhere near your heart."

"I thought you hated me," I say, not looking at him. "For betraying you a third time. You were so angry when I took Remi, and I didn't have time to consult you like you wanted."

"I was angry, definitely," he admits. "But only at first. Once I understood what was going on, I didn't fault you for a second. My only concern was for your safety."

I stare. "But you injected me with the poison. I was

there, Ryder. You picked up the needle, as clear as water, and you stabbed it into my heart."

"You mean, a clear syringe like the one you're holding?" Callie asks, walking forward.

I look at the tin cup in my hands and gasp. Because I'm not holding the cup anymore. Instead, my fingers are wrapped around a needle...with clear formula swimming in its barrel.

I drop the needle, and it lands on my lap. Liquid seeps into the blanket, wetting my legs. Not sticky enough to be a formula, and too much volume to be inside a syringe. I blink, and the syringe on my lap turns back into a cup again.

The dots connect in my head. Oh holy Fate.

"That's why you were there," I say to Callie, my voice high-pitched and breathy. "Because of your ability to create illusions, to make people see what you want them to see."

She nods. "Guilty. We were all being watched, so we couldn't tell Tanner. We couldn't even tell Jessa." She stops, wets her lips. "I'm sorry, Olivia. We made a mistake. As I told you before, my ability is not without limits. We needed to inject you with an actual object, in order for my illusion to work. Ryder and I thought the smartest thing to do would be to inject you with the amber formula. Everyone walking through the window had an extra dose yesterday. Something about how it will keep our minds attached to our bodies, so that we won't get lost in time when we travel through the ether.

"You hadn't received a drop of the formula yet, so we wanted to make sure you were properly prepped." She moves her shoulders. "Clearly, something went wrong."

I massage my temples, trying to keep up. "Yeah. I thought I was being scorched from the inside out. Is that how it felt for you?"

They shake their heads. "I felt a little burning," Jessa says, "but nothing like the pain you're describing. Everyone else says the injection doesn't hurt at all."

I reach into the future. It's an automatic reaction. Need an answer, search the future. Except this time, the blurred and patchy pathways I'm getting used to don't flit through my mind. Instead, nothing happens at all.

I try again and hit the same frustratingly blank wall. I'm about to try a third time...

And then I remember. Oh dear Fate, do I remember.

54

This moment had been predicted my entire life. The one thing in all my pathways that's Fixed. I lose my vision on May Fourth. And lost it I did.

I suck in a breath. "That's it. This was always the answer."

"What is?" Ryder asks.

Moisture springs to my eyes, and I can't tell if it's joy or relief, sorrow or the deep, long-awaited satisfaction of finally understanding. "I was wrong. I thought I hit the blank wall in my vision because I died. But I'm not dead. Maybe I was never supposed to die. It's just my precognition that's gone."

Something clicks in my mind. It's as though I'm thinking clearer now without all those future pathways clogging my brain. "The amber formula. That's what did it. It's designed to treat Asynchronicity, when the mind and body are not tethered to the same time. But that's precisely how my precognition exists.

"My mother traveled to a parallel world when I was an embryo in her body," I continue, working it out in my mind. "Somehow, I gained the ability to detach my mind from this time, to send it flying into different pathways, different futures. The formula must've stripped me of that power." I look at each of them, my excitement growing. "The amber formula blocks my precognition! That's why I stopped being able to see into my mother's future ten years ago, when she started receiving a dosage. That's why my visions have become increasingly blurry, as more and more people started receiving a dosage. And when you injected me with the formula, it ate away at my precognition until there was nothing left."

"She's right," Jessa whispers. "I haven't been able to see into the future, either, not even a few seconds. And it started the moment I was injected with the formula. I didn't make the connection until now. I thought it was because our world was so unstable that nothing was fixed anymore. I had no idea my ability was gone altogether."

She puts her hand on my shoulder. "I'm so sorry. I can only imagine how you must feel, losing your power. It's different for me. I've blocked my psychic ability half my life. But you...you must feel like you've lost one of your senses."

I try to smile, but my lips won't curve. She's right. My precognition was a part of me, so central to my identity that sometimes it felt like the *only* thing I was good for. It might be months or even years before I feel whole again.

But the issue is moot. The world won't be around that long.

Boom.

The noise is so loud it shakes me to my bones.

"What in Limbo is that?" I ask.

"The rebellion," Ryder says shakily. "All the Mediocres who weren't granted passage through the window. Word got out about the realm machine, and now the whole world's in a state of panic. They must've found out about this location somehow, and now they want in, too."

"Can't we let them in?" I ask.

Jessa's eyes widen. "Do you know how many of them are out there? Hundreds. Probably even thousands. They can't access the window because they don't have a bracelet." She holds up her wrist, and I see a metal band imprinted with an intricate design, just like the one Mikey showed me a little over a week ago. "But if we open the doors, they'll overrun the place. The machine will be destroyed before it's even activated, and everything we've worked for will be lost."

As if on cue, a loud whirring fills the warehouse, and a robotic voice blares over the commotion. "Window open in T minus two minutes. Window open in T minus two minutes."

"We have to go." Ryder jumps to his feet. "Come on. You're walking through that window with us."

All of a sudden, I realize that he's wearing a metal band, too, and so is Callie.

"I can't," I say helplessly, vocalizing what should be obvious to all of them. "I don't have a bracelet."

"I'm going to carry you," Ryder says. "Like a child. The same way Angela is going to carry Remi. Remi has her own bracelet, but the tunnel has been programmed to allow one set of footsteps through with each metal band. I'm so big that it might actually work. The sensor might actually think we're one person. Albeit an awfully lumpy and misshapen one."

"You really think we can fool it?" I ask doubtfully.

"I hope so. It's the best idea we have." His eyes pierce me. "Believe me, I would do *anything* to get you through that window with me."

It's brilliant, really. And it might actually work. I could be with all of them again. With my newfound brother. With my friends, Jessa and Callie. With this large, broad-shouldered boy, the one who is strong enough to carry me through the tunnel, the one who means more to me than

I ever thought possible. I could have what I've always wanted. A family.

And yet...I was okay with Ryder getting through the window at all costs. I'm not sure how I feel about me.

"This is cheating," I say. "It's just as bad as using a manufactured memory to gain passage. There are a lot of people who want to walk through that window, and they won't get to. It's not fair."

"That's awfully noble of you," Jessa says. "And maybe a few days ago, I might've even agreed with you. But the window is *now*. There's no way we're opening those doors, so you're not taking a spot away from anyone. So I suggest you put your morality aside. Besides..." She takes a deep breath. "I'm not walking through that window without you."

"Me either," Callie pipes up.

"At the risk of sounding like an imitation bot," Ryder says in a rumbly voice, "neither will I."

"Window open in T minus five, four, three, two, one second..." the robotic voice intones.

"No more arguments." Ryder bends over and scoops me up, pulling me close to his chest.

"I can walk," I protest.

"I'll be carrying you soon enough, anyway. And if you're not sure, we're not taking any chances." He strides out from behind the partition, Callie and Jessa at his heels.

And then, he stops short, almost dropping me.

"Are you—" I start to say.

The words die in my throat.

My mother stands outside the sectioned wall, her hands on her hips, as though she's been listening for a long time.

"Clever plan you've got there," she says. "But I'm afraid it's not going to work."

55

We freeze. Me. Jessa, Callie, Ryder, their faces locked in an expression of horror and despair. My mom's been the enemy all their lives, and once again, she's proving just how evil she can be.

I climb out of Ryder's arms and plant my feet on the floor. But just as I open my mouth to confront my mother, I catch sight of the scene behind her.

Huge metal arches still stretch across the length of the warehouse, and an electric fence surrounds the entire structure. But above the fence, I can see that the realm machine's been activated. The open space underneath the arches has been replaced by a filmy gauze of energy. The air seems to shimmer, and although I can barely detect this wall of power, I know with every cell in my being that it's there. The window into another world.

Guards line either side of the tunnel, wearing neon-yellow vests and waving neon-yellow lights, trying—and utterly failing—to direct traffic. People rush around, chaotic and disorganized. There's no longer a line in front of the tunnel, if there ever was. Panic has set in, and Superlatives mob the front of the entrance, pushing and shoving to gain access.

I swallow hard. A sense of awe starts in my belly and radiates outward. This is...incredible. I've never seen anything like this field of energy, in all the pathways I've seen in all the people's lives. And yet, this window is real. Travel to a parallel world is actually happening.

And then, two things happen at once. The loudest thud yet rattles the warehouse, and the gauze of energy wavers, shrinking by ten percent.

"Potts," Ryder bursts out. "His hold on the window is slipping. The rebellion is distracting him. We need to move now."

Jessa steps forward and faces the chairwoman. "What are you going to do to stop us?"

"I'm not the one stopping you," my mother says calmly. Behind her, the double doors buckle, as the battering ram hits it once again. Dear Fate. The rebellion's going to get through. It's only a matter of time. "Your plan's not going to work. It's not just a scanner you're trying to fool. The intricate code on the bracelet is more than just a pretty design; it also contains technology that will help you get through the window intact. Just as the amber formula makes your mind sticky, so that it wants to stay with your body, the bracelet sucks in energy from the ether that wants to rip your body from your mind." She takes a breath. "You could attempt the ether without a bracelet. But the chances of you surviving intact are very slim."

My mind whirls. "But you didn't have a bracelet the first time you traveled to a parallel world."

"I was lucky. More importantly, I was the only one traveling, which meant I was in the ether for only a fraction of a second. Here, with so many people funneling through, it will take time to move through the realm. Two seconds. Four seconds. With each passing instant, more energy attacks your body." She presses her lips together. "I give you about a one percent chance of surviving without the bracelet."

My stomach plunges to my feet. I knew it couldn't be this easy. Everything I've always wanted, right at my fingertips. I knew it was too good to be true.

"You have to try," Jessa says fiercely. "What's the alternative? Staying here and fading away? You never know. Maybe you'll be that one percent."

"I have a better idea." My mother unsnaps the band from her wrist and puts it in my hand. "Take mine."

I gape. Shock flows through my bloodstream, numbing my senses. I can no longer see the people pushing and shoving as they make their way to the entrance of the tunnel. I can't hear the ever-increasing thuds of the battering ram as it weakens the doors. I don't smell the fear that's permeating the air, a heady mix of sweat and oil. I don't even taste the blood that's pooling in my mouth, where I must've bitten my tongue.

All I can do is stare at my mother. The woman who's placed me second (or fifth or tenth) my entire life. The one who's offering to sacrifice everything for me now.

"Why?" Out of my hundreds of thoughts and thousands of feelings, it's the only word that finds its way from my mouth.

Her eyes travel up, up, up to the window near the top of the warehouse, one that's accessible by a flimsy revolving ladder. "Another point of entry," she says. "If they haven't already spotted the window, they will soon. We have a matter of minutes before they swarm the place."

She looks back at me. "The people have always needed

something larger than themselves to reassure them. To make them feel safe. In the pre-Boom era, this took the form of religion, an all-powerful God, the Universe. And in our era, this wisdom came in the form of future memory, if only for a little while. Before it all went wrong, before the world came tumbling down around us."

She sucks in a mouthful of air and then another, but the action is too fast, too…wet. She's not just breathing, I realize. She's holding back her tears.

"For the same reason, they need a hero or heroine. A symbol of strength and goodness and hope, which is what the Underground had in Callie. Which is what the Mediocres had, just recently, in you." Her shoulders become still. "They also need a scapegoat. A face of evil. Somebody or something to hate. This is what I've given to the world. This is what my life has stood for. They'll never forgive me for what I've done. The people I've killed. The sins on my hands. But I hope you do. You…and your father."

Her eyes drift to the red shed. My father lies inside, holding the window open for as long as he possibly can, saving as many people as he possibly can. "I love him," she continues thickly. "Did you know that? I love him with all my heart. As I love you. But you know what? I love this world more. And I did everything in my power to preserve even a portion of it." She takes a few stomach-deep breaths. "This is my gift to you, Olivia. To all of you. You won't get through that window without my help. They'll swarm the place first and destroy the arch. They need a distraction. Me. Perhaps this is the only time I've ever been able to show you how I truly feel. I hope you'll accept this gift."

"Mom, no." In three strides, I close the distance between us and seize her hands. Her fingers have always been so cold, so clammy. But now, they're as warm as the fire burning in her eyes. "You don't have to do this. We can find another way. I know there's another answer. We just have to find it."

She pulls her hand from my grip and places it on my cheek. "Please, Olivia. All your life, I've never been able to be the mother I wanted to be. The mother you deserve. Give me this moment. Let me do what I've always wanted to do: sacrifice for my child." She looks over my shoulder and meets the eyes of my friends. "Sacrifice for the people whom I've always admired, even as they tried to defeat me."

With one last smile, she walks away and climbs on the rickety revolving ladder.

"What is she doing?" Callie steps forward, panic whipped into her voice. "Olivia, what is she doing?"

The doors surge as the battering ram hits it one more time. Three more thuds, tops, and the entry will burst wide open.

"She's distracting them," Ryder says. "She's trying to buy us time."

My mom reaches the top of the ladder, and it all becomes clear to me. Not just this moment, but also the rest of my life. I was right to believe in her. I was right to love her. She has her faults—maybe more than most people. She's made bad decisions—definitely more than everyone else. But she's my mother. All those times I indulged in an alternate future, I wasn't wishing for a different mom. Because those pathways are a part of her, too. They may not be the woman she was, but they comprise the woman she wanted to be.

And now, in the final seconds of her life, that's more than enough.

My mom pushes open the pane of glass, and the rebels' yells blast into the warehouse.

"Mom! *Mom!*" I wave my arms, desperate for a few more words.

She turns, pushing back a strand of hair that's fallen onto her cheek.

"I love you, Mom!" I shout. "I love you!"

She smiles, as beautiful as she was in that old holo-image, the one where she cradled me as a newborn and looked into my eyes. "I love you, too," she mouths.

Turning, she pokes her head out of the open window, and her hair whips wildly behind her. "I'm the one you want," she screams. "My name is Chairwoman Dresden, and I'm the one who killed you all."

And then, she jumps right out of the window and into the mob.

56

For a moment, none of us speak. Maybe because all our mouths are still open. Outside, the rebels roar, primal and frenzied. Their excitement is so loud, so all-consuming, I can't hear anything else—and I'm glad. I don't need to hear the sounds of my mother being ripped apart. Imagining it is bad enough.

And then, the emotions hit me. My knees buckle, and I stuff a fist into my mouth, damming up the cries. My heart mourns. It yells and screams and rages, and if it were outside my body, it would slice through the air, leaving bloody red streaks everywhere. I want time to stand still. I want the world to cease spinning, so that I can properly grieve my mother.

But it doesn't, and I can't.

"The window is closing," the robotic voice intones. "The window is closing."

I jerk up my head. The voice, from wherever it emanates, is right. The filmy gauze of energy is now half its former size, and the crowd waiting to walk through the tunnel has diminished to a few scattered clumps.

Logan rushes up to us, his eyes bulging. "Where have you been? We have to move, now! Let's go, let's go, let's go!"

He grabs Callie's and Jessa's hands, and the three of them take off toward the tunnel at top speed. Tanner's words flit through my mind. *It's a good thing Logan already won his gold star. He's so weak now I doubt he'd be able to swim a length of the pool. You need muscles for that, and his are...faded.*

So, if Logan's fading away, where is he finding the energy to sprint? Is it just adrenaline? Or something else?

Shakily, I slip my mother's bracelet around my wrist, and Ryder starts to sweep me up.

I shake my head. "I can run. I promise. It'll be faster."

He nods, and hand-in-hand, we run. Images flash through my mind, no longer pathways from the future, but memories of the past. MK's redheaded little boy and his wistful hope that he'll someday swim as well as Logan. The blond girl in detainment who continued to sing in spite of the excrement in her hair. The memory technician, Kanya, who was so concerned about losing her job.

These people's lives intersected with mine for only a few minutes, and yet, they left an indelible mark on my heart. That's who we'll be leaving behind when we walk through that window. Those people—and millions of others like them.

A feeling rises within me, washing over me, threatening to pull me under. An underlying edge of fear. A vague sense of things ending. I can't quite grasp what it means. I reach for it, I stretch my mind for some kind of understanding, for even a handful of words.

It's big. Bigger than me, bigger than my life. A decision point. The weight of the world resting on the fragile point of a pin. Like a house of playing cards, like a long line of dominoes. Something that took a person a lifetime to set up. One false move, one wrong action, and it could all come crashing down.

My dream. The recurring nightmare I've had. It's here, now. The backdrop is different—an enormous realm machine, pulsing with energy, hundreds of people trying to break down the doors of this warehouse—but the feeling is the same.

I have to do…something. I have to take one decisive action, but it has to be the right one, or the entire world will end.

We proceed through the tunnel and join the group on the other side, right in front of the window. Tanner arrives a few seconds later, breathless, probably from searching the other side of the warehouse for us. Jessa's family is all there, all waiting: Mikey, Angela, and Remi; Preston and Phoebe; even Zed and Lauren, whom I heard were on the list on account of Zed's physical strength, but whom I haven't seen until this moment.

Panic rises inside me at seeing my former kidnapper and would-be batterer, but just as quickly, it fades away. I have much more pressing concerns.

Phoebe presses her lips against Jessa's forehead. "Thank the Fates you're here in time."

But there's no time for any other greeting. The screen of energy is now inches from my face, and my skin tingles with the enormous outlay of power. More importantly, the window has shrunk to a third of its original size—and is dwindling fast.

Zed and Lauren move through the window first, perfectly unified even though he towers over her by at least a foot.

"We'll see you in our new world," Preston says to all of us, although his eyes are only for his daughters. He and Phoebe walk forward—and disappear.

Angela's next, snuggling Remi to her chest.

Mikey's right behind her. I watch his foot move forward, as though in slow motion. Time decelerates to a crawl, and with every inch that Mikey moves, I'm able to think a million thoughts, feel a million emotions. Everything flits through my mind at the speed of the pathways, and yet, I don't feel overwhelmed. I don't feel like I'm able to focus on only one element or another. Instead, all my thoughts and emotions coalesce in my mind in one single resolution.

"I can't walk through that window," I blurt out.

Time speeds up to normal again, and everyone turns to me. Mikey freezes, with one foot inside the window, and Ryder picks up my hand, squeezing it as though he's not willing to let go. "Why not?"

"I just can't abandon this world," I say, struggling to put into words what I know in my head. What I feel in my heart. "I can't walk out on these people. All our leaders are fleeing, leaving the Mediocres behind without any information. Other than their sorry attempts to decimate the population, the International Council hasn't done anything to help them. Maybe they believe that the situation's hopeless, that these people will disintegrate in a matter of days. But what if that's not the case? What if there's a way to save this time stream?"

I lick my lips, afraid to continue my line of thought. Afraid it'll sound ridiculous when I say it out loud. "What if the time stream isn't unraveling because of future memory, after all? It could be a more easily solvable problem. It could be...me."

I take a deep breath. "Think about it. You're *all* healthy now, when you were weak and fading away a few hours ago. What's changed?" I move my shoulders. "Lots of things, perhaps. But one big thing that's different is me. I lost my powers of precognition, which means I haven't reached into the future for the last twelve hours." I stumble through the words, working it out in my head. "We were certain that future memory was the cause of the virus because the symptoms slowed during the ten years that future memory was delayed. Well, I went into isolation those same ten years. I saw very few people, so I had very few opportunities to use my precognitive powers. The virus gained new life again six months ago. That was when future memory was discovered; but that was also when I rejoined society."

My voice gets softer and softer, until I'm no longer sure they can hear me. But the group of them presses closer, and the expressions on their faces tell me they've heard every sentence, every word.

"Maybe I was the one making the time stream unstable all along," I say. It is such an enormous conclusion, with such enormous implications, that I almost can't bear to say it. I almost can't bear to think it. Me, a single girl. The cause of the entire world's destruction. But it's too late to hide now. And if it was my fault, I need to make things right. "Maybe now that I've lost my abilities, time can heal itself and return to normal."

"That's a lot of 'maybes,'" Logan says. "You would risk your life on these what-ifs?"

"I owe it to them." My hand is so sweaty that it slips in Ryder's grip. He simply readjusts his fingers and holds on more tightly. "Whether or not I'm the cause, they at least deserve to learn everything I know. So I'm staying."

Saying the words knocks the breath out of me. Not because I fear for my own life, but because this was my mother's gift to me. This was her sacrifice. And yet, I know her death was not in vain. Because she launched herself into the mob, many more people were able to walk through that window. Lauren and Zed. Phoebe and Preston. Angela and Remi. And more I don't even know about. One life to save many others. The greatest good for the greatest number of people. Right up to her last moments, my mother lived her life according to that philosophy.

"What if you're wrong?" Ryder asks quietly. "What if there's nothing you can do to save them?"

"What if I'm right?" I shoot back. "You were the one who taught me I was more than just a shadow, Ryder. You believed that I was fully capable of action. And that's what I'm doing now. Acting."

Another flicker, another waver, and the window shrinks again. It's a five-foot-by-five-foot square now. My friends will still be able to make it through, but they need to hurry.

"Go," I say. "Don't miss this window because you're talking to me. My mind's made up, and there's no changing it. So please, go. Now."

"Not a chance," Ryder says. "I'm staying here with you."

My heart stutters. I never expected this. This is a decision about my own life. I never thought to persuade anyone else to stay.

"You don't need to do this, Ryder," I say haltingly. "The people you love are what's in your heart." I repeat his words back to him. "So, go. Be with them now. Be with your family."

He brings up my hand and brushes his lips over my knuckles. And when he looks down at me, I know exactly why he is superlative, and it has nothing to do with his offer to execute a girl. He's smart and resourceful. But more than that, he's steadfast and loyal. His heart is kind. And once he's given it, he will never, ever take it back.

"No, Via," he says. "You are my heart. You've always been my heart. I just didn't know it until now."

Via. A nickname. For only the second time in my life.

I smile, and he smiles, and he leans forward until his lips are an inch away from mine. But he doesn't kiss me. Not yet. There'll be time for that later, or maybe there won't, but at least we'll be together.

Behind him, Jessa and Tanner whisper furiously to each other. And then, they turn to us with broad smiles on their faces.

"Didn't I say we were in this together?" Jessa asks. "We'll stay, too."

"And so will we," Callie says. One of her hands is intertwined with Logan's, and his other hand is splayed on her belly.

The energy screen wavers and contracts by another foot.

I step forward and put my hand next to Logan's on her stomach. "Are you sure?" I ask in a low voice. "We're risking only ourselves. You would be risking your baby. If you walk through the ether with an embryo in your body, you'll have a baby like me. A true precognitive. Maybe the only one in the new world. Do you really want to give that up?"

She regards me, her eyes steady. Logan's hand on her belly doesn't move. "That's all the more reason to stay. If you're right that your precognition was the cause of all our problems, then maybe it's better if we don't bring that wrinkle into the new world." She winks. "Looks like you're stuck with a family, Olivia. Through the rest of this time and all of the next."

And then, there's Mikey, with one foot inside the window, and the rest of him outside.

"Angela and Remi have already walked through the window," he says, his voice anguished. "My family…"

I go perfectly still. He's faced this same choice before,

between his wife and baby and his nearly grown son. It tore him apart then, and it's tearing him apart now.

The window shrinks, until it's a tight outline around Mikey's body. He'll have to make a decision soon—or it'll be made for him.

Ryder approaches his adoptive father, placing his hands on Mikey's shoulders. "Go. I can take care of myself, but Angela and Remi need you. And Preston and Phoebe... they'll be devastated when their daughters don't walk through the window. You'll need to explain to them why. But most important of all, the new world needs a good leader. I believed it when I was six years old, arriving in Harmony for the first time, and I believe it now. Mikey, you're the best there is."

Mikey nods, his cheeks wet. "I love you, son. You've made me...so proud." His voice cracks.

Ryder embraces him tightly. "I love you, Dad."

Mikey's gaze drifts to me. "Take care of each other," he says.

He ducks his body through the rapidly contracting window. And then, he is gone.

The last shred of the energy screen disappears, and the machine shuts off. In the absence of the whirring, I hear the shouts of the rebels. They're still out there. They still don't know what's happening in their world.

"Come on," Jessa says gently. "You're the symbol of the rebellion, Olivia. You gave them hope; you inspired them to fight. You validated what they knew to be true in their hearts. They're waiting for you."

I swallow hard, wiping at my face. At the tears that have fallen on my cheeks, and at the ones that reside in my eyes and in my heart, waiting to be shed.

We make our way to the entrance of the warehouse,

where a rickety ladder leads to an open window. Where my mother sacrificed herself to save her people. Where I'll address the ones who killed her now, without hate in my heart.

We've all suffered. We've all wronged or have been wronged. The only way to move forward now is with forgiveness.

I climb on the ladder, with Jessa behind me. When we reach the platform, I take a sharp breath. So sharp that it pierces me all the way to my soul. "This is what I meant when I said I saw us fighting together. The actual vision may have depicted a different time, a different scene. But the fight is the same. We weren't trying to defeat my mother, to tear down a system. We were fighting to save the world."

She holds my wrist, and I know that Fate has placed a true friend in my path. "You can always count on me, Livvy," she says. "Always."

I glance at the floor, where Ryder is holding one side of the revolving ladder and Tanner is steadying the other side. And then, I take Jessa's hand and step onto the sill.

"The window has closed," I shout to the hundreds, maybe thousands, of people below. "But we're still here. And we're ready to seize what we have left of today. We're ready to fight for our future!"

I grip Jessa's hand and lift it into the air. And the crowd cheers.

Epilogue

Two years later...

Mikaela slaps her dimpled hands in the oval tub, splashing us with a tidal wave of water. "More, more!" the eighteen-month-old squeals.

"More water?" Her mother, Callie, pats her own face dry with a towel and then picks up a toy watering can to sprinkle drops onto Mikaela's curls.

"More play." The toddler grabs both of her aunts' hands—mine and Jessa's—and with surprising force, pulls us forward so that we fall into the tub, too.

My shirt soaked to my elbows, I catch Jessa's eyes, and we burst out laughing.

"She looks so much like Remi, don't you think?" I ask when I can talk again.

"Well, of course she looks like Remi." Callie pulls one of her daughter's curls straight—and then lets it spring back again. "They are cousins, after all."

A flush highlights Callie's cheeks, and her stomach is round, once again. Twins, this time—just like her and Jessa.

Only, Callie won't be removing one of the embryos to be implanted eleven years later. She's leaving the babies where they belong: together. They'll be born together, they'll grow up together, they'll live and play together. Still, it's hard for me to imagine any pair of siblings who love each other more than Callie and Jessa.

The sun shines over our heads, and we're on the grass in front of Potts's cabin. Well, I suppose it's my cabin, too, since I live here now. I don't know how long I'll stay, although my father has said this will always be my home. For now, we're just enjoying getting to know each other on a deeper level.

The tub belongs to one of Potts's bloodhounds, but little Mikaela was so enamored, Callie gave the basin a good rinse and stuck her daughter inside for an impromptu bath.

Potts and Ryder sit on the porch, their heads bent toward each other, talking. My heart warms at the sight of my father's white mane brushing against Ryder's black hair. So, my wish came true after all. I was able to introduce my father to the boy I love.

Now that Potts has fulfilled his lifelong purpose as the realm machine's anchor, he's much less stringent about sticking to a routine. He still eats the same meals, at the same times—fifteen years of habit, after all, is hard to break—but these days, he'll pass an afternoon chatting on the porch. Just because he feels like it.

As I watch, Ryder glances up, his lips twitching. The warmth in my heart spreads to my stomach. Two years later, he still has the power to make my skin heat with a single curve of his mouth.

The time stream has been restored. Turned out, I was right about the cause of the deterioration. After that fateful day, when I lost my precognition and five hundred of North Amerie's citizens walked through a window into another world, the symptoms of the virus began to disappear. The rest of the formula sustained us until the time stream completely healed.

It wasn't an easy transition to the post-virus world. All of our former leaders had left, and there was a lot of confusion, anger, and chaos. But I convinced MK to help us guide the people, and eventually, she became the Chairwoman of the Committee of Agencies. She was my mother's assistant for so long that she was able to pick up the reins, if not seamlessly, then at least smoothly. Under her watch, our society is crawling back to a version of the world it used to be.

Future memory still exists, but it's no longer compulsory for every seventeen-year-old to receive one. The vision is no longer embedded in a black chip implanted under our wrists; it's no longer used to determine credit loans and job applications and admission into university.

In fact, if you choose to receive a future memory, after completing a course on its hazards and benefits, you are encouraged to keep the vision private. The future, after all, is yours to embrace or defy.

The realm machine remains operable, and Potts could reopen a window…but we have no way yet to control which parallel world we connect to. We have no way yet to find the world to which our families traveled. But Tanner's working on it, along with his research on communication with parallel worlds. We hope, someday, to have a breakthrough. We hope, someday, to be able to send a message or even visit the families who have traveled to a different world, a different time. Tanner's so brilliant that I'm sure he'll figure it out sooner or later. After all, he invented future memory. I have no doubt he'll be the Father of Parallel Worlds, too.

Fate couldn't have given me a better brother if She

tried. And it looks like I'll be gaining an amazing sister, too, if our conversation yesterday is any indication.

"She'll like it, won't she?" Tanner asked me nervously, as he passed me a circuit chip ring of his own design.

"Jessa will love it," I reassured him.

Now, I glance at Jessa's unadorned finger and smile, wondering when I'll see the ring there. Dropping a kiss on Mikaela's sudsy head, I leave Callie and Jessa to finish her bath and wander into the woods.

There weren't enough of my mother's remains to incinerate, but maybe it's better this way. Maybe her presence isn't just contained in the ashes of her body, but in all of us. In the people she killed, as well as the people who ripped her skin apart with their teeth. She would've liked that, I think. After all, that's what she lived her life for: the people.

Still, Potts and I come to these rocks, next to this little stream, and he tells me stories about their early life together, about the way she used to be before the mission took over her life. The way she used to visit him when he first retreated to the cabin but then had to stop. He was her anchor, too— her moral anchor. So long as she was still connected to him, she couldn't make the decisions she needed to make. Couldn't take the actions she needed to take. So, in a way, she gave up more than their love when she committed to saving the world. She gave up herself.

I may not have precognition anymore, but I can so clearly see the woman, the wife, the mother she would've been if our world had handed her a different fate.

I sit on my usual rock, the one with the flat, cracked surface near the water, and pull my knees to my chest. Hearing a twig crack, I turn, thinking it's my father. But it's not.

Ryder slithers toward me, as sleek and powerful as a predator, but I know now that impressions can be deceiving.

What predator would make me split my cheeks with a grin? What predator could make me yank him onto the rock and kiss him until a fish leaps in the stream, splashing cold drops of water on my bare arm?

I ease back and trace his mouth with my finger. "You and my father were having a pretty serious conversation back there."

"Well, I had a serious question to ask him," he says solemnly.

I shiver. I love Ryder's jokes and his lightheartedness, but it's when he's at his most somber, like now, that chills run up and down my spine.

"Oh really?" I ask. "Anything I should be worried about?"

"Yes." He gathers both my hands and kneels on the pebbled shore in front of the rock, right where water meets land. "I have to ask you something that will make you reevaluate the way we've lived these last two years."

A bird swoops low in the sky, and the stream gurgles as it flows around rocks big and small. My skin is both warm from the sun and wet from the water, and my heart—oh, my heart. It might burst right out of my chest. "You...uh, your knee is getting wet."

He glances down. "Maybe you should join me, then." He tugs at my hands, and I slide off the rock onto the ground, onto the pebbles, onto the dampness. If anything, the textured sensation against my knees makes my heart beat even faster.

"These last two years have been rough," he says in a low voice. "In some ways, they were the toughest of my life. But they've been the happiest, too. Sometimes, I miss Mikey and Angela and Remi so much it hurts to breathe. But then I look at you, and somehow, you take out the shards in my lungs and you smooth the holes. Just by being here. You taught me how to find joy from one moment to the next. You taught me how to live, not in the past or the future. But for today. I'm grateful for every single moment I've had with you, and if that's all I ever have, I'll never regret the decision I made to stay in this world."

He licks his lips, and I hardly dare to breathe, much less talk or move.

"But I'm selfish. So I'm going to ask you for more." He turns one of my hands over and presses his lips to my palm. "Are you scared yet?"

"No," I manage to say. And it's true. I know there's nothing to be scared of. Not with Ryder.

"I'm asking you to look beyond today. To make a decision about the future." He lets go of one of my hands and takes a ring out of his pocket, one that is made from the stalks of a plant, twisted together.

"My uncle Logan gave his heart to Callie with something very similar to this," he says. "And I'd like to think we can be as happy as they are."

He slips the ring over my finger, struggling a little over my knuckle, and I look at it wonderingly.

"Olivia Dresden. Joy of my life. Via," he says. "Will you marry me, not just for today, but for all the days to come?"

"Yes," I burst out. "In every pathway, and every time, yes."

He lowers his lips to mine. In all the futures I've ever seen, my precognition never showed me this scene or anything similar to it.

But you know what? I'm glad. I'm beginning to think, more and more, that it's better to live life this way. Squarely in the present, seizing each moment, since no one knows for certain what the future will bring.

ACKNOWLEDGMENTS

This is it—the third book in the FORGET TOMORROW trilogy. I've lived in this world and with these characters for years now, and I am so proud of how each individual story and the overall arc turned out.

First and foremost, I'd like to thank my wonderful readers. I've treasured every kind message you've sent me, and your enthusiasm for the series has spurred me to write a fitting conclusion for these characters whom I love so much. I hope you enjoy Olivia and Ryder's story.

I am blessed to continue working with my editor and publisher, the wonderful Liz Pelletier. Thank you, as always, for your many insights and for your support and belief. Thank you, as well, to the rest of the team at Entangled, especially Melissa Montovani, Christine Chhun, Stacy Abrams, Heather Riccio, and Melanie Smith. You all are amazing, and I am so lucky to be part of the Entangled family!

Thank you to agent extraordinaire, Beth Miller. I know you don't agree with my statement that I couldn't do this without you—so, let me just say that I wouldn't want to do this without you.

I am so thankful to be on this journey with my writing partners in crime. Danielle Meitiv, you give me chills (literally) with your brainstorming brilliance. Meg Kassel and Denny Bryce, I love your insights—and I love your friendship even more. Darcy Woods, I wouldn't be half as productive without your beautiful presence. Vanessa Barneveld, thank you for your unconditional support, and Brenda Drake, thank you for your daily support. I couldn't ask for better friends.

Speaking of which...I am writing these acknowledgments during a reunion weekend celebrating twenty-two years of friendship. Thank you to Kai, Bo, Aziel, Mahira, Joydip, Aruna, Francis, Amy, Josh, and Grace for being here for me through the years. Also, I can't mention long-standing friendships without a shout-out to my dear Anita.

My stories are deeply rooted in love, and I have the best example in the Hompluems, the Dunns, and the Techavacharas. I highly doubt I could write the stories I do without the lifetime of love and affection you have given me.

Thank you to my children, Aksara, Atikan, and Adisai. You make me smile every day of your lives, and your presence makes every moment sweeter, every feeling sharper.

Antoine, I love you to the depth and breadth and height my soul can reach. I first said these words to you at our wedding ceremony, and I mean them more with each passing day.

GRAB THE ENTANGLED TEEN RELEASES READERS ARE TALKING ABOUT!

27 HOURS
BY TRISTINA WRIGHT

Rumor Mora fears two things: hellhounds too strong for him to kill, and failure. Jude Welton has two dreams: for humans to stop killing monsters, and for his strange abilities to vanish.

But in no reality should a boy raised to love monsters fall for a boy raised to kill them.

During one twenty-seven-hour night, if they can't stop the war between the colonies and the monsters from becoming a war of extinction, the things they wish for will never come true, and the things they fear will be all that's left.

OMEGA
BY JUS ACCARDO

One mistake can change everything. Ashlyn Calvert finds that out the hard way when a bad decision leads to the death of her best friend, Noah Anderson.

Only Noah isn't really gone. Thanks to his parents' company, the Infinity Division, there is a version of him skipping from one dimension to another, set on revenge for the death of his sister, Kori. When a chance encounter brings him face-to-face with Ash, he's determined to resist the magnetic pull he's felt for her time and time again. Because falling for Ash puts his mission—and their lives—in danger.

Black Bird of the Gallows
by Meg Kassel

A simple but forgotten truth: Where harbingers of death appear, the morgues will soon be full.

Angie Dovage can tell there's more to Reece Fernandez than just the tall, brooding athlete who has her classmates swooning, but she can't imagine his presence signals a tragedy that will devastate her small town. When something supernatural tries to attack her, Angie is thrown into a battle between good and evil she never saw coming. Right in the center of it is Reece—and he's not human.

What's more, she knows something most don't. That the secrets her town holds could kill them all. But that's only half as dangerous as falling in love with a harbinger of death.

Hide From Me
by Mary Lindsey

"We all hold a beast inside. The only difference is what form it takes when freed."

Something's not right about Rain Ryland's new hometown. On the surface, it's a friendly, tight-knit community, but something deadly lurks underneath the small-town charm. Everyone he meets is hiding something—especially Friederike Burkhart, the hottest girl he's ever laid eyes on. Rain's determined to find out her secret, even if it kills him...and it just might.

Ancient magic and modern society collide in a sexy, spellbinding romance perfect for fans of C. C. Hunter and Maggie Stiefvater that proves sometimes beauty is the beast...

entangled teen

an imprint of Entangled Publishing LLC